## Acclaim for
## Tell Me Something True

"[A] poignant tale of truths hidden and laid bare."
—*Booklist*

"[A] novel of forbidden love and its repercussions...Cobo smoothly imparts the importance of familial ties and family honor in Colombia, alongside American priorities of success and security... *Tell Me Something True* is a bittersweet journey about coming to understand and forgive the indiscretions of one's parents through the simple act of living one's life."
—*Miami Herald*

"With a story that leaves the reader wanting more, journalist and pianist Leila Cobo enters the literary world on the right foot with her first novel, *Tell Me Something True*." [Translated]
—*Semana*

"Raw, passionate, honest, and fearless."
—Examiner.com

"The smooth prose and authentic Colombian settings provide a unique spin to familiar territory."
—*Publishers Weekly*

"[*Tell Me Something True*] is a well-told story. The characters are alive and maintain a reader's interest until the last word."
—*Midwest Book Review*

"A good story, delicately told with pathos and compassion."
—BookLoons.com

"This heart-wrenching story focuses on how memories permeate the everyday, the relationship between mothers and daughters, and the role family plays in our most intimate relationships." —*RT Book Reviews*

"This first novel, one of the best that I have read all year, throws question after question at the reader and tosses us all back to our first loves and the choices we may or may not have made...Relentless and absolutely honest, the surprise ending is unbeatable. Wonderful writing, content, themes, and characters...this novel is a must read. Bravo!"
—TheReviewBroads.com

"*Tell Me Something True* is an utterly wonderful and riveting book that had me in its clutches from the first page. It is lyrical and sensual with no word out of place. The character development is perfect, deep and meaningful, bringing the reader into the heart of the protagonists and their lives. In a sense, this novel sang to me in its poignant story of great loves." —www.MostlyFiction.com

# *The* Second Time We Met

## LEILA COBO

**GRAND CENTRAL**
**PUBLISHING**

NEW YORK   BOSTON

Grand Central Publishing
Hachette Book Group
237 Park Avenue
New York, NY 10017
www.HachetteBookGroup.com

Printed in the United States of America

RRD-C

First Edition: February 2012

10  9  8  7  6  5  4  3  2  1

Grand Central Publishing is a division of Hachette Book Group, Inc. The Grand Central Publishing name and logo is a trademark of Hachette Book Group, Inc.

The Hachette Speakers Bureau provides a wide range of authors for speaking events. To find out more, go to www.hachettespeakersbureau.com or call (866) 376-6591.

The publisher is not responsible for websites (or their content) that are not owned by the publisher.

Library of Congress Cataloging-in-Publication Data
Cobo, Leila.
  The second time we met / Leila Cobo.
    p. cm.
  ISBN 978-0-446-51938-0
  1. Birthmothers—Colombia—Fiction.  2. Young men—California—Fiction.  3. Adoptees—California—Fiction.  4. Mothers and sons—Fiction.  5. Psychological fiction.  I. Title.
  PS3603.O26S43 2012
  813'.6—dc22

                                                    2011029519

*To all adoptive families who have opened their arms to children who need homes and love. And, as always, to the Hanlon circle: Arthur, Allegra, and Arturito.*

# The
# Second
# Time
# We Met

"If I am not for myself, who will be for me? And if I am only for myself, what am I? And if not now, when?"

—*From "Chapters of the Fathers," The Talmud*

# Chapter One

Rita, 1989

It rained that night, and it made all the difference.

In her dream she was on a boat, and the wind and the ocean mist fanned her face, even though she had never even seen the sea. But when she opened her eyes, she realized it was just the rain, trickling slowly in heavy droplets that settled on the innermost corner of the open window before sliding lazily onto her pillow, which lay directly below.

It was very cold.

With a sigh, Rita peeled off the heavy blankets and knelt on the twin bed, the mattress thin and hard under her legs. She opened her arms wide, and with each hand grabbed the heavy wooden shutters that, when closed, sealed off her bedroom completely from the outside world.

They lived in the second-story apartment of a small, three-century-old structure of white stucco walls with its wooden windows and doors painted a dazzling blue. It was a home of long, dark, narrow hallways and cramped rooms with creaking floors. There'd come a time when these same homes would become trendy, when the wealthy people from nearby Bogotá would start scooping them up and remodeling them, tearing down walls and putting in new wooden floors and vast skylights that made up for the undersize windows. But right now her family's threadbare, lower-middle-class existence was evident in the scratched floors, in the living room with the worn, plastic-covered couch, in the bathroom—shared with her little brother—that housed a sad, square shower with broken tiles and a white sink with a perpetual brown stain around its edges that refused to go away even with the most abrasive detergent.

Downstairs was her father's modest sundry shop, right off the main square in this town of expansive landscapes and small imaginations. She knew the minutiae of every client and neighbor: the notary public across the street who paid for his daughter's school supplies with public money; the pharmacist who still didn't know that his wife dyed her hair because she ordered it straight from Rita's father's shop rather than getting it at her own store and risking her husband's learning she was going gray; Rita's older school-mates, who stopped here after school to shop for condoms on the sly, paying her instead of her mom or dad; Georgie, who was thirty-five years old and still lived with his mother next door because he was retarded but was given permission to shop here every afternoon for little trifles as he looked in awe at her classmates' legs, their blue uniform skirts hitched up high above their knees the minute they were off school grounds.

Doors were always locked here, but that still couldn't stop the secrets from leaking outside, like a thousand little minnows set loose in the water.

This secret, though, was so quiet it could have kept for the night, at least if Rita hadn't been up at two in the morning trying to close the window that she opened in the evenings, just to see the stars through the ornate black grille.

She didn't hear the voices at first. She was still half asleep, still taking in the cold wetness of the dark outside. But she realized they were there the minute they stopped, and she—recognizing that something had changed—looked down.

They were wearing fatigues, but of course here in the countryside that could mean anything: army, leftist guerrillas, right-wing paramilitaries, or, worse, thugs who'd decided to scare people off with uniforms.

Rita froze, her arms spread wide, fear making her grip the windows' edges for balance. They were standing in the middle of the damp, empty street, their faces shadowed but still clearly visible under the yellow glow of the streetlights. There were five of them, but her gaze zeroed in on only one. It was less about the levity in his gaze—she couldn't even discern the color of his eyes from the window—and more about the narrow, aquiline nose visible underneath his cap, the confident arrogance of his stance.

He smiled when he met her eyes behind the bars that shielded her from him, a bold smile of utter self-assurance—the assurance that comes from being armed and in a group and…simply from being assured.

Rita hurriedly shut the windows, fumbling with the old latch but finally managing to secure the lock, then sat back on the bed, stunned and scared. Armed men in the middle of the street, in the middle of the night, casing the town. Whoever they were, it couldn't be good. And they had seen her. And she had seen them. She closed her eyes for a second, her pulse quickening with increasing panic. Her first instinct was to be quiet and pretend it hadn't happened. But even at sixteen Rita knew she couldn't do that. Doors here were locked for a reason. It was 1989, and the country was in the midst of civil strife, its rural areas dotted with pockets of violence, as unpredictable and surprising as landmines. Theirs was a false sense of security, brought by the picture-perfect landscape, the cobbled streets, the familiarity of those around them.

But always, always, there was the possibility of danger, lurking anywhere, ready to prey on a small, out-of-the-way town that boasted three overweight policemen (cousins) and no military outpost. They all knew each other here, and they had all been indoctrinated for as long as Rita could remember: "You see anything out of the ordinary, you report it."

Rita took a deep breath and stood up, shivering slightly when her bare feet touched the cold wooden floor. She opened her bedroom door slowly, careful not to make it creak, and tiptoed down the hall to her parents' room with growing trepidation.

She stood outside their closed door, her hand up, hearing her mother's rhythmic breathing and her father's loud snore. They slept in separate beds, virginal twin beds with dark blue spreads, and over each of them a simple wooden cross.

How many nights she had stood quietly in this spot, hearing the sounds of their sleep, hoping to hear some inkling of life beyond their breathing, wondering how in the world she and her brother could have been conceived in this sterile room.

"Do they really do that?" she'd asked her best friend, Jazmin, in horror when Jazmin showed her the sex-education pamphlet they distributed at the health center in the next town over. The black-and-white sketches depicted the man and the woman in a warm embrace, their mouths curved up in gentle contentment, while below, his penis clearly entered the opening in her vagina and little arrows marked the path of the sperm to the womb with cartoonish emphasis.

Rita had looked surreptitiously at her father's crotch for days, trying to divine any sign of lust that could override the utter indifference, sometimes laced with quiet contempt, with which he treated her mother.

Even so, her presence inside their room was strictly verboten, as was her waking them up at night, for any reason at all, from having killed a rat to dealing with a fever.

This time she gathered her courage and knocked, very softly.

"Father," she whispered, her voice breaking. Rita cleared her throat, then called him again, louder this time.

"Father!" she repeated urgently. His snoring stopped, then resumed a second later.

"Father, wake up!" she called again, rapping the door sharply.

This time he heard her.

"What!" he answered loudly from behind the door. "What is it?"

"There are men outside!" Rita whispered loudly. "Armed men."

"Wait there," he answered tersely after the briefest pause.

Rita heard him shuffling inside, opening and closing a drawer, mumbling something to her mother.

He opened the door abruptly, his heavy black hair—which he always kept impeccably swept back in place with a touch of gel—standing out in all directions. She would have giggled—if he hadn't been carrying the heavy shotgun she had seen only twice in her life.

"What happened?" he asked gruffly.

"I . . . I got up to shut the windows because it was raining, and I saw them down in the street. There were five of them," said Rita.

"Did they see you?" asked her father immediately.

Rita cringed. "Yes," she said softly, averting her gaze.

Her father looked at her, at the white cotton nightgown, at her long, loose hair and her bare feet.

"You stupid, stupid girl," he said, shaking his head, raising his left hand, then thinking twice about it. "Get in there with your mother, and don't come out until I say so," he added, pushing her inside his room and shutting the door behind him. Rita stood there numbly, her ear against the door, straining to hear him as he walked down the hall to her brother Sebastián's room, also admonishing him to stay inside.

She felt her mother's presence behind her, close but not touching her, a woolen blanket wrapped around her like a shawl.

"Rita, what did you do?" she asked anxiously, her face creased in worry, as it often was.

"We can't leave Sebastián alone," said Rita, not bothering to answer. Her brother was only ten. "He'll be scared!"

"No he won't," said her mother quietly, resigned. "He's a man. He'll know how to take care of himself. What did you do, Rita?" she asked again, and this time her tone left no room for evasion.

"Nothing, Mother!" Rita replied in a ragged whisper. "I looked out the window. That's all I did."

Her mother looked at her blankly. "Well, you shouldn't have," she said at last, shaking her head.

Rita opened her mouth, wanting to defend herself, then thought better of it and instead crouched next to the door, clutching her arms around her waist in a vain attempt to keep warm as she tried to discern movement in the floor below.

After a few minutes of silence, her mother handed her a blanket.

"Come on, cover yourself. The last thing I need is for you to get sick," she said gruffly.

"Thank you, Mother," said Rita, bringing her knees close to her chest so her bare feet were covered by the warm wool. She leaned her head against the door and remained perfectly still for what seemed an eternity, wondering what little Sebas must be thinking across the hall, hearing the quiet rumble of her father's voice on the phone downstairs and then nothing at all, until her initial fear gave way to exhaustion and she slumped asleep on the floor behind the door.

Her mother sat stiffly on the edge of her bed, one hand holding her blanket around her, the other hiding the handgun inside the folds of her nightgown. Only her eyes moved as she looked from the door to Rita and back to the door again.

*       *  ·  *

The man on the street lingered outside her window, hoping against all logic that the girl would open her shutters again. Long minutes passed as he stood, immobile, then motioned his squad to get a move on.

They called him El Gato, The Cat, but his name was Lucas and he wasn't a man. He was just a boy, but he had the chiseled features and exposed cheekbones of someone who had long shed the vulnerabilities of youth. None of them really knew how old he was; he'd told them he was twenty-four, but he was barely eighteen, a birthday he had taken note of, but not celebrated, just a week before.

They walked more quietly now, familiarizing themselves with the silent streets, enjoying the feel of firm ground underneath their feet after months of mud and marsh. He didn't mind the rain. It had been far wetter up in the mountains, and colder, too. There the early-morning mist penetrated your slicker and your sweater and felt as if it were forever impaled inside the marrow of your bones. At night it didn't matter how close you sat by the fire; the cold seeped in, insidious, its icy fingers creeping under your skin.

Part of their crew had already taken a hot shower—the first in nearly a year—and were already settled in at the lonely police station, the first place they'd gone to enlist cooperation. Others were at the church. It was always harder to make the priests see things their way, but after all, what was the use of resisting? Once the connection was established, they'd be under protection and unbothered, save for the monthly collection.

Lucas liked to walk the town as soon as he could. Get a feel for the land, at night, when the lights were still low, before the sunshine stung his eyes after months spent in the jungle's shadow. He believed fiercely in auras and insisted that the wrong energy could make the best-planned mission fail. This town was steeped in resignation. He'd come here two weeks before, alone, and quietly paced the cobbled streets, letting his hands run over the wooden doors and the low stone walls, covered with moss. He'd walked the perimeter of the town square, his lithe figure barely visible underneath the starry mantle of the sky, but he soon realized there was nothing to worry about. This was a place that collapsed into itself after a certain hour. There were two bars here, and a handful of cafeterias and restaurants, more extensions of homes than business establishments. There must be holidays celebrated here, birthdays, graduations. But that night, from his vantage point at the top of the steps leading to the locked church doors, he couldn't see a single light glimmering behind the shuttered windows.

He pictured her again in his mind: the long dark hair accentuating the white nightgown, the slender arms as she reached for the shutters. Her face was a pale oval, with huge, liquid brown eyes, almost a blur, but he would remember.

He made a mental note of the house, the window, the number. He was in no rush. No rush at all.

# Chapter Two

Rita and her brother didn't go to school that day. Or the next. Or the next. In fact, they weren't allowed out of the house at all, not even to go downstairs and help out at the store.

The two of them spent hours sitting on the floor next to the door that connected their apartment with the stairs that led to the store, straining to hear the muted voices of the men who walked in and out. Rita had neatly piled her notebooks and textbooks by her side and passed the time writing chapter summaries in her tidy little print. She figured that with midterm exams only two weeks off, she might as well get a head start in her studying, and she enjoyed it anyway. She reveled in the orderliness of the printed word, the nuggets of information encased in color-trimmed boxes, the pictures of presidents and leaders and places like China and India and Pakistan, countries whose names she would repeat under her breath as she looked at the photographs in her history book. She copied the highlighted information into her notebooks, writing page after page, the lined paper filling up with the words and exclamation marks and stars and suns and smiley faces—or frowns—that she added on the margins.

She had always been a good student: attentive,

organized, quiet. The kind of student who teachers forgot existed until they graded her papers and her tests, shining receptacles of excellence. It usually took a while for teachers to adjust to her, to reconcile the invisibility of her classroom presence with the forcefulness of her assignments. In the beginning of the term, they would call out names as they distributed graded tests in class and invariably pause when they reached hers, taking in the perfect score, then, looking around the classroom with a touch of bewilderment, trying to match the grade to the girl.

"Rita?" they would say, and her name was always accompanied by a question mark, a tinge of incredulity, until, weeks later, they'd finally get that the languid girl with the Madonna features and downcast eyes was the same person who aced chemistry exams and essay assignments.

Rita didn't care. She'd long ago perfected the art of invisibility, of drawing the least possible attention to herself through her actions. She was a girl of few words, even with her friends, who gravitated to her in spite of, or perhaps because of, her stillness, her ability to listen and finally say just the right thing.

Today she wrote in silence as the afternoon wore on, and Sebastián fidgeted, despite the marbles and the top and the messy stack of magazines with easy crossword puzzles that his father had brought upstairs the night before.

"Rita, I'm bored," he whined, throwing the pencil against the wall in an ineffectual act of small rebellion.

"Go watch some television," she replied, not bothering to look up.

"There's nothing on," he said, his voice rising and falling with ten-year-old indignation.

Rita sighed. He was right. They received only three channels here, and the early-afternoon programming had the bureaucratic dullness of a brick wall.

"And today," he continued, "my friends all went to play soccer. They went with Carlos's dad. Nothing's going to happen, Rita. I'm the only one who's stuck here!"

"And what do you want me to do about it?" she asked calmly. "You know I can't change Father's mind about anything."

"You could come with me and keep me company, and then maybe they'd let me go. But you like being inside and just reading!" he accused. "This is fun for you! You're weird," he added huffily, laying his head on his folded arms and turning his face against the wall.

Rita tilted her head and looked at his skinny back, the small shoulder blades sticking out like stunted angel wings. She loved him. Loved his wet-puppy smell when he came home after playing in the fields with the boys, loved his cold little hand snuggling into hers when she walked him to school in the mornings, loved that he could still speak his mind and make their father smile, as Rita had once done, long ago. He was the opposite of her: spoiled, loud-mouthed, a terrible student, and a brat, really, quick with his affections and mercurial in his moods. It made others go to great lengths to please him, and even at ten years old Sebastián took note, manipulating situations with the natural cunning of smooth talkers who always manage to get their way.

He was their miracle baby. After they'd had Rita, her parents had tried unsuccessfully for years to have a boy, but her mother's body violently rejected the notion of a second child, miscarrying three times, the last after a painful thirty-week pregnancy that yielded a fully formed baby, strangled by his own umbilical cord.

Rita didn't remember much of that time, save for vague recollections of tiptoeing around the house and occasionally being allowed inside her mother's darkened bedroom, the wooden shutters closed against the afternoon sun. Her mother would lie there for hours, grasping a crucifix as she stared at nothing, her eyes briefly lighting up when she saw six-year-old Rita, her hand wanly reaching up to touch her daughter's long hair.

"Your mother isn't feeling well," her aunt—who came and spent a month with them—would say, gently pulling her away from her mother's touch, leading her downstairs to the store, where Rita sat painting on the floor underneath her father's desk, listening to old boleros on the radio.

What Rita remembers most is that her father loved her then. He would let her pick special candy and Chocolatina Jet from the counter, and he would carefully post her drawings alongside the boxes of cigarettes so no clients could miss seeing them when they paid.

In the evenings he would put her to bed and say her prayers with her—*Ángel de mi guarda, dulce compañía, no me desampares ni de noche ni de día*—his deep voice lulling her to sleep like a gentle bass drum. Her mother lay semicatatonic in the bedroom across the hall, but her father's love—enormous, omnipresent—did not allow for spaces to grow in the landscape of her affections.

Rita was cherished then. She was still cherished when Sebastián was born, less than a year later. She wondered about that ever since she read the sex-education booklet. How her mother couldn't climb out of the bed to take care of her own daughter but still managed to have sex with her father and within two months of miscarrying one child—miraculously, it seemed—conceived another.

It must have been their last act of true passion, Rita thought, because how else to explain their unfettered love for Sebastián, even as their affections for her seemed to diminish the older she grew, until she lost the awkwardness of childhood and began to walk with a sway in her hips. That's when her father had stopped looking at her.

But she had loved Sebastián, too. Fiercely and immediately, with the certainty of someone who knows that others can change. She would look after him, she thought when she first saw him, sleeping at her mother's breast, and her then-chubby hands reached impulsively to touch his tiny head, covered with hair the color of soot, only to be slapped away by her mother's hand—the first of so many rebukes—with an admonishment of "Don't touch him, you'll make him sick."

Rita didn't care. Grown-ups slept. They got careless. For them, children were like gnats, pests that were swatted away and eventually ignored and forgotten. In the lazy afternoons, when her parents minded the store and the baby slept upstairs, she would creep into his room and watch over him. Hers was the first face he saw every time he woke up.

The first word he spoke was "tata," aimed at her as she walked toward him with his bottle.

"He's so smart, Sergio," her mother marveled to her father. "See? He's asking for his bottle!" But Rita, at seven years old, knew better. He was saying "tata" because he couldn't pronounce the *Ri* in "Rita." He was talking to her. "Tata," he repeated, and clapped his little hands spastically. He smiled at her, and Rita's heart opened up with an overpowering sense of joy, unlike anything she'd ever felt, far more thrilling than any of the carnival rides that occasionally made it to their town.

She now looked at Sebastián, at his skinny arms folded in indignation, at the black hair that had only seemed to get darker with the years, at the sliver of vulnerable pink skin that lay exposed between his socks and his scrunched-up corduroys.

"I'll fix it," she said quietly, with a certainty she didn't feel, but still she got up and called downstairs from the hallway phone.

"What's the matter, Rita?" her mother asked without preamble, not bothering to say hello.

Rita took a deep breath, then simply put it out there. "Mother, Sebastián wants to know if he can go to the soccer game," she said, cutting straight to the point. "I'll go with him. I'll make sure nothing happens. I promise."

Her mother was silent on the other end of the line. Rita knew she was torn between being overly cautious and giving in—not to her, but to Sebastián. After all, how many days could they keep them inside as the world resumed its pace around them?

"Wait," her mother said tersely, and even though she covered the mouthpiece with her hand, Rita could hear her whispering to her father, could hear their intense arguing, she cajoling, he adamant—because he feared what the guerrillas could do to his children.

"Rita?" It was her mother again, startling Rita, who had begun a quiet game of catch with Sebastián, rolling a little yellow rubber ball down the long hallway so their parents wouldn't hear them below.

"Yes, Mother?"

"Come downstairs. Alone. Your father wants to talk to you," her mother said brusquely, and hung up.

Rita placed her receiver carefully back on the hook. She knew that the guerrillas collected money—a tax, they called it, for protection. She knew they tried to recruit children, to make up for ranks thinned by heightened army activity.

She'd heard that some of them had already left, but a handful had remained behind indefinitely and set up their post at the police station, under the guise of keeping the peace in an area of relative calm but occasional disputes, stolen cattle, a gunfight or two over land boundaries.

Nothing too dire, but she knew they targeted people like her family, people who'd tried to remain neutral during the conflict. She knew they targeted towns like hers, compact but isolated, like random wrinkles on starched linen shirts.

Sometimes when she rode in the back of the pickup

truck that went twice a week to the next town over—the town with the closest bus stop—she'd look out at the winding hills and wonder just how the path of the main road had been decided. There was no rhyme or reason she could discern. Her town was just as beautiful, the fields around it just as fertile, the layout of the land designed for growth yet stunted by lack of easy access. She wondered if the man who'd plotted the route—because she'd never considered that it could be a woman—had succumbed to political favors or if he'd just simply, capriciously, let his pencil slide in one direction of the drawing board and not the other.

Rita didn't muse now. She looked at Sebastián, crossed her fingers, and shrugged with a smile before bracing herself and heading downstairs.

Her parents were behind the counter, her father smoking and drinking sweet black coffee from the thermos Rita's mother prepared for him each morning and each afternoon. He looked at her as she walked in, and in his eyes she caught a glimmer of surprise, as if he didn't quite know what he expected to see. It wasn't the first time she'd recognized that expression when he watched her, and Rita wished she could see herself as he saw her, because perhaps then she could figure out what so irritated him about her. Instead she hunched her shoulders slightly, trying to look less imposing, less whatever it was he thought of her.

"These thugs could be here for a long time, so we're going to have to learn to live with them," her father said with no preamble. He wasn't given to preambles or explanations. Just orders.

"They've assured us they won't hurt anyone, they promise they won't touch the children, but they're criminals and I don't trust them," he continued, looking straight at her for emphasis. "You are responsible for your brother, so pay attention now. You can go to school on Monday. You can take him to play soccer now. But you don't let him out of your sight for a second, you hear me?"

Rita nodded dumbly.

"You don't talk to anyone you shouldn't talk to. You don't stop and chat with your little friends, you don't go around flirting with boys. I don't want any of that to come back to me."

"No, sir," Rita said.

"You'll take your brother to that soccer game today, you'll wait for him, and you'll come back."

"Yes, sir," she said quickly.

"On Monday, when you go to school, the rules are the same. Sebastián is not to be alone. Ever. If he's not with your mother or with me, he's with you. Do you understand me?"

"Yes, sir," Rita said again.

"I expect you to act like an adult, Rita," he added. "Nothing stupid this time."

"Yes, sir," she repeated, frowning slightly. She had acted stupidly a single time, and the protest rose up in her chest, but she quelled it; she was a master of suppression. She didn't want to wreck Sebastián's outing, after all, and, like him, she now yearned to set foot outside, get out of the stale air inside this house.

Her father peered at her intently, then motioned with his head for her to go.

"Excuse me, sir," said Rita, her voice barely a whisper. "Ma'am," she added, glancing at her mother, who had already turned away, busying herself behind the cash register.

"Tell Sebastián to stop for his blessing before you go out," she told Rita, not bothering to look up as she spoke.

"Yes, ma'am," Rita said, and hurried back to the stairwell, carefully closing the door behind her before dashing up the stairs.

He was waiting for her expectantly at the landing, and his eyes lit up when he saw the smile on her face. Rita so rarely smiled openly inside this house; the news had to be good.

"You're a miracle worker, Tata!" he exclaimed, throwing his arms around her waist.

"No miracles, silly!" she answered, pulling him close to her, inhaling the sweet, crisp smell of soap from his little-boy hair. "You just have to ask. Now, come on, hurry, put on your shoes, let's go," she said, pushing him gently toward his room.

Rita changed into jeans and a red T-shirt and brushed her long black hair until it gleamed, then pushed it back with a red hair band that matched her shirt. The only mirror inside her room was a small, poorly lit rectangle on the inside of her closet door, rusting on the edges despite her best efforts to make it gleam. She peered into it now, fingering the lustrous ends of her dark hair, her biggest source of vanity: heavy, luxurious hair, like her father's, which she got trimmed only twice a year and which she deep-conditioned with a mixture of mayonnaise and avocado she wore to sleep once a month.

Rita smiled at her reflection. She didn't care that her teeth were slightly crooked, didn't care what her parents thought; she liked what she saw today.

"Tata!" Sebastián called.

"Coming," she said, hurriedly tying a sweater around her waist as she walked out of her bedroom, leaving her door wide open, a requisite in this house save for when someone was asleep or changing. They walked downstairs together, and Rita ushered her brother toward her mother for his blessing, her face impassive as her mother cupped his face between her hands and kissed his forehead with gentle care. Her father reached his arm over the counter and brusquely pulled Sebastián toward him, patting his cheek softly with his hand.

"Stay close to your sister, son," he admonished.

"Yes, Father," answered Sebastián, smiling broadly. "Your blessing, sir," he added, lowering his head for the sign of the cross.

"Rita, your blessing, girl!" her mother called irately.

Rita came up to her, surprised. It wasn't often that she received her blessing anymore, and she both relished and shunned the feel of her mother's hands on her face, her touch so unexpected that it felt insincere. Up close, Rita looked frankly at the face whose soft, round contours and fine features mirrored hers, but whose still-unlined skin had gone coarse and thick, like a leather sole. Her mother's eyes were her own, liquid drops of dark caramel that had once been soulful but now were simply resigned to the routine of her existence.

"What are you staring at, girl?" her mother asked suddenly.

"Nothing, Mother," Rita answered guiltily, and then, on an impulse, she added, "It's just that you look beautiful, Mother."

Her mother, caught off guard, arched her eyebrows at the unanticipated compliment.

"You do, Mother!" Sebastián piped up.

"Okay, run along now," said their mother, embarrassed, looking sideways at her husband. They were not given to flattery in this household. "You have to be back before it gets dark," she reiterated. "Be very careful."

"Yes, ma'am," said Rita, ushering Sebastián out the open door. She looked back and saw her father's gaze on her, his measuring, speculative gaze. Rita automatically brought her shoulders forward, lowered her head, fixed her eyes on the very next stone her feet were to step on as she took her brother's hand and walked away with him, attention on the road, following the tread of foot on stone, foot on stone, until she turned the corner into the town square and was no longer visible from her father's vantage point by his storefront window. Only then did she pull back her shoulders, toss back her hair, and untie the sweater she had loosely tied around her waist.

By the time Lucas's eyes found them, he saw the skinny little runt of a boy, his right hand swinging from that of his much taller companion—a girl whose black hair floated behind her like a shiny banner, undulating down her back in a languorous rhythm that connected the certitude of each of her steps with the sway of her full hips encased inside tight jeans. Even before Lucas caught up to them, before he grabbed her arm and turned her around, he knew her face, knew the slight curve of her narrow nose, the haughty tilt of her head, the liquid caramel of eyes that seemed to melt when they calmly met his, almost as if she were expecting him.

Rita stood perfectly still and tightened her hold on Sebastián's hand, automatically pulling him behind her. After five days confined with her brother, she was acutely aware of this man's smell, of the mixture of sweat and cigarettes and strength and anxiety that emanated from his body, from the hand that gripped her arm, from his hair.

"You shouldn't be walking alone around here," he said simply.

"We know our way," Rita replied steadily, even as she looked around for someone else, her pulse quickening with the realization that they were alone, midway between the town and the fields.

"I think I'd better escort you," the man said, ignoring her words, his hand running firmly down the length of her arm, to her hand and through her fingers before letting her go. Rita didn't move, paralyzed by a mixture of fear and headiness. She resisted the urge to touch the skin his hand had just grazed and reached inside herself to find the voice she had momentarily lost.

"Please. We'll get into trouble if they see us with you," she said softly.

His face fell, and in that brief, unguarded moment, she

saw him for what he was, for what his companions of over a year in the jungle had missed. He was just a boy. A boy with a crush who was now being turned down. Rita was only sixteen, and her experience with men was limited to a single innocent, catastrophic relationship. But she knew, with the certainty known by thousands of women before her, that right now, for this small moment at least, she had the upper hand.

"Maybe you could follow us, at a prudent distance." The words came out of her mouth unbidden, unnecessary, because he could do anything he wanted and because it was extraordinarily foolish of her to prolong the contact. But she wanted to see how far she could go, wanted to see his reaction, and she did see it, in the eyes that lit up, in the confidence that returned to his stance.

"I'll be your bodyguard, then," he said seriously. "And who am I guarding?"

Rita looked at him levelly, at his fatigues, at his boots, at his weapon, slung over his shoulder, at those strange brown eyes flecked with yellow, and at the full lips, so at odds with his sharp, angular face.

"I'm Rita," she finally said, and wondered if he could hear the resignation in her voice. He looked pointedly at Sebastián, who had quietly moved up to stand alongside her, but she just shook her head.

"What kind of gun is that?" her brother asked, oblivious, cutting to what had been the object of his fascination from the moment this man had grabbed his sister's arm.

"It's an AKS-74U, a Krinkov. It's Russian," said Lucas proudly.

"We're not touching guns, Sebas," Rita said coldly, pulling him away before his hand could reach out and feel the shiny muzzle.

Lucas slowly pulled the gun back, his face blank.

"Guns are only for protection...Sebastián," he said, smiling very slightly, taking note of her brother's name. "But you're protected with me, so you don't need one here," he added.

"What's your name?" Sebastián asked.

"Lucas," he replied, his real name slipping out as he looked from the boy to the girl. "I'm Lucas," he repeated, this time fixing his eyes only on her. "But you can call me Gato."

"Come now, we're already late," Rita said simply, and set forth again without looking back at him, afraid to even guess the distance between them, her brother's hand held tightly in hers.

For years afterward she would remember this moment, remember the smell of burned wood and coal that drifted toward them from the town, remember the sharp clarity of the afternoon air underneath the piercing mountain sun and the faint shouts of the children as they got closer to the playing field. She would remember his silhouette, just his silhouette—because the sun blazing behind him blinded her to his features the one time she dared looked behind her.

She didn't know then that words, more than actions,

determine the course of destiny, didn't know that there would come a time when she would give anything to take back those impulsive words—*Maybe you could follow us, at a prudent distance*—so uncharacteristically forward for her, spurred by the vanity of being made to feel beautiful again with a simple touch and a simple glance.

# Chapter Three

Lucas kept his distance. He set up post on a small hill overlooking the makeshift soccer field, listlessly watching the game out of the corner of his eye but focused really on her. She was sitting down below him with a group of friends on the grass. Another girl leaned into her, and a few minutes later he saw her look up toward him before bringing her hand quickly over her mouth to stifle a laugh—or an exclamation—before turning back toward Rita.

Lucas's hand tightened around his rifle. He'd always been self-confident, a natural leader, even while growing up in the most squalid conditions in the outskirts of the city. Being armed gave him even more assuredness. Rarely did anything that anyone said or did perturb or deter him.

He looked at the group of girls below, at one in particular who was clearly the alpha female, a busty blonde with milky skin. In his present position, he could have any girl he wanted, anywhere he went; it was one of the perks of the job.

But he wanted this one—this Rita. He had never seen a girl quite so beautiful, quite so clean, quite so precise and perfectly arranged, her T-shirt tucked neatly inside her jeans, her fingernails clipped short and painted the lightest pink, with not a touch of grime underneath them.

Lucas sat down, propped his gun between his knees, and lit a cigarette, inhaling deeply and savoring the taste of the smoke and the feel of the sun's warmth on his face. He waited.

\* \* \*

"Don't look!" Rita chided Jazmin, pulling hard on her hand.

"He's cute!" said Jazmin, stifling a giggle.

"How can you tell from here? He's too far away," Rita said reasonably.

"Because I've seen him, silly," said Jazmin. "He hangs out around your dad's store all the time."

Rita blushed, delighted. He hung out around her house? Surely it was because of her. Or was it? He had given her no inkling that he'd recognized her from the other night, although she had recognized him, immediately, and her almost visceral reaction to him surprised her. She'd never been particularly interested in the boys around here, except for Alberto, and look where that had led her.

She glanced surreptitiously up toward Lucas, saw him take a deep drag from a cigarette, and blushed when Jazmin elbowed her in her side.

"Just don't let your dad catch you," she whispered to Rita. "He'll kill you!"

"No kidding," said Rita softly. "He already gave me a lecture this morning." She smiled, trying to make a joke of it, but Jazmin just squeezed her hand comfortingly. They were complete opposites—bright, open, quirky Jazmin and the quiet, beautiful, serene Rita—but had been friends forever. Some of Jazmin's most cherished childhood moments were of times spent helping Rita restock the shelves in her parents' store. When they were finished, Rita's father would reward them with candy, sometimes a piece of gum, even though everyone knew that chewing gum would give you cavities, which meant going to the dentist two towns and three and a half hours away and having him use that awful drill. But Rita could do no wrong then.

It was later, when she grew into her face, into her hips, into that glorious mane of hair, and the men started noticing, that her father, too, noticed that he no longer had a little girl of his own.

Only Jazmin knew what had really happened with Alberto. She had forced it out of her after Rita was abruptly grounded, indefinitely, all of her social interactions outside school severed without possibility of appeal.

Because Alberto, he never said a word, and in that, Rita found a measure of solace. Whether out of decency or sheer fear, he never blabbed, as far as Rita could tell, never bragged of how she'd melted into him inside the storage closet of her parents' own store, how she'd allowed him to kiss her and run his hands up and down her body and finally lift her T-shirt over her head and unclasp her bra. Perhaps he never said a word because Rita Ortiz was Rita Ortiz, as aloof and untouchable as a princess. But for the first time in her life, Rita fancied herself in love, and her boundaries simply shattered. Her relationship with Alberto had progressed slowly but relentlessly, from coy glances during church to furtive hand-holding to quick kisses stolen in the nooks and crannies of their school.

Lots of people kissed—at fourteen Rita had known this, but she had no idea if they felt the way she did for hours afterward, restless and flustered and ready to scream for more. But anything more, she knew, would make her a slut. Only sluts, her mother reminded her, let men fondle them and treat them with what she deemed "lack of respect." Rita wasn't quite sure what constituted "lack of respect." Was it allowing his tongue inside her mouth? His hand to linger on top of her sweater, over her breasts? On Sundays, during church, Rita would pray for forgiveness for whatever it was she could have done wrong and for the strength to resist whatever it was she might do wrong. But she brought none of those doubts to confession, incapable of baring this part of herself to Father Pablo, who'd baptized her, who gave her candy after Mass on Sunday mornings, who was, after all, a man, and how then could he possibly understand what a woman felt? Maybe, she thought, she was indeed a slut, and the thought filled her with a mix of regret and shame.

But alone with Alberto, all her misgivings fell by the wayside, not entirely forgotten but brushed aside, like a pile of dirty laundry that's swept under the bed to be dealt with at some point later, just not now.

That Saturday afternoon Alberto went to see her in the store, where she was manning the register while her mother and Sebastián went to her cousin's house and her father napped upstairs. It was not uncommon for him to be there, but never outside the vigilant supervision of one of her parents, who knew, as only parents know, that girls of a certain age simply cannot be left alone with boys, not unless one can accept the inevitability of an embrace, a touch, the contact of lips against lips and anything else that time allows.

But Rita's parents also thought, as all parents think, that their child, this unusual blend of reserve and shyness and haughtiness, was too special a child, too innocent, and yes, too superior, to allow herself to be sullied by a boy, and certainly not by this boy, the son of a notorious sleaze who was always trying to gain an unfair edge in business dealings. This boy was four years older than she was and already a well-known womanizer, known for promising, promising, but then simply moving along to the next one. Even at fourteen Rita was too smart for him, they thought, and certainly too smart not to know better. Most important, her father, especially her father, believed her to be above reproach, believed that if common sense ever abandoned her, fear of reprisal from him, sheer respect for her father, would keep her in line.

That Saturday, Sergio Ortiz woke up abruptly from his nap, although he couldn't say why. Hot and bothered, he called out to Rita from the landing on the second floor and, hearing no answer, walked quietly down the stairs. He eyed his empty store with mounting dread and silently, suspicion rising in the pit of his stomach, made his way to the storage closet in the back. He heard them before he saw them, Rita's voice saying the right words—"No...I don't know.... Not now"—but her breathless tone was all wrong. It was a certain yes, to Alberto's entreaties, to his "Come on, Rita, it's nothing, just relax."

Sergio thrust the door open without preamble, anticipating what he was going to find but nevertheless shocked to see her—his Rita, *his* Rita—with her top off, her bra off, her pubescent breasts exposed to Alberto Castillo's

probing, obscene hands, the tableau made all the more sor-
did against the backdrop of stacked boxes, liters of soda,
and cigarette cartons.

Sergio lost it. That evening when he recounted the
events to his wife, he couldn't tell her exactly what had happened, couldn't recall exactly what he'd done.

Rita could, though. She'd let Alberto convince her to
go back, just for a minute, but once in the isolation of that
closet, with his mouth on hers, with his hands on her hair,
she forgot all about minutes, forgot all about rules and
admonishments, forgot that if he ever opened her blouse,
she would automatically become a slut. All she could hear
were his words, all she could smell was his Saturday-best
cologne, all she could feel were his hands, hot and clammy
on her breasts. All she could see was his white shirt, freshly
washed and ironed for her, when her father burst through
the door and in a single movement hauled Alberto from
on top of her, shoved him against the opposite wall, and
punched him, hard, on the face.

Alberto Castillo fell to the floor and felt his nose burst
in a kaleidoscope of pain and color, the blood gushing onto
his white shirt, lights exploding before his eyes.

"You fucking bastard!" bellowed Sergio at the top of his
lungs. "In my home? In my store? With my daughter?" He
punctuated every last word with a hard kick that pushed
Alberto Castillo across the floor to the door of the closet.
He caught his breath for a second as Alberto tried to strug-
gle back to his feet, then kicked him again, out the door,
as if he were a bag of trash, kicked him down the rows of
products, kicked him all the way to the front of the store,

until Alberto was finally able to scramble to his knees and get a grip on the door handle. But before Alberto could pull himself up, Sergio grabbed him by the collar, pushed him violently against the counter, and rammed his knee hard into Alberto's crotch.

Alberto grunted in pain and felt himself go slack in Sergio's grasp.

"You ever get close to her again," Sergio said softly, twisting Alberto's shirt so the boy's ear was millimeters away from his own mouth, "and I will kill you. I'll kill you," he repeated.

He opened the door and tossed Alberto out like a rotting fruit, not bothering to wait for him to get up and run, oblivious to the looks of his neighbors playing Parcheesi across the street.

In the closet Rita struggled to put on her bra, her fingers fumbling as she missed the clasp again and again, until she simply gave up and stuffed her bra into her jeans pocket and put her shirt back on. She looked at the smudges of blood on the doorjamb and recoiled. She knew that her father was capable of violence, but not like this, not against her, not because of her, and she stood uncertainly inside the closet, petrified, wishing she could disappear, be anywhere but here, thinking she would give anything, anything, to take back the last half hour. Outside the now-open closet door, she could hear her father's heavy breathing, his slow footsteps as he walked closer and closer toward her, until he stood framed by the door, his trim figure suddenly gigantic against the backdrop of the afternoon sun that came in through the front window.

Sergio looked at his daughter. His only daughter. His pride and joy. He grimaced as he saw in his mind her naked breasts in that bastard's hands, and he felt the anger rise again within him, strong enough that he had to stop himself from lunging at her and beating the beauty out of her face. Instead he took a step back and looked away from her, at the place above the cash register where her paintings hung.

"You," he said firmly. "You are not to see him ever again. Ever. You are not to see any man alone ever again until I say so. I am not going to raise a whore."

Sergio took a big breath and felt a small thread of regret permeate the rage that consumed him.

"Now, go to your room and wait for your mother," he added, and turned his back on her and walked toward the cash register, never looking back as Rita scurried up the stairs.

The next day Jazmin waited for Rita in vain at the monthly communal party, piecing together the fragments of what had happened from tidbits of gossip passed around in between dances. "They wouldn't let me go," Rita told her Monday at school, her face swollen from a full night of tears.

"Don't worry," Jazmin had said, hugging her close. "They'll let you go to the one next month. You'll see."

But they didn't. Not the next month nor the next nor the next.

It had been eighteen months now, and for Rita time had stood still.

"Don't worry," Jazmin said now, laying her head on her

friend's shoulder. "Once we finish school, we can leave and you won't have to deal with them anymore. You'll see. We'll make our own rules."

* * *

That night dinner was more animated than usual, as Sebastián regaled his parents with tales of a victorious match and a scored goal.

When their father asked if they had encountered any trouble, he simply shook his head solemnly.

"You cannot ever, ever tell Mother and Father that we talked with that man," Rita had admonished intently before they'd turned in to their street. It was almost dark, and they were hurrying to get back in time, but before he could round the corner, she grabbed his arm and crouched down beside him, serious.

Sebastián nodded uncertainly. "But why not?" he said. "Nothing happened."

"Because I'm asking you not to, Sebas," Rita said, trying to quell her panic. "And because if you do, they won't let us out, ever again, while those men are here," she added, and she knew that at least was true. "You don't want that to happen, do you? They'll lock us both up."

Sebastián shook his head more fiercely now, his small-boy's brow furrowing with rare concern.

"So promise me," Rita insisted.

"I promise," said Sebastián earnestly.

Rita looked at him unconvinced. She needed way more insurance than that.

"Swear to God," she said, putting her hands on his shoulders.

Sebastián brought up his fist to his mouth and kissed his thumb.

"I swear to God, I won't tell them we spoke with anyone."

At the dinner table, Rita sat quietly, nibbling on her chicken stew as her brother lied for both of them.

Lucas.

She liked that name.

# Chapter Four

Sundays, after early-morning church, was her time. Her parents had to mind the store together—it was their busiest day of the week with the traffic to and from the market—and Sebastián was shuttled off to her aunt's small farm to play with the cousins.

And Rita walked alone. She would change out of her Sunday-Mass dress into jeans and tennis shoes and pick up the huge woven market basket and set forth, an overgrown Little Red Riding Hood dispatched to buy the family's weekly supply of food, her long hair braided back from her face, the wad of carefully counted money nestled inside her bra so it wouldn't get lost or stolen. On Sundays everybody from the surrounding farms and tiny townships came here, to their square, where they set up shop by 6:00 A.M. so that they were up and running by the time the first Mass let out. The day was a procession of people, spilling out from the church onto the square and from the square up the steps to Mass, announced by the toll of the bells sharply at 6:00, 8:30, 11:00, and at 1:00 P.M.

Rita was in the square by 7:30, when the crowd was still light, not just to pick the best produce of the day but to prolong her time outside, making her way as slowly as possible from stand to stand, sorting through the fresh white cheese wrapped in plantain leaves, the piles of freshly pulled herbs with their roots still attached and clinging to moist soil, and the mounds of fruits and red and yellow and white potatoes as the market filled up with people and animals—hens and goats and pigs tethered to trees or bleating in protest at their confinement in makeshift pens. The odor of frying food mingled with that of fresh-cut flowers and hot chocolate and tangy oranges and fresh mint in a cacophony of smells that impregnated Rita's hair and clothes, as the smoke from the burning woodstoves stung her eyes. Rita, the most fastidious of girls, reveled in this messy, dirty, sometimes stinking disarray. She couldn't say why, except that her memories of this market were uniformly warm and welcoming, like a security blanket, and as time had passed, her parents had allowed her to keep this one indulgence, in no small part because she was a smart shopper and a ruthless bargainer who could stretch the weekly budget to surprising lengths.

She was sifting through a sack of oranges, picking them out in various stages of ripeness to last the week, when she felt his hand travel the length of her arm, a caress so light it gave her goose bumps, and she closed her eyes, just for a second, despite herself.

"Please don't do that," she said softly, not looking up. She didn't need to; she knew with absolute certainty it was him.

"Why not?" he countered. "No one is watching. Even if they were, they can't see. Rita." Lucas paused before saying her name and ran his fingers over her arm again.

"You look so pretty," he said under his breath, sorting through the oranges beside her. "Come walk with me."

"I can't," said Rita, keeping her eyes studiously on the oranges, counting them haphazardly, wondering if no one was really looking and no one really could see.

"Sure you can," he said, turning away, tossing an orange up in the air. He caught it and shoved it into his pocket before taking another in his hand. "I'll meet you inside the church. In the sacristy. In five minutes." Only when he walked away did Rita finally look up. She stood there dumbly, an orange in each hand, watching his wiry frame move easily through the crowd until all she could see was his sandy hair receding to the other side of the square.

Rita hastily finished counting her oranges and packed them into the basket.

"I'm taking forty," she told the stand owner. "That guy took two. Did he pay?" she asked impulsively.

"Are you kidding me?" said the man with a snort of disgust. "Who's going to charge those sons of bitches for anything? We're already paying *them* as it is." He counted her change and gave it to her. "I do have to say, there's been no robberies around the farms since they got here. But I just keep my mouth shut and mind my own business," he said, shaking his head.

Rita nodded and hoisted her basket up to her hip. She waded through the crowd until she found Jazmin's stand. For the last six months, her friend had been weaving bracelets out of colorful threads and selling them for a dollar a pop, saving, she said, for their graduation and planned emancipation. The bracelets had started simple, like those that so many others wove, but Jazmin had been perfecting her "proprietary technique," as she called it, weaving single-thread designs into the braided pattern. It was an Indian secret, she claimed, known only to the women in her family.

"Hey, Jazzy, can I leave my basket with you for a bit?" asked Rita, setting it down beside Jazmin, who sat cross-legged on the blanket, braiding threads, her wares laid out neatly before her.

"Sure, Tata," she said, not bothering to look up. "You taking a little walk?"

"I'm actually going to church for a bit," said Rita.

"Really!" said Jazmin, smiling widely. "Twice in a day. How very pious of you."

"I want to go light a candle," said Rita, feeling just the slightest bit of guilt. "I need to ask for a miracle."

"Okay," said Jazmin happily. "Say a prayer for me, too. And here, take...hmmm." She paused, looking through her stash before picking a bright red-and-fuchsia weave through which a golden thread danced in disarray. "Take this one. Reds are lucky colors," she said, motioning for Rita to extend her arm so she could tie the bracelet around her wrist.

"How about blues?" asked Rita, fingering a weave of different shades of sapphire and indigo.

"Protects," said Jazmin. "It's supposed to ward off the evil eye."

"I'll buy it," said Rita, picking it up with her free hand.

"Just take it," said Jazmin, frowning as she tied a second knot.

"No," said Rita. "I want to buy it, okay? Let me contribute to the fund." She plucked the bill from between her breasts and handed it to Jazmin.

"Thank you, Tatica," said Jazmin, smiling, putting the bill between her own breasts in turn. "Take all the time you need, okay? I'm not going anywhere."

Rita shoved the bracelet inside the pocket of her jeans and walked briskly toward the church. It was eleven-fifteen, and the Mass would be less than halfway through. She walked through the wooden doors and blessed herself. Then, instead of going inside the church, she turned right, toward the sacristy at the end of the hall.

She raised her hand to knock on the closed door, but it opened before she could do so, and Lucas pulled her in, locking the door behind her. Despite her trepidation, despite the rattling of her heartbeat, which surely he could hear, Rita looked around curiously at the familiar room with its tall wooden beams and book-lined walls. She hadn't been here in years, since she'd worked as an acolyte after her First Communion. She and Jazmin had loved coming here because Father Pablo would give them the left-over wafers from the Holy Communion and allow them to read the children's Bible, the one full of pictures that felt more like a comic book than a boring book force-fed to them by adults. Now she took a step back, until she stood against the locked door, a safe distance between herself and him.

"Are you allowed here?" she asked Lucas, perplexed.

"I'm allowed everywhere," he said with a touch of smugness. Rita remembered the words of the man at the orange stand who kept his mouth shut and minded his own business. She wasn't sure if she was supposed to be scared or not, and now, face-to-face with Lucas, she couldn't quite read him. His light brown eyes were aloof in that chiseled face—cold, even, as they looked now, like flat pebbles. But he had a soft, beautifully shaped mouth with a full lower lip that gave him a childlike pout. His physiognomy, like his personality, was elusive; he could look and sound like her peer one second, like a grown man the next. He gazed at her proprietarily, this arrogant child-man, his hand resting lightly on his weapon, and now she didn't like what she saw or felt.

"What?" she asked, slightly annoyed. "You're trying to impress me with your big gun? You're trying to scare me?

"I have to go," she added, shaking her head, feeling foolish and now just a little scared.

"Don't," said Lucas, a touch of pleading in his voice, and in that instant he was a boy again, rushing to explain. "I promised Father Pablo I wouldn't mess with his church or with him. I like priests. So he lets me hang out here. When I need to be alone."

"You like priests," repeated Rita, still debating what to do. "That's...a strange thing to say."

Lucas sat on Father Pablo's desk and pulled his gun strap over his head, laying his weapon down carefully beside him. "I went to a priests' school when I was little. Before I joined my comrades," he explained matter-of-factly. "The priests were good to me. They treated me right. My father would beat me all the time. He was always high on something. But the priests, they found the positive side of everything. So I try to reach an agreement with the priests, wherever we go. It's bad karma to fight with priests."

"Oh," she said. "And is it bad karma to fight with girls?"

Lucas slid off the desk and walked up to her, reached behind her neck, and slowly pulled her long braid from behind her back, winding it carefully around his wrist until his face was just inches from hers.

Rita stood very still, her arms akimbo, mesmerized by the utter unfamiliarity, by the tangible danger of the situation, by the heat of his orange-laced breath as it fanned her face. She wondered if he was going to kiss her, and she wondered what she would do if he did. Her experience with men was limited to Alberto, and yet here she was, alone with a man again, in the most unlikely of places, the sacristy of her church.

"It's very bad karma to fight with girls," he said softly, "especially with beautiful girls." Lucas brought up his other hand and very slowly caressed her cheek, then tracked the outline of her eyebrows, her jaw, her lips.

"And you're the most beautiful girl I've ever met," he said simply.

"Maybe you're saying that because you've been in some godforsaken camp for too long," Rita replied, her voice barely a whisper.

"I *have* been in a godforsaken camp for too long," he said, laughing a very small, mirthless laugh. "But you're still the most beautiful girl I've ever met."

Rita looked at him wide-eyed, and now she could see that *his* eyes were no longer flat and expressionless but a clear light brown framed by a yellow iris—like a cat's—their depths flecked with the faintest golden sparks. He leaned in and kissed her, and this time she closed her eyes, obliterating everything else but the feel of his chapped lips on hers, and all she could think of was how sweet, how delicious, it was.

She didn't know how long they stood there, just kissing, her braid twined around his hand, until the Communion hymn brought her back to who she was and where she was. Rita opened her eyes to the sight of Father Pablo's crucifix, clearly visible over Lucas's shoulder, and she instinctively recoiled, pushing Lucas away from her so violently that he stumbled back into the desk.

"This isn't right," said Rita, putting her hands up. "I can't do this. We're in church. And you..." She stopped herself from uttering the words.

"I what?" asked Lucas, his eyes fading to opaque again, his face hardening.

"You're a guerrilla!" she blurted out, putting her hands over her eyes. "I'm sorry," said Rita, feeling completely out of sorts. "I shouldn't have come. I don't know why I came. I'm really, really sorry. I like you, but I really can't see you. I can't," she said, her voice slightly firmer now. "I couldn't."

"Are you afraid of me?" asked Lucas, as if he hadn't heard a word she'd said.

Rita started to shake her head again, then stopped, realizing how palpably idiotic it was to pretend.

"Yes." She nodded. "Yes I am. A little. Sometimes."

"Why?" he asked, still keeping his distance.

Rita shrugged at the obviousness of it. Did she even

have to explain it? She wanted to leave yet seemed incapable of mustering the will to turn around and take the two steps that led to the door.

"You think I'd hurt you?" he pressed.

She licked her lips and was immediately sorry, because the gesture reminded her of *his* lips. She opened her mouth, closed it again.

"Yes," she said finally. "I think you would. I think that's what you and your people do. You carry guns and you kidnap people and you intimidate people, and you *would* hurt me. I think you could get angry at me and hurt me and hurt my brother and hurt my family."

Rita immediately put her hands up to her mouth, horrified at her uncharacteristic lack of restraint. Everything about him made her go against her nature, made her veer from excitement to distress, both unfamiliar emotions for her, but this time she hated her lack of control.

She met Lucas's steady glance, and then, before he could reply, she abruptly turned around, opened the door, and walked out of his sight.

Rita stood at the top of the church steps. From up here the plaza sprawled before her, dotted everywhere with the colors of the market, and beyond she could glimpse the roof of her house, could identify the bend of the road that led to her doorstep. She could, in fact, identify every single house in her picture-perfect town, now held semi-hostage by men with guns. There was nowhere to hide here.

As if reading her thoughts, he materialized beside her, pausing for just a fragment of a breath before heading down the stone steps.

For that instant he looked her full in the face and spoke very softly but very clearly.

"I will never hurt you. Or your brother or your family. Never," he reiterated, and walked assuredly down the stairs, his rifle hanging low over his chest, unhurried, as if he were right at home.

*      *      *

He filled her thoughts.

Completely.

At home and at school, she was quieter than usual, not just drawn into herself—in the inside looking out, as was her habit—but in the inside looking further inside, to a place only she knew existed, a place inhabited by his touch and his smell and the perfect fit of his lips on hers, opening up her pores and heightening her senses to an irrational degree of expectation that left her exhausted and anxious by the end of the week.

She hadn't seen him since Sunday, and on Thursday afternoon as they passed the church on the way home, she impulsively turned to Sebastián.

"Sebas, I want to go light a candle in church," she said calmly. "You go ahead home and tell Mother I'll be there in about half an hour, okay?"

Sebastián shrugged, unconcerned.

"All right, then," said Rita, relieved at his lack of interest. "I'll wait here until you turn the corner." She stood there quietly at the edge of the square, watching him intently as he walked briskly to the end of the street, his backpack hanging haphazardly from a single strap. At the corner he stopped obediently, a small figure in brown corduroys and white shirt, his dark hair spiking up in a state of perpetual defiance, and waved at her before rounding the corner to go home. The minute he disappeared from sight, Rita quickened her pace as much as she could without drawing any attention to herself and walked briskly up the church steps, only to find the sacristy door closed. She stood there irresolutely, shuffling her feet, losing her nerve. She had no way of knowing if he was in there or not. And if she knocked and Father Pablo came to the door, she would choke on an explanation, she was sure of it.

As if reading her mind, the voice from inside the door called out, "Father Pablo isn't here!"

"I'm not looking for him," Rita replied, inching closer to the shut door.

For a second she heard nothing at all, then his footsteps as he strode across the room and opened the door for her. She stood still under his gaze, feeling awkward in her school uniform—the blue pleated skirt down to her knees, the white button-down shirt and the blue sweater, the saddle shoes and the ankle-length white socks.

"Rita," he said simply, and she walked in, dropped her backpack on the floor, and let him put his arms around her and very, very gently draw her in, until her head rested right on his shoulder. She allowed his arms to envelop her and felt his bone and sinew through the thick, rough fabric of his shirt.

She knew she shouldn't be here. She knew that beyond the taboo circumstance of his provenance she shouldn't be alone in a sacristy with a man, with any man. But she didn't care.

She raised her face and let him kiss her, as he had the other day, until the five-o'clock church bells rang, and she broke free, picked up her backpack, and ran all the way home.

# Chapter Five

Rita had always kept her secrets well guarded, her serene exterior smothering them like a thick woolen blanket. She became better at it now, a master of near lies, the little kernels of truth that she could place in her tales fueling her ability to deceive. And it was easy, so easy to do it. Nothing changed on Mondays, Wednesdays, and Fridays. But Tuesdays and Thursdays, the days Father Pablo went to minister in the neighboring towns, she would drop Sebas off from school and walk to the church, climb the stone steps slowly, savoring the delay, and first—always first—go to the altar by the door and light a votive candle. The church was St. Isidore, commemorating the patron saint of farmers and laborers, but she prayed to her namesake, St. Rita, praying with as much strength and concentration as she could produce, her hands pressed tightly against her furrowed brow, although she was never quite sure what exactly she was praying for, save perhaps for the opportunity to breathe, to exist, to not look over her shoulder every minute. And then she would light another candle, for the Holy Mother, and ask for forgiveness for what she'd done, for what she couldn't help feeling, and for what she was about to do, and she would walk out of the sanctuary of the church and into the vestibule and down the hall and knock on the sacristy door.

Sometimes, lying on the blanket Lucas placed on the floor behind Father Pablo's desk, Rita would look up at the crucifix on the wall, unflinching, as he lay on top of her, and wondered if she would go to hell for this. Certainly she would have to pay in some way, for taking part in this aberration, for it was an aberration, an obscenity, fornicating on the floor of the sacristy where she'd been baptized, where she'd taken her First Communion, received her Confirmation. But there was nothing obscene in the way he touched her, in the reverence with which he knelt in front of her, so gently unbuttoning her blouse, turning the plain cotton fabric into the finest silk, his hands—the callused hands of poverty and hard work and cruelty, because he had seen and caused plenty—moving so softly over her collarbone, her breasts, her stomach, making her cry out loud in pleasure, in sheer joy. Those afternoons, as the setting sun gleamed through the tinted panes of the windows, his eyes would turn yellower still, the flecks within them dancing with new vigor as he looked at her, and for the first time in years Rita felt loved. She felt adored by a man, and no matter what happened or what she felt before or after, she could do—would do—nothing, not a thing, to change this moment, this feeling.

Afterward they would lie together on the floor and he would undo her braid, wrapping her hair around them like a shawl, inhaling the smell of fresh shampoo, because she always washed her hair on their rendezvous days. He had never been this close to a girl who smelled so good. His sexual experience was limited to uncomfortable encounters up in the mountains, dirty and hurried and scared, born out of sheer necessity for sexual relief more than anything else. His attempts at love had always been accompanied by the sight of his gun within easy reach in case of emergency and had always ended with him wiping his hands on his camouflage pants, a quick, embarrassed good-bye replacing the intimacy of a kiss.

With Rita he had time. Precious little time, but nevertheless more than he'd ever enjoyed. He'd turn on Father Pablo's radio, loud enough to muffle the sounds from within and without and, screened by a curtain of ballads and vallenatos, Marco Antonio Solís and Camilo Sesto, they would talk in hushed whispers until dusk and the cooling temperatures and Father Pablo's imminent arrival forced them to reluctantly, regretfully, separate. He would unwrap his arms from around her frame, untwine her hair from around his neck, allow his hand to linger until the last possible moment over her breast, finally letting her go, piece by piece until they stood, apart, their backs to each other as they hurriedly dressed, just two kids, the shadow of his gun incongruous against their adolescent nakedness.

Sometimes he'd look at her in her school uniform and feel a pang deep inside, a remembrance of how his life used to be, once upon a time when he was someone else. Only when he was back in camouflage was he truly himself again, a soldier, a fighter, who could hold her close one last instant, promise silently to protect her against God-knows-what, even if he never said the words out loud.

For the rest of her years, Rita would associate sappy ballads, the voices of Julio Iglesias and Roberto Carlos, with furtive lovemaking and the delight of discovery.

Lovemaking because it never felt like sex, this seeking and finding with Lucas.

"Do you have a girlfriend in every town you visit?" she whispered one afternoon.

"No, you're the first," he said absently, his former displays of macho bravado long since put aside.

"Why?" she pressed.

"Why what?"

"Why don't you have more girlfriends?" she asked.

"I'm not supposed to," Lucas said matter-of-factly. "My captain says it distracts us from our mission."

"You don't have a mission now?" she queried.

"Of course I do," he said, a tinge of guilt steeling his voice. "My mission—our mission—is to effect change. To keep order. To protect you. To make the people aware that rich or poor, their rights are the same. Do you see military here? Do you see infrastructure? There is no law in these provinces. That's what we bring. We bring law and order and a sense of mutual respect to the people!" Lucas's voice rose with his rhetoric, but few speeches can persevere before a naked body.

Rita let the words that didn't interest her dissipate and asked again. "But why, then, am I your first girlfriend?" she asked, her tone of voice never changing.

Lucas looked at the serenity of her face, propped up against her arm, at those eyes of liquid brown he wanted to jump into and swim in. He wanted to tell her that the mere sight of her soothed him like a balm, that something in the way she spoke, the way she listened, made him feel that anything was possible. He wanted to tell her that as tough as he was—as strong, as fast, as cocky—he'd never felt truly comfortable with girls, certainly not with girls as pretty as she. He wanted to tell her that he lived for her visits, that every aspect of his life had become rote, except the hours with her. He wanted to tell her he'd had sex so many times, with so many different people, that he'd forgotten what it felt like to really feel—to feel a woman's mouth cushion his, feel her lips move beneath his, more alive, more intense, almost, than any sexual act.

"You're my only girlfriend because you're the only one I've liked," he said simply.

*     *     *

On Sundays she brought him copies of the old magazines left over from the store the week before. They sat and devoured *Reader's Digest* and *Vanidades* and *Cromos* and old newspapers and talked softly while Father Pablo gave Mass, too intimidated by his voice and the choir and the overwhelming aura of holiness that permeated the church that day to go beyond a mere kiss, although they sat side by side on the floor, shoulder to shoulder, thigh to thigh, feeling their mutual warmth flow from one body into the next one, giving them just enough of a charge to last for nearly three more days without each other.

On Sundays he told her things. Told her how he'd grown up poor, so very poor, in a two-room tin shack in the out-skirts of the city. The streets were unpaved, and every time it rained, the roads would turn to mud, thick, sticky mud that would seep into his toes as he carefully trod his way down the hill to school, trying to find stones and pebbles to step on in a desperate attempt to salvage his only pair of decent shoes. By the time he got to the classroom, he was invariably a mess, the mud clinging to his shins and his knees, invalidating the cleanliness of his freshly washed face, his slicked-back hair, the impeccable white T-shirt. Impeccable because no matter what, his mother washed their clothes every single day, scrubbing them clean of grime with a bar of blue soap in that little kitchen sink, then hanging them out to dry on a nylon string that stretched from the kitchen window to the other end of their tiny concrete patio.

"We're poor, but we're clean" was his mother's mantra, one of her few vestiges of pride, for in their impoverished neighborhood they were among the poorest of the poor. His mother worked as a maid, gone twelve hours a day at least, and his father walked in and out of their lives with cataclysmic effect, always leaving behind him a trail of tears and bruises.

"He broke my arm once," Lucas told her, "because I got home late. We were playing soccer, and I just forgot about the time. I really did," he said with a mirthless laugh. "I wasn't trying to piss him off or anything. We were just having fun, and we forgot."

Lucas shook his head and ran his fingers lightly over her arms. His life had been one of precious few cherished memories. But he was an optimist by nature, and even though he didn't know it, his capacity to think of the day ahead had kept him alive longer than would have seemed possible for someone of his provenance and circumstance. Even now, even when he looked back, when he looked forward, he intermingled the good with the bad, the possibilities with the risk, and the direst of stories, the most perilous of plans, acquired a sheen of hope.

"I was the oldest," he continued. "And my little brother, Julián, he walked in first, and my father just got up from the table and slapped him. I mean, really slapped him hard. A slap doesn't sound like much, does it? It's the kind of thing women do on TV when they get mad at guys. But when a grown man slaps an eleven-year-old? I have to tell you, it hurts.

"Julián started crying. Not just because it hurt like hell, but because it's such a humiliating thing, to be slapped in the face. And I just lost it. I did. I went up to my father, and I started screaming at him, 'Don't hit him! Don't hit him anymore!' And I pushed him and pushed him and pushed, until he punched me and I tripped on the chair and fell really, really hard on the floor. But he was *always* picking on Julián. Always. Julián was really small and kind of delicate. He would call him a marica. A fag. And smack him around. But this time it was so unfair. Poor Julián, he didn't even like to play soccer. He just went because I wanted to. He'd do anything for me. I had to defend him.

"The funny thing is, my father punched me on the nose, right? I started bleeding like a pig, my mom started screaming. Ha. Finally. And my father said I was another marica, to get up and act like a man, and then he grabbed me by the arm, and *that* really hurt. And I started screaming, too."

Lucas shook his head and smiled.

"Oh, he was such a bastard, my father. He didn't believe that anything was wrong with me, and the next morning my arm was huge—it was all swollen and it hurt like hell.

They had to take me to the emergency room, and it turned out it was broken."

Lucas rubbed his arm, rotated it and looked at it, as if he could somehow still see the cast or the bruise or the swelling.

"But"—he brightened up as he continued—"the thing is, when we went to the hospital, everyone was so nice. It didn't matter that we were poor, that somebody had beaten the shit out of me—they cared. They paid attention. They asked me how I felt. They talked to *me*," he said, pointing fiercely at his chest.

"Did they ask how you broke your arm?" she inquired.

"Oh, they knew," he said dismissively, rubbing his arm. "It was so obvious. My mother was scared out of her wits, told some stupid story about me tripping. My father didn't even go. They knew," he repeated. "I think that's why they were so nice, actually, because they knew but they couldn't do much more than set it straight and put the cast on. They couldn't fix everything else that was wrong. The doctor even gave me his card. His personal card," he added with a small touch of pride. "He told me to call him if anything like this ever happened again."

"Did you?" she asked.

"No," he said flatly. "The next time it happened, I just left. He punched me, and that time I just left."

Rita looked at Lucas, her boy-man, still a child and yet trying so desperately to act as if he didn't care, as if everything that had happened hadn't left a scar, like that broken arm, long healed and now intact.

"I'm sorry," she said quietly.

"Don't be," replied Lucas defiantly. "Look at me. I'm better off now. My comrades, they saved me.

"They saved me," he said again for emphasis.

He didn't tell her that the last night his father didn't just punch him. He kicked him in the stomach, driving Lucas to his knees until he spit out blood and bile and fourteen years of hate that splattered onto his mother's clean floor, her measly little badge of honor. He didn't tell Rita that he hadn't planned it. That he'd slipped into the bar down the street and snuck three shots of aguardiente, just for the heck of it. By the time he got home, he was buzzed and ornery and uncharacteristically fed up with the cards that life had dealt him. And there he was, his father, his nemesis, this loser of a progenitor who was not only unable to provide for them but who also felt compelled to beat out his frustrations on Lucas. He didn't tell her that when his father raised his hand against him, it caught him by surprise, and, slowed down by the effects of alcohol, he just took it, took the blows, falling to his knees like a repentant little girl, until his father delivered that last kick to his gut, right above his groin, and Lucas started retching violently, watching his courage fly out of his mouth in a spray of blood and just as quickly reclaiming it. He didn't tell her that he was consumed by a rage so blinding, so complete, that for the first—and only—time in his life he truly couldn't see or hear, but he clearly remembered taking out the little pocketknife he always hid in his sock, and from his prone position on the concrete floor he lunged at his father in one last, desperate motion, stabbing him in his thigh, in his stomach, in his groin, again and again, until the blood spurting everywhere wasn't Lucas's anymore.

He didn't tell her that then—and only then—did he scramble up in panic and run for the door and down the hill to the road below, running until he reached the perimeter of the city and found shelter in an empty shed. The next morning he continued his trek, walking farther out into the country, away from his crime, away from the police he imagined were chasing him, until he encountered a group of guerrilla fighters who recognized the hunger in his eyes and the need in his belly and took him into their ranks.

He didn't tell her that his father survived. That an ambulance took him to the same hospital where Lucas had been treated, and there he received four blood transfusions that returned him to life after he'd nearly bled to death from a stab wound to his femoral artery. He didn't tell her that his mother had never called the cops, because the next night, while his father convalesced in a hospital bed, she packed her meager belongings and, with Julián in tow, took a bus back to her hometown.

He didn't tell her any of this, because he never went back and he never knew. But he didn't tell her either that killing gets easier with practice. That once you've felt blood flow from another man's body into your hands, taking away a life can become a job. He didn't tell her how many times he'd stood over a man and watched the light drain out of his eyes, until they were just blank slates looking up at the perpetually brooding jungle sky. He didn't tell her that in his nightmares it was sometimes him on the wet ground, trying to get a last glimpse of sky, to catch a sliver of moon peeking through the foliage.

"Do your parents beat you?" he asked abruptly.

Rita drew back, horrified. "No!" she said, then paused. "Well," she considered, "they don't beat me. They just slap me sometimes, if they get really mad at me."

"Huh," said Lucas. "Then I guess you know what I'm talking about."

Rita didn't answer. The voids in her affections sounded so superfluous compared to his. Yes, her parents slapped her around, but that wasn't what hurt the most. It was the wall of silence, the refusal to speak to her or even meet her eyes, for days on end, when they deemed she had done something wrong. On those days Rita began to doubt her own existence, looking for validation in her reflection in the closet mirror, peering closely, very closely, at herself so she could see her breath steam up the glass before her and then be assured that she was still a living being, that she still mattered.

And yet she had a home, a nice home with her own bedroom, a living room, a formal dining room, parents— a store, even! Rita was no fool. She knew there was a world beyond hers, a world where her reality would be deemed seriously lacking. A world she would get to, soon enough. But Lucas had lived—still lived—in hell, even as he whiled away his free time in the confines of a house of God.

Beyond the closed door and the shuttered entrance to the church, Rita heard the strains of the Communion hymn and began to gather her things. As she checked her pockets for her keys, her hand connected with a wisp of string, Jazmin's blue bracelet, the one she'd impulsively bought for Lucas and forgotten to give to him several weekends ago. She took it out carefully and admired again the intricacy of the weave, a triple braid in six hues of greens and blues.

"Give me your arm," she said.

"Huh?" Lucas said.

"Come on," she said impatiently, and pulled his hand toward hers, turning it over and carefully tying the ends of the bracelet in a cross knot, like Jazmin had taught her, so it couldn't be undone.

"It's blue, for protection," she said.

Lucas touched it uncertainly. He wasn't a man of ornaments or talismans, save for the leopard tooth that hung around his neck on a thin leather cord, a gift from an Indian shaman he'd met in the jungle.

"I don't know," he said. "Doesn't it look girlish?"

"No, of course not," she said, and impulsively grabbed his wrist, looking straight into his eyes. "It's for protection," she repeated with conviction. "You can't take it off. When it's ready to come off, when it no longer needs to protect you, it will come undone on its own."

Rita leaned into him and cupped his face between both her hands with a possessiveness she unwittingly tempered by kissing him full on the lips, so softly, so completely, that Lucas forgot to protest.

"I'll see you on Tuesday," she said, and swiftly rose to her feet, straightening her blouse and adjusting her braid. Quietly, she opened the door a crack, checking to see that no one was in sight. Satisfied, she walked out, nonchalantly, never looking back.

On their off days all Lucas could do was watch help-lessly as she walked to and from school, her pleated skirt swishing behind her, her averted gaze and disdainful back a public rebuke to his intent gaze as it followed them— tall Rita and little Sebastián—meandering through the cob-bled streets. One time Sebastián saw him and involuntarily raised his hand in greeting, but she immediately slapped it down, loudly, so there could be no room for doubt among those around them that any association with the interlopers was disliked and discouraged.

What neither of them reckoned with is that love and lust are transformative, that they peel back layers of your self, surreptitiously, like the softest caress. Before you know it, fragments of you are exposed for all to see, little pieces you didn't know you carried within you until they found their reason to exist.

Rita had lost her common sense with Alberto, a mistake she wasn't about to repeat. With Lucas she was careful, to a fault. Every meeting she had with him was orchestrated to the last detail, taking into consideration the schedules and habits of Father Pablo, her mother, her father, and even Sebastián. Too many things had to go wrong, too many plans had to change, for anyone to find them together. But Rita couldn't control what she didn't know. She couldn't run a check on that slight shift that takes place in women when they fall in love: the loosening in their gait, the increased profoundness in their eyes that only manifests itself when one's primary focus is to please a partner.

Her mother picked it up almost immediately, the way women do, and she peered suspiciously at Rita when her daughter brought her hand to her hair, languorously pulling it back behind her ear as she absentmindedly picked at her food at the dinner table. Susana Ortiz tried to make sense of her daughter's shift—minuscule, but a shift nevertheless. Something was happening, but what, exactly? Every one of Rita's waking hours was accounted for. Perhaps, thought Susana, it was something Rita was reading in school, and she made a mental note to speak with her teacher at some point.

And Lucas—careful Lucas, reliable Lucas, ruthless Lucas—for the first time in a long time, looked at himself in the mirror. He saw a face hardened beyond its years, saw the wispy growth of a beard that had never quite taken off, noticed little bumps on his forehead when he swept back the straight hair that fell in uneven strands over his eyes. He frowned at the flaws. He had no idea if he was good-looking or not; no one had ever told him anything either way. He liked his eyes, though, his cat eyes that gave him his nickname, with that weird yellow iris, like a ring of fire, containing the brown.

Lucas took off his shirt and looked at himself dispassionately. He also liked his body, the strong, reliable body of a fighter, a survivor; limbs lean and sinewy, muscles and tendons clearly defined as much from the natural strain that being in the jungle demanded as from the hours he and his comrades spent in camp working out with makeshift weights. It was his one vanity, his body, his instrument, the skin and bone and muscles that kept him alive. He now

looked at it differently, not as a utilitarian piece of equip-
ment but as an object of desire. She liked to touch his arms,
his stomach, his back—his back especially, running her fingers down from his shoulders to his waist and up again.
Lucas brought his hand to the nape of his neck and closed
his eyes, just for a moment, imagining it was her hand there.

Tomorrow, he thought, he'd go to the barbershop and
get a haircut, a proper haircut.

Rita would like that.

# Chapter Six

Later he would be the first to acknowledge that it was his mistake. But that Saturday, sitting in the barber's chair in anticipation of the Sunday ahead, Lucas felt important. With a long white bib tied around his neck, he watched as the barber carefully snipped his hair, shearing and layering so that one by one his features acquired more prominence, his cheekbones became more pronounced, his mouth fuller, his eyes lighter. Lucas was not motivated by vanity of any kind, but now he liked what he saw. And that tiny moment of vanity made him careless. Had he been more aware of his surroundings, he would have monitored the street outside from his vantage point before the mirror. He would have noticed the worried looks of the other customers as they looked out the window. He would have had his hand on his gun before, but as it was, he had no alternative save to stay in place when he heard the door clang open and the shouted order:

"Out! Everybody out except the fag in the chair!"

Lucas's commander wasn't expected for another week, and automatically, like the soldier he was, Lucas braced for the worst at his surprise appearance, sitting very still as everyone except his men left the shop. Under the long bib, he slipped his hand inside his left boot and pulled out his knife, simply as reassurance, because he knew that if push came to shove, he was a dead man.

"What do you think you're doing, asshole?" asked the commander, cuffing him on the side of the head.

"Getting a haircut, sir," answered Lucas, stone-faced.

"Don't get clever with me, asshole!" screamed the commander.

"I'm not, sir," answered Lucas, then adding, truthfully, "I'm not sure what the issue is, sir."

"The issue," answered his commander, bringing up a chair and leaning very close to Lucas, "is, you've been neglecting your duties."

"I'm not neglecting my duties, sir," said Lucas stoically.

"Oh, you're not?" asked the commander. "Let's see. Do we have any recruits?"

"Not yet, sir," replied Lucas. "We've been taking care of other matters, sir."

"'Other matters,'" parroted the commander, his voice heavy with sarcasm. "Like what? Like recruiting women?"

So this was what it was all about, thought Lucas, feeling his pulse quicken in sheer fury as he sought his roommate's face in the mirror, his comrade-in-arms, who was conspicuously looking straight ahead. Lucas couldn't tell if he saw the beginning of a smirk or a grimace, but either way, he thought, the man would pay sooner or later for not keeping his mouth shut.

"Some women can make good recruits, sir," Lucas said with no emotion, feeling much less conviction than his words indicated.

"But I understand that this one isn't one of those, Gato,"

said the commander swiftly. "I understand this one's a little princess. I understand that her brother was ripe for the taking and you haven't done shit about it. Have I understood right, or is this all bullshit?"

"I don't consider the brother to be good recruit material, sir," said Lucas firmly. "And, sir, I had to stabilize the area before going for recruits."

Without any warning, the commander's fist shot out and punched Lucas on the side of the face, his knuckles connecting with Lucas's cheekbone in a *thwack* that resonated across the shop. Lucas flinched but forced himself to suppress the tears that threatened to well up, forced himself not to move, not to bring his hand up to his cheek, his eyes looking at his reflection as if watching a movie, noticing how ridiculous the white bib looked now, how his head rebounded, how the skin on his right cheek immediately turned a bright cherry red. His hand tightened around the knife, and he wondered if he could fight for the time needed for the red to become black and blue and the swollen skin to subside onto his facial bones.

The commander walked slowly around the barber's chair and looked at Lucas appreciatively.

"Everybody out," he said abruptly, never taking his eyes off Lucas.

In the mirror Lucas saw his roommate's eyes flicker in surprise, and he made himself breathe, thinking it would be an ignominious death, this one, with a slit throat in a barbershop like something out of *The Godfather*.

"What? Are you idiots deaf? Out!" screamed the commander, walking behind them and securing the lock on the door after they filed out. He drew the curtains, blocking any view from the street outside, and walked slowly back to Lucas, who remained immobile.

The commander brought over a chair and sat facing him, his gun lying loosely across his lap but nevertheless pointing squarely at Lucas's forehead. Lucas looked at the muzzle of the gun and then at its owner, and it dawned on him that he had spent a large portion of the past two years fighting, training, walking alongside this man, and yet all he knew was his nickname—Zurdo-Lefty.

"Gato, Gato, Gato," said Zurdo, shaking his head, but there was no sarcasm in his tone this time, simply inevitability. "In our business we don't get attached to anyone. To anyone," he repeated. "Least of all to some woman. Women will get you killed. They'll make you get careless, they'll make you make mistakes. No woman is worth it. You screw them and you move on."

Lucas didn't say anything. With each of Zurdo's words, Rita's essence faded just a little bit, like an entity of light that is suddenly shattered, the particles scurrying in all directions despite your best attempts to gather them back.

"Your men noticed," the commander went on. "It's bad enough you're involved with someone outside the force, but you can never let your men notice. That's not good. You can't make mistakes like this anymore, asshole, you hear me?" The commander spoke with clenched teeth, his words once again etched in fury, but in the question Lucas recognized the possibility of a second chance.

And then there it was.

"Gato, you and me, we've been through a lot. You saved

my life," the commander said, and only then did Lucas
remember the cold fear that would still envelop him every
time they were there in the jungle and the shots would suddenly ring out, unseen, impossible to pin down. He remembered how one day they were paying more attention to the
ground below them than to the possible dangers around
them, because it had rained and the path was slippery and
treacherous and the fall to the engorged river below would
have been almost impossible to survive. One of two lonely
shots hit Zurdo on his left shoulder, throwing him off balance, making him stumble until he teetered on the brink of
the ravine. Before he could free-fall down the cliff, Lucas
reached out and grabbed the strap of Zurdo's rifle, feeling himself slip in the mud, but instead of letting Zurdo go
he desperately clawed at the bush to his left, holding on
fiercely with one arm and pulling Zurdo in with the other,
gathering strength from God-knows-where to draw him
in and thrust him into the thicket. They stayed there until
the jungle quieted again, Lucas pressing down on Zurdo's
shoulder to stem the blood flow, aware it would be so much
easier just to leave him behind, save his own skin, because
they were at least two hours from camp and Zurdo could
still die on him, despite Lucas's best efforts.

"You should have let me go that time," Zurdo now said
quietly, putting his elbows on his knees, leaning into Lucas.
"But you got attached. You still have"—Zurdo pounded his
fist on his chest, nodding—"heart. You have heart. But you
can't get attached, Gatico. Not to me, not to some bitch, not
to anyone. You won't last long if you keep this up, man."

Lucas still didn't reply. Zurdo was now close enough to

him that he could whip his knife up and stab him easily in the stomach and leave through the back door.

"But I'm grateful," Zurdo added, oblivious, or perhaps just cocky, looking him straight in the eye. "And I want to return the favor. Good soldiers don't forget. You're lucky you're a good soldier. You've paid your dues. You've given yourself to the cause. But you need a colder head if you're going to lead these civilian missions. I'm not gonna discipline you, this time, but you go back to camp tonight."

"Yes, sir," Lucas said firmly, his mind already going forward, measuring the possibilities: another year in the jungle, probably, before he would be allowed long-term contact with civilization again. But he could hone other skills up there, maybe train with the medic; there was always something to do, after all. Despite the humiliation he'd just gone through, he was alive, he was still whole, he hadn't lost his rank.

Only then did he think of Rita, of how everything about her had become a liability. He didn't dare mention her now, didn't want to break this fragile truce he had suddenly gained.

Zurdo did it for him.

"Don't let this happen again, Gato," said Zurdo, his eyes cold. "It's a problem. The girl, you can bring her—if she submits to our rules of coexistence. Exclusive relationships aren't condoned. You know that."

Lucas looked down for the first time, finally aware of just how stupid, how deluded, he'd been with his little power trip.

"Actually, might be better for her if she comes," said Zurdo, standing up. "If anyone knows you've been messing with her, she'll be meat for the army or the paramilitaries once they get here."

Lucas looked at Zurdo in the mirror, at a weary, lined face that surely was younger than the years it projected. It was a face of present action, of no illusions or long-term plans. *My face*, thought Lucas, *just like my face*, and Rita's image dissolved a little more until he fully grasped what Zurdo was saying. She'd be meat for the army. Or she'd be meat for his men up there. But at least she'd be with him.

Zurdo looked at him, head cocked, rifle cocked.

"We leave at one in the morning. If you bring her, she's your responsibility, so don't do anything you'll be sorry about later. And a word to the wise, Gato: Watch your back with that roommate of yours. Accidents happen out there in the jungle."

"Zurdo," Lucas spoke finally. "I don't care what happens to me. But please keep her and her family out of it. They have nothing to do with this."

Zurdo snorted mirthlessly and shook his head.

"You're really pussy-whipped, aren't you, Gatico?" he said. "I didn't know you had it in you." Zurdo shook his head again. "These things never turn out well, my man. I know what I'm talking about. Nothing's gonna happen to them under my watch." He sighed. "But whoever comes after, it's out of my hands. You realize that promises are hard to keep around these parts. I hope you were discreet with the neighbors. The less they know, the better."

Zurdo turned to leave but flung a parting shot: "And put that knife away and take off that fucking bib. You look like a fucking fag, not a commander of the people's army."

Lucas ripped the bib off and hurled it to the floor. He stared at the mirror for a long time after Zurdo left, rubbing his bruised cheek, then looked at his eyes until the yellow flecks subsided and they turned brown again, the way they were when he first set foot in this town, like pebbles. Only the yellow band around his irises remained, eerie against the dullness inside. Like a cat. El Gato, he thought, recalling how thrilling, how rousing it had all sounded once, when he'd fancied himself a fighter, a man among men, before he got sucked down by the unbearable monotony of their daily existence. Tomorrow at this time, he would be trekking up the mountain, his boots again digging deep into the mud, taking a shit in some freshly dug hole, like a dog, waiting days for a clearing in the river to at least wash the grime from his hands and face, eating beans and cold rice for weeks on end. When all was said and done, he could be wasted any minute by a bullet, but alleviating the sheer drudgery of his existence was just as daunting. Lucas remembered the sweet taste of that orange in the market-place, the sticky juice rolling down his chin, and his mouth watered. How casually he'd treated his brief rule, the luxuries he'd so quickly taken for granted.

He was a fool.

\*     \*     \*

A shower of pebbles woke her up, landing with a small clatter inside the open window and stinging her sleeping face. Rita woke up, scared more than startled, her hand coming up to touch her cheek. Only then did she hear his voice, calling from outside in a hushed whisper.

"Rita!!"

She quickly sat up and knelt on her bed, like she had that very first night, and looked at the street below through the wrought-iron bars of her open window, to where he stood on the cobblestoned road, his cap obscuring his face as it had done before.

"What are you doing?" she whispered.

"Come down," he whispered urgently.

"Are you crazy?" Rita whispered back, looking anxiously down the empty street, then back at her door.

"Come down!" he repeated, panic creeping into his voice. "I have to leave. You have to come down. Now!"

Rita narrowed her eyes, forgetting her own anxiety and for the first time registering his. She had never seen Lucas lose control, and the sight frightened her.

"Lucas, they'll hear me. I can't!"

"You have to, Rita. Just be really careful. Come on!" he insisted, gesturing angrily with his hand.

Rita stayed as she was for a minute, straining to hear a sound inside her house. She finally signaled him to wait and stepped carefully onto the wooden floor with her bare feet. She opened her bedroom door quietly, easing it shut with the utmost care, and stood for a few seconds, reassured by her father's loud snoring and her mother's steady breathing. She remembered that night three months ago, when she'd stood in the same hallway, trying to wake her father, pounding on his door. So much had happened, yet so little had changed. Here she was, still creeping around her own home, invisible, like a ghost, seen and heard only under duress.

She tiptoed past their door, down the hall to the

connecting door, reached up and cautiously turned the double lock, cringing as it snapped open, but its sound didn't interrupt the steady beat of her parents' slumber.

Rita took a deep breath and pulled the door open, stepping on the landing and shutting it quietly behind her, her confidence rising with every step that separated her from her parents as she walked down the stairs. She unlocked the second dead bolt and stepped out into the dark store, closing this door behind her, too, sealing off the sound as best she could. She walked quietly to the delivery door on the side, unlatched it, and silently drew it open, recoiling as the frigid night air penetrated through her flimsy cotton nightgown.

"Lucas?" she whispered, and he turned from where he stood in front of the store's main door.

"Rita," he said simply, and drew her quickly into the shadows, into his embrace, trying to take all of her being into him in one movement, taken aback by the intensity of his relief, by the very tangible fear he'd been carrying for the past twelve hours, the fear of not being able to touch her again.

Rita let him, sensing she needed to let him, bringing her arms up around his neck as he breathed in the scent of her, his mouth and nose buried in her hair, in her neck, in her arms.

"What happened?" she said, her voice muffled by his chest.

"They know. They know," he said, shaking his head against her neck, and then, to his horror—and hers—Lucas started to sob.

Rita held him very close, instinctively rocking him back

and forth even though she had never seen a grown man cry, and her mind was racing in a million directions, guessing at the implications of his words. Behind his shoulder a quarter moon sat high in the sky, lighting up the thin, cold night air, illuminating a path for a flurry of stars, diffused through the heavens like a capricious game of pick-up-sticks.

Inside her embrace Lucas took in a deep, shuddering breath, the way Sebastián used to do when he was younger and still cried in her arms.

"Come with me," he said, his face still pressed against her.

"What?" asked Rita.

"Come with me," repeated Lucas.

"Come with you where?" she asked dumbly.

"Up. To our camp," he said. "There are other women there. I'll take care of you, and we can be together."

"You want me to go away with you? To be part of the guerrillas?" Rita asked incredulously.

"Why not?" asked Lucas, finally drawing back, looking at her through red-rimmed eyes, thinking again, against all logic, why not? She was miserable here, a nonentity, but even as he thought it, he saw her shake her head no, felt her shift in his arms, her pliant limbs stiffening between his.

"I couldn't, Lucas. You know I couldn't."

"You couldn't or you don't want to?" he asked steadily, holding her now at arm's length, knowing he was being unreasonable; a few hours earlier, after all, he'd been thinking about her welfare, her safety, but now, face-to-face with her again, he couldn't bear the thought of parting, even if it meant dragging her into his little hell. They'd have each other, wouldn't they? That made all the difference.

But Rita was still shaking her head, her eyes bright but dry, her shoulders flung back in an animal's predatory stance. "I'm not going, Lucas," she said. "I'm sorry. But that's not the life I want. And I have a family."

"No you don't. No you don't," he declared disdainfully. "You don't have a family. Think about it. You have a loveless house where you have to look over your shoulder to even open your window. But you have me. Can't you see that?"

Rita just shook her head. She was so close now. So close to finishing high school, turning eighteen, and then no one could stop her. She wasn't planning to stay here, her breath squashed out of her every day, so stifled that she had to hunt for a trace of it on her closet mirror. She was biding her time. But her plan didn't involve risking her life, pledging allegiance to Lucas's movement, and, quite frankly, it didn't involve going into the jungle and living like an animal, without a bed or a bathroom, her head shorn like a man's. Unconsciously, she brought up her hand to her hair.

"I can't do that, Lucas. That's not what I want. Why don't you stay?" she asked, putting her hand on his arm, the idea hitting her with sudden clarity. "You can get out of there, and we can start again together. We can work. We can go to school."

Lucas stepped back from her, gently removed her hands from his arms, and shook his head, surprised at the person he saw before him.

Lovemaking made people supple, compliant, and in the past two months all his interactions with Rita had taken place within the framework of their sexual encounters. He now saw someone whose detached resolve he had failed to recognize before. *Why*, he thought wonderingly, *she's just like me. She will do anything she has to do, just like me.*

He stood before her, only their fingers touching, feeling the night air quietly seeping into him through every pore. He was unfettered in all directions. He could start again, he supposed. He could desert—they'd look for him, but he was good at hiding—and the army could use someone with his skills. But then what would he be fighting for? He thought of Zurdo's words: He was a good soldier. A good man. And he knew in his heart that it was so. Yet no one had called him that before, no one had believed except his comrades. And now her. But what did she know about him, really?

Lucas looked at Rita longingly, with the same wonderment of the first day. In the shadows of the moonlight, she looked like a creature from another world, the white nightgown glowing in the dark, her long hair framing a face that reminded him of the Holy Mother's in church. He reached out to touch the curve of her cheek, where it melted into her neck, feeling how soft it was, thinking he might never again touch something so soft, never return to a part of this world he had been allowed to step into so wondrously, so briefly. In his mind he was already gone.

"I'll come back, okay? I don't know when, but I will," he said, and yet even as he spoke, he knew they were just words, knew there was no guarantee he could keep that promise. He took a deep breath. "In the meantime you can't tell anyone about me, you hear me?" he said. "I'll be long gone by tomorrow, but no one can know we were together. Ever. It's dangerous for you and for your family."

"I know that, Lucas," said Rita.

"No, I don't think you do," he replied earnestly. "If the paras or the army ever come here and find out about you and me, they'll punish you. No one can know, Rita. No matter what happens, tell no one about me, you understand?"

Rita nodded, remembering how she'd made the very same admonition to Sebastián, made him cross his heart, swear to God. Now she stood awkwardly with Lucas in the dark, uncertain of the next step.

"So that's it?" she said finally.

"I guess so," mumbled Lucas. He stood with his legs apart, balancing his rifle across his chest, feeling the reassurance of its presence. It felt comfortable. *He* felt comfortable, and the thought singed him with guilt.

"Take care," said Rita softly. She didn't know if she was supposed to cry right now, hug him perhaps, beg him not to go, but it just wasn't in her. She felt empty.

"I will," said Lucas, attempting a half smile. "See?" Remembering, he lifted his fist to display the blue woven bracelet. "I have your protection. Hey!" he said suddenly. "I have something for you, too."

Lucas reached behind his neck and tried to untie the leather cord that held his leopard tooth, but years of wear and moisture had fused the knot into a solid ball. He finally pulled, hard, until the cord broke, and he came over to Rita, placed the tooth with its broken cord carefully in the palm of her hand and closed her fingers tightly over it.

"It's a talisman. The shaman who gave it to me said it wards off the evil eye. Use it," he said earnestly. "It works."

"And you?" Rita asked.

"I have your bracelet. It's your gift. That's more powerful than anything, isn't it?"

Rita smiled weakly and this time felt her lips tremble involuntarily. "Yes," she said softly, although she was far from sure.

"Okay, I should go," said Lucas at last, and from the tone of his voice Rita could tell that he was already imagining the trek ahead; he had already moved beyond her.

"I'll wait until you get up to your room," he said matter-of-factly, already issuing orders, like a soldier. "Go on." He nodded, giving her the saddest of smiles. "Wave to me when you're up there."

Rita turned silently and walked to the door, glancing back at Lucas, who stood there on guard. He looked so certain, she thought. So aware. Under his cap his face was barely visible, and on an impulse Rita ran toward him and, still holding the leopard tooth in one fist, grabbed his face between her hands, looking at it intently, trying to discern his yellow eyes in the darkness. She ran her fingers over his cheekbones, pressed them hard against that mouth she loved so much, against his head, against his shoulders, then brought them up once more to his face and kissed him softly, fully on the lips.

Without waiting for his reaction, she ran back and shut the door quietly, firmly, behind her. She ran up the stairs stealthily, locked the upper staircase door, and finally, shut the door to her bedroom inside the sleeping house. Rita knelt on her thin mattress, opened her arms wide, and with each hand grabbed one of the heavy, wooden shutters that guarded her window. Below her she saw Lucas, unfamiliar save for that stance, that stance she recognized the very first night she saw him. She raised her hand to him, and Lucas nodded back at her. Then he turned and walked away, briskly, firmly, his boots clicking on the stone-paved road until he rounded the corner into the town square and was no longer visible from her window.

Rita took a deep breath and closed the shutters firmly, bolting them, sealing herself off from the world outside. She looked at the leopard tooth on her bed, tracing its shape, thinking of an appropriate hiding place. Only then did she realize that she didn't have a single photograph of him.

# Chapter Seven

Two weeks later, as she walked Sebastián to school, Rita threw up.

She'd ignored the nausea that began at the bottom of her throat during breakfast, provoked by the aroma of bacon. Ignored it as it rose up to her mouth, flooding it with saliva, and tried to squelch it with each step as they left the house, taking in big gulps of morning air. Just as they rounded the corner, she let go of Sebastián's hand and turned to the wall, spilling everything inside her stomach over the sidewalk.

Rita leaned against the wall, touching her cold face with clammy hands, then slowly allowed herself to collapse until she sat on the curb, her face in her lap.

"Rita, are you okay?" asked Sebastián, alarmed. "Shall I call Mother?"

"No, no," answered Rita, the thought sobering her. Anything but, she thought, although she longed to rinse out her mouth and simply lie down. "Must have been something I ate," she told him brightly. And it must have, for by the time she dropped off Sebastián and got to school, she felt perfectly fine.

The next time it happened, she was at school. She had just eaten her midmorning snack when it all came bubbling up, as before, except on this occasion, knowing what to expect, she made it to the bathroom in time.

"We're going to the infirmary," Jazmin informed her as she patted Rita's face with cold water. Rita didn't protest, allowing Jazmin to lead her quietly to the bare little room behind the office, where she lay down on a clean white cot and simply closed her eyes, surprised at how very tired she was.

She didn't know how much time went by before the principal's voice awakened her.

"Rita, how are you feeling?" the woman asked, the concern in her face real as she stood next to an anxious Jazmin. Rita Ortiz had never been sick, not since the first grade.

"Good!" said Rita, slowly sitting up, and she was. "The same thing happened a few days ago," she went on, unthinking. "I left home in the morning and started to feel nauseous, threw up, and then it was as if nothing had happened. I think I just have a stomach flu, Mrs. Rodríguez."

Fanny Rodríguez was a small, plump woman who favored tight brown slacks and cardigan sweaters over starched white blouses. Unlike most people in this town, she'd gone to college—in Bogotá, no less—but ended up here, encapsulated in the mountains, after working as a teacher for the school as part of the community service required for her to graduate. When the slot for principal opened, she grabbed it, holding on to the romantic notion that one person could make a difference. After fifteen years her ambitions were tempered; in a pool of ordinary students, already subdued by geography, poverty, and the inherent unfairness of their place in life, there were few gems to choose from, although she prided herself on her ability to single them out.

Jazmin Sodi was a gem, the principal had long ago decided. The daughter of peasants, she possessed a resolve and an ingenuity that confounded Mrs. Rodríguez. Something in that home had to have sparked Jazmin's creativity, her relentless optimism, her dogged ambition, but how, when her barely literate parents could hardly sustain a conversation with their child, Mrs. Rodríguez couldn't imagine. Jazmin was her project, earmarked for something different, although she wasn't quite sure what that would be.

Rita Ortiz, on the other hand, she couldn't decipher. A sly, secretive girl, she thought, who hid her true intentions behind downcast eyes and earnest study habits. Mrs. Rodríguez still wasn't convinced of Rita's much-talked-about intelligence or her ostensible piety, so at odds with her undulating walk and her surreptitious displays of vanity. She couldn't quite grasp why Jazmin was so taken with her. More than taken. They were best friends. Inseparable in school. It was Jazmin who had sought out Mrs. Rodríguez and insisted she look in on Rita. And now Rita was rather cavalierly saying she felt perfect.

Mrs. Rodríguez looked at Rita appraisingly, registering her words.

"The other day?" she asked. "How many times has this happened before, Rita?"

"Well, I've been feeling a little nauseous lately, but I've only thrown up once," Rita replied, her brow furrowing, her chin lifting up with a touch of defiance, wondering if she should have kept her mouth shut.

"Jazmin, would you step outside for a minute, please? I need to talk to Rita alone."

A surprised Jazmin glanced from Mrs. Rodríguez to an immobile Rita and started to complain before the principal cut her off.

"Now, please, Jazmin."

Jazmin left without a word, and Mrs. Rodríguez once again regarded Rita measuringly, taking in how lushly feminine she looked, like an overripe peach, even with the prim school skirt that fell to her knees, the length Fanny Rodríguez required.

"Rita, are you pregnant?" she asked without preamble. She watched her student's face closely, taking in the surprise, the realization, and then the horror. In that instant, Mrs. Rodríguez wished she could take it back, wished she could start the conversation again, hold Rita by the hand and walk her through the possibilities until they arrived at the irrefutable conclusion.

Instead she had pushed the girl into a free fall.

Rita began to sob.

"Now, now," said Mrs. Rodríguez, dismayed now at her own lack of pedagogical skills. "No one is accusing you of anything." She put her hand on Rita's shoulder. "I'm just asking if this is a possibility."

Rita shook her head, but deep inside she already knew. She had already known. She remembered the first time. How Lucas had hesitatingly undressed her, taking off her clothes piece by piece until she lay beneath him clad only in her white cotton panties—how vulnerable she had felt, how exposed, until he began to talk to her, to marvel at her body, reverentially touching her neck, her breasts, her stomach, and eventually she softened to his touch. But even then Rita couldn't help being Rita—studious Rita, thorough Rita—and she'd actually remembered to ask if he had protection, and he had answered no but just as quickly assured her that it didn't matter, because girls couldn't get pregnant the first time.

She'd believed him.

Now Rita sobbed. It didn't matter if it was a possibility or not. Didn't matter that Mrs. Rodríguez was saying something about a test, about false alarms, about not getting hysterical, please, now, Rita.

Rita knew. Now she understood why her breasts were constantly sore, as if she were about to get her period, but come to think of it, she hadn't gotten her period in a long time. Now she understood why her jeans were so tight, no matter how little she ate.

The thought brought a fresh wave of sobs to her chest, and she wrapped her arms tightly around her body, rocking herself rhythmically back and forth in a pathetic effort to quell her rising panic.

From somewhere very far away, she heard Mrs. Rodríguez's voice, insistent, and realized she'd been talking to her for some time now. Rita looked at her blankly. Unlike Jazmin, she'd never bonded with Mrs. Rodríguez, and she'd tried to avoid her as much as possible, as she avoided her father and her mother. Rita was perceptive. She sensed the strong current of dislike that Mrs. Rodríguez felt toward her. But right now she didn't care. Right now Mrs. Rodríguez's plain, round face and her small, bright eyes, sympathetic for a change, were Rita's lifeline.

"Mrs. Rodríguez," Rita interrupted quietly. "What am I going to do?"

*     *     *

She walked home from school like an automaton, convinced that surely something extraordinary would happen that would make things revert to the way they were before he appeared. It wasn't about Lucas, not really. It wasn't about that moment when she and Sebastián had walked to the fields that first day, and it wasn't even about that afternoon when she had first given herself to Lucas under the watchful gaze of Christ on the cross.

Because now he was gone, and it was all about her and about this *thing*. This thing she knew she'd been carrying inside for nearly three months. She could get an abortion, she thought, looking around her cautiously, amazed at the fact that everything was the same as ever: the same sky, the same homes, even though she half expected someone to miraculously appear and offer to make it all go away.

She could get an abortion, and her parents would never know, she thought, her hand tightening around Sebastián's. They never noticed anything anyway.

There were healers in these mountains who crafted potions that made you expel anything inside you. Her friends talked about it in hushed tones, with the reverence reserved for the unknown, for it was always someone who knew someone who knew someone else. But Rita instinctively closed her eyes against the very idea. What would that make her? she thought, looking at the church. Not just a sinner. A murderer.

"Are you okay, Tata?" asked Sebastián, wincing as she tightened her hand around his again.

Rita opened her eyes with a start and took a deep breath.

"I'm fine, Sebas," she said, speaking firmly, thinking she would tell them. After everything that had happened, she could deal with them. "I'm fine," she repeated.

\*　　\*　　\*

She couldn't. She couldn't do it. Not that night nor the next nor the next. Not the following week, when Mrs. Rodríguez called her to her office and asked if she'd gone to see a doctor.

"It was a false alarm, Mrs. Rodríguez," Rita lied breezily. "I got my period that same day."

"Oh," replied the principal, puzzled. It just didn't feel right, but she wasn't in a position to do much. It was a public school, and she had little jurisdiction over what happened outside.

"I hope you know what you're doing, Rita," Mrs. Rodríguez finally said. "You can always come to me for help," she added, but she realized that it was a hollow gesture.

"Thank you, Mrs. Rodríguez," said Rita, looking down, thinking that the woman was not someone to be trusted. "Please don't tell my mother about this," she added, looking the principal in the eye this time, her plea genuine. "I promise you, I swear to you, that something like this won't happen again."

Mrs. Rodríguez paused, infinitely uncomfortable with the situation. She hated to conceal information from a parent, but as a woman who prided herself on her progressive mentality she also hated the conservative impositions of the community and the church. The expectation of raising celibate girls, she thought, was patently absurd, and one of the reasons she insisted on providing basic sex education in her school. And of course Rita's pregnancy scare had nothing at all to do with school. Still…

"Please," Rita repeated. There were only two more months left until school let out. If she could hide this pregnancy for two more months, she would be only a year away from graduating. If she could hide this pregnancy for two more months, then she'd somehow know what to do.

Mrs. Rodríguez nodded dubiously.

"Thank you, Mrs. Rodríguez!" exclaimed Rita, elated. "I promise you, I'll study like I've never studied before. I'll be your absolute best student this year!"

It wasn't hard to do. Without the lure of Lucas, Rita focused her entire energy on school, studying with renewed impetus, as if the absorption of knowledge could somehow cleanse her of the other sins, the ones visible to the human eye. And they were visible, to her at least. In the mornings, in the shower, she would press her hands against her increasingly tender breasts with a mixture of awe and fear. She'd recoil at the inflexibility of her round, taut stomach, at the slight yet inexorable widening of her hips, the increasing arch of her back. No matter how little she ate, how much she walked, how deeply she sucked in her stomach, she couldn't control her metamorphosis, her transition from beautiful butterfly to ugly moth cocooned inside herself, her shoulders perpetually hunched over her growing bosom in an effort to conceal her misshapenness.

She was still young enough, supple enough, slim enough, to hide a first pregnancy for months on end, covering it with a slightly larger T-shirt, forgoing the tight jeans without raising too many eyebrows, always wrapping that omnipresent sweater around her waist. And this seemed to be, after all, a new Rita phase, one of less vanity and more intellectual pursuits. If Rita was adept at passing unnoticed before, she became an expert now, invisible in her home, invisible on the street, silent in the classroom, an insipid girl incapable of eliciting a second look, a second thought.

She finished the school term unperturbed. And then she gave up.

She stood half dressed in her bedroom one morning, struggling to fasten a bra that could barely contain her breasts, and recoiled at the sight of the brown line forming between her belly button and her pubic hair. She'd noticed it a week earlier but had decided she would ignore it; it would go away, after all, wouldn't it?

But it hadn't faded. Quite the contrary, it was darker than before, branding her like a scarlet snake emblazoned in her flesh. She wished she'd had the nerve to stick a needle up there, to simply puncture this thing out and carry on with her existence. She used to pray for a spontaneous abortion, for her period—*Please, God, let me have my period*—for nights on end. But there was nothing to do now, she thought, shaking her head. This other being was firmly implanted inside her, like a root that couldn't be pulled out, staining her, straining her. She couldn't pretend that this was happening to someone else, couldn't will it away or hide it in one of her secret places. Rita raised her hand in a futile fist, then pushed her hair back with both hands and sat down heavily on her little bed. For the first time, she felt genuinely heavy, bloated. She felt helpless. She leaned over her bed and opened her wooden shutters just a crack, enough to let the early sunshine in, enough for her to peek outside and see how blue the sky was against the whitewashed homes across the street.

She got up slowly, finally managed to fasten her bra, and pulled up her skirt as far as it would go. She slipped on an oversize T-shirt and, on top of that, a sweatshirt. Then she took a deep breath and walked along the hall to the phone and called downstairs.

"What is it, Rita?" answered her mother—shortly, same as she always did.

"Mother, can you please come up? I have something I need to tell you."

# Chapter Eight

Rita always knew she didn't have much, but she hadn't known how little she had until she fit everything into a single suitcase. She sat on the small wooden chair by the locked front door of the store, the worn black bag on the floor staring accusingly at her. It hadn't been nearly as bad as she'd imagined, really, except for when her mother had started slapping her.

"Who?" she screamed. *Slap!* "Who?" *Slap!* "Whore! Who was it?" *Slap!*

Rita involuntarily brought her hands up to her cheeks, still reddened from the blows. She'd fallen onto the bed, curling up as tightly as she possibly could while her mother rained down her fists over Rita's arms, which she'd brought up to cover her face.

"Stop it! You don't know him!" she finally shouted, and just like that, her mother stopped.

"I don't know him?" she asked, her voice dangerously calm. "I don't know him? You tell me who he is, or I swear to God, tomorrow I'll stand you in front of the church and tell everybody that you're a whore and we're looking for the father of your baby. I swear to God, Rita. I'll do it."

Rita regarded her mother incredulously. "But you're my mother," she said softly. "You're my mother!"

"Yes, I am," said her mother coldly. "And I have the right to know who the father of my daughter's child is. My daughter may be a whore, but she isn't going to have a bastard."

"But, Mother," said Rita, shaking her head, "I can't tell you. It's dangerous for you. It's dangerous for Sebastián. I can't tell you."

"Oh, Rita," said her mother, her voice choking, realization dawning on her. "How could you? How could you? You selfish, selfish person. Always selfish. Always thinking only of yourself. You..." Her mother's voice trailed off as she stood there, her arms dangling uselessly at her sides. "Oh," she moaned, looking around her in slight confusion. Then she ran out of the room and to the hall phone.

"Sergio," Rita heard her say to her father, "close down the store."

They were both at the church now, talking with Father Pablo. Rita had been packed for hours, ever since her mother had tersely told her to gather all her belongings.

"And Sebastián?" Rita had asked then, her voice barely rising above a whisper.

"He's staying at your aunt's tonight," said her mother, not looking at her.

"But I need to say good-bye to him!" said Rita, her voice rising in panic.

"No you don't," her mother spit out. "You don't need to say anything to him. You are not to get close to him."

"Please, Mother," said Rita, for the first time realizing the enormity of what she'd done. "Mother, I beg you. I can't just leave him!"

Her mother hadn't even bothered to answer this time.

"Pack your things," she'd said tersely, turning her back to her. "Just pack your things."

Rita did, carefully folding her T-shirts, the jeans that no longer fit her, her sweat suit, the headbands and the ribbons. She packed her notebooks and her colored pencils and her mini boom box—her aunt's present when she'd turned fifteen years old—and hid Lucas's necklace in her pocket. At the last minute, she took off her gold chain and cross—her only valuable pieces of jewelry—and wrapped them around a sheet of paper with a note to Sebastián.

> *Dear Sebas:*
> *I'll be back in a few weeks. I'm leaving you my cross so you can remember me and be good.*
> *I love you always. Please study.*
>
> *Tata*

Rita stood uncertainly at the entrance of Sebastián's room, seeking out a hiding place her mother wouldn't think of. In his small armoire, she found his soccer cleats on the floor and buried the cross and the note deep inside one of them, her hand hovering over the shoes for an instant; she wanted to write something more but was at a loss for words. She looked around her one last time, at the sparse, clean rooms, almost monastic in their severity, like their lives themselves. She couldn't bear the thought of Sebastián wilting here on his own. Although, as her mother had said, he was a man. He would somehow survive all this.

Now Rita waited in the chair by the door, acutely aware of the pregnancy she'd been hiding for so long. She put her hand tentatively over her stomach, then probed it more firmly, feeling how hard it was. She wondered what was inside. A boy? A girl? She wondered how she could possibly give birth to it, wondered if it would hurt a lot. She wondered if her mother would come with her. Maybe, she thought, it wouldn't be so bad after all.

She heard her parents' steps outside and sat up straight again, folding her hands on her lap, looking directly ahead.

Her father came in first, walking right by her and up the stairs without acknowledging her presence. Rita sat perfectly still until her mother gave the order.

"Come on. We're going to see Father Pablo. Leave your bag here for now."

Rita stood up silently and followed her out the door, down the cobbled street, and around the corner.

She walked slowly across the plaza, up the stone steps of the church, the same path she'd taken three times a week, every week, for three months of her life.

In the dark vestibule, she crossed herself and, responding to her mother's nod, went inside the confessional, pulling the curtain closed behind her. Rita knelt and uttered the words she'd avoided uttering all this time, from the moment she gave her body to him, from the moment, she now knew, that the child inside her had been conceived.

"Forgive me, Father, for I have sinned," she whispered. But the rest of the words got stuck in her throat, as if there were cotton glued to the roof of her mouth. She couldn't do it, she thought. She couldn't do it before, and much less now.

Unnerved, Rita rose, but Father Pablo's voice stopped her.

"Child, unburden yourself," he said firmly. "We don't judge in the house of God."

Rita paused and knelt again, aware of her mother's eyes boring down on the shuttered screen door. She spoke as softly as she could, as much to God as to the priest who had baptized her and given her the First Communion. The priest in whose office she'd conceived this baby, something, Rita thought, that she would never confess to. Never. "Father, I have sinned," she offered. "I was with a man. And now I'm pregnant."

Father Pablo was silent behind the confessional screen. He'd heard this story before, but he hadn't expected it from Rita Ortiz.

"Were you raped, my child?" he asked evenly, because he had to ask.

"No," said Rita, too late realizing that crying rape could have saved her, but still, she couldn't bring herself to tell such a lie.

"Then that's all the more reason for the man who got you pregnant to answer for the child. He has to do right by you. Does he know?"

"No," said Rita flatly. "He's gone. I wouldn't know where to find him."

"Everyone can be found, child," said Father Pablo.

"Not this man, Father," said Rita simply. "This man knows how to get lost."

Father Pablo considered this piece of information, and in a flash he remembered. Remembered coming back to church one afternoon and, from afar, glimpsing Lucas slouched against the entrance, appearing nonchalant but gazing intently across the square. Father Pablo had followed the glance until his eyes alighted on Rita, beautiful Rita, walking sedately in the opposite direction, toward her house. Father Pablo had quickened his step, practically running up the stairs until he faced Lucas.

"Lucas, you and your men are not to touch any of the women here. You promised," he admonished urgently.

"I keep my promises, Father," Lucas drawled. "I said no one is going to get raped under my watch."

No raping indeed, thought Father Pablo now, remembering the precise choice of words. How blind he had been. *Forgive me, Father*, he thought, closing his eyes in prayer, *for Satan tricked me into allowing one of his into our midst.*

"Child, you've had sexual relationships out of wedlock," he said finally. "That is a sin. But now the most important thing is your unborn child. I know you haven't considered abortion. Let me remind you that abortion is also a sin. More than a sin. It is taking away a life. Nobody but God can do that. Now it is your responsibility to bear this child and provide it with a Christian baptism and make sure it is taken care of." Father Pablo paused, weighing his next words carefully, just as earlier that day he'd weighed the safety of a family against the well-being of this girl and her child.

"You cannot have this child here," he said bluntly. "If word got out, it would be terribly dangerous, for you and for your family. You understand this, don't you?"

"Yes, Father," replied Rita meekly, all fight long gone from her.

This wasn't the way it was supposed to be, she thought,

picturing this church she knew so well, the altars where she'd lit so many votive candles the past months, asking for forgiveness because she couldn't say no. It was a sin, but it was so beautiful, she thought. It was almost holy. And yet she hadn't wanted a baby. She hadn't wanted anything, really, other than the rare chance to feel coveted, to feel alive. Sheer vanity. And look at what had happened. Surely it was divine punishment.

She started crying again as she'd done this morning, the helplessness of her situation overwhelming her.

"Rita," said Father Pablo firmly, as if reading her mind, "a baby is not a punishment. It is a gift. And it is your responsibility. That isn't a punishment. But if you don't do the right thing, child, I promise you, God will punish you. Now we are going to pray for forgiveness. You must ask God to forgive your lack of control, your loss of virtue, your disregard for those around you. You have to repent, Rita," he said, leaning his face closer against the confessional window. "And then I will tell you what you're going to do."

\*　　\*　　\*

They waited until it was dark, until the town was asleep. Only then did Father Pablo come by in his little jeep and silently load her suitcase in the back. Rita's father stayed in his room while her mother stood quietly inside the door, her face impassive.

"Rita, your blessing, girl," she said, and Rita walked reluctantly toward her, her hand protectively rising to her face, still feeling the sting of the earlier slaps. But she lowered her head for her mother to give her the sign of the cross, in the name of the Father and the Son and the

Holy Spirit, then felt the small envelope pressed into her hand.

"This is all I can give you," her mother said brusquely. "But you won't need much money where you're going."

Rita clutched the envelope uncertainly. For years she'd dreamed of leaving, but never like this.

"What should I do when it's . . . when it's over?" she asked in a small voice. Her mother raised her chin slightly, and Rita thought she saw a measure of softness enter her eyes.

"No one can ever know you're pregnant, and no one can ever know you have a baby. No one. Ever," her mother said. She closed her eyes briefly, and when she opened them again, Rita saw them glistening with repressed tears.

"We expected so much more from you," she said, shaking her head, and her palpable disappointment drove a hole into Rita's insides. "We thought you were an honorable person," her mother added. "But this?" She made a contemptuous gesture toward Rita's budding maternity. "With one of those bastards? Even if you no longer had respect for your father and me, we assumed you would at least think about your brother's well-being."

Rita didn't say anything, pushing her anger way inside, going to that place in her mind she visited so often in this home. She fixed her eyes on her mother's hands and marveled at how rough and worn they looked, hands of labor, even as her mother continued to pelt her with accusations, unaware that nothing she said or did could make Rita feel any worse now, that her words were months, years too late.

Susana looked at her daughter. At the face that was now deliberately blank and the figure whose roundness she had missed simply because she never looked at Rita enough, and from somewhere inside herself she finally found the right words to say.

"We are your family, and this is your house, Rita. Once this is over and taken care of, you can always come back," she said, resigned.

Rita looked up, surprised at the words and at the unexpected relief that came with hearing them.

"Thank you, Mother," she said with the slightest of smiles, and she leaned forward haltingly in anticipation of an embrace, a kiss, any physical contact between her mother's being and her own. But she could have been standing a mile away. The moment passed, so quickly that Rita wondered if she'd imagined that glimmer of warmth.

"Well, good-bye," she finally said, drawing back, angry at herself for daring to still hope, and this time she walked out to the car. The door to the house closed even before Father Pablo set the car in motion, and by the time Rita turned around, her home was already shuttered, a minuscule fortress from which she was sealed off.

She rode quietly beside Father Pablo, taking in the strangeness of her town at night, as the streetlights petered out and all she could see outside was the darkness of the fields, illuminated only by a sky thick with stars. When she looked back again, the only thing visible from the winding road was the church tower, its white stucco glowing dimly against the pitch-black sky.

# Chapter Nine

*Asher, 2009*

Asher Stone jumped forward to meet the ball and felt the satisfying *thwack* as it connected with his temple. Coach blew his whistle, and almost instinctively Asher bounded back on the balls of his feet and allowed himself to fall onto the grass.

It was one of those glorious autumn days in Santa Barbara, where the sun has managed to disperse the slight layer of fog that sits forever low in these skies, allowing the curtain of blue to emerge with stunning brilliance after a season of gray.

He lay there for a few moments, watching the white plumes of a distant plane cutting across the expanse of the horizon, feeling the crisp, newly cut blades of grass prickle his legs and the palms of his hands, extended flat beside him. On an impulse he flipped around and buried his face into the green moistness. He loved the smell of freshly mown grass. Sometimes he thought that's why he got into soccer: to be close to that cherished smell.

"Damn, Asher, what are you doing?" his friend James called out. "Get up, man. You look like a dog!"

Asher grinned and sprang up, unfazed. He ran over to

James and punched him, not too gently, in the gut, then set off, his small, lithe frame moving—gliding, almost—through an intricate obstacle course of bodies as he maneuvered the soccer ball between his feet with the dexterity of a ballet dancer. He shifted from the midfield to nearly the goal until he was tripped by another player and fell hard, his body splayed facedown over the grass.

Asher felt the breath sucked out of him, and the anger surged up sudden and fierce, like bile. Before anyone could react, he sprang up again and pushed the other player, hard—his rage making him oblivious to the fact that it was just a practice game, that he was pushing back one of his own.

His teammates surged around him, but before a melee could erupt, Coach Duggy barked something from the sidelines and blew his whistle, even as James pulled his friend back. Asher strained against James's arms and then, without warning, relaxed against him, almost as if the belligerence had been drained from him like air from a popped balloon. He gave the other player the finger, then broke out in a big smile that neutralized the gesture.

Coach Duggy shook his head but let the incident pass without comment. Asher's antics on the field were notorious, but his temperament was also part of what made him UC Santa Barbara's most effective starter and a major draw for fans. It was a weird dichotomy, Duggy often mused with fellow coaches, but one he'd seen several times over the years with key players: unflappable types who transformed on the field as if a switch had been flicked on.

Asher concentrated once more on reaching the goal,

even as the clock ticked down to mere seconds, trying to get past the fact that if he hadn't fallen, they'd already have won.

"Just a practice game," he muttered under his breath, but of course regardless of how often he told himself that, it was still a matter of life and death.

*Ah, well*, he thought when the whistle rang out, signaling the end of the match: 0–0. Asher jogged slowly to the sidelines, scanning the perimeter for Alessandra until his eyes found her red coat and he saw her cautiously making her way down the bleachers, one hand holding on to each step for balance.

Asher couldn't help laughing at the sight; he would have leaped down the bleachers two at a time. But everything about Alessandra Lowe had a hint of daintiness: her petite frame, her fine features, the hazel eyes, and the long brown hair she held back with a collection of headbands, making her appear younger than her twenty-one years.

Asher wouldn't have looked at Alessandra twice in high school. He was way too self-absorbed then, way too cool for such a bookish, unapologetically intellectual girl, and one with zero interest in sports to boot. On the surface there was nothing to bind them together—the affable, charismatic jock and the focused academic who favored late-night, in-depth discussions. Indeed, they'd come together by obligation: She was his assigned tutor. That their relationship had evolved into more—going smack against college rules—was a fact Coach Duggy had decided to overlook as long as he could, and as long as Asher delivered what he had to.

And with her he did. She completed him, Asher found, filled his spaces, anchored him, balanced him outside the soccer field. And, like him, she never played games. With Alessandra, what you saw was what you got.

Asher picked up his gear and ran after her, catching up as she neared his car in the parking lot.

"What up?" he called, reaching out to pull her close.

"No, no, no," she cautioned, taking a step back. "You're sweaty and stinky."

"I never stink," he replied with a smile, leaning in and planting a swift, wet kiss on her neck, then grabbing her hand and pulling her eagerly toward his car. "I'm cooking tonight," he declared.

"Not for me, Ash. I have to study," Alessandra said firmly.

"Well, you gotta eat, don't you?" he said matter-of-factly, reaching into his backpack for the car keys.

"I can't tonight, Ash," Alessandra reiterated. "I shouldn't even have come to practice today. I'm really behind."

Asher finally stopped and turned to look her full in the face, taking in the petulant set of her mouth. "What is it?" he asked, slightly confused. "You're still mad at me over draft?"

"I'm not mad at you over draft, Asher," Alessandra replied impatiently. "I'm behind in school." She paused, looking for the right word. "Okay, I'm not *mad*," she elaborated. "But I'm... disappointed."

Asher was deliberately quiet, finally forcing the explanation from her with his silence.

"I'm disappointed that you won't let me be part of the conversation," Alessandra said, looking at him levelly.

Asher made a tremendous effort not to roll his eyes.

The season had wound down, the scouting was over. All he had to do now was wait, then decide. And it was driving Alessandra nuts. There was a high likelihood that he'd be drafted into a major-league team come January, but there was no way of knowing which one. And if everything failed and he didn't get into the league, he could choose either going to play in Germany or finishing up his senior year. Alessandra hated that his life was moving ahead, possibly without her. She wanted to sit down, make a plan, chart a course that would ensure they'd travel this road together even if they were physically apart.

Asher knew this, but he had no intention of initiating that conversation. Yet. He was superstitious about things like that.

"Ally, I'm not going to talk about this before I get an offer," he said, shaking his head. "I'm not gonna nix things."

"Ash, all I'm talking about is going over different scenarios and possibilities. How does that nix anything? It affects my decisions as well, you know?" Alessandra said with a touch of annoyance. She hated to sound clingy, but she couldn't help herself. She liked to plan ahead, and if she wasn't going to be part of his plan at all, she wanted to know sooner rather than later. But of course that's not what she wanted. What she wanted was an assurance from him, something more than just a sign that there would still be a place for her beside him, even if he moved on to a much bigger stage.

Asher didn't take a step back, but he might as well have. He found all this analysis such a turnoff.

"Ally, at this point I'm doing the best I can. You know

that," he said, gently but with the slightest trace of frustration. "You know how this is. And if you don't know where you stand with me by now, then I don't know why we're even talking about it," he added, shaking his head.

He spent all his free time with her, soothed by her presence alone. She'd sit cross-legged on the bed reading and absently stroke his hair until he fell asleep, the way his mother used to do when he was a child. He'd never allowed anyone in so far before. Never. College sports had turned him into an ascetic with little time for emotional attachments. It wasn't simply the time either; he didn't have any energy for it. And it surprised him, because he'd partied and slept his way with impunity through the ease of high school, always falling back on his credo of noncommitment.

But Alessandra just seemed to align all the pieces for him. She was dazzled by his playing, but in a quietly proud way—no squealing, no hanging on, no fawning—tacitly acknowledging what he'd been through to get there, in the same way he thrived on her academic brilliance. There was no need to spell things out between them, or so he used to think.

"I'm sorry," Alessandra capitulated with a sigh, but already thinking of a better time to bring the issue up. She pushed his wet hair back from his forehead and leaned forward to kiss him softly on the mouth, her hand lingering on his cheek. She felt him relax under her touch, and she smiled in relief. "But seriously," she added, "I need to work tonight. I have to speak at Professor Dillard's seminar Saturday, so I have to be done with my thesis syllabus by tomorrow."

Asher allowed his cheek to rest against her hand and breathed in the scent of chamomile shampoo and Vera Wang perfume, Alessandra trademarks.

"Okay," he said regretfully, kissing her upturned palm and pulling back until they were simply holding hands, like two schoolchildren. "Let's see what I can do with my sorry ass," he added, finally pulling away and turning toward his car.

Alessandra laughed and shook her head. "I don't feel the least bit sorry for you, you know that?" she called out.

"You should." Asher laughed, waving as he got into his Jeep, a gift from his father when he made dean's list the year before, and cranked up the volume as he drove to his off-campus apartment. It wasn't that the ability to be contemplative eluded him, he mused, his mind still on Alessandra. But in his experience, dissecting things to death was usually a big waste of time.

The year he turned thirteen, coinciding with his bar mitzvah, his parents had decided he needed psychotherapy, to fully comprehend that although he was adopted, he was truly, unconditionally loved. Asher remembered daydreaming about soccer practice as he sat uncomfortably in that office, its plaid couches and thick cushions ostensibly affording it the look of a living room, but he knew, of course, that he was there to get his head set straight, although he couldn't figure out why. The shrink was named Dr. Hoover but insisted on being called Sandy and gave him hot chocolate or soda, which Asher sipped with quiet trepidation, a little cowed by the grown man who sat in front of him on a tiny stool that made him look like a dangerously overgrown schoolboy.

After three sessions Sandy folded.

"He doesn't need me," he informed Joseph and Linda Stone grudgingly.

"But surely he had questions and issues he's not raising with us?" Asher's mother asked.

"Not really," said Sandy. "He's perfectly clear about everything. He knows he's adopted. He knows you love him. And as far as he's concerned, that's life and it's fine."

"Accept it," Joseph whispered so Asher couldn't hear, placating his wife as they walked toward their car. "You've raised him well, and from somewhere he's got good, sensible genes. Let's count our blessings rather than make up curses."

But Asher did hear, and he still laughed out loud at the memory. As he liked to remind his mother, those silly psychotherapy sessions probably cost nearly as much as his bar mitzvah a few months later.

Nope. He had no complaints, and now he raised the volume of the music even higher. "'I hear Jerusalem bells a-ringing,'" he sang, as loudly as he could, letting the wind and the sound of traffic and just the aliveness of the moment wash over him. He was a starter on the soccer team. At twenty-one years old, he could legally drink anywhere he wanted. In a few months, God willing, he'd be drafted onto a pro team. He ruled the world.

\*    \*    \*

Asher got into his apartment, tossed his car keys on the kitchen table, and put his iPod on the dock, raising the volume on Eminem. He took off his T-shirt, cleats, shorts, and socks as he walked to the shower, leaving everything in a trail that followed him to his bathroom, where he turned on the water full blast and as hot as he could possibly stand it. He stood there immobile, just letting the water beat down on him.

And it came to him. The draft was in two weeks. His mother's birthday was tomorrow. He'd drive down and surprise her. Why not? His parents would help him think—they always had.

Asher quickly turned off the shower and dialed his father before he could change his mind.

"Hey, Dad, what up?"

"Asher," Joseph Stone replied, surprised at the early-evening call. "All good here. What's up with you?"

"Not much. Just got finished with practice for the week."

"Yeah? How's it going? No news yet on the draft front?"

"No, nothing yet. Hey, Dad, I was thinking about driving down tomorrow morning and surprising Mom for her birthday. What do you think?"

"That'd be great," Joe replied. "Is Alessandra coming?"

"No, just me this time," said Asher, trying to sound nonchalant.

"Very good," said Joseph. "Your mom's certainly not expecting it. I'll make reservations for dinner, all right?"

"Please," said Asher. "This tryout diet is killing me."

Joe laughed. "Don't worry. We'll take care of that. Drive carefully, okay? I'll see you tomorrow."

Asher snapped his cell phone shut and opened the fridge. *Nothing there*, he thought, feeling slightly sorry for himself, then thinking it was a good thing after all that

Alessandra had declined his invitation to cook. He started to call Domino's, then thought better of it and shut his phone again.

He hated being alone, a quirk he attributed to some kind of early-childhood separation anxiety born of being left behind. When he was a kid, he'd often crawl into his parents' bed in the middle of the night, snuggling next to his mother as quietly as he could so his father wouldn't wake, just to feel the safety of her hand on his hair. Even now he couldn't sleep alone unless the television was on. He'd never told Alessandra this, that he slept with two pillows—one to hug, one to lay his head on—simply because he needed that presence beside him. He'd never told her that he always roomed with someone else when the team traveled, because being alone made him anxious to the point of affecting his game.

*What the hell*, he thought, looking around his apartment with the cheap futon and vintage posters—unframed, of course. "If I'm not doing anything I might as well leave tonight," he said out loud. It was nearly 9:00 P.M. He could be home by 11:00, early enough to get a good night's sleep, work out the next morning, and have the entire afternoon with his parents. He hadn't spent quality time with his dad in months, truth be told. The holidays had been truncated by the tryouts and the stress of physical strain and uncertainty.

Now, with his fate completely out of his hands, he could breathe, have a nice dinner tomorrow night, drink a couple of beers—God knows he needed them. Asher packed his overnight bag quickly, put in his cell phone charger, iPod,

and cleats, and took a last look around. He'd grab something at Whole Foods and eat in the car, then barrel on
down to Santa Monica. He shut the door behind him and
walked briskly to his Jeep, not looking back once.

After weeks on end riding a bus, he was a good traveler,
particularly at night, even when he drove himself. Just as he
hated to sleep alone, he enjoyed the solitude of his car, listening to loud music, drinking Red Bulls to stay alert, and
littering the inside with impunity, nothing a good weekly
car wash couldn't take care of.

Friday-night traffic was slow, and at eleven he was just
nearing the junction to the 405 that would take him to Los
Angeles's Westside. Asher took a long swig of Red Bull as
he put his blinker on to get on the ramp. He didn't see
the truck veering toward him as he caught the curve, just
captured the flicker of a shadow in his peripheral vision
and instinctively slammed the brakes, even as the front of
the truck crashed into the driver's side of his Jeep, sending the car spinning like a top into the side of the free-
way, where it rebounded against the guardrail and then
lifted off the ground to come down with the resounding
clang of metal against concrete. Asher's head hit the ceiling of his car, and he felt his insides literally jar inside him
in a dull thud that reverberated through his body like the
metallic gong of a bell, and then the air bag exploded into
his face.

*     *     *

Joseph Stone answered the phone on the first ring and
then noted the time: 4:00 A.M. Even before the voice on the
other line spoke, he knew that it couldn't be good. "Asher

Sebastian," they said. "Is this the home of Asher Sebastian Stone?" And Joe Stone thought innocently that it had been years since anyone had called him Asher Sebastian; probably not since his bar mitzvah, and that it was a fine name, a dignified name. Asher Sebastian Stone.

# Chapter Ten

Linda Stone wasn't a romantic. When she found out she couldn't conceive, she took off for the weekend and mourned her barrenness alone at her parents' cabin in Big Sur. She was a tall, large-boned mass of energy with a generous figure, and a winning smile, who spoke loudly and authoritatively. As a producer of television specials, she was used to commanding instant respect in almost everything she did, and she was devastated by the lack of control she exerted over her own body

"We can try fertility treatments," Joseph had said before she left. But as she mulled her options, the prospect of failing yet again, and this time with outside help, was untenable. Linda drank a bottle of wine on Saturday night and the following morning took an arduous, five-mile hike up the mountain, way past the camping grounds and beyond where the barely trodden path ended. She sat at the summit of Mount Manuel, allowing the blend of sun and cold wind to blanket her, and calculated that the descent would take at least two hours and that the chances of encountering another human being for most of the trajectory were mighty slim. If she were to be attacked by a mountain lion, or if she simply slipped and fell off one these ledges on her way down, no one would know for hours. And if she were never to make it back, who would seriously miss her? Her parents would mourn her, of course, but they, too, would eventually die, and she held no illusions about Joe. He loved her, but he wasn't the type of man who could live alone. In a year or two, he would certainly find another wife. And if that were to happen, what would be her legacy in life? She was a successful woman who had no tangible output to call her own. Her work was about collaborating, about putting people together to create short-term projects, television segments that aired once, maybe twice, then evaporated into that ethereal landscape of used pop culture. If she were to die, it wouldn't take long for her imprint in this world to quietly fade, as if she'd never been here at all.

Linda was no romantic, but neither was she willing to simply disappear. And in a flash it came to her: She would adopt. She would make a difference in a child's life, and that child would be the heir to her legacy, to her truth. If she couldn't disseminate her genes, she would at the very least disseminate her personality, her drive, her intelligence, her capacity to do good.

Joseph didn't object. Although he was taller than Linda, his slighter frame and horn-rimmed glasses made him a yin to her yang. When it came to his work as a tax attorney, he was rapacious, capable of squeezing out savings and exemptions that were nearly impossible to contest. But when it came to Linda, he was almost invariably her running mate, supportive and acquiescent, his initiative quietly suppressed. He would drive, if needed, but it was she who steered.

And steer she did. She flung herself into the adoption

process with the same relentless impetus with which she seized every task that ever came her way.

A week after her return from Mount Manuel, as Joseph absentmindedly looked for a calculator in the study desk, he found instead a self-assessment adoption quiz, the answers written in Linda's neat, cursive script.

1. Why do you want to adopt? My husband and I have tried unsuccessfully to have a baby for several years now. We are a stable, loving couple who feel we have much to give. We are educated, we have good jobs, and we live in a beautiful neighborhood and are surrounded by close family and friends. We have a wonderful marriage, full of laughter and travel and love of life. We are religious and try to live our lives in a meaningful manner that seeks to make an impact on the world around us. We are two very different people but very supportive of each other, and we respect each other's identities and wishes as only two people in love can. And yet there is a void in our home and in our hearts—a void that would be filled with the presence of a child. We are so ready and eager to give and to share our love, our good fortune, our religion, our values. If we can do that by providing a needy child with a new chance in life, perhaps that is the path God has set forth for us, and we will also fill that void that now makes our life a little less meaningful.

2. On a scale of 1 to 10, how badly do you want to adopt? 10

3. Who is the driver in this adoption? Myself.

Joseph read and reread the words in wonderment. It wasn't just what they said, but the fact that he hadn't been included in the process. Indignation suffused his chest and made his face flush in uncharacteristic agitation as he rifled urgently through the drawer until he found it, the second set of papers, neatly clipped, bearing a small Post-it note with his name written on it. His mounting anger subsided as rapidly as if he had turned off a light. How could he have doubted her? Linda was impulsive, righteous, but never consciously unfair. Already the mere notion of the adoption was driving a wedge between them. He looked at the questionnaire again, this time at his own yet-unfilled set, his mind as blank as the empty lines before him.

Why did he want to adopt indeed? He hadn't known he wanted to, not until Linda had decided for both of them. He skipped to the next question: On a scale of one to ten, how badly did *he* want to adopt? Joseph looked around at his spacious study, at the telescope and the wall-to-wall books, each with a story, with a reason to exist within the wooden shelves. The rug was a nineteenth-century Baluch Persian, purchased at a flea market in Morocco during their honeymoon. The painting over the mantel was a Richard Estes piece he'd impulsively—irrationally really, but he couldn't help himself—fallen in love with at Marlborough Gallery in New York, then given to Linda for her birthday, the most extravagant gift she had ever received. The wooden globe that sat in the middle of the room was her gift to him, a carved antique from the seventeenth century, purportedly used by navigators to chart their routes before launching out to sea. Every year they took turns spinning it and then, with eyes closed, pointed to a place on the globe, the site of their vacation for that season.

So many places seen and so many beautiful, useless things, he thought, all at the service of two people who had the luxury to be hedonistic and indulge in pleasure for the sake of pleasure. Inside this house he'd never needed anything beyond her company; even at her most annoying, she steadied him, compensated for his little quirks, was happy to voice everything, be their mutual front while he kept to the background, the happy concave to her convex.

A baby? He'd never felt like a baby was missing from their lives. Although that was quite different from not wanting one. He went back to the first question: Why do you want to adopt?

He didn't. That was the truth. But he would, for her.

*"I want to adopt to support my wife and to make a difference in a child's life,"* he wrote, in his typically succinct prose. He paused and read the sentence back. He supposed he should be more eloquent, more elaborative, but there was nothing more to add. Joseph went down the list to the next question: On a scale of one to ten, how badly did he want to adopt? He hesitated, the pen poised over the paper, almost bracing for her criticism.

"Oh, hell," he said, and carefully sliced a neat *"5"* onto the paper.

During the year they waited for the adoption to come through, it never changed for him.

It was Linda who did the research, who finally ventured into Colombian adoptions, because a Latin child, likely olive-skinned, would stand a better chance of resembling their Mediterranean, Sephardic heritage. It was Linda who deemed it should be a girl, so the child could be more compatible with her only niece and because, despite her own self-sufficient nature, she believed that a girl was more vulnerable, more likely to need rescuing from the world. Although she never spoke the words out loud, she also believed that a girl would be more malleable to her mother's wishes and teachings, more likely to emulate her, to take her at her word.

They filed the piles of paperwork and waited, the months stretching their resolve, drilling little pinpoints of doubt into the armor of conviction she had acquired up in the mountain. They didn't take their yearly vacation, for fear of missing that crucial call announcing the coming of a child and because they now had to think about day care and private school and college, all those elephantine investments that had up to now existed only in other people's realities.

Each passing day seemed to take Linda further from Mount Manuel, from her lofty plans, from her desire to pass on a piece of herself to someone else. Some nights she would sit in the study, calculator in hand, trying to figure out exactly how much they had to save for retirement from this point onward if a child indeed came through. She watched the little zeros drop out of their combined income with each year of baby food, diapers, clothes, nanny, tuition, and her palms would begin to sweat, the uncertainty insidiously creeping into her open pores. For the first time in her life, her circumstances scared her. A child! What in the world had she been thinking? How could she have dumped this on Joe? Her moods fluctuated like a kite struggling to fly. Some days she was ecstatic, imagining the possibilities. And then, in the space of less than a week, the doubts would inundate her again, until finally, after six months, Linda caved and called the orphanage: They would take a boy or a girl, as long as the baby was healthy, she said in uncharacteristic resignation. Whatever was quickest. Who knew, thought Linda, that this was a competition, fiercer than finding entrance to an elite college? Who knew, Linda thought, that there were so many like her, lined up like sheep, waiting for a baby—any baby—to appear and save them?

It took six more months for the call to come in—naturally in the most anticlimactic way possible, as she was furiously scrubbing down the kitchen sink, finally yielding to the insistent ringing of the phone, which she normally wouldn't have been there to pick up, except for the fact that they'd worked late last night and she got to sleep in, only to end up cleaning house.

"Mrs. Stone?" asked the lilting, accented voice on the other end of the line. And Linda knew that this was it, even before she shut off the water, before she removed her plastic cleaning gloves. Before the voice could say, "A baby has come in," she was already looking around, thinking, *Nothing is ready, we're not ready*, and her heart dipped in small dismay because she was all alone here, there was no one she could embrace, no one to scream together with, and it was so petty, so banal in the face of this great, marvelous thing that was happening to her, but she couldn't help it. She would have wanted Joe standing beside her, to hold her hand, and the realization that she really couldn't do this alone, didn't want to do it alone, jolted her.

"Mrs. Stone?" the voice at the other end of the phone asked again.

"Yes," answered Linda, steadying herself against the sink.

"We have a baby for you, Mrs. Stone. A baby boy."

\*       \*       \*

He woke up to an excruciating headache—the worst headache of his life. He tried to raise his hand to his head but couldn't muster the effort to lift it from the crisp white sheet under his fingers. Asher let his gaze travel down his body, saw that he was all there—two arms, two legs—even though the left leg hurt with a dull, throbbing pain. He managed to wiggle his toes and flex his fingers, then tried to turn his head. He couldn't. He narrowed his eyes slightly and attempted to sit up, but moving an inch felt as onerous as wading in a sea of sand.

A grunt involuntarily escaped from his throat as he looked around with rising panic, his eyes darting side to side from the limited vantage point of his immobilized head. Out of the corner of his eye, he saw his mother, fast asleep on an armchair across the room.

Asher tried to speak, but his throat felt parched, as if the sand that had weighed down his body had also gotten inside his mouth, sucking up all the moisture, turning his lips to parchment. He cautiously ran his tongue over them and tried again, until the word came out—a croak, really, but the word was out there nevertheless.

"Mom." He cleared his throat and tried again. "Mom," he whispered. "Mom" he insisted, and this time his mother woke with a start.

"Asher," she said, and her voice was like an answered prayer.

She rushed over to his bed and placed her hand very gently on his face, running her fingers over the light growth of beard that now covered his cheeks.

"Oh, Asher," she said again, kissing his forehead gingerly—and then Linda couldn't help herself. They'd all been given explicit instructions on what to say when he woke up, on how to reassure him, on the nature of his injuries and the positive prognosis for recovery. She'd been told to act calm, be in control—she was his mother, after all, his pillar—but every one of her good intentions fell by the wayside, and she covered her face with her hands and began to cry.

\*     \*     \*

He couldn't remember a thing from that night. Only the strains of "Viva la Vida," which he imagined must have been playing on his iPod when he got hit. He couldn't remember the door that crushed his leg or the car twirling around like a crazy top, smashing into the side rail, then rising clear off the ground and crashing down with a thud, the jolt ramming his head up into the car's roof, sending shock waves down his spine, fracturing the second cervical vertebra in his neck. It was a tiny fracture, they said. Tiny. He was so lucky, they repeated. So very lucky. The impact could have broken any of his vertebrae—*should* have broken all of his vertebrae. Had he seen his car? It was totaled.

Yes, he was a very lucky young man, very lucky. He'd been in a medically induced coma for the week since the accident until the swelling in his brain subsided, but he was healthy. He wasn't paralyzed. He had full mobility. Had he read about that football player from UCLA who'd gotten into a car accident last month? That boy had rolled out of his car, severed his spine right at the waist. He'd be in a wheelchair the rest of his life.

But Asher was a miracle, really. One of those flukes. You never knew who got lucky or who didn't in these cases. He should be walking out of here in a couple of weeks, would be running in no time. Probably six months to a year. Of course, he had to wear the halo, but that wasn't a big deal. It was a very common thing nowadays for injuries like this. And it was great fodder for conversation. The girls would be all over him, just wait and see.

The onslaught of words made Asher dizzy. He closed his eyes and removed his hand from his mother's touch, which he suddenly couldn't bear.

"I'm tired," he said softly, interrupting the doctor's flow of explanations. "I'd like to be alone for a while." There was a short, uncomfortable silence, and then they all began to speak at once: his parents, the doctor.

Only Alessandra stood quietly in the far corner, by the window, the outsider, sharing this rare moment of family vulnerability which, she now thought, she should never have been invited to. Because if she'd spent the night with him, if she'd even had dinner with him, this never would have happened; he would never have gotten into his car that evening, or at least he would have been with her, and just picking her up would have delayed them, would have altered his course on that road and prevented him from being in the path of that truck, at that curve, at that precise moment in time.

"Of course, baby, you have to rest," said his mother, silencing everyone, her authoritativeness fully recovered now that it was clear that Asher would recuperate. "We'll get going. You just relax. Call the nurse if you need anything."

"Okay," mumbled Asher as they filed out. Alessandra stopped by his bed and reached for his hand, squeezing it gently.

"What up?" Asher asked, mustering a little smile for her.

"Hey, you," she answered, smiling back. "I programmed new music into your iPod, some Bach and Mozart. Don't roll your eyes at me," she admonished when she saw his expression. "It's music to heal the mind and the body. There's been tons of research into that. It helps connect all your senses."

"You just want to make me smarter," Asher grunted, a trace of humor back in his voice. "Okay, I'll listen to your tunes."

"I highly recommend Bach's Goldberg Variations—Glenn Gould's later version," Alessandra said. "Here, I'll cue it up for you. Try and rest, okay? This should help."

" 'K," Asher managed to reply. He would have preferred to nod rather than speak, but his head was immobile. They had screwed—literally screwed—pins into his skull and the side of his head, to attach the halo and keep it firmly in place. Four stabilization bars connected the halo to a vest, keeping everything fixed. He'd have to wear the halo for approximately three months, the doctor told him, and then he should be fine, good as new. With this treatment the recovery rate for injuries like his was 85 percent—more, even, taking into account the shape he was in as an athlete.

Six months to a year. Six months to a year. He could run again in six months to a year. He could dribble a ball again in six months to a year. Asher felt a few drops of moisture collect in his temples and automatically reached for a pad of gauze moistened with hydrogen peroxide and brought it up to the oozing sore. White liquid or blood was okay, he'd been told; anything yellow or green was a sign of infection and merited immediate attention. Asher looked impassively at the gauze with its red patch of blood on and tossed it in disgust onto the nightstand.

"Six months to a year," he said out loud, because it wasn't about the holes, or his now-freakish appearance— like the son of Frankenstein—or even the waves of pain that came and went with stunning ferocity, immune even to the painkillers that flowed into his veins from his IV drip. None of that mattered. In the end, as the doctor had said, he'd get better, he'd forget the pain, take the body's natural route of self-defense against injury. But he'd lost the draft, and nothing could change that. No one would take him. Not if he was going to be sidelined for six months in the best of cases. And if he made it back, he'd have to start all over again, become valuable all over again, condense the work of a lifetime, or at least of the past four years, into a pinch of time.

Asher felt tears begin to well and fought furiously to hold them back, clenching his hand into a fist and pounding as hard as he could on the hard hospital mattress. He wasn't a spoiled jerk, he wasn't, he told himself righteously. But it wasn't fair!

He resisted the urge to scream. If he could have, he would have turned around, buried his face in his pillow, and shouted at the top of his lungs, until his voice ran out, until at least part of his indignation, of his outrage, was swallowed by someone other than him. For the first time in his life, he had no idea what to do next.

He breathed in deeply, almost reveling in the pain he felt in his bruised rib cage every time his lungs expanded, and he began to concentrate simply on that window of pain, blocking out all else. His sense of the corporal, his body's natural ability to adapt to any circumstance, had long been his most remarkable quality, his passport to the world. Asher had always been the fastest runner, the most agile climber, the kind of person who jumps from six feet above the ground and intuitively knows how to land, how to soften the blows, how to roll with the punches with those innate reflexes some people simply possess. His physical prowess had long defined him, not only as an athlete but also as a person. Asher knew that his body would never betray him; it was the foundation of his easy confidence, of the way he effortlessly navigated even the most challenging circumstances. He knew who he was, what he was. And he liked it.

He was broken now.

Asher turned on his iPod, and Glenn Gould, about whom he knew nothing, showed up on the screen, his face brooding and almost angry. Intense.

Asher clicked PLAY, and the piano came in, so slowly,

each note so carefully, lovingly spaced out, almost fading and then, at the very last minute, connecting with the next, like a small thread in charge of joining scattered pearls that must be strung together. What he did with the ball, what he did on the field, that was beautiful, too, he thought. He could take that ball, propel it, stop it, make it accelerate, make it slow down, turn, twirl—anything he wanted—with the softest, barest touch of a foot, with the swerve of his hips, oh, God, with a well-placed hit on his head.

He could do other things, he thought. He was more than a field of grass and a ball. He just didn't know what right now. He breathed slowly in and out, and in, and out, until he felt his mind finally go somewhere else, first to that intangible, delicious stupor that precedes sleep, and then, finally, everything was gone, except for the music, making its way through his brain.

# Chapter Eleven

For the first time in years, Asher had the luxury of time. Time, stretching endlessly before him as he lay on his hospital bed, time that outlasted his daily physical therapy, his parents' visits, and Alessandra's more sporadic visits now that she'd gone back to school.

One of the nurses suggested audio books, and suddenly the world opened up for him, the stories dripping into his ears from his iPod headset. He heard books he'd never thought to read before: books by Graham Greene and Thomas Hardy and even ridiculously fun kids' series like Percy Jackson.

When he could, he actually read books, propping them at eye level on a stand in front of him, and that's how Coach Duggy found him when he stopped by two days before Asher's scheduled discharge from the hospital.

He stood silently by the door for a moment, getting used to the sight of his star player with his torso immobilized by that freakish brace, and as if compensating, his left hand, distractedly squeezing an exercise ball. A soccer ball sat on the table next to Asher, but its mere presence was incongruous, a reminder of all that had gone wrong.

Asher, sensing a shadow in the periphery, looked up from the book.

"Hey, Asher," Coach Duggy said quickly, stepping into his line of vision.

"What up, Coach?" said Asher, his pleasure at the visit dampened by having been caught so totally unaware. "Sorry I didn't see you there," he said, trying to make light of the situation. "It's hard work staying still."

"I can only imagine," said Coach Duggy, shaking his head as he pulled up a chair to sit directly across from his player. "You look good, Asher," he said after a moment, a touch of surprise in his voice. "Really good, in fact."

"Thanks, Coach," said Asher, feeling relief seep into his bloodstream. The last thing he wanted was for coach Duggy to deem him vulnerable or fragile. "It's not so bad, actually. I've been walking like crazy, doing strengthening exercises. Once you get used to wearing this crown, it's really not so bad."

"Last time I came here with the team, you were in that coma. The guys all sat around and told the most outrageous stories," Coach Duggy said ruefully.

"Too bad I don't remember a thing," Asher said, raising his eyebrows, a newly acquired quirk that conveyed everything from a nod to a shake of the head. "But I should be out of here in a couple of days. And I'll be playing in a year," he added confidently.

Coach Duggy looked at him blankly for a second, then managed to come up with a smile of encouragement, but it was little more than small parentheses around his lips, a timid, worried smile that was a pale memory of the light that had infused his eyes when he'd laughed out loud at Asher's goals.

"Of course," he said, but his words lacked conviction.

"I'm going to be fine, Coach," Asher stated, making it a fact in his head, raising his chin up a notch, repelled by the pity in his trainer's eyes. They'd been together three years, had known each other for two more, when Duggy first went to Palisades High to scout the phenomenon the local coaches kept raving about, that "little Jewish boy from Santa Monica who dribbled with the elegance of a Brazilian."

"It's just a bump in the road," Asher continued, looking him straight in the eye and quoting one of Duggy's favorite phrases. "It's just a bump in the road," he repeated.

"Asher," said Duggy, forcing conviction into his voice, "I have no doubt that if anyone can return to a soccer field after this, it's going to be you." He paused to let the words sink in, much as he did when he coached them after a match. "I came to tell you that we're saving your spot on the team for as long as you need. And your scholarship remains intact until you finish all your course work."

"Thanks, Coach," Asher replied, stone-faced. He'd never fully realized the importance of the hundreds of minute movements controlled by his neck—the ability to nod, to look down and up, to glance away, to avoid eye contact— all those little motions that acted as a buffer between one's feelings and the world. Now he was forced to meet every-thing head-on, with a relentlessness he hadn't encountered even on the field.

"I'll be playing with the guys in no time," he reiterated, forcing a smile. "I realize that it's hard to imagine when I have this cage on my head, but I know my body better than anyone else, and I'm feeling good. I've already been kicking that ball around," he said, patting it protectively on the table beside him.

"I know, Asher," Coach Duggy said as he stood up. "The guys are anxious to see you at the UCLA match next month. You'll be there?"

"I wouldn't miss it for the world, Coach," said Asher.

Long after Coach Duggy left, Asher sat stock-still, staring blankly at the book he had repositioned in front of him. When his cell phone rang, he answered automatically, not bothering to look at the caller ID.

"Hey, Iron Man," Alessandra greeted him.

Asher knew that it was corny, but he still had to smile every time she called him that.

"Hey, yourself," he said quietly. "How's the paper coming along?"

"Good, good, good. Almost done," Alessandra said cheerfully. "I accomplish so much more without you, my friend. You're a major distraction. What's up?"

"Not much. Catching up on my Stephen King."

"Is it creepy?" asked Alessandra. "Is that why you sound kind of in a funk?"

"Coach Duggy came around today," he replied flatly.

"Oh. Well, that was nice of him," said Alessandra, oblivious.

"I guess. He wants me to go watch the guys play next month against UCLA. I'd love for you to come with me."

"That'll be fun, Ash. It'll be so weird watching a game with you beside me instead of on the field, though," she added innocently.

"Yeah, it will, won't it?" Asher said pensively. "You know, Coach Duggy doesn't think I'm going to play again."

"He said that?" Alessandra couldn't keep the shock out of her voice.

"Nooo," Asher said slowly. "Not in so many words, but it was obvious."

Alessandra, usually the voluble one, was momentarily stumped.

"What?" asked Asher, a trace of belligerence creeping into his voice. "Do *you* think I won't play again, too?"

"Did I say that? Ash, I think you can do whatever you set your mind on doing," said Alessandra calmly.

"You know, that's almost exactly what Duggy said. Is that the company line or what? Are you all talking about how I won't play soccer anymore?"

"Asher, I don't know what anyone else is saying or discussing," Alessandra said carefully, but still, a trace of impatience creeping into her voice. "Your coach and I aren't exactly friends, you know? I'm just saying that the person I know—the Asher I know—has always pushed things to the limit." She paused. "Honestly, it's never crossed my mind that you won't play again."

Asher closed his eyes and held the phone tightly against his ear, listening to her soft breathing two hundred miles away. *It's never crossed my mind either*, he wanted to reply, but he was too tired to continue with this suddenly monumental conversation.

"I need to lie down, Ally," he finally managed. "Don't forget the game, okay? Mark your calendar."

*Wouldn't it be great if this halo were off in time for the game?* thought Asher as he stared at the calendar on his iPhone. But he knew it wouldn't be. No matter how hard he tried or how long he wished for it, he knew that it wouldn't happen.

*        *        *

He shunned the wheelchair the next morning, walking out of the hospital unassisted with as much grace as it's possible to muster when one has a seven-pound metal structure permanently attached to one's head. Asher navigated his way carefully into his mother's car—his father's sports car wasn't big enough to fit his head—getting in butt-first, then gently easing in his shoulders, and finally his crest of steel. He rode stiffly in the backseat, literally and figuratively, entirely dependent on his mother. It had been two weeks, he reminded himself. Only two weeks. He had ten more to go. It really wasn't that much.

"We've set up the study for you, honey," his mother said, her hands manipulating the steering wheel with an ease he envied. "We got a big desk so you can work comfortably, we have the physical therapist coming over every day, and we'll just make the best of it."

"Thanks, Mom," said Asher, placing his hand briefly on his mother's shoulder. Although he could have taken a leave of absence for the remainder of the semester, he'd decided to keep on course, simply as a way not to lose his mind. "I'm actually looking forward to some quiet time."

Linda regarded him through the rearview mirror and smiled a little surprised smile. She still hadn't figured out how to deal with this altered Asher. He had never been a talkative boy, but he'd always been blessed, she thought, with a naturally sunny disposition and the ability to shrug cares away.

This post-accident Asher was more introspective. Weeks of inactivity had opened up a different level of awareness for him—the very awareness she'd always wanted from him—and now that he had it, it confounded her. It was as if her familiar boy had suddenly sprouted a tail.

"You do whatever you want to do," Linda said now. "Just take advantage of this chance to rest."

Asher grunted, his new version of a nod now that he couldn't produce one. He sat stiffly, looking outside the window at the ocean that stretched before them, at the small groups of people playing volleyball on the beach as the car neared the curve leading to Santa Monica. Three months ago his team had played a state final at UCLA. They were the underdogs, the visitors at their rival's home field and barely able to hear one another above the din of the fans' shrill screams. They were tied, 0–0, and there was Asher, alone, close to the UCLA goalie by accident, when one of his teammates miraculously recovered the ball and turned it around; he kicked it, high, and it flew toward Asher in a beautiful, elevated arc, the black pentagons and white hexagons glittering against the blue sky of a perfect California afternoon. Asher stood beneath the ball, his heart racing, then flipped his body into a bicycle kick, his right foot whipping the ball over his head as he fell onto his back, holding on to the grass for dear life as he twisted his head around and watched incredulously as the ball slammed into the net.

It had felt good, so very good, and that night he and his teammates had come down to this very beach and played soccer barefoot in the dark until Coach found them and chewed them out for being so stupid as to play without cleats—did they want their fucking toes broken before the next tournament?

In the car now, Asher closed his eyes until he could feel the rough texture of sand underneath his feet, the ice-cold water of the evening Pacific lapping against his ankles.

# Chapter Twelve

They settled into a routine.

Most days Joseph left early so that he could work from home Wednesdays and Fridays. Linda's production schedule began late in the morning, allowing her to help Asher do the little things he couldn't manage on his own: clean his pins, wash his hair, sponge his back underneath his vest. Together they tore apart his T-shirts to enable them to fit over the brace and under the vest, so the itchiness wouldn't drive him mad. He gradually adjusted to his new, submissive morning routine, to his mother's firm, gentle ministrations.

He had always been closest to his father, more comfortable with Joseph's quiet affection and tacit approval of everything that Asher did. He'd never doubted Linda's love either, but he balked at her hypercompetitiveness, at her great academic expectations, her unspoken desire for him to have gone to a place like Harvard or Princeton instead of UC Santa Barbara.

She was the daughter of a physician and a scientist; she'd never figured she'd have a jock for a son, and somewhere down the line she'd figured out that there was only so much molding she could attempt; something already inside Asher was steering his course in life.

Now Linda tended to him as she had when he was a

little boy, constantly coming home with scrapes and cuts and bruises from his rough-and-tumble games, and she was disconcerted by the grown man's physique that was under her care. Like most mothers she'd lost contact with his body as he grew; by the time he was ten, Asher refused to allow her to see him even in his underwear, much less naked. This man she touched was physically a stranger to her, someone whose muscle and bone had been trained to perform in strenuous settings for maximum yield.

The first day she bathed him, Linda sponged Asher's shoulders and back, feeling his shoulders flex under her touch, the small recoil when she neared the pins or the places where the vest strapped onto his chest and back.

"I used to do this when you were little, remember?" she asked, the memory making her smile. "You hated to bathe. Hated it. You'd just sit in the tub and put your hands under the faucet and pout when I soaped your back."

Asher smiled despite everything. He loved to hear stories about himself.

"And your hair," his mother continued. "Oh, my God. If it had been up to you, you'd've washed it once a month. Maybe! You'd scream every time I put on shampoo, scream every time I rinsed it, scream if anything got into your eyes." Linda shook her head. "Your dad and I would laugh afterward. Never in front of you. You'd be so offended." This time she did laugh. She remembered how vulnerable Asher had looked as a little boy—like all little boys do—with his bony shoulder blades, his sharp ribs sticking out, the look of affront in his eyes every time she dipped the small bucket into the bath and poured the water over his head. Then she'd pull him from the tub and wrap him in a towel and hold him close until he stopped crying and finally hugged her back, his thin arms encircling her neck as she carried him to his room, his wet hair pressing against the side of her face.

Linda laid both her hands on Asher's shoulders and squeezed them gently before dropping the bath towel over them.

"I love you, baby," she whispered.

"I love you too, Mom," replied Asher, reaching his hand up to hers. "Thanks for doing all this."

"Oh, it's my pleasure, my love," Linda replied. "Just think how good it will feel when you can take a proper shower again!"

He did think about that. He thought about all the minor things he'd taken for granted all his life, of how startling it was to be helpless, dependent on someone else's whim to satisfy the most basic of needs.

Alone in his parents' house, Asher had time to think. He could finish his schoolwork in two hours, tops. The first few days, it came as a surprise to him how effective one could be with no distractions, no friends, no girlfriend, no soccer, just the emptiness of a house and the outside lure of little more than a coffee at the nearby Starbucks.

So he putzed around the house most of the day, like an unsupervised baby who sticks his fingers into whatever is within reach. And that's how he ran into his past again, entirely by accident as he rummaged through his old high-school desk up in his bedroom.

It all fit in a small manila envelope: the woven red

bracelet, the letter, and the picture of the girl with dark hair and big mournful eyes that looked back at him impassively. His mother.

He brought the photo up to eye level and stared at it for a long time. When he was little, he used to stand in front of the mirror and hold her picture next to his face, trying to discern a similarity where—truth be told, he now thought yet again—there was none. Her oval face had the old-fashioned beauty and aloofness of a collector's doll, albeit one endowed with a hint of haughtiness in the narrow, slightly aquiline nose. It registered for the first time that although her lips held the beginning of a smile, it wasn't enough to reach her eyes, almost as if someone had asked her not to grimace but rather to concentrate on looking pleasant.

Asher narrowed his eyes and tried to see beyond the superficiality of the picture. She looked not only entirely foreign to him but so young and so...detached. Like a surly sister or somebody's baby-sitter, but not like a mom. Certainly not like *his* mom, with her ample smile and generous hugs and clinking bracelets.

Asher carefully drew out the original letter and was taken aback at how very neat and precise the writing was, the kind of detail he never would have noticed before. When he was a little boy, Linda would read the note from the attached translation and he'd listen raptly, until he learned the words by heart.

*Dear Sebastián:*
*I hope you can keep the name I gave you. It's the name of my brother, whom I love very much,*

*as much as I love you. I can't take care of you. I'm
all alone, and you need a family that can give you
time and care and lots of love, with a mommy and a
daddy, so you'll grow up to be the best possible child
you can be. The red bracelet is for good luck. It's
very beautiful, isn't it? It was made by a very good
friend of mine who makes beautiful things. I gave a
blue one just like it to your father. So he can be protected, wherever he may go.*

   *Study very hard. You have to do well in school.
And be a good person, Sebastián. Be kind and be
good, and may God bless you always, my baby.
Have a wonderful life.*

*Mom*

He used to look at the picture and the letter all the time,
but then soccer and college and life consumed him and it
just wasn't that important anymore. Asher's eyes went back
and forth between the original letter and the translation,
wondering how exact the latter really was. Now, after so
many years, the simplicity of the letter, its almost infantile
content, struck him. Then again, she'd been young when
the picture was taken—eighteen when she got pregnant.
All he'd done at eighteen was party and play soccer. God
knows what kind of letter *he* would have come up with.

   Asher looked more closely at the original and marveled
yet again at the penmanship. He could understand some
of the basic words—Dios, bebé, papá, mamá, familia—but
his Spanish, despite his being raised in California, was way
too rudimentary to explore any nuance that could possibly

lie beyond the blue ink on the yellowing paper. He slowly folded the letter and gingerly put it back in its envelope, along with the photograph and the bracelet. He tapped the envelope against his hand for a moment, and then he slid it back into the file and closed the bottom desk drawer behind it.

# Chapter Thirteen

Joseph Stone stood in the corner of the examination room, making every effort to look nonchalant as Dr. Stein carefully examined the pins drilled into Asher's skull for any sign of infection.

He still hadn't gotten used to this immobilized Asher, probably never would, he figured with a twinge of guilt, because he was so insanely proud of everything his son had accomplished and because he was everything Joseph wasn't: athletic, popular, gregarious.

Joseph had so often wondered if he'd seen all those qualities in the brown little baby that had been thrust into his arms so long ago. He couldn't have, and yet what were the chances of finding his alter ego, in the best sense of the word? He knew that Linda still yearned to make an intellectual out of Asher, but there was no bigger thrill for Joseph than watching his son play soccer—soccer! Who'd ever heard of a Jewish soccer player? But there was Asher, unstoppable, relentless, focused, and Joseph's heart would fill and overflow with a warm burst of pride, like a tree suddenly expelling all its leaves, that left him weak with sheer joy.

*His* Asher. His responsibility, he reminded himself now.

"This is healing very, very nicely," Dr. Stein said as he

walked behind Asher, his fingers palpating the base of his neck. "The X-rays show that the bone is fusing very well, faster than we expected. And your motor strength is improving greatly, too, although I was hoping for that, given your physical condition," he added. "So I think we can have the halo off slightly earlier than we planned. Let's see...you've had it for six weeks, correct?"

"That's right," said Asher, who'd been crossing off the days in a calendar on his desk.

Dr. Stein nodded. "Our original projection was twelve weeks with the halo. I think we might be done with ten. We'll assess on your next visit in two weeks, but it looks like you'll be ready to take this off in a month, Asher," he said with a smile. "You're a very lucky young man," he repeated, for what felt like the three-hundredth time since the accident.

Joseph hadn't realized he was holding his breath until he exhaled and allowed a smile to spread over his face.

"That's great news. That's great news!" Asher said, his smile reflecting his father's as he looked at him and Linda. "When do you think I can start playing again, then?" he asked.

Joseph stood a little straighter, all his senses in full alert. He'd been bracing himself for this conversation; it was one of the reasons he and Linda came to every single checkup.

"Playing? Playing what?" asked Dr. Stein, clearly confused.

"Soccer. I'm a soccer player, Doctor, remember?" said Asher testily.

"I'm sorry, yes, of course, Asher, I remember."

Dr. Stein, clearly uncomfortable, took off his glasses, polished them, and put them on again. The examination room was suddenly very quiet.

"Look," he finally said, glancing from Asher to his parents and back at Asher. "The way you're recovering, and the way these fractures heal when they heal properly, which seems to be the case here, you should be able to resume all your activities, even physical activities like running, bicycling, weights. But soccer—especially at the level you play—is a contact sport. You have to literally use your head," Dr. Stein said with a mirthless little laugh. "I'm sorry, but given the kind of injury you sustained—you have a cervical fracture, Asher—I cannot recommend that you return to your sport."

Joseph knew that the words were coming, although he'd told himself over the days that they weren't, that doctors loved to present the worst-case scenario only to invariably be proven wrong, but in his heart of hearts he'd known—how could he not? He knew how Asher played, he knew what it took, he'd been with him every step of the way. Now he forced himself not to flinch as his son looked at him accusingly across the room.

Asher tried to shake his head and couldn't, so he closed his eyes instead until the words came out.

"This makes no sense. You're not making any sense," he said eventually, his voice rising to a shout. "You never said anything before. And I've been asking, and asking, and talking about soccer from day one like an idiot! And you never said anything about not playing!" Asher banged his hand uselessly against the hard metal of the examination table, and the sound reverberated in the now-silent room.

Joseph moved toward his son as Dr. Stein's nurse hurried in, her face grim with alarm.

"Is everything okay, Doctor?" she asked.

"What, you honestly think I'm a threat to anyone?" Asher snorted. "Look at me. I can barely move. I can't do shit!"

Joseph came up protectively to Asher and placed his hand on his shoulder, feeling his son's muscles tense beneath his touch. Linda stood immobile in her corner spot, for the first time in her life uncertain as to what to do. They both began speaking at once but Dr. Stein finally took control of the situation.

"Doris, everything is fine," he said firmly to his nurse. "You can step outside and close the door."

In the silence that followed, Asher brought his hands up to the bridge of his nose, a part of his face he could touch easily, and shut his eyes.

Joseph wanted to say the right thing—he had always said the right thing. He wanted to put his hand not on his son's shoulder but on his head, as he used to do when Asher was a little boy, feeling the bone structure of his skull underneath his hands, the ripple of his buzz cut as he ran his fingers through the top of the boy's hair. Just as he had never missed having a child, once he had Asher, he couldn't conceive of the world without him and he doted on him shamelessly, the lenient half to Linda's far more rigorous agenda of homework, rehearsals, practice, and birthday parties, all scheduled with minute precision, in order to provide every last drop of opportunity to a child who could have had none.

*What now?* thought Joseph. *What now?*

"Asher," Dr. Stein said quietly when the door closed again, "you've gone through a very serious, very traumatic accident. You are recovering far better than I ever expected. But going back to competitive or professional sports after this kind of injury...frankly, no. I'm very sorry."

"You can't keep me from playing again," Asher said, his eyes still shut.

"No," agreed Dr. Stein. "And you're free to seek a second opinion on this. But I hope you come to the realization that being alive, being able to walk and function, is a lot more important than playing one more soccer match and risking another injury that could kill you or leave you in a wheelchair. And I'm sure your coach would agree."

Asher dug his finger further into his brow and took a deep breath, his shoulder rising against the hand that Joseph kept firmly in place.

"You're not alone," continued Dr. Stein clinically. "We see many injured athletes who can't return to their sport. It's hardly the end of their lives—or yours. You're not incapable, and you're luckily not disabled either. There's much to be thankful for, Asher."

Asher didn't say a word. He carefully stood up from the examination table and made his way to the door.

"Let me help you, Ash," Joseph Stone said, reaching for his son's elbow.

"Don't," said Asher curtly. "I'm sorry," he amended. "But please don't. I don't need anyone's help."

*     *     *

They didn't talk about it. He didn't want to talk about it. Instead he spent more and more hours in the makeshift gym he'd set up in the backyard, doing the strengthening exercises for his arms and legs, increasing the weights and the repetitions until his quads were on fire. Even under the benevolence of the mild California weather, he pushed himself until the sheer physicality brought him some semblance of what it felt like to use his body, until he drenched his T-shirts and halo vest with sweat.

He almost relished the itching that came with it, derived secret pleasure from seeing Linda cringe when she passed the sponge over the angry red rash that erupted violently under the plastic armor.

"Let me call Dr. Stein and see what you can use to make this better," she said with a frown the first day the rash cropped up.

"I'm not an invalid, Mom," he told her. It was his new mantra, one he repeated over and over to the beat of Eminem as he did his leg presses. "You work out, things happen," he added stubbornly. "You'll see. Dr. Stein has no idea how powerful the mind can be. Look at James Blake," he added, his words stumbling over each other in his rush to explain. "He broke his back, got shingles, and went back to the court and became a top-ten tennis player. The guy wasn't supposed to walk again."

"It's a different kind of injury, honey," Linda said, quietly but firmly.

Asher felt his mother's hand pause on his back, and his impatience rose upward. They'd always parried, his mother and he, and he'd always brushed her off, always ended up getting his way. Who the hell cared if he got B's instead of A's, after all? As Joseph Stone was fond of pointing out, anyone could have a 4.0 average, but most people could only dream of achieving an ounce of what Asher did on a soccer field.

"You always underestimate me, you know that?" Asher said belligerently, and immediately wished he hadn't, even as a small part of him rationalized that it was true, that Linda always wanted a little more than what he had to give.

"How can you say that, Asher?" his mother countered in a tight, hurt voice. "You've made me infinitely proud. You make me proud every single day of my life. You do," she added quickly, but still didn't manage to catch the break in her voice.

Asher shut his eyes with a mix of anger, resignation, and shame. It seemed all he did lately was apologize—to his mother, to Joseph, to Alessandra, to Dr. Stein.

"I'm sorry, Mom," he said, as if on cue, one more statement of regret to add to his litany of errors. "It's just... you're not an athlete. You wouldn't understand."

Asher knew that his mother would hate that comment; he knew that over the years she'd resented being marginalized from his soccer conversations, the discussions on performance and pushing one's limits. She had always argued that striving for excellence was the same across the board, but he knew it wasn't so. He knew that nothing was as daunting—or exhilarating—as being on the field, shoulder to shoulder, your rival so close you could feel his breath against your sweat-stained face, so close you could see the hunger in his eyes, feel his spit as it singed your cheek. And that made the difference, made Asher want it more than anything, made him better.

"All I'll say, my love, is that I'm here to support you," Linda finally ventured, intuitively knowing that his mind had wandered to a place she couldn't begin to reach. "Your father and I are here to support you through this, through anything. Okay?"

Asher flexed his legs and felt the familiar ache—in his calves, his arms, even in his waist. His muscles protested against the onslaught of sudden strain he'd put them through. He relished it and wondered what his neck would feel like when they took off the halo. Everyone said that it would feel strange at first, as if his head were too big, too heavy for his body.

He silently squeezed his mother's hand.

\*      \*      \*

The brace was still on a week later when he sat on the sidelines at the UCLA game.

"Last time I sat on the bench was after I flunked that math test, remember?" he asked Alessandra, nudging her leg with his knee.

"Well," she said, ever pragmatic, "that's what happens when you don't study and you call your girlfriend a nag."

Asher laughed. "Hey, I fixed it, didn't I?" he said cockily. "One hundred percent the next time around. What did Duggy call it? Ah, yes. A brilliant comeback."

"Did you tell him I tutored you daily for your brilliant comeback, O genius?" Alessandra parried.

"Baby, there's no need to state the obvious," Asher said happily. He felt good. He'd visited the guys in the locker room before the game and was still empowered by the swell of their support. It was almost as if he were the one preparing to march onto the vast expanse of grass any second now, and it would be, he told himself, it would be him. Soon.

The crowd roared, and Asher stood up carefully as his team ran into the field. For several seconds he couldn't speak, wasn't even aware of Alessandra, of the "Oh, Asher," that escaped from her lips, of her hand reaching for his limp one, then dropping it and settling instead on the small of his back.

He only had eyes for the halos—the wispy aluminum-foil kind you get in costume stores to go with angel outfits— that each member of the Gaucho squad wore on top of his head. The halos bobbed over the running figures, and the aluminum strands twinkled under the stadium floodlights. As the team circled the field, he was able to see the backs of their jerseys, emblazoned not with their numbers but with the words HALO EFFECT.

Asher felt his heart pound faster against the constraint of his vest as he watched his team, his guys, salute him from across the field, like brothers-in-arms. He tried to smile, but his lips wouldn't obey; they just trembled involuntarily against the pressure of the tears that he tried to squelch but couldn't. He raised both his hands dumbly, acknowledging the cheers from the crowd, and thought, what the hell, he could cry, couldn't he? He could allow himself the tears—of pride, of regret, of inevitability—as they tossed their little wire halos aside and plunged headfirst into the game. Asher stood on the sidelines as he watched the battle unfold before him, the furious running from one end of the field to the other, the bodies flung against one another with fearless abandon, knees bending, backs contorting, the cleats digging into the soil in front of the bench so fiercely that dirt and mud spattered onto his sneakers, the action so close to him that he could smell it, could touch it if he wanted.

And yet he knew he couldn't be farther away. It would take weeks once the halo was off to strengthen his neck. Weeks to regain full mobility, his stamina, to rebuild his muscles. No matter what he did, no matter what superhuman effort he put into it, there was simply no way to make that draft, even for the following year. One of his teammates leaped up to greet the ball with his head, the motion defiant, aggressive, and Asher cringed, recalling Dr. Stein's little pictures, all laid out next to the X-rays, the arrows pointing to the fractures and indentations that were now an indelible part of the map of his bones.

"It's not going to happen, is it?" he said suddenly, turning toward Alessandra.

"What?" she shouted, trying to hear over the din.

Asher opened his mouth to say something, thought better of it, and forced himself to smile weakly.

"I'm not feeling that great," he said instead. "Let's leave after halftime, okay?"

\*     \*     \*

He didn't ask Alessandra to come in, feeling the faintest twinge of guilt at having made her drive all the way down from Santa Barbara for such a truncated date.

Instead he stood alone inside his bedroom, taking in the endless rows of medals and plaques and trophies. For an insane moment, he felt like sweeping the spoils of his junior victories off the shelves, as enraged people did in the movies, but it felt like sacrilege. His eyes turned to the life-size poster of Lionel Messi pasted on the back of his door: the last thing he saw every night before falling asleep, the first thing he saw every morning when he woke up, his endless source of inspiration. Asher had put him up there because they were almost the same height, Messi five feet seven to Asher's five feet nine—short, scrappy, fast. Messi was an elegant player. That's what they'd always said about Asher, too. How elegant he was on the field.

In the beginning, when he first started to play, when he realized how good he truly was, he used to fantasize about the possibilities. He'd become a champion, he'd play around the world and in South America, and then his mother—the mother who'd given him up—and his father, they would recognize him, they would know his likeness from the pictures in the newspaper, and they'd look for him, celebrate his success, tell him how proud they were of the man he'd turned out to be.

He knew it was all wishful thinking, but there'd been no harm in it either. Now the mere thought felt like mockery. What if—as Dr. Stein had pointed out—he'd died in that accident? They wouldn't even know about it. They would never know. It would have been as if he'd never existed at all.

Without preamble Asher lifted both hands and tore Messi from the door, crumpling up the poster between his hands until it was much smaller than a soccer ball and tossing it with precise accuracy into the wastebasket on the other side of the room.

# Chapter Fourteen

He dug out her picture again the following morning and once more tried to plumb the depths of the girl's solemn eyes. She had him. She gave him up. How could one do that and never look back? he wondered.

"Impossible," he said out loud.

Almost on a whim, he walked down to his computer and Googled her.

*"Rita Ortiz."*

The name alone yielded 8,150,000 results.

"Well, that was useless," Asher mumbled to himself.

*"Rita Ortiz, Colombia,"* he typed. Over 4 million results.

*Okay,* he thought. *There must be a better way.*

This time he typed, *"Rita Ortiz in Colombia."*

A little over a hundred thousand results. He clicked on the first one, a personal profile from a social-networking site. Name Rita Ortiz, from Antioquia, Colombia. A photograph of a blond, middle-aged woman with a scrunched-up face, hefty cleavage, and a green tattoo lining her left arm popped up.

Asher grimaced and sat back. It could be her, he thought. If she'd been eighteen years old, she'd be thirty-nine or forty now. This woman looked the right age. God forbid. On an impulse he signed in to his Facebook account and typed the name again. Rita Ortiz.

This time it was far more palatable: 157 results.

Asher began clicking on photographs, narrowing the possibilities to 74. If he clicked on their friends, the only option open to him as a nonfriend, all he could determine was that most of their Facebook circles consisted of other Latin names, some with countries attached, some not.

It was hard to tell if any of the Ritas looked like him at all. The small profile photos offered glimpses of mostly dark-haired, olive-skinned women whose features began to acquire a startling sameness after he looked at them for the fifth, sixth, seventh time. If he were to place his own photograph next to most any of these, there would be *some* resemblance to grasp in each of them.

But there was *some* resemblance to his adoptive mother as well, from her olive skin and hazel eyes. Asher unconsciously looked at the family picture that sat on the desk before him: he and his parents on a ski trip, their caps and fur-lined parka hoods encasing their smiling faces. Asher stood between his parents, almost cheek to cheek with his mother, displaying the same dazzling white teeth over the bronze skin. No one ever thought he was adopted until he offered the information.

He looked again at the array of women on the computer screen, almost twenty years younger than the only mother he knew. Were they rich? Poor? Depressive? Funny? What kind of houses did they live in? Did they have other children? He thought of all the little quirks he had, how he hated the smell of cooking oil and incense, how he couldn't stand dark houses and narrow hallways, how he needed to see books on shelves, like the ones they had in this house, even though he wasn't a big reader himself.

Why, he thought, couldn't he just get a little file that detailed who she was, where she was, and what she did? And then it would all be over with. His cell phone rang, and Asher looked down at the caller ID. Alessandra. He flexed his hands, his new relaxation technique now that he couldn't run his fingers through his hair.

"What up?" he said simply, injecting some measure of enthusiasm into his voice.

"Hey, Ash, how are you feeling?" asked Alessandra, concern over the previous night audible in her voice.

"I'm good," he replied, and the moment he said it, he realized that he actually was. "I'm sorry about last night, Ally." Asher paused for a moment, debating what else to say, then blurted it out. "I'm actually looking for my birth mother online."

"Oh!" said Alessandra, not bothering to hide her surprise. "That's...hmmm, interesting," she said after a beat. "Why are you doing this now? I mean, I thought you'd told me you guys had tried the Internet route before."

"We did," said Asher slowly, looking at the roster of Facebook Ritas before him. When he had first expressed real curiosity for his birth mother, back in his junior year in high school, Joseph and Linda had input what little information they had into all the adoption registries, but nothing had ever turned up, and not a single e-mail had ever come in from all those websites since then. "But there was no Facebook when we did that," he said thoughtfully. "You know, Ally, she could be right here. There's a bunch of Rita Ortizes. No reason one of them couldn't be her."

"I suppose," said Alessandra dubiously. "But what are you going to do? Are you going to write to each and every one of them?"

"Well, why not? It's easy enough," said Asher, brightening at the prospect. "I have plenty of time. Worst-case scenario, they'll think I'm a lunatic and not answer back."

His fingers hovered above his keyboard. "You know, it's not possible to simply disappear," he continued. "People are born, they must leave behind some kind of trace, no matter how faint. If she lives in the twenty-first century, she has to be online. She has to. Somewhere."

"If she were, don't you think she'd have tried to connect by now?" asked Alessandra uncertainly. "I don't mean to be a downer, but…"

"No, no," Asher conceded. "You're right. Let's assume for a moment that she doesn't want anything to do with me. But what if I'd died in that accident? She'd certainly want to know something like that, don't you think? I'm her son. Surely she's wondered what became of me? She has to. Unless *she's* dead," he added quickly, wanting to gloss over that possibility. "But even then. Someone in her family would be…I don't know, *intrigued* about the fate of her child."

Asher could hear the building excitement in his own voice and thought Alessandra must have noticed it, too, because rather than try to talk him out of his research, she offered advice.

"Well, if I were you, I'd go to the source," said Alessandra, ever practical. "You were born in Colombia—why don't you start there? I mean, not physically. You can narrow your online search to Colombia, can't you?"

"I guess I could," said Asher, "but I can't read all the results. My Spanish sucks. It's ridiculous. I'm a Latino raised in Los Angeles, and I speak no Spanish."

His parents hadn't been the type to ram his birth country down his throat. They hadn't taken him there, taught him the language, fed him the food. When Sebastián became Asher Stone, he became Asher Stone, no strings attached, and Asher, being Asher, never looked back.

Now it was as if an invisible thread were pulling him in the opposite direction, like a fish fighting a line, his brush with mortality more powerful than any lure.

"Ash, just being born someplace doesn't make you belong to that place," Alessandra said. "Although it would have been nice if you'd taken that Spanish course I recommended. And it was super easy, too!"

"Baby, who had time to do anything in the middle of soccer season?" Asher replied testily.

"Well, as you just pointed out, *now* you have the time, don't you?" she parried.

Asher looked again at the list of Facebook names. Half of these women probably spoke no English.

"Okay. Okay. You have a point," he conceded. "My excursion of the day will be to the bookstore to buy a Spanish version of Rosetta Stone. Happy?" he asked.

"Extremely," said Alessandra. "Ash, you're really serious about this, aren't you? Have you spoken with your parents?"

Asher flexed his fingers. The thought had circled his mind since the night before, but for now he wasn't about to lose his nerve.

"No," he finally admitted. "But I will. When the time is right."

Asher clicked the phone shut pensively. He didn't want to come across as an ignorant fool by writing in poor Spanish, but he didn't want to delay the task at hand either. He went slowly down the list until he found the first Rita Ortiz in the United States, in Arizona to be exact. It was a long shot, but what was there to lose, after all?

*"Dear Ms. Ortiz,"* he wrote. *"Do you by any chance have a son named Sebastian?"*

Asher looked at the message for a long time, reading and rereading the name, Sebastian, until it became gibberish. He looked at the plump woman in the picture, standing stiffly alongside a portly older man in a Hawaiian shirt, who appeared to be her husband. They looked nice enough, he supposed. Not relaxed, but content, perhaps. Asher took a deep breath and pressed the SEND button. Only then did he realize he was actually sweating, the rivulets dripping into his vest, making him itch. Before he could lose his nerve, he went on to Rita in Philadelphia and then Rita the vampy blonde from Orlando whose picture oozed attitude and whose friends all looked like party types. Asher gazed at the picture carefully. His mother could almost be his peer, like those high-school teachers who were barely a decade older than he'd been at the time, but looked young enough to imagine them as so much more.

Asher was suddenly exhausted. He got up and walked

to the couch, then sat down stiffly, rotating his body and lifting his legs up. Slowly he lay down, placing a pillow underneath his neck for support.

He closed his eyes and tuned his iPod to Vivaldi, the most joyous music he could come up with right now, and tried to imagine what it had been like to be a baby, to be born in the place one is conceived and nurtured and meant for, and then to be transplanted to another reality, almost like switching the channel on a television set.

Of course it could be done, he mused. Thousands and thousands of others had done it, and from places far more removed than his. He at least was connected to his home country by the mountain range that ran from California all the way down to the tip of South America. If his arms were only wide enough, he could open them and touch both places with the tips of his fingers and still remain in the middle of the two.

*     *     *

The last time he'd seriously dwelled on his origins, it had been as part of a social-studies assignment in his junior year in high school. They were asked to explore the story behind a historic family picture, and Asher chose Rita's, quite simply because he thought it could get him the better grade.

Once enlarged, the photograph looked different. *She* looked different, prettier yet plainer at the same time, like girls who know they're pretty but try to pass unnoticed. The picture showed her from the waist up, wearing a red woolen, V-neck sweater with the collar of a white shirt peeking out from underneath. Her skin was a light olive tone that looked slightly sallow.

"This is my birth mother," said Asher as he stood in front of his social-studies class, the photograph on an easel beside him. "I don't know much about her, except that her name was Rita. Rita Ortiz. This photograph was taken when she was eighteen years old, a year older than I am now. That's how old she was when she had me. She's from Colombia, and this picture was taken in the orphanage where I was adopted from, which is called La Casa en el Campo, which in Spanish means 'The House in the Country.' My mother was probably about to have me when the picture was taken, or she had just had me. Like I said, I don't know much about my birth mother, but this photograph tells us a little bit. She's standing in front of a cross. She was probably Catholic—most people in Colombia are Catholic—which is kind of ironic, considering I'm Jewish. In fact, I don't think I look like my birth mother at all. Actually, I think I look more like my mother, but...whatever."

Asher paused for a moment and realized that the classroom was very still. It wasn't just that everybody was listening; they were simply not moving. There was no rustling of papers, no shifting of legs, no tapping of pencils.

It suddenly occurred to him that his being adopted was probably news to many people. All his good friends—the remnants from his elementary and middle schools—knew. But it was such a given, in fact, that no one would have thought to carry the information on into high school. All the other adopted kids he knew were Chinese or African, or Russian kids who had Russian names that immediately revealed their provenance. But Asher Stone looked like... well, Asher Stone.

Asher cleared his throat. This rapt attention was making him self-conscious.

"I know this isn't really a historical photograph," he went on, "but it's the furthest I can go with my birth family. And it marks the beginning of my life with my real family. With my mom and dad. But she started it," he said, pointing quickly at the girl in the picture.

"That's it," he added, glancing at Mr. Monroe, his social-studies teacher.

"Well," said Mr. Monroe. "That was very interesting. Any questions?"

"How about your dad, Asher?" asked Nina Rowley from the front row. "Do you know who he is?"

"Nope," said Asher, shaking his head. "Nada on him."

"Hey, Ash, maybe your dad was some famous celebrity and they had to keep it a secret," said Steven Thorne from the back of the room.

"Dude, maybe he was an ax murderer," said Mike Avila, who was Asher's best friend.

"Hey, hey," drawled Asher. "He can't have been that bad. Look at me!"

He got an A. And he started thinking about it, really, for the first time in years. Not about his mother. Her, he could take out of a box at night. But him. No one ever said anything about him, as if he'd never existed. Asher wondered why his father was unmentionable. He couldn't have been that horrible; after all, his birth mother had mentioned him in her letter. They had to have been boyfriend and girl-friend, thought Asher, and they'd messed up. End of story.

"Why do you think my birth father's name isn't in any of my adoption papers, Dad?" Asher asked after Joseph had picked him up from soccer practice one afternoon.

The question came out of the blue, and Joseph was momentarily stumped.

"I honestly don't know, Ash," he replied, and it was the truth.

"Is that weird? I mean, is it common not to know any-thing about the father?" asked Asher.

"I think every case is different," Joseph answered carefully. "When we adopted you, there wasn't that much information. And the thing was, Ash, we didn't care. All we cared was that you were healthy and that we could have you. Everything else was irrelevant."

Joseph paused, his eyes on the road.

"What we were told, however, was that your birth mother refused to give out your father's name. She said she'd had a relationship and she said they were in love, but she couldn't disclose who it was."

"She said they were in love?" interrupted Asher, pounc-ing on this new detail.

"Yes," said Joseph emphatically. "She did. I don't know anything else. I'm sorry. I do know this, though," he added with a small laugh. "Whoever he was, he had to have been a good man, a handsome man, and good at soccer, because you sure didn't get it from me!"

Asher smiled at that one.

"Yeah, I guess I didn't," he said, looking at his father's

slight build, at his little horn-rimmed glasses. Joseph stopped at a red light, and Asher impulsively leaned over and gave him a hug.

That night, after Asher went to bed, Joseph whispered in Linda's ear: "They were in love," he told her. "Just remember to always say that."

*       *       *

Asher couldn't bring himself to say anything to his parents that evening after sending out the first Facebook message.

He waited until the next morning, until it was just him and his mother alone, his back to her, his confidence bolstered by the love that flowed from her hands to the scars that she cleaned for him every day.

"Mom?"

"Yes, honey?"

"I've been thinking—you know how everybody is always telling me how lucky I was? How I could have died? What if I *had* died?"

"But you didn't, Asher. That's the miraculous part of this. You've been given a second chance."

"I know, Mom," said Asher, hesitating slightly as he gathered his courage to continue. "And maybe part of this second chance means finding who my birth parents were."

Linda was always on the alert for these very words, but they still caught her by surprise. She stared at her son's shoulders, watched rivulets of water roll down his back. His hair had begun to grow in again, and now it looked like a military buzz cut, exposing a vulnerable neck that had lost the luster gained from hours in the sun. She felt an overwhelming urge to protect him, to shield him from all these things that had happened and could continue to happen.

"Honey, we've tried to find her before," she reminded him. "We can most certainly try again, but—" Linda stopped, trying to find the right words. "We've always hit a roadblock in the past. You know that. We sent letters. We called the orphanage. It always seems to dead-end. I don't know what else—"

"Mom, I don't need her. I don't miss her," Asher interrupted. "But I'd like to find her, and my father, too. Do you know what I mean? I just need to know and move on and not feel like I'm still lying on a hospital bed and having regrets."

*But you're mine now,* Linda thought with a pang of jealousy.

"Mom." Asher turned, slowly swiveling the chair around so he was facing Linda, his eyes earnest inside the frame of his metal halo. "I want to find her."

In the seconds it took for him to painstakingly turn toward her, Linda forced herself to compose her face, not to recoil against words she found odious.

"Asher. We've never told you not to look for her, honey," she said, placating—defensive, even—but she couldn't bring herself to utter anything more enthusiastic.

"I know you haven't, Mom," Asher pressed. "But I need to hear you say it's all right. I need Dad to say it's all right. I want to do this properly this time. Not just simply put my information out there. I want to do everything I can to track this person down. And I need to know that I have your blessing. Not just your approval. Your blessing."

Linda looked at her son. Here he sat, defenseless, with that monstrosity around his neck and chest. She couldn't doubt the seriousness of his purpose.

"Asher," she said, leaning forward and placing her hands on his, "you have my blessing. You have my unconditional support, and I will give you my help with anything you may need. But this is your journey now. Yours. I can help you, my love, but I can't do it for you."

"I know. I know, Mom."

They were both silent, and Asher looked down at his mother's hands, her color almost matching his.

"I love your hands," he said simply.

Linda smiled. They were beautiful hands, her pride and joy, smooth and elongated, the slender fingers always boasting different rings that sparkled around her plain white gold wedding band, that shone brighter against the simplicity of her pale pink nail polish.

"You always used to say that when you were little, do you remember?" she asked him softly.

"You know I'm not looking for anything more than I have," Asher said, covering her hand with his. "I just want to tie all the pieces together."

Linda nodded ruefully. She'd finally come face-to-face with inevitability. She'd had twenty-one years of him all to herself, she thought. That was better than many.

"You do what you need to do, Asher," she said firmly. "And we'll be there for you."

That night he checked his Facebook. No messages. Emboldened, he sent out ten more, then thirty the following day, running the gamut of Rita Ortizes. He checked for answers daily, a captive of Facebook inside his metal halo. It took three whole weeks. And then, finally, one Rita Ortiz wrote back, his question framed in bold letters inside the subject heading: "Do you happen to have a son named Sebastian?" The answer below blinked at him in gray letters:

"No."

# Chapter Fifteen

*Sebastian and Rita*

Asher reaches for Alessandra's hand in the seat beside him.

"It's so gray here," he says quietly, looking out the window of the SUV they've hired exclusively for the duration of their trip. The day is overcast, and the clouds loom low over the city as they attempt to make their way out of it through desperate traffic, an arduous task that's already occupied forty-five minutes of driving time.

Bogotá sits high in the Andes, more than eighty-six hundred feet above sea level, the third-highest capital city in the world. Its mix of piercing sunlight and perennial cold, of blue skies intertwined with the smog of a plateau location, has yet to sit well with Asher, who's grown up between the ocean and the mountains of California.

"Oh, I think it's beautiful!" Alessandra says sincerely, taking in the mismatch of green foothills against the daunting rise of apartment buildings lined up close against one another. Behind them the buildings stretch for miles, lining the thoroughfare and climbing up the mountaintops to the left, buildings perched in the most precarious of positions, overlooking the urban sprawl below.

It surprised Asher, how easily she had agreed to come

with him, setting aside one entire month of her summer, of her life, to accompany him on his quest. Because it was a quest, they both agreed on that. And once he set his sights on finding Rita, he was relentless, using the same energy he'd applied on the soccer field to dissecting and analyzing the scant information they had, for months, until there was nowhere else it could take them, nowhere else but here. He could have come with his parents; they, too, were willing to put their lives on hold for him. But it just didn't feel right, opening up his entire family to the uncertainty of what he could find. Plus, what his mother had said was true: This was his assignment to undertake, not theirs anymore. Alessandra, he thought, was neutral, a step removed, with no prejudices or fears to mar her ability to guide him through this terrain.

"Look, it's so pretty," she says now, as the traffic begins to clear, in sync with the thinning of the structures around them. As if a curtain were very slowly parting, the scenery begins to open up before them, the rolling, impossibly green hills, dotted with crops and whitewashed farms with reddish brown tiles topping their roofs.

"Señor, ya llegamos?" Alessandra asks in halting Spanish.

Asher grins and shakes his head.

"Hey, bum!" she complains, elbowing him in the side. "At least I'm trying to string two words together!"

"Ya casi. Almost," replies the driver—a burly man with an officious manner that is at odds with his imposing figure—in equally halting English. His name is Fidel, and although it's only their second day with him, they've come to a mutual linguistic agreement: He speaks in English as much as possible, and they do the same in Spanish.

"Thees is Sabana de Bogotá," Fidel now says carefully. "Many flower cultivated here," he says, gesturing to the extensive tarps outside that seem to cover acres of land. "Roses. Also strawberree. Ah, here we go!" he adds satisfied, pointing to a side road that snakes into the thoroughfare from the left. Ally's hand grasps Asher's and holds on as Fidel slows the car to accommodate the narrower road and the curves that lead gently down the hillside until they see the complex nestled below them. First Asher spots a small, unassuming house that seems to have sprouted ungainly legs—new additions, he can tell from up here—but the central house is what draws his attention. He's seen it a thousand times, in his photo album. It's the backdrop of his very first picture—the one where he's in his mother's arms wearing a little blue suit, his dad embracing both of them, and behind them this house.

"Look at the playground!" Alessandra cries. "Look at all the kids. Oh, my God, Ash. They probably took you there when you were a baby," she says in wonderment.

Asher looks in awe at the children clambering over the jungle gym and the swings, their voices and shouts getting louder the closer the car approaches.

"I can't even begin to fathom that," he replies, but for the first time he can. He feels like he's been having an out-of-body experience, and now it's over. Now he can start again.

*     *     *

Asher's first thought, absurdly, is that Carla Bernotti reminds him of his mother. The executive director of La

Casa en el Campo is a tall, imposing woman whose mere presence seems to spur her minions into action. She wears a red pantsuit and a black turtleneck above which her carefully frosted blond hair curls in deliberate contrast.

"Asher," she says, enunciating each syllable carefully as she lowers her reading glasses to look at him and Alessandra from across her desk. "That is not a very common name, is it?" she asks in accented yet perfect English.

"No, I guess not," says Asher easily, yet already he feels his head beginning to throb, an unfortunate side effect of the accident that seems to appear at the slightest insinuation of stress. "It's a Jewish name," he adds, because Carla is clearly waiting for an explanation. "My adoptive parents are Jewish."

"Yes. It says so here," affirms Carla, pointing toward the paper on her desk with her pen. She speaks in short, punchy sentences that lend import to every remark. "It says they are Jewish—an accountant, a television producer, nice home, no health problems…hmm."

Asher looks at her expectantly, not certain what he can contribute to this, but before he can articulate the thought, Carla speaks again.

"As you know, we have tried to find your birth mother— Rita Ortiz," she says, still looking down at the papers. "But nothing. The information we have for her is no longer up to date, and we've been unable to find anything with what we've got.

"We have nothing on her. Nothing at all. No birth certificate, no death certificate, no copy of her ID, no current address, no named relatives. In fact," she says slowly, going over the papers to make sure she's got this right, "she had no visitors during her time here. Nothing logged at all. No emergency contact. Nothing. Now. This is not uncommon. Many of the girls who come here are hiding. They don't want anyone to know they are pregnant. They don't want anyone to know they were ever pregnant. This was particularly true twenty years ago. They provide the wrong information. They don't leave forwarding addresses. I say this because it may very well be the case with your birth mother. You have to be prepared for the possibility that even if you locate her, she may not want to be found. And this is not a reflection on you. It is simply the way it is."

"I understand," says Asher. "I do, really. But I want to make every effort to find her. That's why we're here." He looks at Alessandra for support. "We think there may have been something that was overlooked. I don't mean to be critical," Asher adds quickly, leaning forward. "But we realize you're all very busy, and Alessandra and I have the time to do a more extensive search. And if we do find her, at the very least I would like to send her a message, let her know I'm doing well. Is it possible to do that?"

"Of course," says Carla, "*if* we find her. But right now we have *not* found her. When you were adopted, this place was run by an order of nuns. Their records were not nearly as thorough as ours are now, and they certainly weren't computerized. The rules about adoption, contact, and information in general were much, much laxer, which is why we have so very little to work with in your case. However. As I told you over the phone, the nun who was in charge of this case is still alive and well, and she has agreed to see us. It's a long shot—she's older, you must remember that—but she might recall something."

"Well, that's fantastic news!" exclaims Asher.

"We will leave in a minute," says Carla firmly. "But first I want to make sure that we"—she pauses, choosing her words carefully—"that we manage expectations. People often come to me and say they understand that their search may not produce positive results. But then they are very upset if that turns out to be the case. This is important," she stresses, looking now at Alessandra. "Closure—if there is closure—is not always equivalent to a happy ending."

For a brief moment, Asher's face falls into a frown, but it's gone just as quickly, like a receding wave.

"My expectations are managed, Mrs. Bernotti," he says calmly, although he wonders what gives this woman jurisdiction to decide what he can or cannot handle. "Can we just"—Asher gestures with his hand—"move on?"

"Of course, of course," says Carla, offering a slight smile. "I like your spirit. Oh! I did find a picture. A picture of your mother," she adds, holding out a faded Polaroid.

Asher looks at the picture, as Carla holds it hovering over her desk like a flag, taunting him. He extends his fingers toward it, almost expecting Carla to pull it back at the last moment, but of course she does nothing of the sort. She simply lets him take it into his own hands, and he looks at it curiously. The girl he sees is unquestionably the same girl from the photograph that's implanted in his mind, but here she's wearing a red woolen cap and what seems to be a heavy apron over a bulky green sweater that accentuates her obvious pregnancy. Her olive skin has a ruddy cast, and

the look in her eyes is almost derisive. She's the same, he
thinks, but there's something different, a more intent gaze,
as if her image on the film had been brought more sharply
into focus.

"Where was this?" he asks.

"At a flower farm," replies Carla. "She apparently worked
at a flower farm during her pregnancy. She was named
Employee of the Month. The picture came with the letter,"
she adds, slowly extending a neatly typed piece of paper
toward him.

"But why did it come to you?" asks Asher.

"Oh, I thought you knew," says Carla. "Your mother
lived here. We aren't just an orphanage. We give housing
to girls who have nowhere to go. Your mother was here"—
she pauses and looks down at her notes—"the last three
months of her pregnancy. She had you, and then...hmm.
And then she left."

*        *        *

The job numbed her mind and numbed her fingers, but at
least she got to sit down. They had given her the option of
working at the home after her school lessons, but she chose
this instead, because it paid so much better and because
she was naïvely lured by the beauty of the product. What
could be more perfect, more distracting, than a rose?

But it was nothing like that. It was pure drudgery, this
picking and choosing—seated, yes, but seated at a wooden
table under an enormous tarp, the roses piled in a towering
mountain before her, replenished in an endless stream. She
had to trim the thorns and measure the stems, and those
that were pristine she would encase in a clear plastic sheath

to protect their fragile beauty when they journeyed abroad, to the United States or to Europe. The very best got sent away; only the mediocre ones stayed in Colombia.

It was always cold here, the temperature near frigid to ensure the health of the roses. Rita worked with thick plastic gloves so she wouldn't be pierced by the thorns, but the cold still penetrated her hands, settled insidiously between her joints, and by the end of the day the tips of her fingers were always lacerated anyway, bleeding in tiny pinpricks that made the gloves stick to her skin. A giant boom box hung from one of the rafters, perpetually tuned to a vallenato station whose music, she was certain, could not in any way benefit the health of the roses, what with the whining accordion and those sorry tales of lost loves.

But the very monotony of the routine soothed her. She was an automaton, cleaning stems, sorting flowers, one after the other after the other. She kept to herself, as she did in the home, deliberately removing her mind from thoughts of her family, of Lucas, of Jazmin, of her brother—especially of Sebastián, because the mere thought of his name made her want to throw up in sheer sorrow. Sometimes she just couldn't help it. At night she would lie in the dormitory bed and swear she could smell him, would involuntarily reach out to stroke his hair before remembering where she was, how she was. She would think about Lucas then, about how he touched her, but that only filled her with anger, with the desire to scream at the top of her lungs, because she had always wanted to leave, yes, but not like this.

When she sorted flowers, she just concentrated on each stem, each bud, each plastic wrapper; that was all she thought, because all she wanted now was to make as much money as possible and move on, forget that this had ever happened to her, forget about the baby that every day kicked harder inside her, pressed deeper into her womb, boldly declaring his right to be—for she already knew it was a boy—the way only a man could. He would probably be taken far away by some foreign couple, like the very best roses, exported, and she would stay here, bogged down by all her interrupted plans, forever defective.

The award took her completely by surprise. She'd been there for only a month, after all, and had kept her head down, tried to make herself as inconspicuous as possible. She was sitting in a corner in the cafeteria, sipping a warm bowl of soup, when the plant manager strode in and motioned for everyone to be quiet. There were about two hundred workers, mostly women, and they sat in little clusters of friends, making her distance all the more obvious.

"Our Employee of the Month is new with us, but she's demonstrated an extraordinary work ethic. She always arrives on time, she is quiet and diligent and careful. She takes obvious pride in her work and strives to do everything she does in the best possible way. And she is, quite simply, our most productive packer. Rita Ortiz!"

Rita looked up in surprise, then glanced around, certain there was a mistake, certain there must be another Rita in the room. But her companions' envious looks told her otherwise. She never got those looks back home when she was singled out for her grades, because there she was Rita Ortiz, pretty Rita whose father owned a shop, who was popular, who had friends. Here she was a snotty, pregnant teenager in mismatched clothes, the poorest in a room of poverty-stricken workers, because they at the very least had homes to go to at night.

Rita heaved herself up and made her way awkwardly and reluctantly toward the front of the room, acutely aware of their stares, of their outright hostility. Now—she suddenly realized—they would be subject to her standards, to her manic meticulousness. Didn't these people realize she wasn't normal? Didn't they realize that only someone utterly devoid of emotion could do this work? she wondered, looking ahead at the plant manager and at her supervisor, a kindly fifty-something-year-old who rarely spoke a word to her but who was now beaming proudly. Rita stood before them and stared down at her hands, noticing how red and chafed they were—hands that were already starting to look like her mother's.

"This is for you," said the plant manager, handing her a check. "A thousand pesos. And two tickets to the movies and a coupon for dinner at Burger King. We'll post the notice up with your photo on the bulletin board for the month. Congratulations!" he added, beaming.

Rita shook the plant manager's hand and took the small envelope. It felt heavy in her hands. The movie tickets, she wouldn't know what to do with them; she had no one to talk to, much less invite to a movie. But a thousand pesos? No one had ever truly validated what she did, what she was worth. Even Mrs. Rodríguez's mouth would turn downward when she gave Rita the excellence award year after year, the expression on her face bordering on distaste when she handed her the pretty little diplomas that Rita's mother would later unceremoniously cram into a drawer under the kitchen counter.

But here she was praised for her extraordinary work ethic. No one had ever told her she had an extraordinary work ethic, and to her consternation Rita felt her eyes involuntarily well up with tears. She bit down hard on her tongue to keep from crying but nevertheless felt a sudden surge of pride that was far stronger than any sense of embarrassment. *Let them be envious*, she thought fiercely, raising her head, pulling back her shoulders, pleased that her picture and her praises would be hung up for all to see. *Let them.* She didn't care. She could work. She could be extraordinary, even like this.

# Chapter Sixteen

Sister Teresa Rivera lives in the old Santa Rosa convent, on the outskirts of the city, closer to their hotel than the orphanage. On his way there, Asher is on pins and needles. He's seen convents and churches and priests and nuns, of course, but mostly in movies. Truth be told, he tells Alessandra, "I've never seen a nun in my life."

"Oh, please, Asher, you're joking."

"No, I'm not! How many nuns do you know?"

"Hmm. Now that you mention it, I think they're all from *The Sound of Music*," Alessandra replies cheerfully.

"Ally, I'm serious," he says, but he can't help grinning. "No kidding, what's the protocol?"

"I don't know," Alessandra says with a shrug. "I think you call them 'Sister.'"

Asher nervously runs his fingers through his hair, which has grown enough to cover some of the scars.

"Ash, it's going to be fine," Alessandra says gently. "It's been just one day, and we've already found out loads of things we didn't know about her before. We know she had a job she was good at. That means she must have been smart. Ash, these are wonderful things to know," she tells him, squeezing his arm.

"I know, Ally, I know," he says, rubbing his eyes, his

forehead, scratching his head. He feels as if pieces of him are peeling.

"And what about Carla?" he asks, his voice rising. " 'Now,' " he says in a high voice, imitating her crisp accent, " 'we cannot have these high expectations. This is not Disneyland.' My God. Does the woman ever use contractions?"

Alessandra laughs out loud. "I know—I felt like messing up her hair," she says. "But, hey, she thinks you have spirit! I bet she doesn't say stuff like *that* very often."

"It's just so strange. It's like opening a door that leads to another door and to another door down a corridor that never ends. I don't know how to explain it," says Asher.

"Don't try," she says simply. "When you're ready to put it into words, you will. For now just concentrate on charming the nun, okay?" she adds, poking him in the ribs.

They wait for Sister Teresa in the sparse sitting room adorned with a painting of a Madonna and a large cross over rows of bookcases. A threadbare carpet sits underneath the coffee table but it does little to warm up the drafty room, despite the hot tea that's been served for them on a plain metal tray.

"I always thought they lived more...opulently," Asher says in wonderment.

"I know. I did, too," muses Alessandra. "I guess it really *is* about chastity and poverty."

"What if she became a nun?" asks Asher, and the thought seems completely logical.

"Nah," says Alessandra firmly. "She doesn't look the type."

"Since when are you the nun expert?" he scoffs.

"I just... She looks like a go-getter. She doesn't look like she'd be happy in a place like this."

Just then Carla leads a frail woman into the room. She is very small, very slight, and very, very wrinkled, like a fruit that's spent too much time under the sun. Beneath her white nun's coif, Sister Teresa's face looks even smaller and browner, and her eyes glitter behind thick glasses.

Alessandra elbows Asher in his ribs and smiles as if to say, *This is exactly how a nun is supposed to look.*

"Sister Teresa, this is Asher Stone," says Carla as Asher belatedly extends his hand toward the nun.

"A-chéh?" she replies, puzzled, with a shaky voice that contradicts the firmness of her handshake.

"Asher," he says slowly.

"*Ache*, like *h* in Spanish," declares Sister Teresa.

"No, no. A-sher. Like *sh*," he says, moving a finger to his lips as if warning the nun to quiet down. Not quite the introduction he'd imagined.

"Such a strange name?" says Sister Teresa questioningly, looking at Carla for help.

"Sister, you can call him by his Christian name, Sebastián," says Carla, cutting to the point.

"Ah!" Sister Teresa's countenance changes visibly. "Sebastián. Much better," she adds as she sits down carefully on a worn olive armchair and looks up at Sebastián, her cocked head giving her the appearance of a brown sparrow.

"So you are one of my babies," she continues in Spanish.

"Yes," answers Asher slowly, unsure how long *his* Spanish will hold out. He shoots a pleading look at Carla, who nods reassuringly and takes over.

"Sister Teresa, Sebastián is looking for his birth mother. He's come all the way from Los Angeles, in California, because there is no record of her. He wanted to see you and talk with you and ask if perhaps you remembered anything about her that could help him."

Sister Teresa continues to look at Asher appraisingly.

"Sebastián," she says. "What a beautiful name that is. Are you also one of my babies?" she asks, turning toward Alessandra.

"No, Sister. I'm a friend of Ash—of Sebastián's," Alessandra replies, the name catching on her tongue.

Sister Teresa peers at her closely, her face expressionless, then turns to Asher again. "Sebastián," she repeats, placing the accent on the last *a* instead of the second *a*, as they do in Spanish, and Asher realizes he's never heard his name pronounced like that before.

"Are you happy, Sebastián?" asks Sister Teresa. "Are you close to your parents?"

"Very much, Sister," he answers earnestly.

"Then what are we doing here?" Sister Teresa asks bluntly. "Bah." She silences him with a wave of her hand before he can even muster a protest. "You are all looking for something, someone, and then it's never what you expected."

Asher narrows his eyes and decides to ignore the comment. "My mother's name was Rita Ortiz," he says smoothly, waiting for Carla to translate as he speaks. "We have very little information on her other than her name and dates. But I'm hoping you can at least remember something about her, something that will help us find her or at least get a better sense of who she was."

Sister Teresa is quiet for a moment, then grudgingly acknowledges his information.

"Rita Ortiz," she repeats, and shakes her head. "There were so many girls. So many girls with so many problems," she says, audibly tsk-tsking.

"We brought you her file, Sister," Carla prods gently, handing her a brown manila envelope. Sister Teresa purses her mouth. It's obvious she dislikes doing this, and Asher can't help but wonder if it's that she's simply old-fashioned and a believer in sealed adoptions or if she's seen too many botched reunions and doesn't want to deal with another one. Whatever it is, she still opens the envelope and gazes at the picture for what appears to be an inordinately long time.

"I remember her," she says at last, and there is conviction in her creaky little voice. "I wouldn't have, except…" Sister Teresa's voice trails off, as if she is trying to make sense of some great, elusive fact. "She was very quiet," she ventures after a long silence. "There is nothing I can remark about her. It was almost as if she didn't exist. Except she came back."

"Pardon?" asks Asher, leaning forward. This he didn't expect.

"This one came back," she repeated. "About a year or two later. She wanted the baby—you—back."

Asher feels his pulse accelerate but remains perfectly still, afraid that any movement will make this tiny specter of a woman vanish into thin smoke. Alessandra instinctively places a hand on his thigh, and he covers it with his own. Without taking his eyes off the nun, he says, "Please translate for me, Mrs. Bernotti. I don't want to miss anything."

Carla begins to speak in English, but Asher keeps his eyes glued to the nun, looking for any insight beyond the meaning of the words.

"She came to see me and said she wanted her baby. She said she had the means to take care of him now." Carla pauses between sentences, letting Sister Teresa's words sink in before she translates further. "I told her he had—you had—already been adopted. I reminded her she had given up the rights to that baby. Here, before the baby is adopted, the mother must go to court and give up the rights to that child," she says, looking at Asher levelly, and he knows she wants the words to register. She wants him to know that his mother walked away on her own. But he doesn't care right now about that. She came back. For him.

"Was she upset?" Asher asks, enthralled.

"I think 'resigned' might be a better word, but it was very long ago. I can't be sure of anything anymore," Sister Teresa says with a shrug. "I did ask her, why now? Why could she do this now? And she said she'd inherited some money and she could raise her boy and go to school. I remember all this because I was very surprised. I mean, a girl like that, suddenly getting a substantial amount of money. It made me think she was involved with the wrong kind of people. But she didn't look the type. She asked if she could get in touch with the baby, but of course I had to say no. I did tell her she could leave her information and if you or your family contacted us, we would immediately call her. But," she says, looking perplexed at the file and shaking her head, "I suppose she didn't do that."

Asher feels his temples throb at the sites of the halo pins and instinctively begins to rub them with both hands. The movement makes Sister Teresa lean closer and look at his forehead with a frown.

"You have scars there," she says, jabbing a finger at his face. "What happened?"

"I had a car accident," Asher replies haltingly, feeling like a two-year-old with his inadequate Spanish. "I broke my neck. And they put this thing"—he gestures at his head for emphasis—"around my head, and inside," he adds, pointing toward the scar sites.

"Ah," says Sister Teresa, leaning back. "You almost died. That's why you want to find her now." She is silent for a moment, then pats Asher's hand gently. "Coming face-to-face with our own mortality is frightening, no? That's why we have the Lord beside us," she says knowingly, adding, "I'm sorry. I know this is very important to you, but it might not have been as important to her. Remember, she was much younger than you when she had you. She was just a girl. Babies are not important to young girls. They are important to people like your mother and your father, who went to great lengths to have you."

"I know, Sister, it's just—"

Sister Teresa waves for him to be quiet. "You don't need to explain," she says dismissively. "I've heard it all before. When I was a girl, if there were no parents, children were raised by their uncles, their aunts, grandparents, friends. It didn't matter who it was, as long as there was love," she adds, raising both her hands out as in an offering. "Love. That is what I looked for when the parents wanted to adopt. I didn't look at their religion or where they came from. I wanted to see the love inside them. Love and a belief in God. Because even if they weren't Catholic—like your parents—they must believe in God. But this thing of wanting to find your roots, your origins, where you came from, blah, blah, blah. Nonsense." She grunts in disgust. "All concocted in America to make more money. Before, all my children who returned, they were here just to say thank you. 'Thank you, Sister, for giving me this wonderful family. Thank you, Sister, for giving me an opportunity. Thank you. Thank you.' Now it's always 'Why? When? Who is she? I need to know. I have'—what do they call them over in America?—'issues'," snorts Sister Teresa.

Alessandra starts to protest, but Carla lifts her hand to stop her. Like a schoolteacher, she gently brings Sister Teresa back to point.

"Times have indeed changed, Sister. But our mission is still to do the best for the child," Carla says patiently, putting her hand softly on Sister Teresa's bony shoulder. The nun manages a nod and peers at Asher with a mix of pity and hostility.

"Look at him," continues Carla. "He is a success story. Intelligent—he will graduate from college next year. He has wonderful parents that he adores. He just wants information, if it's available. Is there anything more you can tell us about his birth mother? Anything at all? Where she came from, perhaps?"

Sister Teresa looks in resignation at the skinny file in her hands. "I wrote a letter of recommendation," she muses. "It's a flattering letter. I wouldn't have written a letter like that if she weren't a hard worker. And honest. Honesty is very important to me. She must have been honest, despite her obvious shortcomings. Oh. Oh," she says abruptly, her small head snapping into alert position. "I do have something that may... it may—I can't promise anything—but it may have some information. What year was this again—1989? Let me see. I have all my datebooks. I may have written something there. You," she says to Asher, "help me up."

Asher stands and extends his arm toward her so she can hold on to him and get to her feet. Her hand grasps his arm like a claw, and he thinks she's made of steel, this seemingly fragile little nun who with the simple stroke of a pen charted his destiny twenty-one years ago.

"Help me to my room," Sister Teresa tells Carla unceremoniously. "Give me a moment," she has the grace to tell Alessandra and Asher. "Just walk around," she adds with that dismissive wave of her hand she seems so fond of using. "The patio is very lovely. Or better still, why don't you go to the chapel and pray for a moment, ask God to illuminate you? You should give thanks to the Lord. Even if you're Jewish. The entrance is through the patio as well."

Asher stands there, still a bit stunned. Alessandra slowly rises beside him, and all of a sudden he turns and embraces her.

"Wow, am I ever glad you're here," he says, drawing her toward him.

"She's rather feisty, isn't she?" says Alessandra, her

head lying softly against his chest. "You think she whipped them?" she asks, attempting to defuse the situation with some humor.

"Ha! I wouldn't put it past her," he says, closing his eyes and burying his face in her hair. He thinks he smells the ocean off Santa Barbara, and for a moment he feels safe, attached once again to some semblance of reality. "She has a point, though," he says uncertainly. "This is kind of scary."

"Of course it is, Ash," says Alessandra, pulling back. "You know, we can go home if you want. At the very least, I think we've determined that you were adopted in the best possible way. That there was order, that there was love, that your mother might have been desperate but she sounds pretty together to me. I don't think this nun would put up with any bullshit, to be honest."

Asher laughs mirthlessly and shakes his head. What was it the nun had said? There was nothing to remark about her, that she wanted to disappear, and he wonders if she was always like that or if he made her that way.

"Let's go to the chapel," he says, grabbing Alessandra's hand.

"Really?" she answers, incredulous.

"Yeah! I've never been to a chapel. Have you?"

"Can't say I have," she says dubiously. "But I've been to tons of European cathedrals. Isn't a chapel a kind of mini-cathedral?"

"A mini-cathedral?" asks Asher, laughing, his first genuine laugh of the day. "Is that like a mini-temple?"

"You know what I mean," she replies, but lets him lead her outside to the patio, which is indeed lovely, cobbled in river stones verdant with the clinging moss that seems to grow wild in this cool climate. A slight breeze stirs the rose trellises that go up the side columns, and in the middle, there's a vegetable garden, overflowing with herbs and tomatoes and zucchini.

"They must grow a lot of their own food," says Alessandra softly.

"Why are you whispering?" asks Asher.

She shrugs. "I didn't know I was," she says, louder this time. "It's just that kind of a place. It feels like time slows down, doesn't it?"

Asher doesn't answer but walks quietly to the chapel door, the chirp of his sneakers sounding unbearably loud with every step. *It's not that mini,* he thinks as he looks around him. It's sparse but beautiful and warm and cold and beckoning all at the same time. The low wooden beams and white stucco walls, adorned with images of saints, ensconce the thirty or so rows of bare, wooden pews, split in two by the pathway that leads to the altar. It is small but magnificent, a wall of wood with gold-laminated statues, and in the center an elaborate, heavy wooden cross, from which the figure of Christ looks at them both with mournful compassion.

Asher stares at it, fascinated. His only forays into churches have been as a tourist in Rome and Milan, but this is different, almost shockingly intimate and made more so by the uncanny silence of the place. He sinks down heavily, and despite the hard discomfort of the pew, he's almost immediately lulled into a sense of serene relaxation.

"It's pretty, isn't it?" he asks Ally, reaching for her hand to sit her beside him.

"It is," she agrees. "Isn't it funny how much a Catholic church can look, and feel, like temple?"

"Yeah." Asher nods. "You know, it just dawned on me, I must have been christened."

"With that nun in control? No doubt," agrees Alessandra.

"That's kind of strange, isn't it? Does that make me a conflicted individual?" he asks.

"No, Ash," she says, leaning her head against his shoulder. "That just makes you doubly blessed."

Asher smiles and glances up again at Christ's sorrowful eyes. *Look at what happened to you*, he thinks. *I am blessed. Doubly blessed. Triply blessed*, he adds to himself, squeezing Alessandra's hand a little tighter.

# Chapter Seventeen

Her water broke a full two weeks ahead of schedule, as she sat on her warehouse perch, slipping plastic casings over a shipment of yellow long-stemmed roses. She felt a trickle run down her leg, and before she could assimilate what was happening, a torrent of water gushed out, soaking her thick corduroy pants and leaking into her rubber boots and onto the cement floor.

"Oh," she said softly, and instinctively clutched her pregnant stomach, looking around in panic at this group of older women to whom she hadn't deigned speak in more than two months. But Rita undervalued the power of her pregnancy, as she had all this time. Before she could utter an actual word, they surrounded her, helped her out of her seat, and escorted her to the manager's office, where she was laid down and given sips of hot tea and a stream of supportive words until the nuns came to take her to the hospital.

"Thank you, thank you," she mumbled in wonderment, looking around at this sea of faces, astounded by the unsolicited show of kindness, mortified that she didn't know a single one of their names and that now it didn't matter. The last thing she saw before they escorted her out the door was her Employee of the Month flyer and photo, pinned to the cork bulletin board in the hallway.

She gave birth to the baby a mere four hours later, an extremely quick delivery for a first-time mother. For Rita it was more an expulsion than a birth. She was too far along in her labor process to be able to get an epidural, and the pain exploded in waves of fiercely sharpened little knives that burst from within her womb to her every nerve ending, piercing each inch of her until she screamed in agony, willing him to come out, to leave her forever.

She heard him cry, but the sound came from very far away, as if she and her son were in different rooms.

"Here he is," one of the nurses crooned, bringing up to her a swaddled bundle with black, black hair that shot straight out like spikes. She leaned forward to place the baby in Rita's arms, but Rita shook her head emphatically. She looked curiously at the tiny figure in the nurse's arms. He was so very small, she thought, and yet he had hurt her so much coming out of her, ripping her apart, it felt. He looked wrinkled and wizened and red, as if he'd been scalded in a pot of hot water. She couldn't tell if he was beautiful or ugly or if he looked like her or like him. All she could really discern was the hair, standing up in all directions the way Sebastián's used to do.

"You don't want to hold him?" the nurse asked, puzzled.

"No," said Rita, turning her head away to stare out the window, even though there was little to see now as the evening shadows slowly enveloped the cold skies.

No one spoke for several moments, and the nurse glanced hopelessly at the attending doctor, who merely shook her head as she washed her hands. "Okay," said the nurse, looking in dismay at the tiny, mewing figure in her arms and at the young, impervious teenager who had mothered him. "Well, Baby...Ortiz," she said, consulting Rita's chart. "Baby Ortiz, let's go find you a crib."

"No, not Baby Ortiz," said Rita suddenly, before the nurse could step out of the room. "He has a name," she said, her voice firm even as she kept her gaze deliberately averted. "His name is Sebastián."

"Sebastián. That's a beautiful name," said the nurse in relief. "It means 'revered,'" she added, looking around at the momentarily silenced room. Even the doctor had stopped what she was doing, her wet hands suspended in the air, the paper towels next to her forgotten.

"It's an auspicious name," insisted the nurse, unfazed, thinking someone needed to speak up for this poor little creature, for both little creatures, the son and this sorry girl whose accusing eyes seemed to damn the entire world for her predicament. "I think your baby will be very loved. We will take care of him, Ms. Ortiz."

*Why won't she just go away?* thought Rita. *Can't she see I have nothing to say?* Rita closed her eyes and willed herself to concentrate on the pain still coming in waves, to keep from screaming out, until she was finally alone. She lay in the dark, relishing this rare moment of solitude, running her fingers lightly over the clean, crisp bedsheets.

She wondered where Lucas was right now, if he ever thought of her at all anymore. She wondered where he spent his nights, tried to imagine what her life would have been like had she gone with him.

At the orphanage they all slept in cots in the same military-barracks-style room. Here it was just her, in this big clean, firm bed with fluffy pillows and water and ice set beside her. She even had her own television set—for the first time in her life—but right now she just wanted the tranquillity of total silence.

Rita closed her eyes. She touched her stomach and felt it still swollen but clearly deflated, empty. *All this*, she thought, *and now it's over, just like that*. And she had nothing to show for it, only a stockpile of lost avenues. As if on cue, she heard the door open again, and this time she turned to see the assistant from the home walk in with a sheaf of papers.

"Congratulations, Rita!" the woman said cheerfully, turning on the lights without asking and pulling up a chair so she was close to the bed. "I saw the baby—he's beautiful! You are a very, very brave young lady, and you're going to make this baby and his new family very, very happy. The good Lord will reward you for this."

Rita nodded. She was exhausted. She didn't want to think about anything right now.

"I'm Mercedes, and I need you to sign this paperwork. Also, this is the time to write a letter for your son, so he can take it with him to his new life along with anything else you'd like him to have. I've brought some writing paper here and a pen, and I can just leave you alone for a few moments so you can write, or you can dictate to me if you prefer."

"A letter?" asked Rita, puzzled.

"Yes. A letter," Mercedes repeated patiently. "Remember, we spoke about this at the home. You can write a letter for your baby."

Rita frowned. She vaguely remembered some mention of a letter, but she must have tuned it out as she did most things these days. She closed her eyes and shook her head against the pillow. "No. I'm not writing a letter. Just give me whatever I need to sign."

Mercedes sorted through her papers and coughed discreetly, making Rita open her eyes again. "Rita, please write the letter," she said, her voice gentle but uncompromising. "For your sake and for your son's."

"Why?" demanded Rita. "He'll have his own family."

"And he'll always wonder about you," Mercedes countered, placing her hand gently on Rita's arm. "Quite frankly, I have no idea if his adopted family will want him to know anything at all. This is a closed adoption. They can choose to show him things from his past or they can choose not to. But we must prepare for the possibility that they may want to give their child a message from you. Now, you have done a lot already. But you must do this last thing. I don't need to know the circumstances of this pregnancy or of this birth, unless you want to tell me, but you have to wish your boy love and good fortune and Godspeed on this journey."

Without asking, the woman pushed the side button on Rita's bed until Rita sat upright, and then she moved the tray table in front of her.

"Here is a pen and paper. I'll leave you alone for a few minutes," Mercedes said, and got up and opened the door.

"But what should I write?" asked Rita, her voice rising in panic.

"Write something beautiful," Mercedes said. "Write something loving. Even if you don't mean it this very moment, I assure you, you will mean it one day, and you'll be thankful that you did this."

Mercedes shut the door, and Rita looked blankly at the white sheet of paper before her. *Once upon a time*, she thought, *I wrote beautiful things and expressive sentences. I told wonderful stories and got good grades.* Now she thought of helpless little Sebastián with his spiky hair lying alone in some crib; he was finally rid of her, and she was finally rid of him.

*"Dear Sebastián,"* she wrote at last in her neat, beautiful cursive writing. Such a pretty name, Sebastián, and such pretty memories attached to it. Rita closed her eyes for a few seconds and resumed her writing.

*"I hope you can keep the name I gave you. It's the name of my brother, whom I love very much, as much as I love you."*

"Liar," she said under her breath as she wrote. It pained her to write the lies almost as much as it pained her to think that one day the baby might learn the truth: that he'd been unplanned, unwanted, that she felt wretched with him inside her, that he'd truncated the small hopes she had harbored of leaving her constrained existence, that the memories of her first—her only—moments of love had already been forever tainted by his presence, marring her every thought of their time together like an enormous wart she could never remove from her conscience, or from her body, even. He was out of her, true, but all else lingered— the stretch marks, the brown line that led to her navel, her bloated stomach. Why was she still bloated when he was no longer inside her?

Rita took a deep breath, then another, trying to calm her nerves, as she used to do when her father screamed at her, until her heart slowed down again to match the unfathomable expression in her eyes.

*"I can't take care of you,"* she continued, and in this, she thought, she was being truthful. *"I'm all alone, and you need a family that can give you time and care and lots of love, with a mommy and a daddy, so you'll grow up to be the best possible child you can be."*

Rita paused. Mercedes said she could give him something of hers, but what did she have? She gingerly touched Lucas's tooth, dangling from the leather strap around her neck, the only thing she had of his. And then she looked at the bracelet, Jazmin's beautiful, intricate bracelet, purchased with her own money at the marketplace. Against the weave of the red and fuchsia hues she saw the gold pattern, dancing in a single thread around her wrist in whimsical arabesques. Rita carefully undid the knot that Jazmin had tied around her wrist, a knot so strong, Jazmin would tell clients, that only lack of further protection would allow it to open up. Rita worked it with her teeth until it finally loosened and fell in a little heap onto her tray.

*"The red bracelet is for good luck,"* she wrote. *"It's very beautiful, isn't it? It was made by a very good friend of mine who makes beautiful things. I gave a blue one just like it to your father. So he can be protected, wherever he may go."*

Rita reread what she'd written. It sounded cold and standoffish, she thought. Not at all like the things her father used to tell her when she was a little girl, when she was loved. But it was the best she could come up with. She removed the necklace from around her neck and looked at it for a long time as she twined it around her fingers. So many afternoons she'd lain next to Lucas, playing with the charm, running her fingers down his strong chest, marveling at his man's body next to hers. She felt so grown up then, so invincible. They were doing something utterly forbidden, but they were untouchable. She thought she loved him, and how couldn't she? How couldn't she when he held her face between his hands and kissed her so gently, but oh, so deeply, and it was so wholly delicious, a slice of air in a life of asphyxiation, moments that lacked nothing, that were almost too good to be true?

She looked at the necklace in her hands, this symbol of his power, now reduced to mere leather and bone. A trinket. A cheap trinket, that's all it was. But it was all she had. If she gave it up, she'd be left with nothing, she thought, and her fingers tightened around her charm, burying it inside the folds of her hospital nightgown. The degree of her own selfishness surprised her, and Rita looked furtively around her, feeling as guilty as if she were stealing a prized jewel. She picked up the pen again, a little less certain of herself now, struggling with the words as if she were wading through logs in a river, clumsy, ineffectual.

*"Study very hard,"* she finally managed. *"You have to do well in school. And be a good person, Sebastián. Be kind and be good, and may God bless you always, my baby. Have a wonderful life. Mom."*

Rita reread the single sheet of paper and folded it neatly in three, as her mother used to do with the letters she occasionally mailed to relatives far away.

When Mercedes returned to the room, Rita extended the folded piece of paper and the bracelet toward her.

"You have to give him both things," she said, the little necklace weighing heavily against her leg. "Everything. The bracelet and the letter."

"Of course, Rita."

"Okay." Rita nodded. "Let me sign, then."

\*　　\*　　\*

That night, when the maternity ward was asleep, she went into the nursery. From the window she could see the rows of babies in clear plastic cribs, all looking exactly the same from a distance.

"You want me to bring him out?" asked the nurse on duty.

Rita hesitated, then nodded. The nurse wheeled the little crib out, and Rita saw the name tag—SEBASTIÁN ORTIZ— affixed to the head of the crib.

"Would you like to nurse him?" the nurse asked softly. "We've already fed him, but you can nurse him, too."

Rita shook her head. "No," she said simply. "I can't."

She regarded the baby dispassionately. He was less red now, looked more like a little person than a monster. His eyes were squeezed shut, like a tiny newborn kitten's, and his breath came in short, quick pants. One hand poked out from underneath the blue-and-white blankets that swaddled him, and she gently placed her index finger on the palm of his hand, smiling despite herself when he clutched her finger back.

"Good luck, Sebastián," she said softly. "May all your dreams come true." She carefully pulled her finger out of his hand and looked away before she gave in to the desire to touch him, to stroke the tuft of black hair, to nurse him. He was just a baby. Just a baby, she told herself. And in no time he would be someone else's baby altogether.

Rita turned around resolutely and, without a backward glance, waddled back to her room, to her big bed, to her clean sheets. She closed her eyes in relief and raised her hand to clasp the little tooth once again dangling from her neck. This time no thoughts or even dreams permeated her consciousness. She slept more soundly than she had in months, despite the cramps, despite the discomfort of her postpregnancy sutures and her sore breasts, despite the steady flow of noise that emanated from the hospital hallways. They allowed her to stay for two whole days, two days in which she thought about nothing, did nothing except watch television—soap operas about pretty poor girls who became pretty rich girls—and go to the bathroom. She never returned to the nursery, nor did she ask to have Sebastián brought to her.

No one visited her, except for Mercedes with her forms and a woman from Child Protective Services. She knew that the nurses pitied her; it was obvious in the way they peppered her with small indulgences—little treats they had baked themselves, magazines, a medal of the Virgin of Chiquinquirá to "light her way." It surprised her yet again, this kindness from strangers, from people who knew nothing of her, nothing at all but the very worst.

On November 2, Rita Ortiz packed up her meager belongings—the corduroy pants, the boots, and the sweater she used for work, her hairbrush and ribbons for her hair—and sat by her bed, as instructed, to wait for someone to pick her up.

She looked out the window, at the cars entering and exiting the parking lot below. A beat-up blue car pulled up, and a man who could have been her father's age ran around the car and helped out a very pregnant woman, who walked very slowly, one hand holding her waist, the other her stomach. A little girl, perhaps ten, got out beside her, carrying a big pink overnight bag with the word BABY emblazoned on its side. The woman was obviously in pain, but she still laughed at something the girl said, still leaned down to kiss her on the forehead.

"Rita?" One of the nurses knocked on the door and peeked in. It was Marlene, the nurse who had first offered Sebastián for her to hold. "Can we come in?"

"Of course," said Rita, perplexed.

She walked in with three other nurses and was carrying a large shopping bag stuffed with colorful tissue paper. "We got you a good-bye gift. Open it," she said, excited, placing the package on Rita's lap.

Rita felt the contours of the bag uncertainly, fingering the soft tissue paper that was almost too pretty to crumple up. She pulled it out gently, smoothing the paper with the vague notion that it could be reused somehow. Inside was a red turtleneck, brand-new, and a knit magenta cardigan sweater. Rita lifted the sweater in front of her, marveling at its length and flowing sleeves. It was striking, finer-looking than anything she'd seen in a store.

"It's so beautiful!" she said in awe.

"I was knitting it for my niece, but I decided to give it to you instead," said Marlene. "And the girls all pitched in for the other one. They thought red would look good on you."

"It's my favorite color," said Rita truthfully, still reveling in the soft texture of the sweater beneath her fingers. "Thank you. Thank you so much. You didn't have to," she said, looking down at the bag, at the sweaters, at the newness, the *prettiness* of it all. It struck her that in two weeks she would turn seventeen, and to her dismay she began to cry. Not a few errant teardrops but a sudden torrent of pity, loss, loneliness, sheer helplessness. She cried at the unfairness of it all, at the assault on her body and on her spirit and on herself because she no longer recognized this person she had become.

"Oh," said Marlene, enveloping Rita in her arms. "Oh, I know, I know," she repeated, as Rita's body shuddered with sobs, her fingers still clutching the lovely, colorful sweaters on her lap, as lovely as Jazmin's bracelets, only now she would never be able to tell her that.

# Chapter Eighteen

Sebastián?" Carla's voice breaks up his reverie. Asher looks away from the altar reluctantly. As much as he hates to admit it, the nun is right: There is something in this room that invites contemplation, even if Alessandra has dozed off with her head on his lap.

"It's Asher, Mrs. Bernotti," he says reflexively.

"Please, with all due respect, that name is unpronounceable here," she says impatiently. "Just deal with Sebastián for a few days. Come along, now. Sister Teresa found her datebooks."

This time Sister Teresa sees them in the library, where she sits behind a tall desk that makes her look even more minuscule. She has her glasses on, and she is peering intently at a leather-bound journal open before her.

"Okay, I found her in my notes. I found your mother, Sebastián," she says, not bothering to look up. "On June twenty-eighth, 1989, a Rita Ortiz came to us, recommended by Father Pablo Quiroga from St. Isidore's. She arrived alone at the bus terminal and was picked up by someone from our staff—I wouldn't be able to say who. She left us on September twenty-fifth for a job as a maid at the home of Colonel Antonio Santos. I wrote her a letter of recommendation, as you already know. And," she adds, looking up at last, "as you also already know, she came back a year or so later, asked for you, and since then no one, at Casa at least, has heard from her. It's been...what, twenty-one, twenty-two years?" Sister Teresa looks at Asher expectantly, her eyes pensive behind the thick glasses.

Asher, whose glance has been going back and forth between Carla and Sister Teresa, desperately trying to keep up with the account, finally reacts. "What's St. Isidore?" he asks.

"It's a church, young man," says the nun, clearly irritated. "I must say, I have met with other adoptees before you, and most have been a little more...let's say in touch with the country and its customs."

Asher feels himself blush, because he truly isn't that clueless, but the barrage of information, in Spanish, is confusing. He turns for support to Alessandra, who's been taking copious notes, but, surprisingly, it's Carla who comes to the rescue.

"He's trying, Sister," she says dryly. "Just give him some time. Do you happen to have contacts for St. Isidore or for this colonel?"

Sister Teresa shakes her head. "Well, the colonel's number is definitely outdated. It has only five digits, and that has all changed. Perhaps he's listed. As for St. Isidore's... no. Nothing. But I would have to guess it had to be reasonably close for him to have sent her here. There's several St. Isidores. You can call them. Well, I hope I have been of some help," she says, closing the book, dismissal clearly in her voice.

Asher looks back at her, the reality of the situation sinking in. It's not as if he expected to come here and simply pluck Rita Ortiz's phone number out of some directory, but this all sounds terribly vague. A church without a town, a colonel without a phone number.

"Is there anything more concrete you can give me?" Asher asks in English, letting Carla translate for him.

Sister Teresa frowns. "Listen to me, young man," she says, even though she clearly feels she's already had her say. "I know that you expect a miracle. You think it was a miracle you survived that terrible accident of yours, the one with the scars," she says impatiently, pointing to her head. "You believe that God saved your life so you could come here and find your mother, yes?"

Asher looks quickly at Carla, waits for her translation, and then says excitedly, "Yes, yes, you see—"

But Sister Teresa interrupts him with a wave of her hand. "There is a difference between miracles and good fortune and excellent medical care," she says, punctuating each item with a stab of her bony finger on her leather-bound agenda. "A miracle was your mother—this Rita—who conceived a child, who was brought precisely here, at the precise time that your parents, five thousand miles away, in the United States, became the next family on the list to receive a baby for adoption."

Sister Teresa allows Carla to translate, so the words fully register. "Very often children and their parents, they don't see eye to eye, do they?" she asks. "They fight bitterly, they say words that they later regret. You have to honor thy father and thy mother. But what happens when you have despicable people as parents? Or despicable people as children? I have seen so many tragedies. And yet here three strangers created an unbreakable bond from thin air," she says, shaking her head. "A family. That, my boy, is a miracle," says Sister Teresa, her reedy voice slowing down.

"Everything else"—she waves her hands in illustration—"all this, the names, the places, the details, all of that is the work of man, and if you wish to find where they come from, then you must do a man's work. But do not expect any more miracles. Do not be greedy."

Asher feels chastised, like a little boy forced to give explanations to the school principal. If he had scant Spanish before, it has now dissolved before the miniature nun's reprimand.

"I'm tired. I have to go rest," says Sister Teresa, getting up heavily, this time supporting herself on the desk instead of Asher.

"Thank you, Sister Teresa," says Asher, helping her nevertheless.

"Mmmm," grunts Sister Teresa, waving her hand dismissively as she walks away, her receding bony frame bent but firm at the same time, like a figure cut from barbed wire.

"Well!" says Carla brightly once the nun is out of sight. "I for one think this was extremely productive. Come on, let's go." She gathers her materials, her jacket and files and notes, and hustles all of them outside, beyond the convent's judgmental walls, to the shaded entryway that looks out at one of the city's many little parks, dotted with flower beds and maids dressed in blue-and-white uniforms walking dogs and pushing strollers in the crisp afternoon air.

Carla leads them to one of the benches at the edge of

the park and carefully arranges her immaculate suit on the wooden seat.

"I meant what I said," she repeats. "This was very productive. You have two excellent leads. You need to follow up on them, and it will be tedious, and I do not have time to do this for you. I have an institute to run. But, frankly, you cannot do this on your own. Your Spanish is deplorable, both of you. Maybe you can take some classes while you're here, hmm? But in the meantime I have a student, very smart, very dependable, very resourceful, who can make these calls for you. She needs extra work, and she's completely trustworthy. I'll have her call you tomorrow and work out some kind of payment for her. Among the three of you, I'm sure you'll get somewhere."

"Carla, why are you doing this?" asks Alessandra. "Do you do this with everyone?"

Carla smiles ruefully. "I need to feel it here," she says, touching her heart. "And when I feel that the sentiment and the desire are genuine, yes, I do try to help.

"I have an adopted son," she adds after a pause. "He is thirty years old now. I adopted him long before I came to work for Casa. But that's how I got acquainted with the program. Sister Teresa and I go way back," she explains with a smile.

"Anyway, like you, he wanted to find his birth parents, which is completely understandable. But our results were not very positive."

"What happened?" asks Alessandra.

"We found his mother, and she had a drug addiction," says Carla quietly. "It was terrible. She wanted to continue seeing him, but always because she wanted money from him. It was a very destructive episode and one that affected my son deeply. But I understand the motivation and the need. So I will continue to help you with this, although you may find nothing, or you may not like what you find. Or," she added with a small smile, "you may have your happy ending. We just never know."

Carla gets up and brushes an imaginary speck from her skirt. "I'll have Inés—that's my student's name, Inés Mendoza—call you tomorrow or Monday. Keep me apprised of your progress. I'll pray for you."

*     *     *

In the beginning her intent had been to return babyless and pristine, ready to resume her life plan and finish school as if nothing had ever happened.

She couldn't say when things changed. Perhaps when she gave birth to the baby. Perhaps when she gave the bracelet and the letter to Mercedes. Perhaps when she realized that in everything she'd done in the past four months she'd left behind little pieces of herself, until she looked in the mirror and could barely see who she used to be. What she did know is that when the time came to go back home, it seemed far more daunting than moving forward. Instead she went to the nun, a tiny woman who for no logical reason filled her with terror, and asked for a job.

Sister Teresa squinted at Rita as if seeing her for the first time. "Weren't you the one working at the flower farm?" she demanded. "You don't want that job back?"

"I'd rather a place that's in the city, so I can go to school," said Rita meekly, looking at her feet, as she was wont to do when she wanted to avoid confrontation.

Sister Teresa shook her head and riffled through the papers on her desk. "So you're another one who doesn't want to go back home," she said, almost to herself. It was her duty to keep them safe, but she had learned long ago to be pragmatic and shed her prejudices. Rita Ortiz said she was eighteen years old, but Sister Teresa was certain she was lying about her age. As most of them did. Too young to live on her own, the nun decided.

"The best you can do, I think, is work as a maid in a home," she pronounced. "At least you'll have room and board. You can go to school at night or on the weekends. Hopefully, do something with your life."

Rita didn't say anything. She'd found that often the act of simply waiting somehow elicited the right words from people.

Sister Teresa folded her arms and looked at her. "Are you willing to work as a maid?" she asked bluntly. "Look at me, girl!" she prodded impatiently, and Rita's head snapped up, her chin automatically rising with a touch of the old pride.

"Are you?" asked the nun again, and her voice was slightly gentler. "It's not what you're used to doing, I'm sure."

Maybe not, thought Rita, but after all, hadn't she cleaned her own house and followed someone else's orders her entire life? Same thing, she mused, just with a different name.

"I'll do what I need to do, Sister," she said levelly.

And as far as maid jobs were concerned, this one had

to be better than most, she reckoned. Colonel Antonio Santos was an eighty-two-year-old bachelor who lived alone in a seventeenth-floor apartment against Bogotá's eastern slopes. His dark, musty furniture contrasted with the panoramic views of the city below. The record of his sixty years of army service was emblazoned in the walls of his study—medals and decrees and rifles and photographs with a dozen of the country's presidents. Even now he cut a daunting figure, all five feet eight inches of him preternaturally ramrod straight, trim, and perfectly groomed from dawn to dusk.

At the orphanage Rita had developed a carefully measured cocktail of half lies, bending what was true just enough to sound plausible. She said she had to leave her home out of security concerns, because her family was threatened by the guerrillas and the paramilitaries. She'd fled in the dark of night, left everything behind. No, she had nowhere to call home. Her entire family was disbanded; she didn't know where they were. She was, for all intents and purposes, a nonentity, a status that didn't clash with the orphanage's mission of protecting the anonymity of single, desperate, unwed mothers.

But her vague explanations didn't sit well with the colonel's sense of order and decorum.

"Girl, the reference is excellent, and I have a good feeling about you. But I need some form of identification," he'd said flatly during their interview.

"I'm sorry, sir," she said in her understated tone of voice, the one that defused conflict, the one that made the other person think he or she had the upper hand. "I just don't have anything I can give you. But I'm eighteen, sir," she said, smoothly adding a little over a year to her real age to make herself a legal adult.

Rita knew her ID number by heart but hadn't given it out to the orphanage, to the flower farm, or even to the hospital. She was terrified that somehow someone would put two and two together and tie her to the baby, to Lucas, to her family and Sebastián. She wasn't quite certain how ID numbers worked, but surely if they were government-issued, they were traceable, weren't they? Such thoughts kept her up at night, for if she were found out, what had been the purpose of leaving?

But in the colonel she discovered an unexpected solution.

"We need to secure you a new ID, then, so I can formally hire you and get your work papers in order," he said. "I'll have somebody from Mr. García's office take you to the registry."

Edward García, the colonel's attorney, was a very thin, very tall man whose suits were permanently rumpled and who was forever forgetting his spectacles in different rooms of the colonel's house.

But he knew someone who knew someone who knew someone, who whizzed them right by the line that wound around the building, right into someone's office. Someone who took her word for it that her ID was lost. Who believed—or pretended to believe—her story or perhaps just didn't care that it was patently obvious that one doesn't forget things like one's ID number. Someone who took one look at the severity of her face and believed her when she said she was eighteen years old, an adult, no longer required to be under the supervision of a guardian and entitled to new documentation. Someone who, in a matter of minutes, provided her with a freshly laminated ID card that duly noted her birthday and this city as her place of birth and assigned her a new number, one that proclaimed, in black and white, that this Rita Ortiz was not that other Rita Ortiz, the pretty little thing with undulating black hair, languorous walk, and coquettish, downcast eyes who came from somewhere else, from a town whose outlines grew vaguer by the day. This Rita Ortiz was from the city. She had no living family, no obligations, and few expenses. She kept her own, very small—but growing—bank account. She was crisp and neat and encapsulated, almost like a nun with her prim white shirts, her face devoid of makeup, her hair rolled up in a bun, and her dark cardigan. This Rita was eighteen, and old beyond her years. There was nothing remarkable about the way she looked or talked or walked or dressed, save for the flowing knit magenta sweater she sometimes wore to class.

And that was essentially it. There was nothing more to it. Nothing.

He expected her to cook, clean, do the laundry, and iron his shirts until the cuffs and collars peaked stiffly under his jackets. The sheets—300-thread-count cotton—had to be ironed, too, the beds made with military corners. A chauffeur picked him up Monday, Wednesday, and Friday afternoons at 5:00 P.M. and took him to his club, where he played cards and drank scotch until nearly midnight.

Those evenings Rita went to night school from 6:00 to 9:00, walking to the bus stop two blocks away, even when it poured, which was often. She'd learned the ways of the city quickly enough. Learned always to take an umbrella, always to clutch her bag close to her side, to be alert, even as she ignored the din and the bustle around her, navigating in a bubble from the peaceful apartment with the doorman and the view to the chaos of the bus to night school, barely uttering a word as the scenery around her morphed from what she wanted to what she was.

Her fellow students were clearly the same ilk, day laborers, like her, forced to work ahead of their time by God knows what circumstance, cramming bits and pieces of high-school curriculum in between punching in and punching out. She often wondered what their day lives were made of, if they were like her, if like her they wore uniforms that branded them to the world, that proclaimed that their duty in life was to clean up after someone else. If like her they were so close to comfort and wealth that they could touch it but couldn't aspire to own it. Yet.

Rita remembered when she'd first arrived at the home, how inferior the other girls had seemed to her, with their swollen bellies, their clothing frayed by poverty, their horrid grammar when they read out loud in class. But these ones, she knew from the moment she first set foot inside the classroom, these ones were like her, looking for a way out, clinging to the notion that there was something out there, just beyond their reach, and scrambling to get to it, even though their means were most inadequate, limited to this downtrodden classroom with the too-bright lightbulbs and the drearily boring teachers who taught simply by the book.

Rita studied. She had nothing else to do, after all. No family, no friends, no boyfriend.

"The perfect servant," she overheard the colonel say to Mr. García one afternoon after she'd finished serving coffee for them in the study. Rita had stopped just outside the study to straighten a tilted painting, and the words had shocked her into stillness, humiliation rising from the pit of her stomach to her face. "She works hard, doesn't complain, keeps her mouth shut," continued the colonel. "Doesn't gab all day on the phone, like most of them do. As a matter of fact, no one ever calls her. Which is just fine by me. Last thing I want is another pregnant wench like the last two I had."

"Seems awfully young," said Mr. García.

"Eighteen," replied the colonel. Rita heard him strike a match and light his cigar, inhaling deeply as his leather chair creaked beneath him. "Better that way. The older they are, the sicker they get and the heavier their baggage. I don't know what this one's story is, but she had good recommendations, and you know what? She's going to night school. Wants to graduate, she says."

"Is that so?" asked Mr. García with a small chuckle. "Doesn't strike me as the sharpest of knives."

"Ah, don't be fooled," said the colonel, much to Rita's surprise. "This one likes to play dumb, but she ain't. She sees everything. Runs all my errands, deals with the repairmen, accounts for every little thing she buys for the house. Smart as a whip, if you ask me. We'll see what happens with that school of hers. In the meantime I got myself the perfect servant."

Rita stood there for a few moments longer, but the conversation turned to a discussion about bonds and investments, something that had nothing to do with her. She tiptoed as quietly as she could all the way to the kitchen and gently shut the swinging door behind her. Her notebooks were stacked neatly on the kitchen table, her pencils lined carefully alongside them, as they used to be when she was at home. She liked to do her homework here, looking out the window at the mountains and the buildings before her. One day, she thought, she'd have one of these apartments. She wouldn't be all alone, like the colonel. She'd live there with her own family, and her apartment would have a view, most certainly a view. And a little terrace with lots of plants. And maybe even her own maid.

# Chapter Nineteen

"How's it going, my love?" his mother asks the following day, five thousand miles away. There's always a half-a-second lag when they chat via Skype, and it drives Asher nuts, even though he's the one who insisted everyone get Skype so they could all chat as often and as long as they wanted.

"Well, a little slow," he admits. "But it's great to be here."

They're staying at a furnished apartment near Bogotá's Zona Rosa, an area surrounded by trendy restaurants and unique shops. Early that morning they bought lattes from the coffee shop next door, and then Fidel drove them to the track at one of the university campuses, where Asher managed his forty-five-minute run despite the blow of the altitude, which had left poor Alessandra gasping for breath within ten minutes.

"Had I known it was so tough to work out in this place, I'd have come much sooner," Asher jokes now.

"How about your strength exercises? You're doing those, right?" asks his father.

"We bought a month's membership at a nearby gym and checked it out last night. It has everything we need. Although it's an overwhelming city. Not really user-friendly like a European city," Asher says with a laugh. "But having the driver is a huge plus. Thanks for helping with that, Dad. It really makes a big difference."

It was Joseph who had put together the logistics, calling his clients until he found the right corporate housing, the reliable driver. It was expensive, but not outrageous, and certainly, he reasoned, something he could afford to do for Asher, whose college had been largely subsidized by his soccer scholarship.

"How's the search going, honey?" asks his mother again, bringing them back to topic.

"It's like doing detective work," explains Asher. "We got off to a good start with the orphanage yesterday. But it's what we encountered back home, Mom," he adds, because now that realization is fully hitting him. "This isn't something you can do over the phone or online. People here need to see you. I don't want to sound corny, but they need to look you in the eye, right, Ally?" he asks, looking over his shoulder at Alessandra, who's reading on the couch.

"Hi, hi!" She waves with a smile, popping her head into the camera's line of vision. "It's a diplomatic mission, Linda. We have to convince everyone of our good intentions."

"Maybe I should come down and help you out," says Linda, worry in her voice.

"No, no, Mom," says Asher quickly. "Trust me. Having two non–Spanish speakers in the same room at one time is enough of a challenge. Anyway, we're not alone. The orphanage director recommended a student of hers who's going to help us with some of the groundwork."

*　　*　　*

Inés Mendoza is an accounting student, and her voice over the phone when they speak later that day is high-pitched and melodic—each word rising and falling like a flute playing an intricate musical passage—belying the methodical nature of its owner.

"Okay, guys. I think our first step is to call all the St. Isidore parishes until we find our church?" Inés begins, speaking in that informal, Americanized English adopted by those who watch too much MTV and end each sentence in a question. It's a far cry from Carla Bernotti's crisp enunciations.

"Sounds like a plan," says Asher. "How about the colonel? Can we look into that as well?"

"Sure, we can do that," says Inés slowly. "But I'm gonna start with the church. They're so much nicer than the military, you know?"

"Actually, I don't know," says Asher, thinking that despite her speech patterns Inés Mendoza has to be incredibly good at what she does. "But, hey. We trust you," he adds good-naturedly. "How can we help?"

"You know, it's probably gonna take some time to hear back from everyone, so why don't you just relax this weekend. You were born here, no? Get to know your city. Your roots."

*　　*　　*

Sundays were Rita's days off, and she would spend them taking long walks through the park in front of the apartment building, devising new routes and pathways to make her outings longer, simply to pass the time. She never went too far. She was loath to admit, even to herself, that the city still terrified her, that in this teeming, interminable maze of concrete and heartbeats she was afraid of getting lost or—worse still—being found. If she was private before, she became practically hermetic now, and yet her loneliness confounded her. In her other life, she had been controlled but she had very seldom been by herself, and she would often catch herself on the verge of saying something to Sebas or Lucas or Jazmin or her mother, even. She took to borrowing books and newspapers and magazines—her favorite was *Reader's Digest*—from the colonel's library, hiding behind the pages as she surreptitiously watched the world pass before her: the families with little children in tow, pulling little wagons and grasping bright balloons; the joggers in matching running suits; and most of all the couples, arms entwined around each other, oblivious—completely oblivious—to anyone near them, even when they kissed, even when the boy's hand wrapped familiarly around the girl's waist or dipped inside her back pocket. Rita watched and wondered how she'd completely missed that part of life, the part where someone like her could simply be with someone else and not even think twice about it. Sometimes, but less and less often, she thought of Lucas. She'd stopped going to church, because everything there—the hymns, the candles, the smell of incense outside and from within—reminded her of him. One Sunday, in the middle of the sermon, she simply got up and walked out, but not before looking back one final time to see if he was leaning nonchalantly against the columns by the door, watching her go.

She forced herself not to think about the baby. Not

consciously, at least. Only when she showered in the mornings and looked down at the marks his presence had left on her body. Eventually those, too, began to fade, and her waist began to shrink and her breasts once again became those of a girl, unsullied by pregnancy and childbearing and pain.

She'd be the first to admit that despite everything she was content. That she liked having her own bedroom, her own bathroom, and her own television. They felt like luxuries, even if her room was a tiny maid's cell. Mostly she relished the modicum of respect she received, because the colonel gradually reeled her out into the world, increasing her responsibilities in bits and pieces until she was the one who fully ran the household, who coordinated his schedule, who encouraged him to start entertaining again; after all, wasn't she there precisely to help with such things?

In hindsight she should have planned ahead while things were going well and her newfound routine was so comfortable that she could finally sleep deeply at night, secure in her corner perch on the seventeenth floor. Instead the colonel's death, three months shy of her real eighteenth birthday, took her completely by surprise. She was in class that night, and someone from Edward García's office was waiting for her when she returned to the building, shortly before 10:00 P.M.

The colonel was dead, García's messenger informed her. He'd had a sudden, massive heart attack during his Monday card game. An ambulance had arrived almost immediately, but there was nothing to be done. Rita was to fix up the house and prepare for the arrival of his family.

"What family?" she asked, perplexed. "I didn't know he had one."

"Of course he does," said the assistant primly, looking at her with a frown. "He has nephews and nieces. They'll be staying here while they arrange all the matters of the estate."

"But what will happen to me?" asked Rita, realization dawning inside her.

"Well, I suppose you'll have to look for another job," said the assistant, although not unkindly this time. "But they'll probably be needing you for a couple of weeks at least. Mr. García will speak with you, I'm sure."

Rita rode up quietly in the service elevator, mulling this unexpected turn of events. She had her meager savings, accumulated after eight months of spending barely a dime. But a maid's salary didn't go very far. She could look for another job, but she'd have to negotiate the right to go to school at night. Only when she opened up the kitchen door and faced the dark reality of the apartment did it strike her that the colonel was irrevocably gone.

She should be crying, she thought, shocked at her own lack of emotional connection. The man, after all, had employed her for nearly a year, treated her fairly, paid her decently. Knowing now that he wouldn't return, Rita opened the balcony doors and sat on the little settee out on the terrace, a liberty she would have never taken otherwise, wrapping her arms around her against the cold night air. Even from up here, the city looked busy. She could hear the whoosh of the traffic below, almost feel the pulse of life in the apartments and houses and streets that stretched below her. It had been so effortless to get to this place—a miracle, really. For what else were miracles but opportunities that appeared at exactly the right moment?

She'd never considered that the colonel might be an angel or the result of some sort of divine intervention. He was too detached from her, too aloof. She was his maid, nothing more, nothing less. A smart maid, but still a servant, with her station in life perpetually decided. Perhaps that's why she harbored little sorrow at his passing. Instead, more than sadness, she felt a pang of regret, like what a child feels who leaves a toy behind in the park and can't find it again.

Rita took a deep breath and walked quietly through the apartment, turning on the lights as she went. She wasn't a timorous person—she'd long ago learned that real people are what one should be afraid of—but still, she couldn't bear the thought of waiting things out in the dark. She stopped momentarily at the colonel's bedroom, appraising how neat he was, how immaculately starched every piece of clothing that hung in his closet. Like her, she thought. And so alone. Like her, too. She'd never heard of these nieces and nephews of his who were supposed to descend on his home and claim his belongings. They hadn't called once that she could remember in all her months here.

"This is the fate of the lonely," Rita said to the dark, empty rooms. "To be pillaged by strangers when they die." She didn't want this to be her fate. She wondered if the colonel had ever been happy, if he'd ever been in love. If he'd ever yearned to have children, or if, maybe, he *had* a child, somewhere in the world, and simply didn't know about it. So many nights she'd sat at the kitchen table and wished she could one day have a place like this, but not alone, she thought. *I couldn't be alone.*

The trilling of the phone interrupted her reverie.

"Colonel Santos's house," answered Rita in an even voice.

"Rita, it's Mr. García," said the man on the other end.

"Yes, sir?"

"You heard what happened?"

"I did, sir," replied Rita. "I'm so sorry, sir."

"Yes, well. Colonel Santos's family will be coming in tomorrow. There are four of them. Please make sure there are rooms and food ready for them."

"Yes, sir."

"You'll also need to choose an outfit for the colonel to be buried in. His uniform, actually. With all the insignias. I'll send someone in the morning to make sure everything is in place."

Rita smarted under the unspoken criticism.

"There is no need to do that, sir," she said calmly. "Everything will be ready. Of course you're welcome to send someone from your staff as well," she added quickly.

"I think I'll do that," he said curtly.

Rita rolled her eyes. "Of course, sir," she said evenly.

"The funeral will be on Wednesday," continued Mr. García.

"Can I go, sir?" Rita asked.

There was a pause on the other end.

"I'm afraid that won't be possible," he said. "We need someone in the apartment at all times. There's going to be too much going on. I'm sorry," he added, almost as an afterthought.

"Mr. García?"

"Yes, Rita," he answered, sounding impatient.

"What will happen to me?"

"Well, you are obviously out of a job, I'm sorry to say. Perhaps the family will want you to stay in some capacity, but until I hear otherwise, consider this your two-week notice."

As obvious as the outcome was, it was no less shocking to hear it so bluntly stated. Alone in her room that night, Rita pored over the classifieds and weighed her options. It would be so much easier if someone could steer her in the right direction, as had happened the first time, but she wasn't about to go back to the orphanage and ask for help—that chapter was closed—and the thought of returning to the flower farm was unbearable. For the first time, she wished she'd been friendlier to her classmates, more outgoing with her teachers. Surely one of them was in some capacity to at least recommend a place for her.

Her eyes went from the domestic positions to the office positions. Why not? she thought. She had a high-school diploma—or she would in a month, at least. She was good with numbers, good with words. Rita chewed distractedly on her pencil, the possibility beginning to take shape in her head.

Why not? she thought again, and carefully, methodically she began to circle her options.

# Chapter Twenty

Asher has delegated sightseeing duties to Alessandra, and she suggests they go to Cerro Monserrate, so he can have a bird's-eye view of his birth city from its highest peak, more than ten thousand feet above sea level. They take the cable car at the foot of the mountain, from a whitewashed Colonial structure right in the heart of the city, and begin an ascent that feels almost heavenly. As they leave behind the din and dirt of the city, the sky opens up above them to reveal in increasingly sharp detail the white church above and the expanse of the city beyond, impossibly vast and spread out so the homes and buildings spill into the mountains like ever-growing tentacles.

"It was originally just a little chapel," Alessandra tells him as they walk the stone path. "It started to grow in importance among the locals, who came up here to worship. It caught the attention of a hotshot priest in the 1600s, and he's the one who decided to build something bigger. A big church, housing for the priests, something much grander. This same priest is the one who built the pathway up the mountain. At Easter, hordes of people make the trek. It's like a two-hour walk."

"I would have walked," says Asher, looking down the steep incline.

"Yeah, but I wouldn't have," says Alessandra, punching him in the arm. "Anyway," she continues ceremoniously, raising her hand for silence, "in the 1800s they had a big earthquake, and they had to rebuild part of the whole complex. And then—in 1917, I think—they had another earthquake, and that's when they built the church we're going to see now. It's the power of transformation. You can change things, turn them into something completely different, but their essence always remains the same."

"What if the essence is intrinsically tied to the physical properties?" counters Asher.

"But it isn't. I wouldn't be here with you if it were," says Alessandra sharply.

Asher smiles and gestures to the statues of Christ that line the path. "And this?" he asks.

"These are the stations of the cross. In each of them we see Christ on his way to Calvary. As you know, our people killed him," Alessandra adds, unable to stifle a giggle.

"I guess our people aren't very popular around here?" Asher asks with a laugh.

"Oh, I wouldn't say that," muses Alessandra. "I like the aura of this place. It's very welcoming. And look!" She points, taking his hand and pulling him ahead. "This is the church. This is where they have the statue of the fallen Christ of Monserrate. He's supposed to be miraculous. That's why all these people come here."

Asher allows Alessandra to drag him along into the church and all the way up to the altar, where the statue of the fallen Christ, lying on his side over a wooden pedestal, lies behind a glass wall, against which groups of people are greedily pressing their hands in a futile effort to touch the figure just beyond their reach. The allure of the church itself doesn't catch Asher by surprise after his visit to the chapel, but he shakes his head at the faithful mingling by the fallen Christ.

"So this is how people ask for miracles?" he asks wryly.

"Well, it's one way," says Alessandra reasonably. "As long as you have faith and you believe, who cares how your miracle comes about? Let me show you something else," she says, taking him by the hand again and pointing toward rows and rows of plaques that line the walls of the church. "These are testimonials of people whose wishes came true. They're thanking the fallen Christ for accomplishing their miracle."

Asher strains to make sense of the messages carved in the stone plaques. "'Thank you for helping me get my U.S. residency,'" he reads out loud. "'Thank you for finding a lung for my father.' Are you expecting me to ask for a miracle here?" he ventures, a little incredulous.

"Not really," says Alessandra, shrugging. "That'd be too weird for a Jew, even a Jew who's been baptized." She smiles impishly. "I just thought the whole story of the place was really cool, and I wanted to see what there was about it that moves so many people. Look at this. It's powerful."

Asher gazes around him, studying the knots of people, heads bowed in prayer, who continue to arrive in an endless wave, parading past the fallen Christ. To his left, a woman begins to sob uncontrollably, and this time he's the one who takes Alessandra's hand and leads her out of the church to the wooden balustrade from which they can see the sprawl of the city below.

"Look at *that*," Asher says. "Imagine if she's there? It'd be like finding a needle in a haystack." He shakes his head. "I've been thinking about what Sister Teresa said. Everyone talks about these miracles. Even my mom keeps talking about what a miracle it is that I survived. But it's not about miracles. What I do with her, with me, how I move ahead, that won't be a miracle. That'll just be me. And finding her won't be the miracle. It'll simply be what's meant to be, or what I—what we—are able to do." Asher turns and looks at Alessandra standing beside him. "But I hope I find her, Ally. I so want to find her."

Alessandra moves behind Asher and hugs him, bringing her hands under his jacket until they touch his chest, feeling the rhythmic beat of his heart. "Rita," she says after a moment. "You have to say her name. Rita. Rita Ortiz. It'll make her real. Say it, Ash. 'I hope I find Rita Ortiz.' "

Asher closes his eyes, feeling like he's preparing to deliver an incantation. "I hope I find Rita Ortiz," he finally whispers, then repeats it louder. "I hope I find Rita Ortiz.

"I hope I find Rita Ortiz!" he shouts, raising both his arms to the sky.

*     *     *

It was a big burial, with much pomp and circumstance, attended by the crème de la crème of the military establishment. The relatives had arrived the day before, two nieces, one nephew, and a granddaughter, who all looked at Rita suspiciously and began barking orders almost immediately. The granddaughter couldn't have been much older than

Rita was, a thin girl with very straight brown hair colored by carefully applied highlights that glinted when she tossed it over her shoulders.

*My hair is prettier*, thought Rita sullenly as she quietly served breakfast in the morning, wishing she could rid herself of this odd mixture of dread and jealousy that had enveloped her ever since they came. It had never bothered her before, working for the colonel. Quite the opposite, she'd felt a quiet pride for her position; even if she scrubbed floors, there was an expectation of excellence and always of something beyond the menial work. The family didn't see this, clearly. She was the help to them, invisible. If someone had asked them to describe her, they wouldn't have been able to; they never looked at her face long enough.

"You wanted to be forgettable, and now you are," she mused aloud as she furiously scrubbed the dishes. The family had been sorting through the colonel's effects almost from the moment they'd walked in the door, dividing up the memorabilia, appraising the contents of his safe—the safe even she hadn't known existed. Friday morning before the burial, they called her to the study.

"Rita, we know you've been with my uncle for nearly a year, and we're told he was very happy with your work," said the nephew.

"I hope so, sir," said Rita, looking down at the tips of her white house shoes, surprised by this turn of events. Did they really mean this?

"We wanted you to have this, as a token of appreciation for your work," the nephew added, and Rita looked up in surprise, taking in the small, rather dainty silver wristwatch that he extended toward her. Rita took it with a sense of wonderment. She had no idea if it was a fine watch or not, but certainly, she'd never before been given anything that looked so expensive.

"Oh, thank you, sir," she gasped, enormously pleased with the gesture until she saw the granddaughter looking at her with a moue of disdain. She looked again at the watch, uncertainly now. Was it terrible? she wondered. But she decided she didn't care; in her eyes it was beautiful, even if clearly someone else had rejected it first.

After they left, Rita tried on the watch, turning her arm this way and that, admiring the way the delicate silver band encircled her wrist. It was a woman's watch, and she wondered if it had been his mother's, or if he had purchased it for someone else and then, at the very last minute, changed his mind and left it there, locked in the safe forever, until it found its way to her. Rita reluctantly put the watch away in her little suitcase, afraid it could get wet while she did her housework. She had no idea what she could wear it for, but surely, this was a sign that someday she would have clothes fine enough to match.

The phone rang yet again, and she answered as she always did. "Colonel Santos's house."

"Rita?" asked the female voice on the other end.

"Yes, ma'am?" she answered, surprised.

"This is Mrs. Cruz, from 1104."

"Oh, yes, ma'am," replied Rita, immediately conjuring the image of the woman, a prim seventy-something-year-old who lived alone with her husband six stories below.

"We heard about Colonel Santos. We're very sorry."

"Thank you, ma'am. I'll convey that to the family."

"This will sound a little strange, but we are looking for a maid," continued Mrs. Cruz. "The colonel always spoke highly of you, and we're wondering if you might be interested."

"Oh," said Rita blankly, caught totally off guard. *No*, she wanted to say, thinking about her carefully circled want ads. But she instantly realized how foolish that was, to reject an offer when she had absolutely no notion of her immediate future. "Oh," she repeated. "That's very kind of you, Mrs. Cruz. I'm not sure when I could start, though. I would need to ask the family how long they need me here for. I imagine a few days at least."

"Well, speak with them and let me know, will you?"

"Certainly, Mrs. Cruz. Thank you, ma'am. Oh, ma'am! There is one thing," she added hurriedly.

"Yes, Rita?"

"I go to school, ma'am. On Monday, Wednesday, and Friday nights. I...I'm not going this week, of course, because they need me here. But...but I do need to finish my school. I can stay with you on the weekends, though," she added hurriedly, weighing the silence on the other end of the line. "I don't usually go out."

"Mmm. That's right. The colonel had his card game, didn't he? Well, I suppose that should be fine, although I might need you on those nights from time to time."

Rita was expectantly silent on the other end. She wanted the certainty of a position, but she wasn't willing to cede ground on this particular issue, not when she was three months short of graduating.

"I'm sure we can work it out," said Mrs. Cruz finally. "Speak with them and give me a call tomorrow, will you?"

"Of course, ma'am. Thank you, ma'am," added Rita, carefully hanging up the phone. She felt a small surge of panic as she began to see how her carefully laid plans were beginning to unravel. She was going to go from being a maid to being a maid. *Why in the world did he have to die?* she thought in a burst of anger. How incredibly inconvenient. How incredibly inconsiderate. Rita kicked the trash can in the corner of the kitchen, kicked it hard, and the flimsy can toppled over, strewing banana peels and coffee grounds on the shiny linoleum floor. Rita looked at the mess, at the incongruous sight of ugly garbage all over such a clean surface. She took a deep breath and moistened a rag under the sink. Then she got on her knees and cleaned up her floor.

By the time she received her second summons into the study that afternoon, she was fully prepared for a dismissal. "Rita," said Mr. García without preamble. "Please sit down."

Rita looked inquiringly around the room, expecting pitying smiles. She saw instead outright anger. Her mind rapidly went back to the events of the day and the previous week, trying to figure out if there had been a misstep, but she could think of none. The watch, she thought then, reflexively looking at her feet. They wanted the watch back.

"Rita, there's been a mistake," said Mr. García, as if reading her mind.

She sat perfectly still, not saying a word, like a deer who senses a predator in its midst. After all, years of living in enemy territory in her own home had made her an expert at defusing aggression.

"It appears that..." Mr. García hesitated, clearly thinking of the best way to phrase what he was going to say next. "It seems that your name was inadvertently placed in some of the colonel's documents."

"I beg your pardon?" said Rita, utterly at a loss.

"There are some documents of the colonel's, some financial documents, that for some unknown reason are in your name," repeated Mr. García, polishing his glasses.

He was lying, thought Rita suddenly. He was telling half-truths, just like hers. And if he was, it meant this was important.

"What kind of documents?" she asked carefully.

"Some certificates of deposit. It shouldn't really be a problem. We can just switch them over to Mr. Santos's name, and that should take care of it."

"But," Rita began dubiously, "why is my name on the documents in the first place?"

"It was a mistake. I think he simply forgot to change them to his name, but now we have to fix that. So if you sign this document here, it allows me to simply change the papers to the right name and we're set."

Rita nodded, and she might actually have done it, despite her mistrust, until she glanced up and saw their faces, looking down at her like vultures getting ready for a feeding, saw the ill-concealed impatience and anger, and, overwhelmingly, she saw concern. And Rita knew, with the instinct of a survivor, that she had the upper hand.

"I'd like to see these..." Rita struggled to remember what they were. Certificates of something. "These documents with my name on them," she said finally.

"It's not necessary, Rita," said Mr. García, his voice dripping with condescension. And she remembered. She remembered the conversation behind closed doors that she had inadvertently heard months before. What was it that he had said? *Doesn't strike me as the sharpest of knives.*

Rita lifted her chin a notch and squared her shoulders back.

"Actually, it is necessary," she said, and, to her horror, her voice squeaked slightly, but she didn't care. "However, I can have an attorney request it if you prefer."

Mr. García stared at her, trying to remain impassive but painfully aware that he—and the colonel—had grossly miscalculated the effects of this particular gamble.

"Why don't you step outside for a moment, Rita," he said, taking off his glasses and putting them absentmindedly on the bookshelf. Rita stood up very slowly. Her knees actually knocked against each other, something that had never happened to her before, not even after the incident with Alberto, but she managed to shut the door of the study behind her. She heard them arguing furiously in harsh whispers, then the nephew's voice rising in agitation, shouting, "She can't do this!" and Mr. García interceding in that maddeningly calm tone of his. Rita's hand went reflexively up to her neck, but she had nothing to hold on to for support—not her cross, or Lucas' amulet, or even Jazmin's bracelet. She had nothing but her wits.

"Rita!" yelled Mr. García from behind the study door, by now all niceties dispensed with. Rita once again entered and stood in the center of the room. This time no one asked her to sit.

"Now, where are my glasses?" said the attorney, looking around hopelessly. Rita walked up to the bookshelf and handed them to him, as she had been doing for eight months of her life. This time, for the first time, his eyes met hers.

Without a thank-you, Mr. García picked up a sheaf of papers.

"The colonel put some money in some certificates of deposit in your name," he said flatly. "That money was not meant to be yours. It was there simply for tax reasons. The correct thing to do would be to return it to the rightful owners."

"Can I see the certificates, please?" asked Rita, assuming a calm that she was far from feeling.

Mr. García shrugged and tossed them onto the desk, staring at her intently as she was forced to walk toward him and pick the documents up. She savored the crisp lightness of the papers, feeling the indentation of the typed words beneath her fingertips. She breathed shallowly through her half-open mouth, as subtly as she could, but still couldn't do anything about the galloping beating of her heart. It didn't register at first, the names and the dates and the percentages and all those numbers, so many that she finally resorted to methodically counting them in her head, to be certain—one, two, three, four, then a period, then two more and a six at the very beginning. Rita forced her breathing to slow down, dragged her eyes away from the numbers, and zeroed in on the tips of her white shoes, where she now could see a smattering of coffee grounds.

"Thank you," she said, not looking up, refusing to meet

their eyes, refusing to open the door that she had mentally shut between them, refusing to let them see that she was certain she was mistaken. "I'll study this and let you know in the morning," she added, gingerly stepping backward, then turning around and rushing out the door. She went straight to her room, closed and locked the door behind her, and sat down on the bed. She clutched the papers tightly in her hands, afraid they could somehow dissolve into thin air. Rita looked down with trepidation. There were percentages, and little bar graphs with codes, and numbers and dates and lots of numbers in parentheses. But there was no mistaking the $50,847.31 that stared at her arrogantly from the box labeled "TOTAL."

Rita shook her head. She had $50,847.31? This was simply impossible, she thought. How could something like this happen? What was it that he'd said? That the money was in her name for tax reasons. She knew nothing about taxes. She assumed that her parents paid taxes, but she'd never been privy to such matters. And she had no idea what a certificate of deposit was either. She had no notion of how these black-and-white papers could become cash, cash in her hand, that she could spend. What was certain, however, was that somehow she had claim over the possibility of this money. And she didn't care if it was a mistake, or a tax issue, or perhaps—and why not—subconsciously a gift. She was going to keep it.

She didn't sleep at all that night. She put the papers underneath her pillow and felt them crinkle through the night, every time she turned around. She wanted to make plans, but she didn't dare until she knew, without a shadow of a doubt, that the money was hers to keep, for she couldn't bear the chance of more disillusionment.

The next morning Rita got up very early, put on her new watch and long sweater, and carefully placed the papers in her little handbag. She waited in line in the cold dreariness of the morning until the nearest bank opened its doors.

She sat across the desk from the bank manager, a middle-aged woman with a navy suit and a no-nonsense look about her. Rita pulled out the papers and carefully placed them on the desk between them.

"My employer died and left me this," she said flatly. "Can you please explain to me exactly what it means?"

The woman's name tag read MISS MÓNICA MARTÍNEZ, MANAGER. She looked the papers over, her face impassive, for what seemed to be a very long time.

"Do you have your ID on you?" she asked eventually, still not showing any expression.

Rita nodded and pulled it out of her wallet.

Miss Martínez compared the names and the numbers, then finally gave Rita a long, probing look before looking back down at the picture on the ID, then back up at Rita again.

"It means that in two months, when this certificate of deposit is up, you will have a little over sixty thousand dollars to your name," said Miss Martínez. "Your employer was a generous man."

Rita felt a roaring in her ears, as if she'd tumbled from a cliff into a waterfall. Miss Martínez was speaking to her—Rita could see her lips move, but she couldn't hear a word she was saying. Rita pressed her feet very hard on the floor beneath her, to make sure it was there and then to simply keep herself from falling. She couldn't even begin to grasp the significance of sixty thousand dollars. She made three hundred dollars a month. How was it possible to suddenly have sixty thousand dollars?

"Ms. Ortiz?" Rita finally heard Miss Martínez ask, concern in her voice. "Would you like a glass of water?"

Rita shook her head no, then yes, realizing that her throat was parched.

Miss Martínez went to get her the water, and Rita began to breathe again, deep breaths, like they'd taught her to do at the Lamaze classes before she had the baby. By the time Miss Martínez came back, she'd regained some sense of composure.

"And this number here?" asked Rita, pointing to the $50,847.31, her finger shaking.

"That's how much you have now," said Miss Martínez, and to Rita's surprise, her voice was actually kind. "See, he put in forty thousand dollars and left it to earn interest for nine months. The amount has been growing. In two months you'll have more."

"Do I have to wait two months to get the money?" asked Rita breathlessly.

"You don't have to, but if you take it out before, there's a penalty. I suggest you keep it there until the term is up. Also, you know that this CD isn't from this bank, correct?"

"Yes," said Rita. "It's just that I have my account here."

"And hopefully you can move the rest of your money here when you cash in your CD," said Miss Martínez. "What you should do," she added, "is make an appointment with one of our financial planners, or with me if you wish, and we can help you go over options."

"Can anything happen to it?" asked Rita tremulously.

"To the money? Nothing can happen to it if it's in a CD. Your investment is guaranteed."

"No, I mean, can anyone else take it away from me?" asked Rita.

Miss Martínez looked at the papers again. "No." She shook her head. "This is in your name, with Mr. Antonio Santos having power of attorney over it. But if Mr. Santos is dead, no one else has access to it except you."

"How about his attorney?" asked Rita.

"No. He'd need to get a new power of attorney to do that." Miss Martínez paused and looked at Rita with some measure of concern, then leaned forward, her voice falling. "Miss Ortiz, this money is yours and yours alone. It's a substantial amount of money. No one can take it away from you unless you sign something. Do not sign anything, you hear me? You can't let anyone take this money away from you. I don't know what kind of arrangement you had with your employer or why he gave you this. But my advice is, the fewer people that know about this, the better."

Rita looked at Miss Martínez anxiously. *Were you once like me?* she wanted to ask her. *Do you see yourself in my eyes, in my clothes, in my fear?*

"What can I do with so much money?" she asked instead, reaching out for the papers. "What do other people do?"

"Some of them pay off debts. Some buy things they've always wanted," said Miss Martínez. "It's a chance to start again," she added, matter-of-factly. "Frankly, you shouldn't be walking around with those papers. I'm going to make a copy and put it in your file here. If anything should ever happen to the originals, you know you have a copy that's safe and sound."

"Okay," said Rita meekly, sitting back. Was she rich? She thought she was rich. She couldn't remember her parents ever bandying about talk of a sum even remotely close to sixty thousand dollars.

Rita started out of her reverie, beginning to grasp the full significance of the moment. She could begin again, the woman had said. She had a second chance.

"I need to go," she said abruptly when Miss Martínez returned with her papers. "Thank you. Thank you so much. I'll be back."

Rita dashed out the door and ran to the thoroughfare, fervently clutching her little bag. Although she had vowed never to go back there, she could still remember the bus line that had brought her here, almost a year before. An hour and a half later, she was walking down the winding road that led to La Casa en el Campo. She'd been pregnant and poor last time. Now, she reminded herself, she was thin and rich. The mere thought made her euphoric, and she quickened her pace to a run until she reached the porch and began to bang frantically on the door.

A woman she had never seen before opened the door. "Yes?" the woman said, annoyed at the ruckus. "What can I do for you?"

"I've come to pick up my baby," said Rita breathlessly.

# Chapter Twenty-one

It rains that weekend. Not the pouring rain of the tropics but the slow, steady, cold rain of the mountains. Fidel drops them off in the Colonial downtown, near the base of the cable car to Monserrate, and they spend the day strolling in a loose embrace under the shelter of an enormous yellow umbrella.

"When I played soccer, I could never do this," Asher muses as they walk around slowly inside the Gold Museum, which houses the bulk of Colombia's prehistoric treasures. "Every trip was about practicing and playing. I went to all these cities, but I never had time see any of them."

His precious time, which he feared would be wasted forever in the wake of the crash, but which he now gradually finds pleasure in reclaiming.

"I love it," says Alessandra simply, her fingers tightening against his, and Asher knows she means his time as much as this place.

It's a blindingly white, almost austere, contemporary building of sleek, clean lines and long panes of glass that provide stark contrast to the sheer richness of the gold figures it displays.

Asher looks intently at an enormous mask of solid gold that stares back at him from a glass case. Save for a pointy little nose, any semblance of facial structure has been pounded flat into the shape of a pancake, turning the mask's fierce eyes and bared teeth—carved into the gold in an angry gash—all the more fearsome.

Asher looks at the inscription below: " 'Mask to terrorize,' " he reads out loud.

"So simple, but it works," says Alessandra softly. "They were used to scare the spirits away, as most terrifying masks have been used through the centuries," she adds, lapsing into what Asher likes to call her "teaching voice," the one she uses when she tutors him.

"The native populations throughout Central America and the Andes are known for their fine metalwork," Alessandra goes on, oblivious. "But here in Colombia they worked particularly well with hammers. See how thin this is?" She points to the mask. "Gold is very malleable. It's the ideal metal to elaborate on. They would hammer it, then cool it in cold water so it wouldn't break. And then they'd run through the cycle again until they got the shape they wanted." She peers more closely at the figure in the case, then catches Asher's smile reflected in the glass.

"What?" she asks defensively, spinning around. "Are you making fun of me?"

"Not at all, Dr. Lowe. You're just such a little lecturer." Asher laughs, raising his hands in surrender. "I love it. However, I must point out, according to my Colombia readings, the mask was intended to transform the wearer, obliterating his own persona and taking on the attributes of animals or deities or monsters or whatever it was."

"Well, sure. Ultimately the objective of any mask is to

hide the real person," Alessandra says. "Although, not to get too philosophical, but I've always thought that there's no better disguise than being out in plain sight. Like a chameleon, you know?"

"I think Rita is here, hiding in plain sight," says Asher abruptly.

"I wouldn't say she's hiding," says Alessandra, moving on to the next piece. "We just haven't tracked her down. Anyway, she could be anywhere."

"The amazing thing," says Asher, going back to his previous thoughts, "is that if I hadn't had the accident, I wouldn't even be here. You realize that?"

"Maybe not now, but you'd have come eventually," says Alessandra, reasonable as ever.

"Nah. I was fine," he says, shaking his head. "I was," he repeats defensively, looking at her arched brow.

"Ash, there's nothing wrong with wanting to know," says Alessandra. "You can use the accident to justify it, but the bottom line is, there's nothing wrong with what you're doing. She doesn't owe you anything, though. Just remember that."

"What's that supposed to mean?"

"It means exactly that," Alessandra replies, unfazed by the annoyance that has crept into his voice. "The fact that you almost died doesn't make you more special in her eyes. It doesn't compel her to commitment after twenty-one years of silence. She's a stranger, babe," she adds, pressing her hand up against his cheek. "Maybe you'll share some quirks, but that's it. Everything else is a bonus, like Carla says."

"Wow!" Asher says snidely. "You used to be my big cheerleader. When did you become a cynic?"

"I'm not a cynic," Alessandra retorts. "It's just the way it is. The fact that she's your birth mother doesn't automatically make her a wonderful person or even someone worth knowing. You don't need to get ornery about it."

"Ornery?" Asher snaps. "That's just the kind of thing you would say, isn't it? Ornery. Who would use such an obscure, pedantic word like 'ornery'?"

Alessandra looks at him, her pale face flushing in sheer anger. "Ornery," she spits out. "Yes, I'm the kind of person who uses the word 'ornery.' You know what other word I like to use? 'Asshole.'"

Alessandra whirls around and walks quickly to the next gallery, leaving him behind. Asher stands there irresolutely, rubbing his temples at the incision sites. He wants to tell her that the anger and regret that his accident introduced into his life are something she can't understand—something no one can. But now he's convinced himself that if he can find Rita, somehow it will make things better, though he himself wouldn't be able to say why. He takes a deep breath and looks again at the mask to terrorize, and now he sees it simply for what it is: a façade. Made out of gold, but just a façade nevertheless.

Asher walks slowly through the gallery until he sees Alessandra's slight figure standing in front of a jewelry display, everything about her posture set with deliberate concentration. He's always loved that she loves knowledge, that she carries facts and tidbits of information on her the way other people carry loose change, that she always fills her days—her minutes, even—with boundless curiosity. Of course she wanted to come, and he couldn't do it without

her, he thinks. He could never bring himself to put his own
mother through this, and he simply doesn't have the guts
to go about it alone. He's here because of her. Asher places
his hands softly on Alessandra's shoulders and whispers
against the chamomile smell of her hair.

"I'm sorry," he says gently. "I'm sorry."

That evening, as they sip mulled wines at a bar around
the corner, Inés calls.

"Hey, guys," she says cheerfully. "I found the church."

# Chapter Twenty-two

Rita shut the door of La Casa en el Campo behind her and braced against the cold dreariness of the day, walking automatically forward up the winding hill, oblivious to the lone car coming toward her until the driver pressed the horn impatiently, making her jump to the side of the road at the last, scary second.

"Idiot!" screamed a woman, her voice audible even through the closed window. Rita stepped quickly back onto the road and looked around her, uncertain. She gazed back down at the house, but now it seemed miles away, unreachable, even though she'd walked only a few yards. She continued to the bus stop and took the long journey home, getting off at her stop by rote. But she didn't want to go to that apartment now.

She started walking instead, aimlessly, buffeted by the throngs of people flowing past her and toward her, to the left and to the right of her. Rita was impervious to the shoves, the muffled curses; she just trudged on, steadily, like a mountain climber. She didn't know how much time had passed before the first conscious thought came into her mind, before she looked back at the winding avenue and saw miles and miles of blocks behind her and realized she had no idea where she was.

Rita looked around, but nothing seemed familiar. The modern buildings had given way to the more Colonial architecture of downtown. For a disconcerting moment, looking at the blue wooden doors and the wooden windows, barricaded with ornate wrought iron, she thought she had somehow walked all the way home. But of course it wasn't home. It was gray and dreary here, as it always was, and this was just a downtown cafeteria, with fresh bread laid out on the glass counter inside the darkened room. Rita realized she was starving; she hadn't had anything to eat since breakfast. She looked at her watch. The pretty watch the colonel's nephew had given her, before the will was read, when he still thought she was just a poor little maid who needed to be appeased with trinkets. It was after 4:00 P.M. She'd been walking for over five hours.

Rita ordered coffee and a ham sandwich and sat down at a wooden table in the corner, hungrily gulping down her snack, warming her hands on the hot cup. Some song played on the radio, and the girl behind the counter sang along softly under her breath, but Rita couldn't recognize the tune. She couldn't seem to clear her head, as if she were underwater, and she wondered briefly if she could have a fever, but her cheeks and her forehead felt cool to the touch. Rita felt her heart begin to pound against her chest again, as it had this morning in Casa, and she forced herself to take deep, long breaths, one after the other. Wasn't she, after all, the calm one, the one always in control? After a while the dots in the world around her finally connected and the words to the song came suddenly to her, like little pellets: *There's nothing after you, no sun, no morning.* She watched the people who came and went, registering for the first time the features of those around her: the leathery skin of the man behind the counter, the colorful bohemian scarves and worn jeans of a gaggle of pretty girls carrying books under their arms; two older men playing dominoes in the back, their buttoned-up vests and tweed jackets giving them an air of propriety that suited this cold city, even in a place as unassuming as this one.

Rita took a sip of coffee and watched another group of girls with backpacks and books come up to the counter. So many students, she thought absentmindedly, then looked across the street and saw the red, unfurled banners hanging from a modern, three-story building with tinted windows that stood in stark contrast to the white stucco walls of the houses around it. The public library. She looked at it curiously, looked at the groups of people milling around the entrance, at the steady flow of foot traffic. The only library she'd ever been to was in her old school, a tiny room overrun by encyclopedias and atlases and the small number of novels the girls were permitted to read on premises. No books ever left the library. One had to go accompanied by a teacher, who would sit idly by while the students did their research.

Rita wiped her mouth with the flimsy paper napkin and got up slowly, her cheap little bag pressed tightly against her as she walked out to the street, with a purpose this time. The library was bigger up close, so big that there were two turnstiles to allow people in and out. Rita stood by uncertainly, trying to figure out what was needed to get in, but people just walked in and out, in and out, showing their bags for inspection in either direction.

She walked shyly up to the guard, who took a perfunctory look inside her bag and handed her a flyer.

"There's a concert at five, if you want to attend," he said automatically, already handing another one to the person behind her before she had a chance to reply. Rita looked up at the imposing marble staircase before her and put the flyer in her bag as she grasped the cold metal balustrade and climbed up. She had never been to such a grand place, with huge oil paintings of serious men hanging on the wall and a vast, towering skylight that allowed warmth to seep into the hushed halls. She walked toward the double doors that read, simply, GENERAL COLLECTION, and pushed them open to find herself surrounded by books.

Rita looked around dumbly. All these years, she thought, she'd figured she was so darn smart, so knowledgeable, so incredibly superior to her parents, simply because she'd memorized a handful of textbooks. She regarded the rows and rows of shelves, packed with books. She couldn't even see the end of it down the carpeted aisles. She walked to the nearest shelf and glanced up, shaking her head in bewilderment—who knew? She ran her hands gently, reverently, over the bindings of the books, leather tomes, the words engraved into their spines like etchings on wood, little numbered papers pasted at the bottom. How could she possibly find anything here?

She remembered all those books she had once wanted to read but simply couldn't find in her town, so she'd finally resorted to reading the magazines in the store. There were newsmagazines, yes, but she also read the gossip and beauty glossies and, of course, her must-haves, the love stories by Corín Tellado in *Vanidades*, her mother's favorite women's magazine. In those saccharine romances, the girl was always beautiful and virtuous, and she always saved herself for that perfect, wonderful, fabulously wealthy man, and of course they got married and were happy.

Rita thought of Lucas, of his rough hands and smooth, hard body, of how gently he'd kissed her, of how he'd unbraided her hair and entwined it around the two of them as they lay naked, of how he'd made her believe there could be nothing more, nothing less than making love with him. Rita looked quickly around the room, one part of her expecting to see him, sitting so still at one of the back tables, staring at her intently, following her with his eyes, always following her, watching her—seeing her—as no one ever saw her.

But of course he wasn't seeing her now. For all she knew, he was dead. She wondered what would happen if she kept to her original plan and just went back. Now there really was no baby. Her parents could tell everyone she'd just gone away to visit an aunt, and she could pick up the pieces of her life, be quiet again, keep her head down, take her brother to soccer practice. And she had money now. Money that could help the family, that should make her father happy, enough to maybe talk to her again, just a little, enough to get her through school. Maybe going back, staying there, wasn't so bad. At least she'd have Sebastián. She'd have her parents, imperfect as they were. She'd have her own bed.

"Can I help you?"

Rita started in surprise at the sound of the voice beside

her. The woman talking to her was older, probably her mother's age, but impeccably dressed, with a gray wool skirt and a plain but soft, clingy black cardigan open over her red silk blouse. Her hair was short and very coiffed and her face perfectly made up, the red lipstick matching the color of her blouse. She wore pearl earrings—big, beautiful round pearls that glowed gently with opaque luster. Despite her nice sweater, Rita felt immediately intimidated, suddenly acutely aware of her cheap bag and ugly, sensible shoes.

"No, no, I'm all right, thank you," she replied.

"Do you need help finding a book?" the woman pressed gently.

"No, of course not," said Rita, attempting a smile. "I... I can find it, thank you."

"It's hard to find things here if you haven't been here before," the woman replied, and it occurred to Rita that maybe that was true. The woman was a librarian, after all, and surely there were other people who needed help. For the first time, Rita noticed the little name tag pinned to her impeccable sweater: BEATRIZ LÓPEZ.

"Tell me what book you need, and I'll show you how to find it," Beatriz López said, not unkindly.

"Mm. I... I would like to read *Love in the Time of Cholera*," said Rita, watching the woman's face carefully. Surely this wasn't a choice to be ashamed about. "And also," Rita added, because the idea simply came to her in a flash, "*Little Women*."

"Excellent," the woman said pleasantly. "So let me show you how this works. Come with me, please," she said, and started walking, Rita in tow, until she arrived at a gigantic wooden shelf housing what appeared to be dozens and dozens of rows of little boxes, each one with a printed tag.

"What we have here..." Beatriz paused. "What is your name?" she asked.

"Rita," she answered, and the name felt awkward as it fell from her lips.

"Rita," Beatriz repeated, looking at the vast wall of boxes. "This is our card catalog. There is a card here for all the books in the library. We have thousands and thousands and thousands of books, and we know exactly where each of them is.

"Now," she continued, "we catalog each book by author and by title. So if you know the author of the book, that's the easiest way to search. With the first book you want, *Love in the Time of Cholera*, there are many, many books that begin with the word 'love.' But there aren't many authors named Gabriel García Márquez, correct?" She looked at Rita for confirmation.

Rita nodded quickly, looking at the little labels on each of the boxes.

"So," Beatriz said, "we arrange the authors by last name, in alphabetical order. We look under the *G* for García Márquez." Beatriz López pointed with a bright red fingernail, the same color as her blouse and her lipstick, to a series of boxes, all of them bearing names beginning with *G*.

"Once you find your author, the author's book titles are also arranged alphabetically. Here, you try it now. Find *Love in the Time of Cholera*."

Rita stood beside Beatriz, her chapped, unmanicured

hands contrasting with the woman's translucent skin, her golden wedding band, her brightly lacquered nails. But she found it! *Love in the Time of Cholera*. Once, twice, so many times she stopped counting.

"Look how many there are," she whispered.

"We have many copies, some hardcover, some paperback, different editions," explained Beatriz. "But they're all together in the shelves. So this is what you do," she said, reaching up into a little tray that contained small pencils and slips of paper. "You write the number that you see on each of the cards," she said, and Rita quickly obliged.

"That's the number assigned to each book. It's based on something called the Dewey decimal system, which organizes all kinds of books under certain numbers in libraries. The number tells you exactly where each book is in this library. The three hundreds are social studies, for example. The four hundreds are languages. This book is a work of fiction, so it falls under the eight hundreds," she finished triumphantly. "Come, let me show you."

Rita followed Beatriz as she walked purposefully toward the rows and rows of bookshelves.

"Here we are. Fiction. See if you can find your book," she said, motioning Rita toward the shelves.

Rita followed the numbers on the book spines with her finger until she landed on the right row. "Here it is," she declared, plucking out a hardcover copy of *Love in the Time of Cholera* from the shelf. She turned it around in her hands, looking at the familiar yellow jacket with the black riverboat she remembered from the other edition she'd once begun to read.

"This is amazing!" she blurted out, her face breaking into a wide, unbelieving smile, her first real smile of the day, perhaps of the last month.

Beatriz gazed appraisingly at the girl, such a somber, dour girl, she thought, and saw what a little attention did. She was quite lovely, really, despite those horrid, worn, depressing clothes.

"So I can come and read it whenever I want?" Rita asked hopefully.

Beatriz seemed confused. "Well, you can do that, of course, but why don't you just borrow it and bring it back when you're done?" She looked at Rita's puzzled face, realizing she had no clue how a public library worked. "You can do that, you know."

"But, they're free?" asked Rita in wonderment. "How come they're not all taken out?"

"Well, a lot of them are," replied Beatriz López, heading back toward her counter. "Sometimes you search for a book and it isn't there, but in that case you can tell us, and we'll let you know when it arrives."

"But don't the books get lost?" asked Rita, feeling unduly concerned at this prospect.

"Of course," said Beatriz. "Sometimes people don't return them, sometimes they get put on the wrong shelf, sometimes they get lost. You swear you put them in one place, and they show up in another, months, sometimes years later. Books are like people, you know that? They're unpredictable. They have a life of their own," she added with a small, knowing smile. "But," she added, "we're beginning to computerize everything. In a couple of years, we'll be able to know exactly who has what and exactly where each book is. The computer will be able to tell if a book is back inside the library, and people like you won't have to waste their time going back and forth between the card catalogs and the shelves. In the meantime, though, we still do things by hand."

Rita didn't say anything. She clutched the book anxiously against her chest, her mind going a mile a minute, trying to figure out how this book lending would work. Surely they wouldn't just give her the book. They would probably ask for money, for some kind of deposit, a letter from her parents, and what would she say then?

"All right," said Beatriz, sliding behind a long counter at the front of the room. "I imagine you're not a member, so we'll begin by filling out a membership form." She took out what looked like a big index card.

"Is it free?" asked Rita dubiously.

"No, nothing's free," said Beatriz. "Nothing should be free. We charge you a very nominal fee to join, and in turn we provide you use of and access to the greatest library in the country, one of the greatest in the world. You decide if it's worth your money, dear."

"How much is it?" Rita asked, and raised her eyebrows when Beatriz told her the sum, barely as much as three bus rides across the city, nothing more. She had money on her, her full week's pay that she had taken with her, thinking, illogically, that she would pick up the baby and take a cab back to the colonel's house, and—and what then? she wondered miserably. What exactly was she going to do with that baby, even with her newfound wealth? Have him sleep on the bed beside her? She didn't even have a crib for her baby, had never sat down to think through what it meant to lay claim to her child, because, after all, she had wanted nothing of him, wanted only to forget he'd ever existed.

She remembered the pity on the faces of the nurses at the hospital and hated it, despite the kindness that came with it.

And now Beatriz was selling her a library membership, was handing her a form to fill out, and in her voice and in her eyes there was no pity at all; there was no baby to distract from her mission, just the righteous certainty that Rita liked books, and therefore she should—she would—buy this membership, even if she was so obviously poor, so utterly unsophisticated that she had never set foot inside a public library in her life.

The realization made Rita stand just a little taller, pull her shoulders back, as she used to do before, long ago when she was a pretty girl, even though she was acutely aware of Beatriz López looking at her hands as she withdrew the crumpled bills from her small wallet and smoothed them out on top of the counter, as people for whom money is very precious are wont to do, and turned them over with a tinge of regret. She then filled in the blanks carefully—her name, her new birth date, her new ID number. She paused before the address entry, then resolutely put down the colonel's address and phone number, for there was nothing else she could give. She paused again under the entry marked "Reference," then filled it out with the only reference she had, the only one she'd ever had, Sister Teresa's.

"Very well," said Beatriz, satisfied. "Let me just fill out the card, and you'll be set."

She sat down at the typewriter and a few minutes later handed Rita a small card bearing the library logo, Rita's name, and an ID number. Rita looked at it carefully, at her name—Rita Ortiz—so stark and clear and neat.

"Now, please sign here, put your ID number alongside your name, and you can take that book with you. Bring it back within two weeks or you'll get assessed late fees. You should know," added Beatriz, "this is a special student fee. Now, please use your card well and wisely."

"I will," said Rita. "Thank you so very much."

"You're welcome, Rita," Beatriz replied. "Good luck," she added, with just that hint of a smile she had that never grew to become the real thing, or at least not here, not with her. Rita wondered if Beatriz ever smiled, broadly and genuinely, when she was home with her family, with the husband who'd given her that gold band on her finger, or if all her smiles were half smiles even as she went about performing acts of kindness. Beatriz looked at her oddly, and Rita felt herself blush as she realized she was just standing there staring, caught up in this bizarre reverie.

"Thank you," she said again, apologetically, lowering her eyes, backing up a few steps before finally turning around and walking as quickly as she could through the double doors. She opened her bag to put the book inside and found the flyer she had crumpled up and tossed there when she'd first walked into the library.

Rita remembered what the guard at the entrance had said—admission was free—and smoothed out the glossy white paper printed in crisp black ink and looked curiously at the picture. There were three of them—two young men wearing tuxedos and a girl, around her age, she guessed, wearing an evening gown. "'Young Artists Concert Series,'" read Rita silently. "Works by Beethoven, Schubert, and Shostakovich for piano trio."

She knew Beethoven, could recognize the Fifth and Ninth symphonies; she had no idea what a piano trio was. She looked at her new watch again and saw that it was almost 5:00 P.M. Rita took a deep breath. She suddenly felt the vastness of the distance between the morning, when she'd set out, and now, as if time had stood still but simultaneously shifted forward in a blur. A lost child, a found book; she couldn't fathom how to bridge the two things, save for the fact that she was exhausted, utterly drained.

She followed the signs downstairs to the concert hall and came upon two heavy, open wooden doors flanked by two women who looked like Beatriz López, dressed in black pants and red formal jackets. "Take any open seat," said one of them, giving Rita a small program.

Rita looked around uncertainly, but this time she was better prepared for the grandness, the utter foreignness of the place. It wasn't that large—maybe three hundred people could fit here—but everything about it—the semicircle of plush leather seats, the elevated stage where the lacquered grand piano reflected the polished floors, the layered wooden panels instead of walls, the high, high ceiling with dots of lights—screamed understated importance. Rita quickly took a seat in a back corner and observed with relief that there were other people who appeared perhaps a little like her, that if one didn't look too closely, she could pass for a student. There were even other people sitting alone, she noticed, and slowly she began to loosen her strained grip on the bag clutched to her chest, leaned back on the chair, let the softness of the seat take her weight in full. She scanned the program now and acknowledged a small flutter of delight at realizing she could understand what it meant. That thanks to a long-ago music class, she actually had a vague notion of keys and tonalities, and from somewhere in the recesses of her mind she pulled out the memory that the Fifth Symphony was written in the key of C minor, the same key as the first sonata on the program, although she couldn't remember the difference between a symphony and a sonata or the other title on the program, a serenade. And then the stage door opened and the girl walked out, followed by the two young men, but Rita had eyes only for the girl, for the long scarlet dress whose fabric shimmered in rippled waves as she walked across to the piano, one hand going up to the pearl choker around her neck. She had her hair tied back in a tight bun, and her bare shoulders and arms looked white and round and alluring, almost like a painting in the soft yellow light of the stage. The girl bowed, and everyone started to applaud, but Rita didn't move; she was mesmerized by the figure on the stage, who must have been about her age, who was just feet away from her, so close that Rita could see her chest rise and fall as she sat on the piano bench and took a deep breath, close enough that Rita could see in exquisite detail the mole on her exposed right shoulder and the way her eyebrows arched upward, like wings, as her eyes looked down at the ivory keys, her fingers stroking them gently, on the surface, before attacking them with quick, surgical precision.

Close as she was, Rita had never felt further away from anyone. She had never heard music like this. The colonel had been wealthy, but his tastes were pedestrian; the music that played in that house consisted of old boleros, Son Cubano, popular trios—the kind played with two guitars and maracas—where the simple melody was enough to lull her into pleasant complacency as she mopped the floor. You could never mop the floor to this. She sat immobile and absorbed the cello's deep vibrato as the man—no, the boy—on the stage dug his bow deep into the strings, until it felt as if he were drawing that bow across the innermost core of her soul, moving like she was, in a slow procession of mournfulness, even as the piano and the violin played over it, lithely, quickly, unconcerned, until she realized that even the melody was profoundly sad, and she finally remembered the difference between a major and a minor key.

Rita closed her eyes, let the music penetrate her, felt it find its way into a part of her brain she didn't know existed, then dissolve, spreading inside her like the mercury from a broken thermometer, the droplets scattering and reaching every cell of her being until her fingers tingled.

Her body felt the change of tempo, from somber to rapid, and forced her eyelids open, and she looked at the girl once more, noticing how she propelled the music and brought it together. From her seat she could see the fine film of sweat beginning to form on the pianist's upper lip, the tiny tendrils of hair that escaped the bun at the nape of her neck. Rita marveled at how beautiful she was, this girl who made beautiful music, at how well kept she looked, as

Rita had once been. She imagined that the musician was the kind of girl who wore lace lingerie and used perfumed cream on her hands before going to sleep every night, knew with certainty that this girl would never have clandestine sex on a sacristy floor, would never bury her face against a jacket impregnated with the smell of cooking oil, would never need to wash the smell of shame from her hands with holy water.

Rita closed her eyes again. She didn't want to think now. She deserved not to think. She let the music creep into her again and sat, immobile, until the people around her got up and started to applaud and she reluctantly entered their realm again. This time the girl in red was smiling and taking a bow. She was real again, just another girl, Rita's age, but then a little girl handed her a glorious bouquet of red roses and marigolds, and the girl held the beautiful flowers against her chest and bowed again before walking off the stage, and Rita knew she wasn't like her at all; she might as well be from another planet. The audience began to file out, and Rita now noticed the couple standing close to the stage, the ones proudly receiving the steady stream of congratulations, and she recognized the similarity between mother and daughter: the same arched eyebrows and sweet smile, the same elegant bearing; the mother exuded the same air of careful tending to.

She looked so happy, thought Rita as an ache of longing began to grow where the music had been just minutes before. Longing and envy, and anger, too, because why couldn't she have any of this? She was one of the last people left inside the hall, and she watched silently from her seat as the girl's family ambled slowly by, their conversation punctuated with laughter.

"Well, she sounded inspired today, Rosi," one of the men told the mother.

"Oh, thank you! I did think she played just wonderfully," the mother replied. "And thank you so much for coming to see her," she continued, laying her hand on the man's arm.

"You know we wouldn't miss it for the world," the man answered, patting Rosi's hand with his own, his voice beginning to fade as the group left Rita behind. "She is so talented. And so beautiful. We're very proud."

Rita stayed in her seat, listening to the remnant of voices echoing off the wood panels of the room until there was nothing but silence. She slowly picked up the program and opened it again, reading carefully this time.

"Piano, Daniela Hart," it read, and Rita looked at the photo again, curiously, at the rather unremarkable planes of the face, save for the intentness of the eyes. Surely her own used to be as determined. And if so, what made the difference? she wondered. Was it simply wealth? Luck? Talent? She had no particular talents she could think of, but she was intelligent, she thought clinically; even in that lame little night school, she was the best student. All that studying, those carefully crafted essays that invariably won her honors at school—the most they'd ever elicited from her parents was a perfunctory "Good job," which could have meant that no less was expected of her, or it could have meant that it didn't matter to anyone anyway.

But perhaps if she'd had a beautiful voice or a knack for theater or painting. Maybe if she'd simply *been* more beautiful, it would have tipped the scales her way. Maybe then they would have let her stay and her mother would certainly have loved a grandson, another little boy to dote on, another Sebastián.

Sebastián. Rita wondered if they ever talked about her to him. To Sebastián her brother. To Sebastián her son. For the first time since it all began, since she first felt the flutter deep inside her stomach and knew with irrevocable certainty that no matter what happened, she was having this baby, Rita felt herself drowning in a profound self-pity she didn't know she was capable of. She despised the feeling, just as she rejected the pity in other people's eyes. She'd always been proud—haughty, even. So many people assumed she was quiet and shy, but that wasn't it at all. She simply wasn't interested in most of the things they had to say. Now she would give anything to have someone ask her for an opinion, or just the time of day, if only to hear the sound of her own voice. Rita looked again at the picture of Daniela Hart and imagined what she must be doing right now, with her family, her friends, all revolving around her, what she did, how she played, where she would go next.

But if Rita were to disappear today, right this second, no one would be the wiser. At the colonel's house, they'd probably celebrate, pack her bag and donate it to charity. Eventually, she imagined, they could claim her money, feel vindicated, pretend she hadn't happened. Her universe was reduced to her son, who would never know her, and her brother, whom she couldn't see. For all intents and purposes, she didn't exist.

The cleaning crew walked in and started to vacuum,

and Rita got up heavily. It was almost seven now, and it would take her at least two hours by bus to get back to the colonel's apartment. She walked down the steps and looked again at the portraits on the walls and felt the eyes of the roomful of stern, painted men following her progress through the long hall. Outside, the temperature had gone down, and she held her sweater closer to her, wondering if she would ever get used to the frigid humidity of this city. She took a seat at the bus shelter to wait and remembered the book, the book she had borrowed with her very own library card. She thought of Beatriz López as she'd handed Rita the card. Use it wisely, she had said, and now Rita suspected that policy probably didn't allow her to simply give someone a book without checking references first. But Beatriz López, with her perfect outfit and prim, forced smile, had looked beyond Rita's forlornness and seen something more, perhaps a trace of who she used to be, or better yet, thought Rita, of who she could be. Because she had money now, Rita reminded herself. She had money. She had her second chance, as that bank woman had said. She could start again, create a new family, on her own terms. It made all the difference.

Rita opened up the book and began to read, and for the first time since she'd been in this sad city of perpetually gray skies, the bus ride didn't seem quite that long.

# Chapter Twenty-three

The narrow two-lane road curves ahead of Asher as they drive out into the countryside, hugging the edges of the mountains in a close embrace, avoiding the deep precipices open alongside. Asher sits in the front with Fidel, while Alessandra and Inés Mendoza ride in back, the latter providing a nonstop stream of chatter.

Inés is a chubby little ball of energy with long, mahogany hair tied back in a ponytail, smooth brown skin, and a round, cherubic face that belies her sharp organizational skills. She's tracked down the church and the school in the small town where Rita Ortiz once lived. Although Father Pablo is no longer there, the school's director is. She has records of all the students who ever attended under her watch and has agreed to see them.

"This area used to be really dangerous before, you know?" Inés says in her singsong voice.

"Until Álvaro Uribe became president, you couldn't drive around. Too much guerrilla and paramilitaries. Now you see all the soldiers?" she asks, a real question this time.

"It's a little intimidating," observes Alessandra, whose liberal inclinations make her automatically leery of anything army-related. While she's grown used to military presence inside Bogotá, the three military roadblocks they've encountered so far make her nervous.

"Yeah, but support for the military and for the current government is overwhelming, isn't that right, Inés?" asks Asher.

"Oh, yes," says Inés. "Me, I was never a big fan of Uribe. But he did make things safer, I have to admit. Like, the town we're going to? No one used to go before. It was too isolated. But then they improved the infrastructure and they made this new road that cuts across many of these little towns. Now a bunch of rich people have been buying houses there, because it's really cute, you know? Like, really old and Colonial, and the square is supposed to be very authentic. It's, like, a hot destination now," she says with a laugh.

In the front seat, Asher has grown quiet. Although he won't say it, his stomach is in knots at the prospect of visiting this unknown destination that looms ever closer with each turn in the road. Certainly if Rita went to school there, if she went to church there, her family could still be there, he told Inés over the phone the night before.

"Sure," Inés replied matter-of-factly. "And it's a pretty small town. Someone *has* to know them. Maybe Rita is back there, too," she pointed out reasonably. "Wouldn't that be great?"

It would, Asher agreed, but he didn't add that the prospect of coming face-to-face with Rita, so quickly, so abruptly, now filled him with irrational terror. It had been one thing to imagine the person, to dream about the person, to build up to this moment, and quite another to realize that in a matter of hours he could actually meet her in person.

"We turn here," Inés announces as they come to a fork in the road with a small sign: El Edén. The road narrows further as they continue to wind up the road, and the cliffs give way to hilly fields, until in the distance Asher sees the white steeple of a church.

Despite the cold air coming from the open windows, he feels rivulets of sweat trickling down his chest and back under his leather jacket. His mouth fills up with saliva.

"Fidel, stop the car!" he says suddenly, but the startled Fidel keeps driving for several more yards until he finds a nook at the side of the road to pull up to, and then Asher scrambles out, running to the very edge of the cliff and bending down, hands on his knees, to take in big gulps of clear mountain air, trying to swallow the bile that is rising up his throat.

*I'm having a panic attack,* he thinks in amazement, because it's never happened before, not even under the most extreme pressure he's felt during the most crucial games. But he was in control then; now everything is up to unknown entities—other people, other places, circumstances always just beyond his control and his grasp.

Alessandra has come up behind him, and he feels her hand on his back but doesn't even have the strength to acknowledge it. Right now he just needs to stop this, to turn off the gush of trepidation that's threatening to suffocate him.

"Look at the farm below, Asher," says Alessandra softly but firmly. "Concentrate on that farm. Look at the cattle in the field. Count the cows. Count them out loud. Come on."

He obeys her, counting one, two, three, four, five heads

of cattle on a pasture as green as the golf courses of Santa Barbara, then counting again, and again, until his heart starts beating normally, the heart of a champion, his heart. Asher allows himself to sit heavily on the grass.

"What if she's awful?" he asks her under his breath, finally able to pronounce the words. "What if they're all awful? Or they don't want me?"

"What if they are?" Alessandra counters. "You are you. You already have a family, remember that. A family that loves you. That's what you have to remember and what you have to believe in. Say it now," she urges him gently, again. "Say it. 'I have a family that loves me unconditionally.' Say it out loud, Asher," Alessandra repeats.

Asher feels for the first time the grass beneath his hands, wet from the fog that kisses the ground every morning, and looks at a sky drooping with clouds that sit heavily on the mountaintops, tendrils enveloping the small houses sitting incongruously on the sides of the sloping hills. From below he hears a faint shout and looks down to see the tiny figure of a man moving the small herd that Asher had been counting just minutes before. The man prods them with a stick, and they begin a slow, leisurely track down the ravine, until they turn and disappear from sight. He has a family, Asher thinks, even though they've never felt so very far before.

"I have a family that loves me. Unconditionally," he says softly, but out loud.

Alessandra moves her hand up his back until it caresses his hair.

"Why is it that I'm always reciting mantras when I'm with you?"

"Because you have me, too," she says gently.

"I do," Asher agrees, and covers her hand with his. "Give me a minute," he says after a pause.

Alessandra nods silently and walks back to the car.

"The accident," she lies smoothly to Fidel and Inés. "Because of the drilling in his skull, the altitude sometimes makes him sick. But it's getting better."

*     *     *

Fanny Rodríguez's plump figure has grown to rotund, and her hair, which she keeps knotted tightly in a bun, is graying. But she still runs her growing school with the same iron fist that characterized her twenty-one years ago, when this was still a tiny enclave whose residents rarely left for the outside world. Now the pictures of her accomplished students, those who have gone on to the army or to jobs in big cities or to college, line an entire wall of her small office.

She's had many visitors, especially in the last five years, since the road opened and Edén suddenly found its place on the map. That was when the rich people started vacationing here, bringing their employees and their money and their needs, which translated to an increase in students, an increase in graduates, and, finally, more success stories than she can talk about.

But she's never had visitors from the United States, she thinks as she appraises the trio seated across from her desk. Never.

She's already made up her mind about Inés; she's seen hundreds of other Colombian girls like her. Girls of modest backgrounds who are smart and ambitious in their resolve and sense of entitlement to an education and a career. Cocky. But then again so was she.

The little gringuita is a wisp of a thing, with pale, lightly freckled skin, but Mrs. Rodríguez can sense the steel that lies inside the outward fragility. She immediately warms up to the frank curiosity with which the girl is taking in every detail in her office, from the photographs to her diploma and accreditation, which hang proudly behind her desk alongside the Colombian coat of arms.

And then there's the young man with the strange yellow eyes. Him, she can't make up her mind about. He greeted her with a firm handshake, looking her straight in the eye and smiling a dazzling smile that she's certain has charmed many before her. There is an easy confidence about him, a strong sense of presence that takes over the room, but also a certain detachment, as if he's holding something back.

"How can I help you?" she asks, folding her hands on the desk.

"We are so thankful for your time, Mrs. Rodríguez," says Inés, and even Asher's untrained ear can detect the shift in tone when she switches to Spanish, all gangly expressions now absorbed into a cushion of carefully enunciated respect. "As I mentioned, this is Mr. Asher Sebastian Stone. He is here from the United States," she says, gesturing toward Asher. "I'm helping them with the language. Miss Alessandra speaks some Spanish, but it is essential that they understand everything we discuss. You see, Mr. Stone is looking for his birth parents. He was put up for adoption here—in Colombia—over twenty years ago. We believe that his mother might have been a student at your school."

There is a long pause as Mrs. Rodríguez digests this information.

"Yes?" she finally says, making the one-syllable word sound interminably long.

"Her name is Rita Ortiz," continues Inés as she hands Mrs. Rodríguez the picture of Rita in her red sweater. "This was twenty-one years ago, Mrs. Rodríguez. It's a very long time. I don't know if you have any records that you can look up."

There is an even longer pause as Fanny Rodríguez looks intently at the picture of the young girl she holds in her hand, her face an inscrutable mask.

"Mrs. Rodríguez," prods Inés, a touch of concern in her voice.

"I don't need to search any records," says Mrs. Rodríguez, at last looking up. Her face is expressionless. "I remember Rita Ortiz. What did you say your name was again?" she asks, leaning forward slightly and looking at Asher with renewed curiosity.

"Asher Sebastian Stone," replies Asher in halting Spanish. "Stone is the name of my adoptive parents."

"He was adopted by a couple in the United States," explains Inés, attempting to clarify.

"Sebastián?" repeats Mrs. Rodríguez, pronouncing the name with the accent on the *a*, as Sister Teresa had.

"Yes. Yes," says Asher haltingly. "Sebastián."

"Sebastián. Like Rita's brother," says Mrs. Rodríguez flatly, but she's thinking that this is Rita's son. And he is like his mother, guarded. *How very curious*, she thinks.

"Exactly," says Asher, oblivious, breaking out in that

winning smile. The recognition seems to obliterate all Spanish from his vocabulary. "Inés, ask her if Rita is here in town. Is her family here?"

Mrs. Rodríguez shakes her head when Inés translates, and she is surprised to see a touch a relief on Asher's face along with the disappointment.

"No, I haven't seen Rita for more than twenty years. Since she was pregnant," she says tellingly, looking at Asher with new eyes, trying to see a piece of Rita in him. "The family moved about five years ago," she adds with certainty. "They had a little store, but they sold it when the price of real estate went up. I don't know where they went."

Asher looks a little bewildered as Inés translates for his benefit, as if he's been waiting for something more.

"But she remembers Rita," he finally says. "It means she made an impact on her, right?"

"This is a very small town and a very small school. I remember all my students," explains Mrs. Rodríguez. "I didn't know that Rita had her baby, although at the time I imagined something like that might have happened."

"You knew about her pregnancy?" asks Inés excitedly.

"I knew she was pregnant. But when I confronted her, she denied it," says Mrs. Rodríguez slowly, her brow furrowing in an effort to bring back the past. "I'm sorry, the details are very hazy. I haven't had a reason to think about Rita Ortiz in years. I don't even know if she's still alive."

Mrs. Rodríguez stops when she notices the shift in Asher, who clearly understands enough Spanish to comprehend what she has just said; this possibility, she sees, hadn't occurred to him.

"I'm so sorry," she tells him, wishing she could take back the words. "Please, tell him I apologize," she reiterates to Inés, who quickly translates. Asher nods dumbly, but his yellow eyes are very bright.

"It's just that I never heard from Rita again," Mrs. Rodríguez continues. "She finished her school year. I'm certain she did. But she didn't return the following term to graduate. I know I asked little Sebastián, and he gave me some kind of explanation. I think he said she had gone to live with an aunt in the capital or some other relative, something like that." Mrs. Rodríguez shrugs her shoulders helplessly. "No one spoke of her again."

"How about my father?" asks Asher in halting Spanish. "Do you know anything about him?"

Mrs. Rodríguez laughs, a short, humorless laugh. "No, my dear. Your mother said very little. Ever. She kept secrets, that one."

Inés frowns as she attempts to translate words that clearly aren't meant to be flattering.

"I don't understand," Asher says in English, speaking to Inés to ensure she translates precisely. "*She* was secretive, or she kept her *pregnancy* a secret?"

"Both," Mrs. Rodríguez says with no hesitation. "I knew she was pregnant, because I just knew. Women notice these things. She never admitted it, but then again with Rita you never knew. She was a quiet kind of girl. I don't recall a boyfriend, and I don't know who the father was," she says after an uncomfortable pause. "I'm very sorry," she tells Asher, and there's something akin to pity in her eyes.

"Mrs. Rodríguez," intercedes Alessandra in her choppy

but functional Spanish. "What else can you tell us about Rita? We know very little about her. Anything you can tell us would be appreciated."

Mrs. Rodríguez looks again at the picture in her hand, at the melancholy face that used to be so proud and aloof. And she begins to speak, slowly, clearly, like the schoolteacher she once was.

"She says your mother was extremely smart," Inés translates. "That she always acted like she knew less than she did but that always, at the end of the year, she won all the awards. That she loved to read. That she was beautiful. Very, very close to her brother, Sebastián. She walked him to and from school every day."

"Sebastián." Mrs. Rodríguez sighs. "They were always so proud of Sebastián. After Rita left, his mother would walk him to school, even when he got older. But it was different back then. Guerrillas and paramilitaries came through this town, and we had to be so careful all the time. And then on top of that, for Rita to have gotten pregnant, I can't even imagine. She begged me not to say anything to her parents, and I didn't. And then she said it had been a mistake, that she wasn't with child after all. And of course . . . well, here you are." Mrs. Rodríguez gestures toward Asher.

"There is one thing," she adds, remembering. "Her best friend. Her best friend was Jazmin Sodi. They were inseparable."

"Jazmin Sodi? The one who makes the bags?" asks Inés excitedly.

"Yes. The very one. She's one of my success stories."

Mrs. Rodríguez smiles, pointing at the wall. "I don't know. Maybe Jazmin has kept in touch with Rita."

"Have you kept in touch with Jazmin, Mrs. Rodríguez?" asks Alessandra.

"Oh, yes," says Mrs. Rodríguez, her voice warming up. "She comes to visit once in a while. She's always doing something to help the school."

"Do you know how we can reach her?" presses Alessandra.

"Oh, yes, yes, of course," says Mrs. Rodríguez, taking out a little leather phone book from which she neatly copies down two numbers on a small slip of paper. "Here is her cell phone and her office. Tell her I gave you the numbers. Tell her you're Rita's son," she says, looking straight at him.

"And, Sebastián?" she says, holding out the paper to him.

"Yes, Mrs. Rodríguez," he answers automatically, respectfully.

"You are doing well? You have good parents?"

"I do. I do," he says, and in his voice she hears the conviction, and in his eyes she sees what she now realizes Rita's had lacked: trust.

"I'm glad to hear that," says Mrs. Rodríguez sincerely. "I'm sure you did better than your mother in that regard."

She stays behind her desk long after they've gone, looking through her window at the children as they file out for lunch, the girls wearing their blue pleated skirts and neat white blouses. She clearly remembers Rita Ortiz, little more than a child back then, the same age as some of the children on the patio, her eyes swollen from crying and her voice helpless as she asked, "What am I going to do, Mrs. Rodríguez?"

*       *       *

The cobblestone square is big for a town this small, and its expansion lends additional dignity to the modest, white-washed church that stands proudly on the other side. Asher walks the length of the square slowly, a steaming Styro-foam cup of coffee in one hand. He knows he shouldn't be drinking coffee when he's ready to jump out of his skin, but he can't help himself, he thinks, running his other hand nervously through his hair.

All he can do is hope this priest has something else to give him, more than just another scrap of useless informa-tion. He's fed up with these vague memories, with someone else's thoughts. He wants results. He wants her.

"Why do we always end up in a church?" Alessandra sighs as she catches up with him at the top of the stairs, the altitude making her gasp for breath.

"Good afternoon," says a soft voice with a British accent.

Asher looks up to see a kid with a priest's collar stand-ing next to the church entrance.

"You're the priest?" Asher asks incredulously. The man looks younger than he does.

"Yes." The kid smiles, extending his hand. "Father Robert Mesa. And you must be Sebastián and Inés?"

"No, I'm Alessandra. I'm—"

"She's my girlfriend, Father," says Asher unceremoni-ously, placing his hand more proprietarily than protectively around Alessandra's shoulders. "Inés is…" He looks around him and spies Inés hurriedly making her way across the square. "She's coming. But I guess we won't need a translator this time."

"I spent two years in Oxford," says Father Mesa, his proper British accent incongruous against his childish visage. "Come, let's wait for Inés inside, shall we?"

Father Mesa leads them to a small room that is surprisingly cozy, with tall wooden beams and book-lined walls as the backdrop to the Vivaldi that plays on the stereo.

"This was Father Pablo's sacristy," explains Father Mesa. "A lot of it burned down in a fire, but between the diocese and the people here, they did a good job of rebuilding it and apparently making it look as close as possible to what it was before. I'm the third priest that's been here since his death."

"So do you know the Ortiz family at all?" asks Asher hesitantly, just as Inés knocks on the door and lets herself in.

"I'm sorry, guys," she says, her breathing as labored as Alessandra's a minute before. "I got distracted looking around. Father Mesa, it's nice to meet you," she says, and plops herself heavily into a chair.

Father Mesa looks expectantly at them. "Well," he declares at last. "In answer to your question, no. As I mentioned to Inés over the phone, I don't know Ms. Ortiz or her family. I did ask around this morning, however. Apparently they moved several years ago, before my time."

"We were hoping you had some kind of records on Rita or the family," says Inés. "Maybe a current address."

Father Mesa shakes his head slightly. "No, we have nothing. All the old records—birth certificates, marriage certificates, First Communions—everything was lost in the fire. Don't you have Ms. Ortiz's ID number?" he asks Asher. "That would make everything so much easier."

"I don't have her ID," says Asher, impatience tingeing his voice. Inés has already asked about the ID, and the mere thought irritates him now. If he had an ID, would he even be here now? "What happened to Father Pablo anyway?" he asks, changing the subject.

"He was murdered," says Father Mesa flatly.

"Murdered?" exclaims Alessandra. "How?"

"He was executed by paramilitaries," says Father Mesa. "They took over the town and decided Father Pablo was a guerrilla sympathizer. Apparently he'd allowed the guerrillas to use his church."

Asher sits up, the reality of Edén, the deceit of its beauty, hitting him.

"Back then," adds Father Mesa softly, "it was like the Wild West. The paramilitaries could take over, or the guerrillas. Father Pablo's job was to keep the faith and to keep the peace, at any cost. He couldn't take sides. He was a holy man. These..." Father Mesa clasps his hands and looks down at his desk for a moment. "These animals," he continues. "They came in here, to his sacristy. They marched him at gunpoint to the square. They shot him there, in front of the entire town. They said it was a lesson for those who played nice with the guerrillas. Then they set fire to the office and left. Thank God they didn't burn down the entire church."

Asher reflexively brings his hands up to his head, to his scars, feeling the comfort of his skull under his fingers. He's alive; he's fared so much better than Father Pablo. He now remembers Sister Teresa's words: The miracle was Father Pablo taking his mother precisely to La Casa en el Campo and Rita giving birth precisely when his parents were up to get the next available baby.

"Father Pablo sent my mother to the orphanage," Asher says thoughtfully. "What if he hadn't?"

"Well, you're in the right place to thank him," says Father Mesa. "I do have something for you," he adds, reaching for a notepad. "The woman who cleans the church, she knew the Ortizes. They lived very close by, just a couple of blocks away." He hands Asher a slip of paper. "Here is the address."

*       *       *

The woman who opens the door to the house with the bright blue windows has frosted highlights in her hair and wears a cashmere sweater over designer jeans. She listens, an expression of dry amusement on her face, as Inés attempts to condense Asher's story and his needs into some concise request.

"I know it's a huge imposition, but could we see the house?" pleads Alessandra in her pidgin Spanish. "Just very quickly. My friend—my boyfriend," she amends with a smile, "he's looking for his..." Alessandra struggles to find the right word in Spanish.

"Raíces," says the woman finally. "His roots," she adds in perfect English. "All right," she adds. "Let me show you around. Quickly."

Asher doesn't know what he expected, but it wasn't this luxurious home of polished mahogany floors, white couches, and pre-Columbian artifacts hanging on the walls.

"We totally remodeled," explains the woman with a touch of condescension, seeing the surprise on his face. "Of course these aren't the original floors or the layout. There was a store downstairs, and we gutted that and put in the common areas. And there was a full home upstairs, but the rooms were tiny and there was very little light. It was all about opening things up."

Asher climbs the stairs with some trepidation, feeling like a voyeur about to observe something intimate, not meant for him but still irresistible.

"Can I see the bedrooms?" he asks hesitantly.

The woman opens a door at the end of the hallway that leads to a very small, but cozy room. She immediately shuts it again and moves to the next one—the master bedroom—which she again opens just wide enough for him to peek inside, then shuts right away. The third bedroom faces the street in front of the house, and when the woman opens the door, light and sky stream in through the open wooden windows.

"This looks like the kind of bedroom a girl would sleep in, don't you think?" Asher asks, pushing slightly forward.

The woman shrugs. "It's the guest room now," she says, and firmly shuts the door behind them.

\*　　　\*　　　\*

Much later, when they get back to the apartment, they look for the nearest Jazzy store, and once they see it, just blocks away, they wonder how in the world they could have missed it in the first place. The centerpiece of the display window consists of purses and belts, leather adorned with layers of brightly colored woven fabrics—patterns that on the surface look like so many that can be found on the street corners where handicrafts are sold, except that upon closer examination these are small treasures, the designs surprisingly intricate, and in every one of them a whimsical line in a contrasting color that snakes in and out of the basic design, not one exactly the same as any other.

"Like yours," says Alessandra in wonderment, and indeed, there are even bracelets in the window, only they're not mere trinkets to tie around a wrist anymore, but complex little structures in silver and wood and bronze and leather, the woven design binding them like a flag. They enter the store silently and walk around as if in a trance. The specter of Rita, all but obliterated in Edén, suddenly reappears, for here is a real, tangible link to this person who has teased Asher's existence, this phantom who leaves impressions behind but who refuses to reveal herself.

Alessandra runs her hand over the bags, each one a unique design, each one labeled with a name: The Jazzy, The Silvia, The Boris for men. On one of the back walls, she finds it: The Rita.

"Oh, Ash," says Alessandra, and turns around, bag in hand, her fingers touching his as he reaches for it, the bag with Rita's name.

Asher gingerly picks up the bag, a dainty little square clutch adorned with silk weaves, clearly the dressiest bag in the store. He runs his hands over the weaving carefully, feeling the luxury of the texture. Everything about the bag is exquisite, perfectly finished, down to the silk lining that hugs the inside of the purse and the designer label, sewn by hand in flowing calligraphy in the side pocket.

"Do you like it?" he asks Alessandra.

"It's like a work of art," she says in awe. "It's perfect."

# Chapter Twenty-four

Rita wouldn't be able to pinpoint when the thought began to take shape. What she did know was that with each passing day it became easier to see, as if she were traveling a winding road that begins to curve into its destination and finally affords a view of what lies just beyond. The day after her failed effort to reclaim the child that was long gone, she moved into the Cruzes' apartment, a mere six stories below the bedroom of the man who, with the stroke of a pen, had placed her on the verge of changing her life.

In an unspoken agreement, she didn't mention her imminent good fortune to anyone, and neither did Edward García nor the colonel's family. The whole situation was profoundly embarrassing for an attorney who prided himself on being the master of crafty arrangements that skirted the law and were designed for maximum profitability. To have such plans foiled by an adolescent maid was infuriating; if word ever got out, it would seriously compromise his practice.

Rita worked hard, with the single-mindedness of someone who had a plan. Whereas a month ago she simply wanted to get through school, it was now clear to her that she could go way beyond that, as she had originally dreamed. She and Jazmin had always planned to leave their town as soon as they turned eighteen and were old enough to be on their own. She would study business or engineering; Jazmin would do design. It was a winning combo, they used to joke: Rita's head for numbers and Jazmin's imagination.

Rita wished she had Jazmin's imagination now, to help her fly, to help her laugh. For the first time in the entire year, she began to socialize in class, to speak with teachers. And increasingly she turned to books. On Sundays she would take the bus to the library, to the room supervised by Beatriz López. It was she who Rita turned to for counsel after her night-school teachers suggested she consider trade school as an alternative to college. Beatriz, thought Rita, was the kind of person who would push for the harder but more rewarding alternative, whatever it might be.

"College." Beatriz said the word thoughtfully as she gazed appraisingly at Rita. The girl no longer looked like a nonentity ready to disappear among the bookshelves. Now Rita stood taller, made eye contact, walked with a purpose; she had a presence about her. She was still understated, but the effect was one of intelligent reserve and even a bit of haughtiness, rather than the slow, subdued girl she had appeared to be before.

It made Beatriz curious despite herself, for this job was something she did out of her sheer joy for books, and she didn't tend to dwell on library patrons. But this Rita intrigued her. One did not simply acquire assurance in a matter of weeks. It was as if she had been suppressing the real her before. And now college?

"College," she repeated. "Well, my first question would be, what do you want to study?"

Rita had mulled it over so many times, alone in her little maid's room at night. The career choices that would surely make her money—like law—versus the ones she loved, the ones that dealt with numbers and planning and precision.

"I think I want to study engineering," she said, her eyes lighting up. "Civil engineering. Or maybe urban planning."

"Urban planning?" parroted Beatriz, surprised. "Now, how in the world do you even know what urban planning is?"

"I...I've been reading, Mrs. Beatriz," said Rita, looking down at her shoes. Beatriz noted the defensive reaction and was immediately sorry she had blurted out something so condescending.

"I'm sorry, Rita. Of course you can be interested in urban planning."

"Don't worry," said Rita unexpectedly. "I understand that you would be...skeptical. I'm just a maid. But I'm not going to be that for long. I'm going to be something different."

"Of course you are, dear," said Beatriz. And although it sounded like a platitude, as she told her husband later that night, it wasn't. "I meant it. She just has this look. I don't know how, I don't know who will help her, but I do believe she'll somehow go beyond her current condition," she told him.

It was Beatriz—unaware that Rita had means—who walked her through college possibilities—public schools and private schools and scholarships for people like her, people with no parents or family or financial resources at their disposal.

But it was Rita who never forgot that conversation. As long as she was Rita Ortiz, she would forever be a maid, a single mother who'd had to give her child up for adoption, the lover of a dangerous man, a failed daughter, a sister who had left her brother behind. People like Rita Ortiz never prospered. They lived up to their expectations and to the destiny someone else decided for them.

One afternoon, on a whim, she looked up the meanings and origins of different names, names she'd always liked, names like Cristina and Victoria and Carolina. Then she looked up Rita, St. Rita. Married at age twelve to an abusive husband, now the patron saint of impossible cases.

"I'm cursed," Rita said aloud to herself. "How can I ever do better if I'm named after someone who adopted suffering as her motto?" The patron saint of impossible cases, she thought incredulously. Then again, she reasoned, getting such an unexpected lump of money was an impossibility, wasn't it? Rita undid the bun at the back of her neck and began to wrap and unwrap her hair around her wrist, as she used to do when she was deep in thought. She'd already gotten a new ID, and that process had been ridiculously easy. What if she changed her name? Then she could be someone else completely. She could really, really, start again.

She opened up the book of saint names again. Surely there was one for her. Agnes, the patron saint of engaged couples. Rita had to smile at that one. Hardly, she thought.

Margarita, patron saint of pregnancy. Worse. Helena, patron saint of difficult marriages. For Christ's sake, she thought, was every single name linked to marriage and children? Joanna, she continued down the list. From Joan of Arc. The patron saint of soldiers and fighters. Joanna, thought Rita. Joanna.

"My name is Joanna," she said out loud, softly. "This is Joanna," she said pleasantly. "Hi, this is Joanna, can I help you? My name is Joanna," she repeated, furtively looking around to make sure no one nearby was listening. Joanna Ortiz. But then she remembered what Beatriz had said about last names: People always searched by last names first. She looked at Beatriz López, attending visitors way on the other side of the room. How collected she appeared. How elegant. How intelligent. Beatriz López, who had helped her simply because she could.

Joanna López, thought Rita. There were so many Lópezes that even if the "Joanna" stood out, the "López" would blend in, one of millions. "Joanna López," she said again out loud. "My name is Joanna López."

She liked that name.

Two months later Rita Ortiz cashed in a sixty-thousand-dollar mature certificate of deposit. She went to a notary public and officially changed her name, a devastatingly simple process that, she was told, could be done only once in this country.

"This name you choose," said the official behind the counter, "will be the one you have to live with the rest of your life. You can't even change your surname."

"Don't worry," said Joanna López as she carefully placed her fingerprints next to her signature on the official notarized document. "I have nothing more to change."

She reinvested most of the money in an account in a different bank, her first official transaction under Joanna López's name. In December, on Christmas Day, she gave Mrs. Cruz her two-week notice.

In January, Joanna López began her first day of class as a civil-engineering student at a private Jesuit college. Although she had savings to her name, her lack of family and home allowed her to qualify for a generous scholarship designed for outstanding students in need. She lived in a women's dormitory a few blocks from school and worked part-time as an office assistant at a construction firm downtown. One Monday afternoon, on Beatriz López's day off, she left a note for her at the library.

*"Dear Mrs. López,"* she wrote, in her impeccable calligraphy.

> *I've decided to go to school out of town. They offered me a full scholarship, which I couldn't refuse. Thank you so much for helping me make my dreams come true. You have been an inspiration to me.*
>
> *Most affectionately,*
> *Rita Ortiz*

Her one regret was never being able to set foot inside the library again.

# Chapter Twenty-five

Jazmin Sodi sits quietly at the bar in Mario's sipping a Bloody Mary as she waits for Asher and Alessandra. She chose the restaurant, which is bright and airy and has an enticing, flower-filled patio that's perfect for sunny days like this one.

Jazmin, who's scheduled meetings all morning to take her mind off this rendezvous, arrived in Bogotá the night before; she alternates her business weeks in the capital with residence in an artists' colony on the outskirts of Medellín, a city whose temperate climate she adores. After living in frigid weather her entire childhood, she's vowed to spend the rest of her days in a place where one doesn't perpetually need a sweater. Immersed in her work in an area where the Internet connection is spotty, she didn't receive the message from Inés for a full day, and then she took another day to think about it and another to get the nerve to call back and set up an appointment here, at a favorite and familiar lunch spot.

"You claimed there's a note," she said tersely over the phone. "Tell him to bring the note, please. And the bracelet."

When Asher and Alessandra walk in, they go straight to the terrace and look around, unaware that Jazmin is watching them from the bar. She would never simply meet two complete strangers without being certain of what she was doing. But she also wanted to see him first, be mentally prepared, before sitting face-to-face. She's already checked out his story and called the orphanage. Spoken with the woman with the Italian name. Jazmin makes a mental note to send her a bag as a gift—she was extremely helpful—and maybe some trinket, perhaps makeup bags, for the pregnant girls.

Jazmin sips her Bloody Mary and tries to appear nonchalant behind her gigantic sunglasses, even though she's ready to jump out of her skin. As soon as they walk in, she knows it's him. Perhaps because he looks so thoroughly Colombian, and yet is standing next to a very slim, very fair girl in worn jeans who is obviously not. But it's more than that, she thinks, deliberately shoving aside her romantic notions to think objectively. He doesn't look like Rita, and yet he is Rita's. She knows. She's certain. It's something in his stance, in his quiet watchfulness, as if processing things mentally before making an assessment. She eyes him as they move to the terrace. And there is something about his walk, she thinks. Something about that easy, quiet walk that she can't quite place.

"Charge it to my lunch bill," she tells the bartender, leaving behind a tip, and walks outside. She wanted to see him in a sunlit place, because, she thinks, it's so much harder to keep secrets in the unforgiving glare of daylight. By the time Asher looks up, she's already standing beside their table.

"Sebastián," she says briskly, and sits down. "And Alessandra, right?"

As Alessandra says hello, Asher studies the woman who was his mother's best friend. She is very small and very energetic, like a little pixie, with very, very short, spiky black hair that draws attention to a bold face with high cheekbones and wide lips. She is rosy and has a light sprinkling of freckles, the same coloring of many of the peasants they saw in Edén and the surrounding mountains. Jazmin wears jeans with a white T-shirt and a black leather jacket, around which she's wrapped an array of colorful scarves that both clash and complement her many layers of bracelets and a wild assortment of silver rings. If she were to go to UC Santa Barbara, thinks Asher, she would pass for a student. He can't possibly picture her as being anyone's mother, can't picture himself with a mother that looks this young.

"Can I see the letter and the bracelet?" she says without preamble.

Alessandra reaches inside her purse and places an envelope on Jazmin's plate. Jazmin keeps her sunglasses on, shielding her reaction as she slowly takes out the contents and runs her fingers over the bracelet.

*Damn, am I good*, she thinks, admiring the fuchsia weave, the work of a beginner, but still the skill was clearly there. All these years, and it hasn't come apart. She remembers the day perfectly, almost feeling Rita's small wrist between her hands as she tied the knot—the knot that should never come undone. She can still feel how warm Rita felt under her fingers and how excited she was that morning, brimming with something Jazmin couldn't quite figure out. She wanted to go to church, she'd said, and she'd taken off with the excitement of someone who's going to a party. Jazmin unfolds the letter slowly, but by now she knows she'll find Rita's neat little writing on the paper, perfect, not a scratch, not an eraser mark, impeccable.

"'Dear Sebastián,'" Jazmin reads out loud softly.

"'I hope you can keep the name I gave you. It's the name of my brother, whom I love very much, as much as I love you....'" Jazmin's voice trails off as she continues to read silently to herself, even though her lips still move. *"I can't take care of you. I'm all alone, and you need a family that can give you time and care and lots of love, with a mommy and a daddy, so you'll grow up to be the best possible child you can be. The red bracelet is for good luck. It's very beautiful, isn't it? It was made by a very good friend of mine who makes beautiful things."*

Jazmin looks at the words on the paper for a very long time, and she can almost smell the scent of fresh mint and burning wood and the cornucopia of fruits and cooking oil that always filled the market air. In her mind she can see Rita with her big old basket, how pretty she had looked that day with her hair in its long braid. She remembers she insisted on paying, to "contribute to the fund," their little private joke, their private plan for something bigger than what they had. Jazmin can still see her, waving as she walked up the steps to the church. Her friend.

She looks at Asher now, at his high cheekbones and full mouth, and now she knows who he reminds her of—he was always watching them with those weird yellow eyes. Jazmin marvels at how she could have been so incredibly blind then. And she wonders, as she's wondered endlessly for twenty-one years, how her best friend could have hidden so many things from her.

Jazmin shakes her head, and when she finally speaks, her voice is choked with tears. "I would have done anything for her," she says, her face a grimace of pain. "Anything. She never said a word."

Asher and Alessandra sit in silence, their hands clasped underneath the table, and Asher looks in wonderment at the woman sitting across from him in this busy restaurant with white tablecloths and bright sunflower arrangements on every table. They were friends, he thinks. They grew up together, they walked together, they studied together. If he were to touch Jazmin Sodi's hand, he might still find a trace of his mother, a tiny reminder embedded in this woman's skin, a speck of Rita for him to absorb, so close, so close, but still a lifetime away.

"Darling!" Jazmin motions to the waiter. "Get me another Bloody Mary, will you?" She looks at Alessandra and Asher, but they both shake their heads. Jazmin shrugs, then finally looks squarely at Asher.

"So you're the reason she left," she states, her composure somewhat restored, her gaze intent on his face. "They said she'd gone to visit an aunt, and then her parents simply stopped speaking about her. Almost as if she had died."

"I'm sorry to ask something so stupid," says Alessandra. "But didn't you notice she was pregnant? Isn't that something that's kind of hard to miss?"

Jazmin frowns but then cocks her head to one side. It's awfully tough to read her with those big Audrey Hepburn glasses, thinks Asher.

"You're right," she concedes. "It's hard to miss, but I can't say she looked pregnant. She got heavier, and she threw up all the time, which in retrospect was a pretty big clue." She laughs with a trace of self-deprecation. "But you have to understand, Rita Ortiz was perfect," she adds, leaning into the table. "She was the prettiest, the smartest, the best behaved. Oh, my God, that girl—she ironed her jeans! She wore little ribbons in her hair that matched every blouse. She had one boyfriend, and one time her father caught them making out. After that he watched her like a hawk. She wasn't even allowed to the school dances. It was just inconceivable that she could get pregnant unless it was from immaculate conception."

"Seriously, all this time you didn't know she had a baby?" Asher insists.

Jazmin shakes her head helplessly. "I don't know what I thought. I kept waiting for her to come back and give me an explanation. We did everything together, like sisters," she says wistfully. "I was an only child, and my parents were very, very, very poor. Rita and I, we had plans. She was my rock, my support. And I was hers. The only reason we didn't spend more time with each other was that she had to take care of Sebastián and her father wouldn't let anyone go to the house with her. And still, we spoke every day. We saw each other every day. It was very hurtful to be abandoned by her and, worse still, to know that something had gone wrong. I..." Jazmin shakes her head and her voice trails off. "It took me a very long time to accept it. I suppose I never did.

"It's funny," she adds, before Asher can say anything.

"You look nothing like her. Just the nose. But everything else—God, even the way you walk—you look like him."

"Like who?" asks Asher automatically.

"Like your father, of course."

"You knew my father?" he asks, his heart quickening. "Who was he? Who is he?"

"He was—" Jazmin stops abruptly. "Wait," she says. "Why do you know who your mother is and not your father?"

"She didn't say anything about him," says Asher, suddenly very self-conscious. "Not in the letter. Well, you saw it. Not in the birth certificate. There's no mention of him at all, except the part about the bracelet. That's it."

He pauses. There's something in Jazmin's expression, even with the sunglasses, that makes him hesitate. He remembers Carla Bernotti and her son and the truths he uncovered.

Jazmin Sodi taps a finger against her Bloody Mary glass, a small finger with a huge ring and the nail and cuticle bitten ragged. She lifts her sunglasses up onto her head, revealing slanted, light brown eyes. Indian eyes that look at him speculatively and frankly.

"Your mother bought a bracelet for him. Paid for it with her own money, even though I insisted that she not," she says pensively. "Rita was always so proper. So by the book. But then she would do something totally irrational.

"I don't know this for a fact," she continued with a small sigh. "But if it is your father—and by your looks I would guess so—they called him El Gato, 'The Cat.' We weren't supposed to know their real names because they were guerrillas. They took over our town the year before Rita went away. They stayed for several months. He…" Jazmin frowns, trying to piece together her memories as best she can because she hasn't thought about any of this in so long.

"He was crazy over her," she says. "He followed her everywhere. Everywhere. Every time we went anywhere, he was watching. She thought he was so handsome." She smiles softly. "And he was. Just like you. My God…it's just uncanny how alike you look."

Jazmin's words sound surreal to Asher, almost as if he were listening to a lecture about someone else, about other people with fantastic lives that have nothing to do with his. He's awed at her nonchalance, at the matter-of-fact tone with which she tosses the words—*they called him El Gato…they were guerrillas*—everything said with polite understatement, almost as if she were mentioning that he was an attorney or an accountant or a doctor. Just another profession, not one worthy of horror or reproach or even surprise.

"He was a guerrilla?" Asher finally ventures uselessly, his voice tinged with regret, because he hadn't expected this. He hadn't expected anything, really, but certainly not this. "What was he like?" he presses before she can answer, because he already knows the answer. "I mean, as a person. What was he like?"

"I don't know," says Jazmin, shaking her head. "We weren't allowed to talk to them. They were the guerrillas. It was totally taboo. And Rita? No way. Her father would have killed her if he ever saw her remotely close to one of those guys. I can't imagine," she adds, perplexed, looking at him frankly, her voice trailing off when she sees his expression, a mix of pain and awe and profound disappointment.

"Listen, I...I don't want to lie to you. Rita was a good judge of character," Jazmin assures him. "If she had a relationship with him, he had to have redeeming qualities. But those were violent days," she says, shaking her head, looking from Asher to Alessandra for support. "Sometimes our boys would disappear. Our priest, he was executed by the paramilitaries. We all lived scared of people like Gato. We were scared of anything that had to do with the guerrillas. I have no way of knowing how he got where he got. People join the guerrillas for different reasons. Many are forced into it. But it most certainly couldn't have been a normal life. He was a fighter. Christ, it's just crazy how much you look like him," she says again. "Your eyes are just like his."

Jazmin waves her hand in front of her face, as if trying to dispel the memory. "Listen," she says, looking down into her drink. "He was very young. We all were," she adds sadly. "Rita thought she knew something about men, but she didn't at all. She was very young for a sixteen-year-old.

"Our birthdays were only a week part," says Jazmin, twirling her celery stick. "I was January eighth, 1973. She was January fifteenth. We pretended we were sisters all the time. Same age, same sign. We thought it was fate," she adds with a little smile.

No one speaks for a moment. The menus haven't even been looked at, and Asher senses that it will be impossible to actually have lunch. He can't imagine being able to chew on anything.

"How about Sebastián?" he asks, the thought just popping into his head. "What happened to him?"

"Oh, that poor little boy," says Jazmin, and her eyes well up with tears again. "He was eleven, you know? He was little, little. He was a terror," she says with a laugh. "Always getting into trouble. The opposite of Rita! But he adored her. She'd take him to his soccer games. She was the one who took him everywhere."

"Sebastián played soccer?" asks Alessandra.

"Yes. Well, all children did," says Jazmin. "But Sebastián was exceptionally good, as I recall. He loved to play. And Rita, of course, thought it was the silliest game. Rita was an intellectual, really. She was most definitely born in the wrong place," says Jazmin shrugging. "But we'd go together, gossip while the kids played. He was devastated after she left. Didn't speak for days. That's how I realized it wasn't that Rita had simply left but that something had to have gone horribly wrong. No one wanted to say anything. Not even Sebastián."

"They told us the family had moved," says Alessandra gently. "Is that true?"

"That's what I heard," says Jazmin. "I left as soon as I finished school, and I lost touch. Rita's parents never talked to me again. I guess they thought I was in cahoots with their daughter or something." Jazmin Sodi shakes her head.

"How old are you?" she asks Asher suddenly.

"Twenty-one. Almost twenty-two," he says.

"It's the age where we really question our place in life, isn't it?" she asks, clearly not expecting an answer. "You came here with your girlfriend." She nods toward Alessandra. "Why not your parents?"

"It's more fun to share a room with Alessandra," he says with a smile, but Jazmin looks back at him stone-faced, dismissing—or perhaps not getting—his attempt at humor. Asher raises his eyebrows and nudges Alessandra under the table. "My parents are . . . my parents," he says levelly. "I didn't feel it was fair to put them through something like this. After all, it really is my search, not theirs. They already found me."

"They're good parents? Truly? You can talk to them?" asks Jazmin, plainly curious.

"Always," says Asher, and his eyes soften at the thought. "They expect a lot from me, especially my mother. But they're very . . ." He looks up, searching for the right word. "They're very unconditional," he says finally.

"That's ironic," says Jazmin with a dry, mirthless laugh. "Rita's parents—I suppose that would make them your grandparents—they were quite the opposite. Very 'conditional,' very judgmental. Very unloving," she says, carefully enunciating the word and looking away, at something inside herself. "I was dirt poor. My parents were peasants, and they had nothing. But they cherished me. There was affection and love in my home. I suppose Rita's parents loved her, but they never displayed it, and it's a testament to her—to the kind of person she was—that she could still rise to the occasion and care for others.

"Well," she says looking up. "I don't know if I've been able to help you in any way."

"Do you have any suggestions on who else to speak

with?" Alessandra asks, leaning forward. "As you know, we went to see Mrs. Rodríguez—she loves you by the way," she adds with a smile. "But everything that has to do with Rita seems to dead-end. We know she came here. We know she worked after having Asher. And after that we have nothing at all."

"She worked where?" asks Jazmin, and Asher remembers she knows even less than he does.

"As a maid," says Alessandra. "Right after Asher was born. That's the last time anyone saw her."

"Actually, that's not true," Jazmin says after a moment.

"What do you mean?" asks Asher dubiously.

"I saw her once. Here in the city."

"When? How?" he asks excitedly. "Here?"

"Please, I don't want you to get all wound up over nothing," says Jazmin. "It was an instant. And it was years ago. Almost ten years ago, I'd say. I could have been mistaken."

"You don't really believe that," says Asher firmly.

"No, but it was so ephemeral," says Jazmin, crossing her arms. "I was in a hotel lobby, and I saw her walk by. It took me a moment to react. She was...very elegant, very businesslike. And her hair was very short. Rita used to have this absolutely gorgeous long black hair. But it was her. It was her," she says with certainty. "I called out to her. I shouted 'Rita!' But she just kept on going. She might have hesitated for a second, she might not have. When time passes, you tend to confuse what you saw and what you think you saw and what you wanted to see. The fact is, by the time I got outside, I didn't see any sign of her. She had vanished. That's when I designed the Rita bag. I figured if she ever came into my store, she would I know I thought about her and maybe she would seek me out."

"But maybe she did," says Alessandra uncertainly. "I mean, why wouldn't she?"

"Oh, please," says Jazmin ruefully. "You two aren't even from here. How long did it take you to find me? An hour? If she wanted to see me, she'd find me."

Jazmin nods, almost to herself. "Anyway," she continues, signaling the waiter for the check. "I made my peace with it. Even before you came along, I figured Rita had to have powerful reasons to disappear. And now I know. A baby. With a guerrilla." She shakes her head. "I'm sorry," she says looking at Asher. "But that was taboo. That wouldn't have gone over well, not in a town that hated the guerrillas. Oh, my God, it would have been a major issue, to put it mildly."

"And now?" asks Asher.

"Now? Oh, now that's all changed. Our town became trendy, it became expensive. The main road now runs practically right through it, and it's completely gentrified. You both saw it. It's lovely, it's picturesque. It's a very different town from the one we grew up in. When we were girls, everybody knew everybody else. Now I only go back to visit Mrs. Rodríguez, to whom I'm eternally grateful. She got me my scholarship, gave me a chance. But it's not my town anymore. Please," says Jazmin after giving instructions to the waiter. "Have lunch on me. I've kept the tab open. And," she adds, taking out a small business card, "if you want to buy anything at any of my stores, just show them this and you'll get twenty percent off."

"Oh, thank you. We already shopped there once," says Alessandra.

Jazmin smiles, a dazzling, proud smile that Asher is sure must have opened countless doors. "I'm so glad to hear that," she says, genuinely pleased. "Buy some more!" She laughs. "Please. And, Sebastián, if you do find Rita, tell her..." Jazmin lifts her hands up helplessly, and her voice breaks. She quickly pulls her gigantic sunglasses over her eyes. "Tell her Jazzy would love to see her. Tell her I've never stopped thinking about her. Tell her—" Jazmin Sodi stops and takes a deep breath. "Tell her nothing matters. It's still me. Just me."

# Chapter Twenty-six

The rain wakes her up.

She feels the drops on her face and the wetness on her pillow and vacillates between lucidity and slumber but just lies there with her eyes closed, listening to the dull, insistent patter until the fact that it's inside the bedroom forces her fully awake. She looks regretfully at the empty pillow beside her, a reminder that her husband is away on a business trip.

Joanna gets up, looking with annoyance at the puddles in the room and the soaked gauze curtains. She walks toward the open glass doors, careful not to slip on the wet floor, and stands there for a moment, her face tilted up toward the darkness of the night. The rain is coming down in sheets now, ebbing and flowing with no rhythm or rhyme, buffeting her one second with a stream of water and the next with a light mist. Joanna reluctantly closes the sliding doors of her bedroom in the tenth-story apartment. She walks to the bathroom and takes out a gigantic towel from the linen closet—towels for hippopotamuses, she always jokes when they buy them in Miami—and goes back to the glass doors and spreads it carefully over the wet floor. They are her pride and joy, these floors, made from caoba wood flown especially for her from Colombia's Pacific jungle.

Almost as an afterthought, she tries to squeeze the curtains dry but, realizing the absurdity of the situation, finally pulls them aside violently, laying bare the expanse of glass that serves as her bedroom wall.

Joanna stands on the wet towel, looking impassively at the storm outside; already, the rain is subsiding, and away on the horizon lightning crackles, once, twice, three times in quick succession, the jagged lines fracturing the black sky.

An electrical storm, she thinks, returning to her bed and getting back under the sheets, eyes wide as she watches the dance of light playing for her against the vastness of the sky beyond.

It's still dark when she wakes up the next day, seconds before her alarm clock buzzes. Unlike the night before, where sleep was rightfully and irrefutably hers, this time Joanna is instantly alert, mentally ticking off the schedule of the day before her, like a finely calibrated metronome. Early workout, in the office by nine-thirty for a meeting with a prospective client who wants the firm to design the prototype for a fast-food restaurant. Then it's off to check on the two projects she's directly supervising: a new housing development and an art-gallery building.

She gets right out of bed—no stretches, no yawns or deliberation—and peels off her nightgown, impervious to the morning chill. She slips into her workout clothes, laid out on the chair at the foot of the bed—bicycle shorts and halter top, because she's long ago decided that sweat suits are synonymous with sloth—even before she sets foot in the bathroom to pee. Joanna looks impassively at her reflection in the full-length mirror, pulling her hair into a ponytail, twisting around to look for signs of cellulite on the backs of her legs. Nothing. She then stands sideways and runs her hand over her still-flat abdomen, her pregnancy still hidden, so hidden she has yet to feel the slightest symptom of morning sickness. Joanna shakes her head and pushes her shoulders back.

"Act and God will act," she says mechanically, and switches off the bathroom light.

When Daniel Soto walks into their home gym half an hour later, still slightly giddy after his overnight flight from Rio, his wife is already immersed in her workout, her eyes glued to the television set, oblivious to his presence by the door, her iPod blaring so loudly into her eardrums that he can hear the beat of the rhythm above the thud and whirl of the treadmill. As she runs, her ponytail grazes the dark blue top that matches the dark blue spandex shorts. Even working out, Joanna is immaculate. Her nails are always beautifully manicured, her shoes are always shined, her shoulder-length hair is always blown out in glossy waves. She is, her assistant jokes in private, the kind of woman who doesn't even have a dirty Kleenex in her handbag.

And Daniel loves this, because it is at such odds with the unrestrained trust and abandon with which she makes love, as if quenching some deep, steady thirst.

He watches her now as she increases the speed on the treadmill, one notch faster per minute, until she reaches the seven-minute-mile mark she always reserves for her last mile and looks up to see him by the door.

Joanna punches the STOP button immediately, her sprint

forgotten as she smiles the smile she reserves just for him, the one that lights her face from within.

"My love," says Joanna simply, stepping down from the exercise machine and walking up to him, cupping his face with both hands, her utter possessiveness disarmed by the tenderness of the gesture. "My love," she repeats, kissing him full on the lips.

She never calls him simply "love" or "baby" or "darling." It's always "*my* love," "*my* baby," "*my* darling," the possessive seemingly an insurance that her endearment won't evaporate or somehow get transferred to the wrong recipient.

Daniel just stands there, feeling the warmth of her hands, the sweat of her body, the very substance of her engulf him. He sometimes lies awake at night, wondering if he could tire of this, if she could tire of this.

"How was Rio?" she asks softly, leading him to the kitchen, where she turns on the coffeemaker. He peeks into the bread basket and smiles when he sees the chocolate muffins, his favorite.

"Beautiful—and stressful—as always," he replies, taking a bite, inhaling the smell of butter and dark chocolate.

Joanna had long ago decided that when Daniel returned home after a business trip, he had to be greeted with a freshly baked treat, because baking was the most intimate, most familiar, and warmest form of culinary art. Joanna carefully planned these treats, as she planned everything else.

"Especially for you," she says now, pleased. "I knew you wouldn't be able to sleep before going to the clinic, so I made your favorite. The conference went well?" she asks as she pours his coffee and follows him into the bedroom.

"My presentation got a standing ovation," he says, shooting back a smile at her. "Being an expert in mestizo noses goes a long way in Brazil," he adds, unbuttoning his oxford shirt, kicking off his loafers, peeling off his jeans, and letting them fall on the floor. Joanna automatically picks everything up and drops it inside the clothes hamper, the neat freak to his incorrigible messiness. When they first started dating, she marveled that a surgeon, a master of precision, could be so extraordinarily disorganized, and she tried, ineffectually, to get him to at least hang up his suits in hotel rooms.

"Please don't tell me what to do or how to behave," he finally told her tersely one afternoon. "I can afford to hire a maid to pick up after me, but I don't want a shrew on my back."

It was the only time he'd ever gotten testy with her, and the words stung her, reminded her of the odious life of incessant reproach she'd buried behind her. It was also her first glimmer into this other side of him, of the man who had a reputation for kicking people out of the operating room if they made a mistake in handing him an instrument.

And yet Daniel doesn't expect perfection from her. There is, of course, the occasional physician's dinner, the end-of-the-year parties at the hospital, the exhausting awards ceremonies, all those little and big events where it is expected, often demanded, that a prominent physician show up with his wife. And he does, and she looks good and says all the right things while standing proudly beside him.

Daniel appreciates that, but those are simply accessories to him. His love for Joanna has nothing to do with her public performance but with her private presence, with her quiet, total acceptance of him and the fact that she could stand alone if he weren't there.

He doesn't know that she needs him far more than he needs her, that he completes her far more than she accepts him. He doesn't know that she stopped second-guessing herself only when he married her.

"The mestizo nose," she now muses as he stands beneath the hot shower, the steam beginning to rise above the half-open door. "What about the mestizo butt?" she asks, raising her voice, turning around to look at herself in the mirror again.

Daniel laughs. Self-deprecating humor is rare in Joanna, and he relishes those small doses when he gets them.

"We love the mestizo butt!" he shouts above the water's flow.

*       *       *

In the beginning, months before Joanna was set to start her freshman year, she spent hours in the university library, simply watching the students who filed in and out, taking in the clear differences in social strata, in popularity, in pecking order, determined by those ineffable details that are sometimes just impossible to pinpoint. She had never cared about such things, because she used to be sure of herself, sure of who she was and where she was going, even when she spent her hours behind the counter of a small-town sundries store. All she knew now was that she was trying to be someone else—she *was* someone else. She just wasn't sure who.

She began with her hair, her defining trait. One Saturday morning she walked into a trendy salon and placed her pride and joy into the hands of a complete stranger. Joanna undid her braid, loosened the dark curtain that nearly reached her waist, and said, unflinchingly, "Redo me."

Tony Bosi, a stylist with the demeanor of a military sergeant, obliged by shearing off nearly a foot of hair, layering it until it fell in feathery waves that rippled around her face and settled just above her shoulders. Joanna looked at her reflection impassively, at the cheekbones that suddenly appeared—seemingly out of nowhere—and at the eyes that seemed suddenly bigger, at the face that finally seemed to look the age she pretended to be.

"I want it shorter," said Joanna.

"No. It wouldn't be you," said Tony Bosi flatly.

"Please. I want to look completely different," protested Joanna, vexed.

"You do already," said Tony Bosi patiently. "And remember, changing your hair doesn't change who you are."

"I just want it shorter," Joanna repeated, and even to herself she sounded petulant. She remembered her mother, who would not relent on even the tiniest of things. One thing Joanna did know: She would not be her mother.

"I just want it to be shorter," she said yet again, but her tone was more placating this time, her words accompanied by a tentative smile that felt strange on her normally severe countenance. Tony Bosi had been right: A haircut didn't change the essence of a person. Neither did a new ward-robe or the braces she wore to straighten out the slightly crooked teeth that had long made her self-conscious about her smile.

Joanna remained a secretive person, aloof, cautious, forever on alert. Very slowly, time began to peel off her lay-ers, until she became a girl again. She started going to the parties she had never been able to partake of in her previ-ous life, and she laughed spontaneously again, as she once used to do with Jazmin, long, long ago, before her mistakes and the pettiness of her world closed in on her and made her a nonentity.

Joanna did what she should do, what she was supposed to do, what she was now able to do. She bought a car and enrolled in a driving school. She made friends who—like her previous ones—appreciated her tacitly quiet nature, her capacity to simply listen. She became respectable and respected, a top student with an uncanny knack for pre-cision and execution that made her a wanted commodity in the group projects that are a staple of civil-engineering studies.

And yet she never stopped looking over her shoulder, always expecting to see Rita, or a remnant of her, appear and tear everything down, expose her sham for what it was. She was careful with men now. Her relationships were clin-ical, concise, and rare. Alone at night in her room, Joanna obliterated thoughts of Lucas and all the yearnings she used to have when she was sixteen and thought she was in love. Instead she planned. Just as she had once dreamed of finishing high school, then college, she now looked ahead at her life beyond, at that place where she could finally settle and work and be self-sufficient and simply be. If she could get there, she thought, everything else would fall into place. She would meet the right person, and then she could create her own family on her own terms. Just one more day, she thought, with every day that passed, just one more month, just one more year, until what she used to be and what she had done truly began to fade, until only occasional glimmers made their way into her memories and her dreams, until she stopped looking for his face every time they covered guerrilla takeovers in the evening newscast, until Lucas and Sebastián and Jazmin and Rita became simply words and no longer the names of people she used to know.

It happened years later, when she was already comfortably settled into her other skin, her other body, her other name. Joanna was walking briskly through the lobby of a downtown hotel after a business meeting, her high-heeled boots clicking in sharp staccato on the marble floor.

"Rita!" She heard the name called, and the first time she heard it, she genuinely didn't register it as her own. But the second time she knew that it was meant for her. Joanna's spine stiffened, and she quickened her pace, her back a shield between the name and her face. She walked beyond the third shouted "Rita," swiftly going through the revolving doors to the street outside and equally swiftly ducking into one of the waiting cabs.

"Just drive," she ordered urgently, never looking back,

telling herself again and again that it must have been her imagination, that no one had shouted "Rita!" and even if someone had, it most certainly wasn't aimed at her, it was nothing. She deliberately put it out of her mind, as she had put everything else before it, and with each passing day she convinced herself that indeed it had all been in her imagination.

# Chapter Twenty-seven

The first thing he does when they get back to the apartment is change into his workout clothes and head for the gym.

Asher gets on the treadmill and runs, without defining time or distance, the music obliterating the day and the week and the past failed months of his life until Alessandra drops by nine miles later and tells him to "Stop Asher, just stop."

They make love urgently that night, until he is truly spent, until he forgets, at least for a moment, everything he's carried the past few days.

After Alessandra has gone to sleep, he stays up on the living-room couch, Rita's paltry little file in his hands, watching the now-quiet streets below him. His father was a member of a guerrilla group, and his mother is probably somewhere in this city, maybe walking this very neighborhood, still hiding after all these years.

His father was a member of a guerrilla group, he thinks again. He was a soldier, a fighter, someone with a certain degree of cool. He was young, handsome face, unusual eyes with a strange yellow tint and slanted like a cat's. Asher has often wondered whom he got his own eyes from; now he knows.

Gato. Asher has been reading up on Colombia's bloody civil war, but who's to know what accounts are accurate or exaggerated? He wonders if Gato was a ruthless guerrilla fighter, a willing killer, or if he was recruited by force. Whatever the motivation, Asher knows he was feared. That much Jazmin said. The townspeople weren't allowed to talk to the guerrillas. Asher brings his hands up to the holes in his skull, which are throbbing in dull, steady waves. He opens the file and looks again at his mother's photo. The headmistress had said Rita was "hermosa," her only kind word about her. He'd never thought she looked lovely in this photo. Not unpleasant, but not all that remarkable. Asher stares at the picture for a long time, until he begins to glimpse the beauty beneath the defeat and the sullenness. *You were lovely*, he thinks. *Until you had me. The mere thought of me was so unthinkable that you made yourself disappear.*

On an impulse he dials his mother, directly from his cell phone, not bothering to fuss with the Skype.

"Linda Stone," she answers on the second ring,

"What up, Mom?"

"Asher! Oh, my God, baby. We've been worried sick. You haven't answered that phone or that Skype of yours in two days." The words tumble out of Linda's mouth in a long roll of relief.

*They miss me*, Asher thinks. *She misses me. She's been wondering why I don't call.* And then he begins to cry.

"Ash?" asks Linda uncertainly. "Ash? Talk to me. What happened?"

"N-nothing." Asher takes a deep breath, horrified. Never

has anything like this happened to him before. "Nothing, Mom. I'm sorry," he says, slowly regaining his composure. "It's just that things have taken a different turn from what I imagined."

"But are you okay?" asks Linda, trying to sound calm.

"Yes, yes, Mom. I'm sorry, I'm sorry. I don't know what came over me."

"Honey, that's why I'm here. Tell me what's going on."

Asher takes a deep breath.

"We met today with Rita Ortiz's best friend, from when they were kids. You know, she's the first person who not only remembers her vividly but remembers her well—in a positive light, I mean. And not even she has any idea of where Rita has gone. It's as if she's literally vanished off the face of the earth. And apparently my father—my birth father—was a member of the guerrilla forces. They took over the town where Rita lived, and that's how they met." Asher laughs. "Those are my birth parents. A guerrilla fighter and a teenager who found her pregnancy so terrifying she made herself disappear."

Linda doesn't skip a beat. "Ash, it doesn't matter," she says calmly. "Your dad and I went through every possibility, including your being the product of the war in some way. It doesn't matter who your biological parents are or what they did. It doesn't affect who you are now, who you are to us."

"How can you say it doesn't matter?" Asher's voice is choked with tears. He leans back into the sofa and runs his hand through his hair. "Her friend says that what she did was taboo. You know what they did, Mom? The priest—the priest who sent her to the orphanage where you guys adopted me—he was murdered because he helped the guerrillas. For all I know, he was murdered because of me. I never imagined some idyllic background, but this isn't what I wanted, Mom. This isn't who I wanted to be."

"Asher Stone, you listen to me," says Linda, her voice that of a woman in command. "You are our son. You are *my* son. My blood is your blood. Everything that came before was before. You hear me? Nothing changes that." She stresses every word. "Nothing. Changes. You. Or us. You were immersed in the mikvah and purified of everything that came before. These are your beliefs, and you have to be strong in your faith, Asher. That's what we taught you. But, most important, you can't forget that you are my son and I love you unconditionally. Unconditionally," she repeats. "And if there's anything you're going to feel for this other person, for both these people, it's gratitude. Because thanks to them we have you."

Asher holds the phone held very tightly against his ear even though the entire apartment is quiet.

"Asher, are you there?" his mother asks, concern creeping back into her voice.

He nods, then remembers she can't see him. "Yes, Mom."

"Ash, you mentioned that nun to me—the one who spoke about the miracles, remember?"

"Impossible to forget," says Asher ruefully.

"Do you have any idea how many times your father and I have looked at you, from the moment we got you, from the moment we first held you, and marveled at the miraculousness of you and of us?"

Linda doesn't wait for her son to answer.

"I feel for Rita, Asher, I do, because my gain was her loss. And if she's hiding, baby, it's because she can't move on. But you have, Asher. Living in the past stifles your future. Aren't you the one who's always preaching about never dwelling on the past, how looking ahead is the only way to win a game? This is where you come from, Asher. This is your foundation. Everything else is only as important as you want it to be. Does that make sense?"

Asher nods silently into the phone.

"Anyway," adds Linda. "A guerrilla fighter. I should have known it was going to be someone dramatic," she says with a little laugh.

Asher smiles despite himself. His exacting mother, who nevertheless is a conciliator, always trying to find the bright side of things.

"Yeah. It's dramatic all right," he agrees. "Mom, by the way," he adds, "they keep asking about an ID number for Rita Ortiz. Could there be anything like that buried anywhere in your files?"

"No, baby," Linda answers without hesitation. "Everything they gave us was in that envelope. Don't you see, Ash? We got *you*. We didn't need anything else at all."

\*          \*          \*

It is sheer coincidence that her drive to work takes her past a Jazzy store every morning. That particular store opened a year after she and Daniel moved into their apartment—the apartment of her dreams—and by then she was unwilling to move aside simply because a piece of her past had gotten in the way. But the sight of the store gnawed at her, made her stomach churn with apprehension, until one afternoon, vexed, she ordered the driver to stop.

Joanna stepped out of the car and stood for a long time just staring at the Jazzy store's window. She'd been to a different store once before, when the chain first opened, and, mesmerized, she had walked in to ascertain for herself that the impossible had become possible: Jazmin had fulfilled her dream. Joanna now let the windows of this store protect her for seemingly endless minutes before she finally walked inside, fingering the weaves, the meticulous handicraft, with quiet pride. She bought two purses that day, somehow exorcising Jazmin's encroachment from her new reality, and gave them away as gifts. After that she would stop in the shop from time to time. She never bought anything for herself, until the day she saw "The Rita."

Joanna cocked her head to one side and looked at her namesake with the coolness of a property appraiser. She picked up the elegant little clutch and turned it this way and that, admiring how it fit perfectly into her hands. The mix of elegance and just a splash of flash was so very her. Only Jazmin could detect and translate such details, she thought.

She bought one. And from that point on she would regularly stop to see what new colors The Rita had assumed for the season. She never contemplated the possibility of running into Jazmin in the store. There were dozens of Jazzy shops nationwide; the odds that her old friend would be in the same store at the same time she was were too small to cause concern. And besides, she told herself, did it really matter? She was just Joanna López, just another shopper.

Joanna doesn't stop today. Fussing over Daniel has made her late, and she hates being late. She pores over her notes from the backseat of the SUV, making a last-minute review of the project they're presenting today, a proposal for the new communications building at her old university.

After she got her master's degree, Alfonso Valle and Alex Acosta asked her to join their firm. A woman, they decided, would be an asset in a field of men. A pretty woman, with exacting standards, would be even more valuable. They got the leads, she clinched the deals with a mix of attractiveness and proficiency that disarmed potential clients, particularly the politicians and big developers who made up the bulk of their business. It was Joanna who insisted they also carry a substantial number of what she called "boutique" projects that netted them just a fraction of what their gigantic endeavors did but which, she claimed, kept the creative juices flowing and acted as oases in a world dominated by bureaucrats.

Dr. Daniel Soto was a boutique project, and one that naturally fell to her. He wanted to expand and remodel his offices, which housed a bustling facial-plastic-surgery practice. Who better than Joanna to steer the design of such an eminently aesthetic project?

"But are you an architect or an engineer?" Daniel had asked, bemused, as he watched her page through the plans, making "little" changes until the original was all but unrecognizable. He'd been hard-pressed to take his eyes away from her since she'd greeted him at the reception area wearing a tailored pinstripe suit and a starched white shirt that resulted in a disconcerting mix of professional and sexy. He almost immediately had visions of her standing next to her drawing board, naked save for her high heels and a Sharpie, and he shook his head impatiently to clear his thoughts. He couldn't pinpoint what it was about her that had him so enthralled. She was pretty, yes, but no prettier than dozens of women he saw every day, many in his office. It was something about the way she held herself, he thought, her face exposed by her short, feathered haircut yet her whole being enveloped in an air of privacy, as if by some invisible shroud that begged to be removed.

Daniel couldn't know then that dozens of other men had sat in that same chair and had contemplated very similar thoughts. He didn't know that she was used to it, so used to it that she practically had a ready-made script for every come-on. He didn't know that men like him were cellophane to her, because she'd learned her lessons well and she wasn't about to repeat her mistakes.

But because Daniel Soto was a decent man, a mindful man, who by the very nature of his occupation always saw the long term, he did what no one else had done.

"Can I take you out to dinner?" he'd asked simply. And before she could protest, before she could launch into her "I can't have dinner with clients" script, he'd added, "When you finish the project?"

Joanna looked at him closely for the first time, at his curly hair, boyish countenance, and the tall, heavyset frame that made him look like a cross between a teddy bear and a gladiator. "I guess that would depend on what kind of job I do," she'd said evenly. Seven months, three weeks, and four days later, they went out on their first date.

                    *       *       *

Inés calls the day after the meeting with Jazmin, bubbling with excitement.

"So?" she asks. "What did she say?"

"She has no idea where Rita is," Alessandra says, feeling slightly defeated for the first time, even though, as she constantly reminds Asher, they've only been here for a bit over a week.

"Oh," says Inés, and that little word, too, carries the weight of the world. As an accountant in the making, she's vexed that the woman has vanished. With so many snippets of connection floating around, she thinks, it's just mathematically impossible that someone can be so completely lost, as if vaporized.

"All this time Jazmin has heard nothing of her?" Inés presses.

"Well, she says she thinks she saw her once. Here in the city," says Alessandra dubiously, because she's seriously thinking that was just a figment of Jazmin's imagination.

"Really?" asks Inés, her voice rising in excitement again. "Saw her…when? What was she doing? What did she look like?"

"She just said she thought she saw her in the lobby of a hotel, like ten years ago," says Alessandra.

"Ten years ago?" echoes Inés, her voice rising to unusual heights. "What did she *look* like? She used to be a maid, didn't she? Was she dressed like a maid?"

Alessandra tries to remember the details of the conversation. None of this had crossed her mind when Jazmin recounted it, but then again she doesn't think like

this, doesn't catalog people in defined little social strata, but
here, she sees, these details matter. Details reveal volumes.

"I...I'm not sure," she stumbles. "But from the way she
spoke, it sounded as if she looked like a guest."

"Mmm," says Inés, and Alessandra feels a twinge of
guilt at her lack of guile.

"There is something," Alessandra says thoughtfully.
"Jazmin mentioned her birthday. January...something. Do
we have her birthday?"

There is a pause on the other line, and Alessandra hears
the click of the computer keys as Inés searches.

"No," she finally says, surprise in her voice. "We just
know how old she was when she had Sebastián, but we
don't have a birth*day*. That's important," Inés adds slowly.
"Actually, that's really important!" she exclaims, her voice
rising again. "Even if we don't have the ID, we can narrow
the search with a birthday. People change their birth years
all the time. They change their names. They change everything. But not the birth*day*. Birthdays are too easy to mess
up. What is it?"

"Oh, God," says Alessandra, racking her brain helplessly. "Asher!" she shouts. "Asher!"

"What!" he answers, annoyed, from the bedroom.

"Do you recall Rita's birthday? Remember, Jazmin mentioned it?"

"January fifteenth, 1973," Asher shouts back without
hesitation. Then he gets up and pokes his head out the
door. "Why?"

"Hold on, let me put you on speaker," says Alessandra,
excited. "Inés, what's the deal with the birthday?"

"We haven't had information to look her up in the National Registry," Inés explains quickly. "You see, here you get a permanent ID when you turn eighteen. Kinda like your Social Security number? I have friends at the registry, and they can look things up for me. But Rita Ortiz is a really common name, and we've never had anything else to go on, so looking her up by her name alone was impossible. But with a name and a birthday, we have a much better chance. I'm sure she's changed something, you know?" Inés adds. "I think she probably lied about her age. But she wouldn't change her birthday. I mean, would you?"

# Chapter Twenty-eight

Joanna doesn't realize that even when you cross to the other side, someone or something can still bring you back, no matter how far you travel beyond that invisible line that divides what was from what is.

Joanna doesn't realize this because she has convinced herself that it isn't so, because she believes herself to be stronger than all the circumstances around her. But she's forgotten that she set those circumstances in motion, that sooner or later, by the very laws of nature, it will all come back to her.

It does, on an ordinary Wednesday afternoon.

"Ms. López," calls her secretary over the intercom, using Joanna's professional, maiden name.

"Yes?" she answers distractedly as she studies financials.

"There is a Mrs. Carla Bernotti on the line."

"Who?" asks Joanna, not even looking up.

"Mrs. Carla Bernotti. She says she's from La Casa en el Campo?"

Joanna stops what she's doing, her No. 2 pencil suspended in midair. Only when her beating heart threatens to explode from her chest does she realize she has ceased breathing, and she takes an anxious gulp of air, then another and another, until her brain starts to function again.

She silently wills her hand to move, to gently set the pencil down, wills her mouth to open, to say the right words, like a talking doll that is wound up again.

"Please take a message, Betty," she says shortly, disconnecting the intercom before her assistant can say another word.

Joanna calmly picks up her pencil again and resumes her review, but five minutes later she's still looking at the same number on the same line on the same page, and her hand is shaking so much she has to put down the pencil yet again. Her heartbeat feels erratic, and she searches for her pulse, thinking this surely can't be good for the baby. She remembers, with stunning clarity considering it's been a lifetime since she thought about it, how another time she prayed for the opposite, for something to happen to that baby, anything, just so she could be free again.

Joanna puts her hands on her desk and tries to stand up, but her legs won't hold her, and she collapses back onto her chair, sending it rolling away until it crashes into the window behind her. The impact has a sobering effect on her.

*Get a grip*, she thinks sternly. "Get a grip on yourself," she says, out loud this time. "Get a grip," she repeats. "Get a grip." It seems to take forever, and she thanks her lucky stars for days without clients. Finally her thoughts gather together, like little magnetic pieces that pull toward each other until something begins to take shape, an idea, a thought, a plan.

*It's just a phone call*, she tells herself. *Just a phone call. They could be looking to hire me for a project. It could be totally unrelated*, she thinks logically. But it is not logical, she knows. The odds are too stacked against her, the likelihood of its being something else is too high.

Okay, she thinks. Suppose they somehow know who she was. She'll just deny it. Joanna's head goes up, her shoulders square. Of course! It's really that simple. She denies it and her life goes on, as it already has for twenty-one years. Joanna picks up her pencil again, and this time it's steady in her hand; this time her thoughts converge solely on the numbers and their meaning as her eyes move back and forth, back and forth across the page.

Later, as she sorts through the little pile of messages Betty leaves for her at the end of the day, she finds the pink slip with Carla Bernotti's name on it. Under "Reason for Calling," it simply states, "Personal."

Joanna opens her top drawer and takes out the hand-painted matchbox she keeps around to light the incense and candles that are part of her office ambience. She goes inside her private bathroom, strikes a match, and watches the slip of paper consume itself until she drops it into the toilet to extinguish the flame, then flushes the remnants out of sight. Joanna turns and washes her hands carefully at the sink, scrubbing between her fingers, as if she had grime embedded in her skin and under her beautifully manicured nails. When she's done, she looks at herself in the mirror impassively, objectively, as she's always been wont to do.

She sees a woman who looks both younger and older than her thirty-eight years, her cheekbones pronounced under the smooth, blemish-free honey tones of skin that stretches tautly over the planes of her face. Her body underneath the formal jacket is trim, her collarbones exposed and vulnerable in the opening of her crisp white blouse. It's her eyes that are older, eyes that are large and dark brown and profound, like pools of water at night, alert, measuring, but with melancholy simmering just below the surface. Joanna remembers how, when she first started college, she would stand in front of her mirror at night and literally force herself to smile again, to laugh, until she slowly began to remember what it felt like to turn her mouth up, not down, and felt the spontaneous joy that comes from not having to constantly look over one's shoulder.

She had crawled so deeply into a shell, and it had been hard to come out again, in spite of the money, the education, her growing confidence.

Joanna leans in toward the mirror and runs her hands over her face, pushes back the hair—now shoulder-length—long for the first time since she cut it all those years ago. She had done it for him, for Daniel, because he was the only one who'd seen beyond her façade, who'd been able to reach deep inside her and bring out not only what she had been but what she had never known she could be. They dated for weeks before he took her to his apartment, the first woman he'd taken there after his divorce ten years before. He undressed her slowly, and she silently gave thanks for the generosity of time, which had finally allowed her body to erase the signs of pregnancy and her heart to fully open up to a man's intentions.

He used to ask her about the family she'd left behind, the family that she told him had died in a fire. She's never provided the full scope of details, but beyond their alleged death she hasn't outright lied about her circumstances either.

"Let's just say you and I come from very different places," she told him bluntly on their second date, because by then she knew that her place was with him and she needed to know, before she went any further, that he would take her—Joanna López—for what she had fashioned herself to be: the small-town girl who had lost her family, who had worked her way through college, who had made it not through her pedigree but through her wit.

"Where you come from is much less interesting to me than where we can go together," he had said simply, and she knew then that it could be. That she could close the circle. God had really given her a second chance. And for three years Daniel has never doubted her. He's never had reason to doubt her.

What would he think? she begins to wonder now, and then covers her face with her hands at the possibility. *He will think nothing*, she tells herself sternly. *He will never know.*

*     *     *

"The birthday?" asks his mother incredulously. "You mean to tell me this person has vanished for over twenty years and you found her simply with her birthday?"

"Yeah," says Asher with a sigh. "Isn't it amazing what two little numbers can do? People change their name, their age, where they come from, but apparently they can't bring themselves to change their birthday. I guess it's the celebratory nature of the date."

"All these things she changed?" asks Joseph, bemused.

"Everything," says Asher. "That's why Inés couldn't cross-reference her name. She always figured that something was off, but she had nothing to search against. Once she had the birthday, she just played with the years until this Rita popped up."

"But her name isn't Rita," says Linda.

"No, that's the irony," Asher elaborates. "If she hadn't changed her name, we might have missed her, because the hometown was wrong; we weren't looking for someone born in Bogotá. But the system flags name changes, because you can legally change your name just once in your lifetime in Colombia. That's the only reason Inés checked further. Because she changed her name. Anyway," he adds, defeated, "technically we haven't found her. I mean, she hasn't returned Mrs. Bernotti's calls, so we can't be a hundred percent sure it's her."

"Of course it's her," says Linda, resignation coming through in her voice despite her best attempt to sound enthusiastic. "What are you going to do? How long are you planning to wait?"

Asher looks at his parents helplessly, their images fuzzy on the computer screen, their speech delayed by the five thousand miles between them. They may be disconcerted, but he's utterly demoralized. He knew that Rita was hiding, but it had never occurred to him that once found she would flat-out ignore him.

Carla has called her. Twice. And she has not responded. How could she not? he now thinks, indignation rising inside him. Not even to say she's not interested or she doesn't want to see him or even to insist that they have the wrong person. It's as if she has simply obliterated any notion of him. And logically it shouldn't hurt, this rejection by someone he doesn't even know. But it does.

"I'm calling her myself," he'd declared angrily earlier today, the impotence of waiting finally reaching a breaking point.

"You are not to call her," Carla said curtly, forgoing her usual gentle approach to him. "While it is my duty to help you as much as possible, it is also my duty to respect the wishes of the women who give up their children for adoption. If you cannot abide by this, I am going to have to step aside here."

"Your first duty should be with me," Asher insisted. "I have rights. You know I do."

"Ash," Alessandra reasons, "why risk scaring her away after we've come so far? Let Carla go through the process first."

"Ash," his father calls again from across the world. "You have to set a deadline, Ash," he says firmly. "This isn't making sense anymore. Come home. If she calls, you can fly back down. But you can't settle and live somewhere else just in case you might get a phone call."

*What the hell do you know about anything?* Asher wants to shout back, and immediately he feels consumed with remorse at the mere thought of the words. While he's had disagreements with his parents, they've rarely dissolved into outright fights before. He instinctively pushes his hair back. It'd been exciting for a while, to be here with Ally, discovering this parallel universe. But enough already, he thinks. Enough. He could stay here forever, and it still wouldn't force her to open the door just a notch. He's underestimated her. They all have, their notion of Rita

Ortiz forever encapsulated in that sad little photograph of the forlorn sixteen-year-old—because now they know she was just sixteen—with the mournful eyes.

This woman, this Joanna López, is completely divorced from that other photo, from those slumped shoulders, from the defeated eyes. She has nothing to do with that helpless, hapless girl. Of course she doesn't want anything to do with him.

"It's Wednesday," Asher says, his mind made up. "We leave Sunday, come what may. At least I know she's okay," he adds ruefully, his voice slightly pleading as he looks directly at his mother. "And she'll know I'm okay, too. Really. That's all I can ask for."

*         *         *

Long after Joe has gone to sleep, Linda Stone sits alone in his studio, mindlessly watching television as she sips a glass of red wine, something she rarely does during the week.

"I didn't think he would find her," she told him during dinner, words that she will never say out loud to Asher. "Joseph, I prayed that he wouldn't find her," Linda added.

"It won't change your relationship with him," he'd replied, picking up her exquisite hand and taking it to his lips. "You have to believe that."

"I try," she'd said, shaking her head. "Really. I tell myself that all the time. But I don't believe it myself. Joe, she's thirty-eight. I'm fifty-two. How can I possibly compete?"

Linda crossed her arms, and her eyes welled with tears. "I'm the one who raised him. Me, and you, of course," she says, placing her hands on his arm. "But you have no competition, Joe. You're his dad. His only dad. Me, though—I'm the other woman now."

"Lin, please calm down," he said, using his rational voice, the voice whose equanimity has kept her by his side all these years. "Asher is adopted, and we made a choice by adopting him and by loving him. We can't do more, Linda. He has to do what he has to do, and he's going to come back to us." Joe sat back and threw his hands up in the air. "Or he's not. Either way, we've done all we can do. I for one," he continued, standing and picking up his plate to take to the kitchen, "think our son will meet his birth mother, he'll find her delightful, and he'll tell us all about it over dinner next weekend."

Linda sips her wine and thinks about the other woman, who now has a name and a place. Joanna López. An engineer, no less. A partner in a well-known construction firm, for God's sake, and married to a prominent doctor. A perfect life. All these years doing her best to change into someone else, and now this.

What could have happened, she wonders again, to transform Rita into Joanna López? It must have taken so much, so very much.

She remembers the long drive to find him, through Bogotá's furious, smog-filled traffic and then the scenic highways taking them from the hotel to the orphanage in the outskirts of the city. They'd told her it was clean and neat, but they hadn't prepared her for the surprising warmth of the rather modest, unassuming house, nestled in a sea of green grass and red peonies, almost like a British cottage.

They had walked inside to a cozy patio, like that shared by so many Latin American homes. The heart of the house, with a little fountain providing a constant, quieting murmur, surrounded by two stories of small rooms, each one flanked by bright red doors that seemed to wink knowingly at the visitors below. The Stones sat in a waiting room adorned with framed pictures of babies and children and smiling parents, the faces a kaleidoscope of black, white, and brown shades. Linda had looked at Joseph and knew with certainty what he was thinking. That they could still say no. They could still walk away, childless, from this little home in the country, with its singing fountain and green-stained fields.

And then they brought him in.

On a rational level, Linda understood that this is how all new parents felt, all equally besotted with babies, regardless of race or gender or beauty. She had prepared for this, had anticipated the thrill despite the uncertainty, despite the doubts, because, after all, she was a decent woman, a woman of principles, even in her worst moments.

And yet she was unprepared for the small bundle ensconced in light blue pajamas.

He was the color of burnished copper, a toasted gold that made his dark hair seem darker still, his gold-flecked brown eyes seem tawnier. Everything about him glowed, from his skin to the yellow irises around his pupils, which, Linda swore, dilated when he made eye contact with her.

She had expected a sleeping newborn, not this alert creature who certainly was a few months old and whose gaze seemed to zero in on everything around him with an uncanny degree of awareness. Linda looked inquisitively at her husband, who sat motionless on the wooden bench. The short, plump woman who carried the baby regarded them expectantly for a moment, then walked over to Linda and carefully handed her the light blue bundle.

"This," she said gently, "is your son. Sebastián."

\*     \*     \*

He's refused to leave the city and do any sightseeing because he's convinced she's going to call. He checks his cell phone obsessively, making sure there's service. "All these mountains," he keeps telling Alessandra. "You just never know."

Fidel takes them to a park where Asher can finally run outside, a vast expanse called Parque Simón Bolívar, hundreds of acres of green spreading out in hills and valleys. Asher runs, five miles, eight, ten, until he feels that his lungs are going to burst, and he marvels that after two weeks here he still can't get used to this place, to the oppressiveness of it, the smog, the altitude that constrains him even in this park, and the clouds that press down relentlessly into the city. He runs without his iPod, and in his mind he can see her, Rita, sixteen and alone, walking those streets that he gets driven through, pretending to be in control when she had nothing to look back at and nothing to look forward to.

Yet somehow something changed and she'd gone back to reclaim him. For the first time, Asher feels a rush of pity, as cold as the air stinging his face. He has Alessandra, he has his parents, for a long time he had an entire soccer team, a retinue of people to call, to consult with and get assurance and love and companionship from, every step of the way.

Rita had no one but herself. A life so lonely she was able to wipe it clean and start again, and no one had even missed her. Until now.

In the distance at the end of the path, Asher sees Alessandra, waiting for him, worry written all over her stance, her hand shielding her eyes from the sun, then breaking into a wave when she finally spots him.

Asher sprints the final yards and grabs her arm, holding on for dear life as he bends over, wheezing for air until he's able to talk, to make her understand.

"She started again, don't you see?" he asks earnestly, grabbing onto the sleeves of Alessandra's sweatshirt, the words tumbling out in a torrent. "She had to. Otherwise she didn't stand a chance. But the first thing she did, the only thing she did before moving on, was make sure I was okay. Don't you see?" he repeats. "That's what she does. She's methodical. And now it's the same. She has to know what she's doing before she does it. She did it before, and she'll do it again. But she has to know. She has to be sure."

That night he makes love to Alessandra slowly, relishing the smell of her hair, of her neck, carefully mapping her shape underneath his hands, feeling the contrast of her slenderness and her softness, the body of girl, not an athlete, no matter how hard he tries to turn her into one. He makes love to her with leisure, leaving aside the desperate urgency that's plagued him since he got here.

"Thank you, thank you," he whispers afterward, and she knows it's not for tonight but everything, for watching over him when he most needed her.

He wakes up much later, when it's still dark outside,

and stands for a long time looking out the window at the city that's still asleep, its chaos almost totally silenced save for the occasional alarm that blares away in the distance.

Asher switches on his computer and looks her up, her firm, her address, her phone. There isn't much, but it's there, everything in plain view now that he knows her name and occupation. He takes out the stack of pictures—celebrating his first birthday, his bar mitzvah, his high-school graduation, pictures in his soccer uniform—the photographs he'd carefully selected and brought with him in anticipation of the grand meeting that now seems to be receding further and further away. He chooses a baby picture and a portrait—his college photo from the previous year—and flips them around and dates them with a Sharpie, clearly printing his name underneath. It dawns on him that he doesn't know if she speaks English or not, but he doesn't have a choice now.

He then takes out a sheet of paper and begins to write.

# Chapter Twenty-nine

Joanna López spends most of the day visiting her construction sites. She returns to her office only that afternoon and immediately goes into a lengthy project meeting that runs until 6:00 P.M., after her secretary has left for her customary Thursday happy hour. Daniel is working late in anticipation of his trip to Brazil Saturday evening, and Joanna pours herself a cup of green tea as she sorts leisurely through her mail and messages, lulled into tranquillity by the rare silence that surrounds her.

The sealed manila envelope, delivered early that morning, is at the very bottom of the pile, innocuous save for the word PERSONAL, written in red, underlined block letters, the mere sight of it as unexpected as an electric shock.

"Ah," she says in recognition, but the word is more a lament than an exclamation. She looks at the envelope, not touching it, and represses the urge to slam the other letters back on top of it or to tear it up unopened. Once she connects with it, once her fingers touch that first lining of separation between herself and him, it will never be the same, she knows, but she also knows now that it was simply a matter of time. No matter how often she hides from this truth, it will find her—it has found her. It's not hers to bury anymore.

After what seems an eternity, she finally reaches out
and places both her hands on the yellow paper. She closes
her eyes for a long moment. She feels like a diver who's
about to leap from the highest springboard, except she has
no clue what dive to perform and she doesn't even know if
there's enough water for her to cut through. But she has to
dive—or be pushed over the edge.

Joanna takes a deep breath, and, using her silver letter opener, the one she bought in the flea market in Paris,
she cleanly slices the envelope open and carefully spreads
out the two photographs before her, his picture and the
baby's. She doesn't need to read the letter to know that
it's him. It's so clearly Lucas looking up at her after more
than twenty years, except his hair is longer and his smile
is so wide, so carefree, so unguarded, the way his smile
never was, not even when they were alone. She unwittingly
reaches her fingers out to touch him, then quickly closes
her eyes again, because all this time she's dreaded coming face-to-face with him, even when it was the only thing
she used to think about. In the beginning she would look
for him everywhere, convinced he would somehow find
her, save her, change everything about himself so he could
make her whole again. And then his face began to fade
from her mind, *he* began to fade, like everyone else, like
the baby in the picture, except he *is* the baby in the picture,
because it suddenly hits her that it isn't Lucas she's looking at.

Joanna looks again, closer this time, less agitated, and
sees beyond that first, shocking resemblance. His skin is
darker, like hers, and he has her thin, haughty nose. But

the eyes—especially the eyes—are Lucas's, as is the surprisingly full mouth and the planes and angles of his face, although they're gentler, rounder. She doesn't know if it's because she's in him or if because this man has had the benefit of care and love and money and attention, all the things that can soften a countenance and replace the possibility of viciousness with the possibility of—Joanna looks intently until the word pops into her brain—hope. This man has hope in his eyes.

She forces herself to finally look at the baby picture, to compare the two visages that stare unblinkingly at her. The baby. He's just a baby, she thinks again. A baby like so many babies. She couldn't distinguish him from any other child, and why should she? She never held him, after all. Never nursed him, never sang to him, never cradled him close to her heart. She'd never even looked at him—really looked at him—as he lay inside his crib. She looks now but feels nothing—no pull, no guilt, no tenderness, even. It's the other photo that draws her: Lucas's eyes, Lucas's mouth, Lucas's face, and somewhere, too, there's a piece of her, more discernible almost by the second, like those digital photos that slowly take shape before your eyes on a computer screen, the fuzziness gradually giving way to sharpness of detail.

Joanna reluctantly tears her gaze from the picture and takes out the note, handwritten in English in black ink:

"Dear Ms. Lopez," she reads. "My name is Asher Sebastián Stone. I was adopted twenty-one years ago from La Casa en el Campo, and I'm looking for my birth mother, Rita Ortiz."

*If you indeed are Rita Ortiz, please know that I mean no trouble, and all I want is a chance to meet you, to see you, to say hello, and tell you that life has been good to me and that whatever led you to give me up so long ago led me to a good place.*

*I was raised in Los Angeles, California, by loving parents who afforded me every possible opportunity. I will graduate from college next year, and I feel I have much to contribute in the future.*

*Over the years we tried to find you several times. It's important for me to know my true origins and understand where I come from.*

*At this point in my life, nothing would make me happier than meeting you in person and knowing a little bit about you and my birth father.*

*I would also like you to know that my birth parents are eternally grateful to you, as am I.*

*I'll be leaving for Los Angeles on Sunday and hope we can meet before my trip. Please find my number below. I'll be waiting for your call.*

*Sincerely,*
*Asher Sebastián Stone*

Joanna reads the letter again. And again. The calls from the orphanage director, those were easy to ignore. But this is a handwritten letter. A letter written by her son. *Her son.* Her flesh and blood. Joanna leans back in her leather chair, made to her specifications, to her height and weight. She looks at the paintings that decorate her office, each done by a specific artist and selected for a specific reason. The candles smell of cinnamon and lemongrass, and she orders them through an exclusive online catalog. Everything so carefully planned and measured and executed. And this, she thinks, holding up one photograph in each hand, was never meant to be. But then again, if it hadn't happened, she wouldn't be here today either.

Joanna looks at the phone number on the letter but can't face the thought of actually hearing his voice on the other end of the line, of actually initiating a conversation with this stranger who is her son. Instead she rummages through her desk until she finds one of Carla Bernotti's multiple messages.

Slowly but deliberately, Joanna picks up the phone and dials.

"Mrs. Bernotti?" she asks without preamble. "This is Joanna López."

\*          \*          \*

In the end, despite the fact that Asher has knowingly gone against her wishes, Carla intercedes.

"She says she will meet you," Carla tells him the next day, "Sunday at the chapel in Santa Rosa."

"But I *leave* on Sunday," Asher protests.

"She is unable to see you tomorrow." Carla sighs. "She knows you are leaving. She said she would be there by ten A.M."

"But why didn't she just call me?" Asher presses. "We can work out—"

"Sebastián," Carla interrupts. "You wrote her, and she responded. I think we have both done all we can do here."

"But what else did she say?" asks Asher, immensely

bothered. If it was his letter that elicited Joanna's response, why was she going through an intermediary?

"Did she ask you anything? Did you talk about anything at all?"

"She asked if you were a decent person," replies Carla with a touch of resignation. "That was the first thing she asked about you, actually. Not if you were wealthy or smart or handsome or artistic. She asked if I thought you were a decent, good person. And I told her you were, Sebastián. Please, let her do what she needs to do. Don't let her down."

"Let *her* down?" Asher asked incredulously. "What about *me*?"

Carla sighs again. She knows it's never enough. Despite all their protestations, their assurances that they just "need to know," it's never only about that. It's endless, this searching, where every tendril of information opens up a desperate hunger for more, until the only thing left is the need to physically see and touch and plumb the depths of the woman herself, looking to find that one elusive, essential piece of her that will make everything fall into place, that will explain away all those unanswered doubts, all the what-ifs of a lifetime. Carla wants to tell him that no one is ever satisfied, no matter which parents life deals you, no matter what their provenance or standing or ambitions, or even the measure of their love.

"She already did the best she could for you, Sebastián," she says instead. "Everything else is a bonus."

*      *      *

"No, you need to go alone," says Alessandra when he asks her to accompany him.

"I thought you could wait for me in the garden or something," says Asher, trying to appear nonchalant while he packs his bags, indecision clouding his face as he tries to decide what to wear the following day. "I don't know, I think jeans and a T-shirt is too casual, but if I wear a jacket, she'll think I've dressed up just for her," he continues, looking pleadingly at Alessandra for help as he lines up yet another T-shirt on the bed beside a growing pile of possibilities. "I don't want to look like I'm trying too hard."

"I think jeans and a jacket are perfect," Alessandra says simply, although she knows of course he wants to impress her, he wants to look his absolute best, make her proud, and in a tiny way make her sorry for what she's lost.

"I think she's going to be so totally proud, Ash," she says brightly. "I can't wait to hear all about it."

# Chapter Thirty

Sunday services at the convent in Santa Rosa are already under way when Joanna arrives at 8:00 A.M. It's sunny for a change, and the startling blue of the sky illuminates the garden, dew still clinging to the vegetables and the roses. Joanna walks slowly toward the chapel, her long sweater wrapped tightly around her in the cool morning.

After Daniel left for his trip the night before, she spent the evening ransacking the boxes where she keeps her old books and notes and college sweaters, looking furiously, unable to believe she's lost it, but uncertain, too, because it's been so very long since she's even thought about it, until she finally found Lucas's necklace wrapped in a little plastic bag inside one of her old makeup cases.

She used to wear the leopard-tooth necklace to bed, back when she still dreamed of him, and it was the last thing she touched before she fell asleep and the first thing she felt for when her morning alarm jolted her awake at 6:00 A.M. She would take it off before donning her maid's uniform, leery of curious looks or, worse, questions she couldn't properly answer.

Sometimes at night, when the anguish of her situation made her snap awake in panic, she'd turn it over and over between her fingers, praying to that shaman of his for protection, for just a speck of magic, enough to at least allow her to sleep, until she finally succumbed to sheer exhaustion, convinced that somehow the amulet worked, that it had the power to embalm her, allow her to last another day.

Even during her early college years, she wore the necklace at night. It grounded her; reminded her where she was going. She can't pinpoint exactly when she broke the ritual. She knows only that some nights she went to bed too spent to even think about rummaging inside her nightstand for it, until its sense of urgency and importance simply faded, along with her past, and one evening, without much thought, she simply put it away.

Now she feels inside her purse to make certain that the tooth, dangling from its leather cord, is still there.

Joanna stands outside the chapel door for several long minutes, listening to the chant of the prayers inside. She chose to meet him here because it's home to Sister Teresa— her only link to the past and the present and her truth— and surely this will somehow act as a redeeming catalyst between what is, what was, and what could have been.

Joanna feels slightly dizzy and takes a deep breath to regain her composure. Save for the occasional wedding or funeral with Daniel, she hasn't been to church of her own volition for two decades. She carefully opens the heavy wooden door and lets herself in, closing it gently behind her, appraising the sea of black-and-white coifs, heads bent, praying on the rows before her. Joanna crosses herself and makes her way to the ornate wooden confessional at the far left corner of the chapel. The door is open, and she knows there is no priest giving confession at this time, but she still kneels down, inhaling the smell of candles and incense, relishing the pressure of the hard wood against her shins.

"Forgive me, Father, for I have sinned," she whispers, and her voice—alone in the midst of the nuns' prayers—is little more than a rustle, but she can hear herself, she can feel the words, she can grasp their tenor and their meaning and the ache and longing of the twenty-one years in which they remained hidden, forever unuttered, until now, and Joanna feels the most immense relief.

\*　　　\*　　　\*

Asher arrives far earlier than their 10:00 A.M. appointed time and paces nervously in the garden, his hands shoved deep into his jeans pockets, stopping every so often to adjust the collar of his white shirt and his blue blazer as he looks around nervously for any sign of her, wanting to make sure that when she appears, he can exude an air of casual nonchalance, as if he hadn't been up all night, as if he'd been able to down more than a coffee this morning, as if his heart weren't beating so terribly hard that he feels he could keel over at any moment. Asher paces around the garden yet again, then makes his way to the entrance of the patio, from where he can see who enters through the convent's great double doors.

When Joanna walks out of the chapel, she is momentarily blinded by the sunlight and searches inside her purse for her sunglasses. Only when she puts them on and looks up again does she notice the silhouette standing at the other end of the patio. Something must alert him, because he turns around just as her eyes grow accustomed to the glare.

For a frightening moment, Joanna feels like she's been

physically sucked into another dimension, back to that path between the town and the soccer field where the afternoon air was so clear you could pierce right through it, when he was walking toward her, his face barely visible from the dazzle of the sun on his back and in her eyes.

And then, slowly, like a lazy wave that has taken her out to sea and now brings her back to shore, she returns, her consciousness adjusting by the second, until it pieces together that it's her, Joanna, right here, right now, in a church garden, and that the man is older than the man she once knew. Even with the garden between, she can discern what she saw in the picture: that he has the same full mouth, the angular face, yet everything about him is gentler, like a retouched painting, save for the eyes. The eyes are his and his alone, looking at her with that same longing of the first day, when all he wanted was her permission.

Later Asher would have liked to tell Alessandra that time stood still, that there was a flash of recognition between them, but the truth is he's thrown off balance by the disconcerting blankness of her dark glasses, by the obvious analysis that's going on behind her shuttered stare, and despite himself he waits anxiously for some sign of approval.

It comes with a slight beckoning movement of her head, and he obliges, walking slowly toward her, unconsciously shifting his shoulders underneath his jacket, and he wonders how it can possibly be that he's so uneasy, the skin around his collar already starting to itch from the starch of his freshly pressed shirt, while she looks so extraordinarily collected, as if it were perfectly routine to see your son after twenty-one years apart.

Asher walks up to Joanna and stops when he's barely a foot away, close enough that she can see the smooth, bronze texture of his skin, the rise and fall of his chest, the chapped lips he licks nervously. For the first time in her life, Joanna wishes she had carried the baby when he was born. *Maybe then*, she thinks, *I could feel a connection, a desire to hold him close.* But this young man standing in front of her is...intimidating, despite the vulnerability of those slanted eyes, a man she can't bring herself to touch, a man she would have deemed too old to go out with had she met him back then, back when she was Rita Ortiz.

She looks at him, surprised at how anticlimactic it feels, and she's wrenched by a pang of guilt and, also, surprise at her lack of empathy.

She instinctively presses one hand against her stomach and wonders if her shortcomings are really at the heart of it all, if she's incapable of unselfishly loving anyone, even the new baby she now carries inside, because she doesn't recognize—she doesn't even like—this person who finally, finally opens her mouth.

"Sebastián?" she asks hesitantly.

He nods, because unlike her he's literally struck dumb. It was one thing to see an old picture, but it's another to see her in front of him. He marvels at how young she looks, too young to be his mother, and he searches in vain for something in her face that will connect her to him. But he sees nothing, and for a moment he panics, thinking it's all been a mistake.

"You are like your father," she says at last, haltingly, as

if reading his doubts, gesturing toward his face in explanation. "I'm sorry," she adds. "My English is not perfect."

"My Spanish either," says Asher with a tentative smile, feeling like a tot before his kindergarten teacher. He wishes fervently that Alessandra were here; she'd know what to say, how to act. She was the only one who'd gotten Rita right, who'd seen the drive behind the desperation.

They stand there for what seems to be many beats, and Joanna thinks she must take control of the situation; she's the mother, after all. And not just that—she's an engineer, a woman used to directing men. Only there are no right words, nothing that she can say that won't sound forced or insincere or even hostile. But looking at him again from behind her sunglasses, she sees all his doubts come up to the surface. He so badly wants her to like him, to approve, and she brings herself to gently place her hand on his arm.

"Come, let's sit down, yes?"

# Chapter Thirty-one

They sit awkwardly next to each other on a little bench next to the rose garden, a bucolic setting in which Asher feels uncharacteristically ill at ease before her quiet reserve. He's not certain if Joanna López has a charming side to her, but right now the most cordial adjective that comes to mind is "aloof." She's more than aloof, though, really. She's shuttered tight. He remembers Jazmin and her bright scarves and bracelets and wonders what she could possibly have found in common with this quiet woman, utterly unreachable despite the fact that she's so close to him he can actually smell her perfume.

Joanna looks at him behind her dark glasses. Already she can see he finds her wanting, and the thought fills her with unreasonable anxiety. She certainly doesn't feel bound to embark on a mother-son relationship, but neither does she want him to leave with a negative impression of her.

*I did the best I could for you!* she wants to scream at him, but instead she pushes the glasses back onto her head and looks at him calmly, with her steady, practiced gaze.

"Mrs. Bernotti said you're a soccer player," she says finally, grasping for the pieces of her conversation with Carla.

"I used to be," says Asher, startled by the depths in her finally visible eyes. "I don't play anymore," he adds, and is immediately sorry when he sees the trace of dismay in her face at having said the wrong thing.

"Oh," she says, disconcerted. "She didn't say that. Your uncle used to play soccer," she adds after an uncomfortable pause, speaking in an even tone that belies her anxiety; somewhere inside her inexperience, her intuition tells her this is the right thing to say. "Well, the last time I saw him, he was very little," Joanna continues carefully. "But he loved to play. His name was Sebastián. Like you," she adds.

Asher nods uncertainly. He knows this, he wants to point out; she wrote it in her letter to him. What he wants to do is ask what has happened to that other Sebastián, but he's unsure of his boundaries, of the line between what's allowed and what's taboo.

"Actually, my name is Asher Sebastian," he blurts out, and is immediately sorry at the lack of tact.

Joanna López looks confused. "Excuse me?" she asks.

"My name," repeats Asher slowly but deliberately. He wants to establish the connection, but also the distinct separation; he's no longer hers, after all. "My name is now *Asher* Sebastian. Asher Sebastian Stone."

"A-sher," repeats Joanna, now remembering his letter. "Asher," she says again. "It's a rare name, yes?" she says with a slight smile, feeling terribly foolish and wondering what kind of name Asher is anyway. She should have at the very least looked it up, she thinks, simultaneously appalled at her lack of curiosity for this person before her yet incapable of mustering the enthusiasm the situation requires.

"My parents—my adoptive parents—are Jewish," explains Asher. "It's a Hebrew name. It means 'blessed.'"

He wants to go into the entire explanation of how he got his name, that it was because his parents were so grateful to have him, grateful to her, but, face-to-face with the reason, he can't bring himself to say words that he fears might sound flat or trite.

"Why didn't you name me after my father?" he asks instead.

Joanna is momentarily speechless. She readies one of her half-truths and then firmly quells the impulse. There is no sense in lying anymore, she thinks. If he's found her, he's capable of hearing the truth.

"It was dangerous," she says simply, looking straight at him, marveling again at his eyes. "Your father was a guerrilla fighter. We weren't supposed to fall—to be together," she adds, amending the words at the last minute. "But you can't help those things. Well," she ends with resignation, "I suppose you can, but we didn't."

Joanna looks down at her hands, at the tasteful wedding band encrusted with diamonds, the only adornment on her fingers.

"My family could have gotten killed—I could have gotten killed—if word got out about who your father was," she tells him.

Asher listens to her steady voice, mesmerized. She speaks like a character in a soap opera—clearly, precisely, narrating fantastical entanglements of extraordinary proportions.

"So I didn't name you after him," she says, oblivious to his train of thought. "And I never told anyone his name." She pauses for a minute. "And you know what? I never knew his last name. I know how that sounds, but I didn't. They called him Gato, because of his eyes. His eyes were like yours. But his real name was Lucas."

Joanna pauses. After so many years, the word feels stiff inside her mouth; her tongue has trouble forming the two syllables that make up the name she once used to whisper herself to sleep. "Lucas," she repeats, and the faintest glimmer of a smile appears on her face. "His name was Lucas."

Asher repeats the name inside in his head. Lucas. Even though it's not an unusual name, he still doesn't know anyone named Lucas. Not Luke. Lucas. He had a father, and his name was Lucas. Asher pushes back the additional barrage of questions straining to leave his mouth, loath to break the moment. He's certain that Joanna has never uttered any of this out loud, and it's quite possible she never will again.

Joanna looks at Asher with a mix of pity and curiosity. He just wants to know, she thinks with amazement, because he is that certain that he comes from a good place. And for the first time, she feels an urge to reach out and touch him, caress his cheek, or at least put her hand on his. She remembers her own father, the love that turned to scorn, so hateful that she obliterated him from her thoughts, scrubbed his words and his actions and—most of all—the way he looked at her from her memory and started anew, fashioning in her mind and in her life another father, one who adored her but died tragically.

Lucas. Impossible to know what kind of father he would have been, and she harbors no illusions. But she won't tell Asher this, she decides. She'll tell him only what she knows. And what she knows is insufficient, but it is still good.

"How old are you now?" she asks, although she knows, but she wants to hear him say it.

"I'm twenty-one," Asher replies. "Almost twenty-two."

Joanna nods. "Lucas said he was twenty-four. But he really was eighteen. He didn't talk too much about himself. What little he told me was...hard," she says lowering her eyes, cringing a little at his memories and at hers. "My parents were very, very strict, very rigid people. But Lucas had a horrible life. That's why he joined the movement.

"They took over our town," she continues unbidden, because now that the words have been spoken, she can't stop them, they need to get out, they need to be uttered, recognized, and left in peace, like the words in the chapel. "And they stayed for weeks. That's how I met him. Edén was such a small, insignificant, petty little place, and Lucas was—" Joanna stops for a moment, her voice breaking. "Lucas was everything else. He was strong, he was confident, he was beautiful. He had power, and he cared about me."

Joanna looks intently at Asher now and says the words again. "He cared about *me*," she repeats with certainty. "Everybody was so afraid of them, but I was never afraid with him. I was never afraid *of* him. He was even kind with Sebastián. Then, when he had to leave, he offered to take me with him, but I couldn't go there. I couldn't live that life in the jungle with those people, fighting their wars. It wasn't my fight, or my life. But I never imagined I was pregnant then either. When you're sixteen, you never think you're going to be pregnant. Maybe if I'd known, I would have made a different choice. I don't know," she says with a shrug.

"But you could have kept me," Asher says. "Couldn't you have kept me?"

Joanna looks at him, taken aback by the question, surprised he even has to ask.

"I had no choice," she declares defensively, squaring her shoulders. "You don't understand," she continues, shaking her head with a touch of impatience, but also regret. "It was the end of the world."

A part of Joanna wants to say she's sorry, but she's not sure what to apologize for. To her it was the end of the world back then, when everything ground to a halt—her expectations, her dreams, her vanity, her ability to love—and it's taken this long to make herself feel again.

"How about your parents?" Asher asks, oblivious. "Your parents didn't want me?"

Joanna smiles and shakes her head, a trace of wistfulness in her look.

"No, Sebastián," she says. "They just didn't want *me*. And you were part of me, don't you see? What happened was unthinkable. *You* were unthinkable. And anyway, what was I supposed to do with you? I had no money, I hadn't finished high school, I had no one. No one. No one came to visit me once while I was at that orphanage. I didn't get a single call, a single card, nothing. I didn't exist. Is that what you would have wanted? To be invisible? Didn't you say you had great parents?" she continues with a touch of sarcasm. "What are you complaining about, then?"

"I'm not complaining," Asher counters, recoiling from her bitterness, dismayed at the turn the conversation is taking. "I just wanted to know, that's all," he adds, feeling

chastised but resentful at the same time, because he is entitled to know, he thinks. He was part of what happened; he
can't simply be dispatched into oblivion.

"I know you were in an impossible situation," he adds
carefully now. "But did you ever wonder what had happened to me? How I was doing? Because we tried to find
you. After all this time, weren't you even a little bit curious?"

Joanna sits stone-faced next to him and after a few
moments brings her big sunglasses back down over her
eyes. She shouldn't have come, she thinks. She should have
trusted her initial instincts, because what good could arise
from a meeting such as this? A litany of recriminations over
a past that wasn't hers to control and that now can only
cause her irreparable harm.

"I went back for you," she pronounces stiffly, and the
moment she says it, she realizes how devastating it was, to
take the bus back to Casa, to walk down the path and past
the playground and knock on that door, to retrace steps she
had thought she'd taken for good, and then to be rejected
yet again.

"Sister Teresa told us," Asher says, feeling a slight tug of
hope. "Why did you?"

Joanna crosses her arms and looks straight ahead,
thinking that this time she can't wish away the question.

"Because I could," she finally says, softly, still not looking at him. "I inherited some money, and it changed everything. I changed my name. How I hated the name Rita!"
she says, pursing her lips and taking a deep breath. "I went
to college. It was a miracle, really. I got a second chance.
But you had already been adopted, and there was no sense

in revisiting the past. Only cowards live in the past. If you haven't learned that from life yet, you should," she adds dryly.

"Believe me, I've learned that," Asher answers. He leans forward on the bench, elbows on his knees, and rubs at the scars on his temples, momentarily at a loss for words.

Joanna looks sideways at him and feels a twinge of remorse for this righteous boy-man with his noble intentions. It's not his fault, after all, she thinks, remembering the little pang of happiness she felt when his tiny baby hand had squeezed her finger, her only physical contact with this person who is her son and whom she now is pushing away again, even as he sits beside her.

*Only cowards live in the past*, she tells herself, *and this is no longer the past. This is now.*

"I brought something for you," she says, reaching into her purse and carefully unwrapping the worn brown paper bag and removing the plastic wrap. "It was your father's. It was the only other thing he valued besides his gun. He said a shaman gave it to him, for protection," she explains, taking out the worn leather cord, exposing the curved yellow tooth. "He gave it to me the night he left."

Joanna closes her fingers over the tooth, feeling its smooth curves caressing the palm of her hand for the last time, then gently opens her fingers again and extends the necklace toward him, the other Lucas, his son, her son.

"Here," she says with finality. "It's yours now."

Asher slowly straightens and looks at the necklace in her hand. A peace offering. He lifts his own hand up to accept it, feeling the leather cord tantalizingly unwind onto his open palm. Joanna closes his fingers around the necklace and leaves her hand there for a moment, wrapped around his—as Lucas once wrapped his hand around hers—surprised at how easy it is to touch him after all.

"Now it's your turn, Sebastián," she says, removing her hand slowly, and this time her voice is gentle, deliberately tempered. "You said you'd looked for me before, but what made you come here now?"

"I had an accident," he finally answers. "I was in a car crash, and I broke my neck." He automatically raises his hand to rub his neck. "I was lucky I didn't die or end up in a wheelchair. People are always telling me it was a miracle," he says, looking at her appraisingly. "I suppose you could call it that, or it could just be very good luck. Either way, I also got a second chance. That's why I came."

Joanna looks at him again in surprise, and for the first time she notices the scars, partially hidden beneath his growing hair. She instinctively reaches out and rubs her fingers over their uneven surface and then allows her hand to travel very slowly down the side of his face and rest heavily against his cheek, feeling him lean unresistingly against her palm, his skin warm against her hand.

"I'm sorry," she says simply. "Were your parents there with you? Did they take care of you?"

Asher nods dumbly, his cheek still pressed against her hand.

"Tell me about them?" Joanna asks, and Asher realizes that no one has ever asked him to talk about them before, because they have always been there, so familiar there's no need to point them out. He begins to talk, slowly at first, then faster as he realizes there's too much to say and so little time left, and Joanna listens raptly, her mere silence an injection of encouragement, until his words slow to a trickle and finally taper to nothing.

Joanna looks at him longingly, a shade of envy in her liquid brown eyes.

"They did so much better than I ever could have done," she finally says. "*You* did so much better than me. My parents were so different. I can't even begin to imagine your life."

"That's what Jazmin said," Asher says automatically.

"Jazmin?" asks Joanna, her voice rising slightly.

"Yes." He hesitates, feeling like an interloper. "We met her. My girlfriend and I."

"You met Jazmin?" Joanna asks.

Asher nods and pulls up the sleeve of his jacket. "I showed her the bracelet," he says.

"Oh," Joanna says as she touches it gingerly, feeling the fibers of the threads between her fingers, and her face lights up with a smile of sheer pleasure. "She's so good, isn't she?" Joanna says, stating the obvious, holding back the sudden swell of tears.

"Why don't you want to see her?" Asher asks, puzzled. "She's been waiting for you all these years."

"It's been too long now," Joanna says with regret, shaking her head. "I could never face her after all this. She'd never take me back into her life."

"But that's not what she said," Asher states urgently, and this time he's the one who leans forward and places his hand over hers. "She said she would love to see you and that she's never stopped thinking about you. She said to tell you that nothing matters. That it's still her. Just her."

Joanna doesn't say anything for a long time, her eyes fixed on Asher's hand, on the snippet of red bracelet that peeks from under his white shirt and his blue blazer. He's so handsome, so righteous, and she thinks of all she left behind because she had to, and all that remained behind because she couldn't face it anymore. *Only cowards live in the past*, she thinks again, and as she looks back up at his familiar and unfamiliar features, she hopes that it's not too late.

"Stay," she says simply. "I know you said you were leaving, but can't you stay? Just a little bit longer."

# Chapter Thirty-two

Linda Stone paces anxiously outside customs at LAX, her eyes going from the door to her BlackBerry, checking for the text messages, missing calls, anything to indicate that Asher will appear at any moment. He hasn't called, not since the Skype conversation, not even to return her messages the day before to confirm his flight information.

Joseph says she's being irrational, but she can't help the apprehension that's gnawing at her with ugly insidiousness. She hates this side of herself that she didn't know she possessed, the insecure, clingy side that demands constant reassurance when she's never required any before.

"I can't stand this. I'm going to Starbucks," she finally says. "Joe, do you want anything?"

"No. You go get your latte, I'll keep an eye on the door," he says with a smile. "Go, go." He waves, leaning against the wall.

So it's Linda, coming back with coffee in hand, who glances up and first sees Alessandra at the end of the hallway, not yet in Joseph's line of vision. She's alone.

Linda stands still, stunned into immobility. There must be an explanation, she thinks, because no matter how much she's feared this, it's simply not possible, and her dismay renders her helpless as the paper cup tumbles to the floor. Flustered, Linda bends down, making a feeble attempt at cleaning by at least picking up the cup itself, but the thought of Joseph alone is too much to bear, and she straightens again and simply leaves the mess behind, walking quickly toward the glass doors.

Alessandra is already there, enveloped in Joseph's generous embrace.

"And Asher?" Joseph asks, and Linda surges forward, focused only on him, when she hears his voice.

"What up, Mom?"

Linda turns around to face her son, devastatingly handsome in jeans, a blue blazer, and a crisp white shirt, his smile lighting up his slanted yellow eyes as if they were lanterns lit from within.

The gush of relief renders her unsteady. If there had been a chair nearby, she would have collapsed on it, but instead she reaches for him, finding her balance in his arms, her bearings in the closeness of his face.

"Oh, Ash," she blurts, out, her face pressed against his jacket. "I didn't see you walk by. I thought you hadn't come back."

"Not come back?" he asks, puzzled. "Why wouldn't I?"

"I don't know," says Linda helplessly. "You didn't answer your messages. I didn't know what to think."

Asher looks at his mother, seeing her, really seeing her, in the same way that he had to bring her up in his mind when Joanna asked about her this morning.

"But, Mom, I never left you," he says, his arms holding her against him, and this time he's the one who soothes her, who reassures her. "I just went looking for something. But I never went away."

*     *     *

A week later, the day Daniel is scheduled to come back from his trip, Joanna cooks risotto for him, reveling in the luxury of the dish and in the time and attention required to prepare it, gently stirring in the saffron and the olive oil and the white wine so the odor permeates the apartment, filling it with warmth, like an embrace.

"What smells so good?" he shouts as he walks in the door, slamming it shut behind him, the clatter of briefcase and papers and jacket preceding his appearance like a page heralding the arrival of the king, and she smiles despite herself when she sees him finally standing in the kitchen, rumpled and bigger than life, his face illuminated with joy.

"Mushroom risotto," she says simply, blowing a stray strand of hair from her brow. "And endive salad and chocolate soufflé."

"All that?" he says, delighted, walking up behind her and encircling her waist with his arms. "What have I done to deserve this?" he whispers into her ear. Joanna leans back into him, relishing the moment, thinking in a flash that it could be the last time, then just as quickly chastising herself for her pessimism.

"Okay," she says quickly, drawing away. "Go wash your hands. This is ready."

She marvels at her own equanimity, watching herself go through the motions, say the right things, ask the right questions as they enjoy the dinner whose every ingredient she has chosen with care. She wonders if perhaps she's been living on autopilot all these years, because how else to explain her detachment? But that's what she always does, she thinks with a start. She simply disassociates, pretends that things are happening to someone else, wills the bad away until it leaves, out of sheer frustration at its inability to pierce her unflappable exterior. For the first time in her life, Joanna wonders what she would have been like if she weren't perpetually running scared. If instead of continuously deflecting conflict she had, just once, met it head-on. Perhaps she would have crashed and burned, bounced off her imaginary walls and ended up curled in a heap at the foot of the hill. Or perhaps she would have crashed right through and kept on going until she reached the very top of the hill. And there, exhausted, she would have looked around and leisurely walked down again or kept going, with the ease of someone who knows she can do what she needs to do.

"I got a call the other day," she says finally, as he takes his first bite of chocolate soufflé.

"Oh, yeah?" he answers, but immediately he tunes in to the shift in her demeanor. He leaves his question open, an invitation for her to go on and tell him what she needs to say.

"It was..." She pauses, her head tilted, and looks curiously at Daniel, sitting across from her, his guileless eyes so rare for someone whose living depends on others' misfortunes. She wishes she had somebody to call on, somebody who could explain to her husband how terribly vulnerable she was back then and how, with the passing of the years, it became easier and easier to pretend that nothing had happened and that she could really start anew.

But now it's just her, completely alone, as always, trying to stave off the juggernaut of her past as it approaches her with the inevitability of a speeding train.

"It was a call from an adoption agency," she manages to say. "They wanted information about someone named Rita Ortiz."

"Oh?" asks Daniel, and this time he puts down his spoon, all his senses fully alert to his wife's words, to her tone of voice, to the sudden pleading he now sees in her eyes. "And who's Rita Ortiz?"

Joanna looks at her beautiful soufflé for a moment, whittling away at the sides with her spoon, her brow furrowed in a small frown, because now that she thinks about it, she doesn't really know anymore, who is—who was—Rita Ortiz.

"She's someone I used to know," she says, softly but firmly, surprised that her voice doesn't shake. "She's someone you should know," she adds, looking up at him, and for a moment he can see deep beyond her eyes, despite the darkness in their depths.

# Acknowledgments

Thank you…

First and foremost to my incredible editor, Selina McLemore of Grand Central, for her friendship, her support, and for knowing how to extract the absolute best from me and having that extraordinary ability of taking the writing, the narrative, the characters, and the essence of the story itself to a whole other place.

To *everyone* at Grand Central: the sales team for placing my books in every nook and cranny in the country; the design team for coming up always with the perfect cover (how do you *do* that??); to the online and marketing team for making sure that every site in the world gets my books! To Kallie Shimek and Maureen Sugden for their incredibly thorough copyediting. And especially to Linda Duggins for her hard work, belief, and infinite patience with me (smiles) and Latoya Smith for her cheerful optimism and support.

To David Peak and David Vigliano at Vigliano & Associates for looking after me every step of the way.

For Kirsten Neuhaus for continuing to be my biggest advocate. The future is bright!

To Agatha León, director of Chiquitines Cali, for her wealth of knowledge on everything adoption-involved and for the truly extraordinary work she does on behalf of so many children in need of homes and love.

To Allegra and Arturito for their constant feedback, ideas, genuine interest, and love.

To Arturo for putting up with so many late nights and long weekends of writing and for always replenishing the supply of sauvignon blanc.

To my mother: Te prometo que los libros se publicarán en español!

To my in-laws, Arthur and Therese, for promoting my books throughout the California Coast.

To my friends Blanca LaSalle and Erwin Pérez for having lent their talents and professionalism to the effort of taking my writing to a bigger audience; I am forever touched by your generosity.

To Nora Comstock, Isabel Lemus, and all the Comadres for their friendship and support.

To all the bloggers and reviewers—there are so many of you—who celebrate good books and keep readership alive and well. Thank you, thank you for reading my books and taking the time to write about them on your pages. What a privilege.

To all my media friends who came through for me with such unconditional support.

Last but not least, to everyone who took the time to read *Tell Me Something True* and turned it into such a big success. Your readership has made this book possible and, I hope, many more to come!

Thank you.

# Reading Group Guide

1. Try to imagine you were Rita's age, living in her world. What would you have done if you were in her shoes? Kept the baby? Given him up for adoption? Sought an abortion? Do you think that if any one of her circumstances had been different—if she'd come from money, if the father had been a boy from town—she might have acted differently? If so, how?

2. How does the Colombian setting affect the decisions made by the characters? If Rita were an American teenager living in a community like the one Asher was raised in, how might her story be different?

3. The characters in *The Second Time We Met* often find their desires and ambitions pitted against the reality of their situations. What real choices did Rita have? What choices did Lucas have?

4. Rita manages to escape her reality, even though doing so was painful because she had to give up people she loved, like her brother, Sebastián, and her best friend, Jazmin. Could Lucas have done the same? What would he have had to risk in order to be with Rita?

5. After she gives up her son, Rita gets a second chance and starts her life anew. If you were given such a chance, what would you do? Would you keep aspects

of your current life, or would you want to do something dramatically different?

6. Whose rights are more important, those of a child who wants to find his or her birth parents or those of the birth parents who want to remain anonymous?

7. Did Joanna have a moral obligation to meet Asher? Or would she have been justified in declining a meeting?

8. Did Asher have the right to pressure Joanna for a meeting she didn't want to have?

9. Does a child's meeting a birth parent undermine the importance of the adoptive parent?

10. How would you react if your adoptive child insisted on finding his or her birth parents? Would it make you feel threatened? How do you think you would cope with such feelings?

11. What do you think happens to Joanna after she tells her husband the truth? Will he accept her? Will she go looking for her family?

12. Do you think Asher and Joanna will develop a relationship? If so, what do you think it might be like? If not, why not?

13. What would Linda think of Rita, and vice versa? Do you see them having a relationship?

14. How would you describe the role of the church in this book?

15. How would you describe the role of the school system in this book? Did the principal have any obligation to be more involved than she was with Rita? For example, was it her responsibility to tell Rita's parents about her suspicions?

# About the Author

Celebrated journalist and former concert pianist **LEILA COBO** is the executive director of Latin content and programming for *Billboard* and is broadly considered the ultimate Latin music insider. Leila is a frequent contributor to NPR and has written liner notes for acts such as Ricky Martin, Shakira, and Chayanne. She is also the host of the television show *Estudio Billboard*, which features in-depth interviews with top Latin acts.

A native of Cali, Colombia, Leila holds dual degrees, one in journalism, from Bogotá's Universidad Javeriana, and one in piano performance, from the Manhattan School of Music. After graduating she won a Fulbright Scholarship and obtained her master's degree from USC's Annenberg School of Communications. Leila got her start in journalism as a writer for the *Los Angeles Times* and later became the pop-music critic for the *Miami Herald*.

Recently named one of Colombia's most influential women by the prestigious magazine *Fucsia*, Leila is a recipient of the Premio Orquídea award for international journalism. She lives in Key Biscayne, Florida, with her husband and their children.

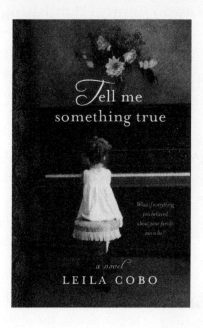

If you enjoyed *The Second Time We Met*, then you're sure to love these captivating novels as well.

## Now available in print and as ebooks from Grand Central Publishing

A professional woman's life is turned upside down when her deceased cousin leaves her an unlikely inheritance: three young children.

"Julia Amante understands the ties that bind all families regardless of culture and nationality."

—Jill Marie Landis, *New York Times* bestselling author

Award-winning author Lorraine López shares the story of a woman who craves solitude, only to find family more fulfilling.

"López imagines believable characters and observes their world with literary insight. An entertaining appreciation of one woman's journey, sometimes ribald and funny, sometimes ironic and self-deprecating."

—*Kirkus Reviews*